Sequestered

I0563362

By Max Overton
And Jim Darley

Writers Exchange E-Publishing
http://www.writers-exchange.com

Sequestered
Copyright 2011, 2015, 2025 Max Overton and Jim Darley
Writers Exchange E-Publishing
PO Box 372
ATHERTON QLD 4883

Published by Writers Exchange E-Publishing
http://www.writers-exchange.com

ISBN **ebook**: 978-1-921636-69-1
Print: **978-1-925574-50-0** (WEE Assigned)

Prologue

August 21-22, 1986

Simon Nkoma, standing silently in the darkness of the African night, gripped his machete tightly in one sweat-moistened hand, and strained to hear the sound again. It had been an odd sound, something akin to a thump and a gurgle, and he could not think what had made it. He was familiar with the animals of the open scrubland and forest, having lived his whole life in the region and most of his adult life hunting a variety of bush meat. Most nights he caught relatively small animals like bush rats or a civet, perhaps a porcupine or a squirrel, but this night he had been lucky and caught a small antelope in a wire noose.

The sounds of the bush continued around him--frogs and insects, the cries of small animals and rustlings in the leaf litter--but none of that concerned Simon. Those sounds were ordinary and every day, while this sound...this sound was something strange. Strange was not good when you lived your life depending on your knowledge of the forest. The sound was not repeated however and he shifted the gutted antelope on his shoulders and moved off down the path again.

The visibility through the scrubland was poor, the faint starlight intermittently blocked by cloud, but his feet found the path unfalteringly. He had a small flashlight but only used it in an emergency or in the deepest shadow, preferring to rely on his night vision. The path was familiar, one he could traverse with his eyes shut, but on this night Simon hurried, his gaze searching the blackness for

1

anything out of the ordinary. He came to a fork in the path, sensing it rather than seeing it, and took the downward route toward his village nestled at the foot of the lake.

The vegetation thinned and Simon looked out over dimly-seen fields to the dark, still waters of the lake, the star field above him cascading down the sky until it met the blackness of the crater rim. The sound came again, much louder, a belch and a gurgle as if a giant somewhere broke wind, and in the faint light he thought he saw the black waters shimmer and lift before breaking into white-topped waves. The hairs on his arms lifted and he stared at a lake suddenly alive. Without a conscious thought he dropped the antelope, turned and ran, stumbling back up the path in the darkness. He passed the fork in the path and continued upward, scrambling toward the valley rim, gripped with a terror he could not explain.

Below him, in his village, was family and friends, but he spared them no thought. He only knew he had to get away. A wind passed him, damp and foetid, smelling of rot, and he felt as if a knife plunged into his lungs. He inhaled deeply and choked, his head swimming as if unaccountably deprived of air. He staggered on a few more paces and collapsed in the middle of the trail, unconscious before he hit the bare earth.

Simon awoke with the dawn, his head racked with pain. He sat for a time, waiting for the pain to recede, and slowly realized that the morning was silent around him. He stood, and looked out across scrub and grass toward the village and lake with dread at the ruin he might see, remembering a watery upheaval in the night. However, the huts were untouched, though no smoke rose from cooking fires and no children played in the dusty streets. Men were normally out in the fields not long after dawn but today the fields were devoid of life. Simon could make out a scattering of brown and black mounds on the grass but failed to recognize them. The lake was placid but discolored, as if rain had washed mud into the still waters. The hairs on his arms rose again as awareness flooded in on him. No birds flew in the air above the lake or fields, no animals moved in the fields or forest, no people in the village.

He prayed, lifting his arms to the sky and then set off down the path to the village. He passed the antelope he had dropped and was surprised to see that there were no flies, nor any of a dozen small animals that might be attracted to fresh meat. He left it where it lay and hurried on. Dead bodies lay on the grass of the fields, cattle with heads thrown back and tongues lolling, eyes glazed. A little farther on he found a village dog, also dead, and an old man, collapsed and untidy in death. He left him where he lay and moved toward the village.

Simon entered the first hut he came to, pushing open the door and calling out a greeting. Silence replied, and bodies, but no flies. No flies. Nothing. Nothing lived in the village, not even insects. He stared at a rat lying in the middle of the floor, cockroaches and spiders fallen from the thatched roof, and superstitious fears gripped his mind.

My wife and children. Simon looked at his home near the water's edge for a long time before going in. *I know what I will find.* His wife lay in bed, as if asleep, and his two young sons on a shared pallet in the next room, also sleeping. He knelt beside them and called their names, praying they would wake. *Miriam, Issa, Tomas.* Simon Nkoma broke down and cried, rocking back and forth on his knees, his wailing cries the only sound in a village filled with the dead.

Chapter 1

July 8, 1997

D r Maxwell Hay received the summons with something approaching shock. He had been a member of the scientific staff of the Northern Coal Consortium based in a backwater laboratory in Edinburgh, Scotland, for two years, and had never expected to meet anyone higher than his section chief, let alone the 'big man' himself.

"Are you sure he wants to meet me?" Max asked. "Perhaps there's another Max Hay."

"Mr Matternicht doesn't make mistakes," said the messenger coolly. He held out a slim envelope. "You're booked on the 5pm flight to London, connecting with a midnight one to Berlin. The exact times are in there. You do have a current passport?"

Max nodded.

"Keep all receipts for expenses and reasonable ones will be reimbursed upon your return. Any questions?"

"Er, whereabouts in Berlin am I going?"

"You'll be met at the airport. Everything you need to know is in the envelope."

Just before nine the next morning, Max was sitting in the reception room of German Coal and Power, a subsidiary of the Northern Coal Consortium, on the Tiergartenstrasse, waiting to be admitted to the office beyond a polished walnut door. On the hour, the summons came and he walked into a small but luxuriously appointed office with floor to ceiling windows overlooking the Tiergarten.

The figure behind the oak desk was slight of stature, bent over papers spread across the polished surface, and Max's first reaction was one of disappointment. James Matternicht did not live up to the image he had of him in his mind.

Matternicht seemed oblivious to his presence, so Max stood on the richly textured carpet in front of the desk and waited. Several minutes passed before Matternicht looked up and fixed him with an ophidian stare. At once, Max felt the power of the other man and even experienced a tiny frisson of fear. Unbidden, he saw himself as a rabbit frozen by the mesmerizing stare of a stoat. Then the image shattered as Matternicht smiled.

"Ah, Dr Hay. So good of you to come. Please take a seat." He waved a hand negligently at a pair of padded armchairs near the window, then rose from his desk and joined Max, sitting opposite him. "May I offer you some refreshment? Tea, coffee, a soda?"

"Er, whatever you're having, sir."

Matternicht smiled. "I only drink non-GM soymilk. I find it's not to everyone's taste."

"A...a ginger ale then, please."

Max did not see or hear a summons, but the door opened and a man in a suit entered, listened to Matternicht's request, and had the drinks delivered within three minutes.

Matternicht raised his glass containing five fluid ounces of soymilk. "Ishkabibble," he said.

"Er, I'm sorry...cheers?" Max flushed, trying to hide his confusion at the unfamiliar word.

"The word was 'Ishkabibble', Dr Hay. It was a toast from the trenches in World War One, and means roughly 'Why should I worry?'. The proper response is 'san fairy ann', which comes from the French *ça ne fait rien* which translates as 'It does not matter'..."

Max grinned suddenly. "And that's a play on your own name, sir, Matternicht--matters not."

Matternicht's eyebrows lifted. "Very good, Dr Hay. I usually have to explain that." He sipped from his glass and regarded the younger man solemnly. "I don't usually bother to meet my employees, but your file intrigued me. Your academic credentials are impressive, Dr Hay. A double first from Imperial College in Biology and Geology, followed by a superb doctoral dissertation in environmental studies, followed by post-doctoral studies in fossil fuels. Your work record is, of necessity, shorter but still worthy lecturing at Bristol and then an associate professorship at Durham University--perhaps I should address you as Professor

Hay? With your brilliant record in academia, I'm surprised that you opted to join Northern Coal. May I ask why you did so?"

"I, er, was made a very good offer, sir." Matternicht said nothing and Max felt he was waiting for something more. "I prefer research to teaching, sir, and the teaching load at Durham was, in my view, excessive."

"You're on a lower salary at Northern Coal, aren't you?"

"Yes, sir, but I hope that'll change in the future."

"I believe in rewarding results...and loyalty." Matternicht sipped at his soymilk again. "You were a member of various environmental groups at university and demonstrated against the use of fossil fuels on more than one occasion. Yet you now work for one of the largest coal producers on the planet. I find that curious."

Max took a drink of his ginger ale while he considered his answer. "I won't apologize for my stand on the environment, sir. I think anyone who views pollution and climate change dispassionately must see that fossil fuels have the potential to ruin the planet. When I was an undergrad, I viewed things in black and white, but as I matured, I gained an understanding for other arguments. I believe the world has painted itself into a corner with fossil fuels. We're utterly dependent on them, yet we know them to be bad for the earth. We need non-polluting sources of energy, like solar, wind, hydroelectric, or geothermal, but these are expensive or only available in certain areas. We could develop more efficient technologies, but if we stop coal and oil production while we do so, the world economy crashes."

"So, what's your solution?"

"I don't have one, sir. Not yet. But that's why I joined Northern Coal. I believe it'll give me the opportunity to research alternatives."

"You think I should subsidize research that'll put me out of business?"

"No, sir, but I think it makes good economic sense to find a way of making coal cleaner while the world finds other solutions."

"We already scrub the exhaust from our smokestacks. In most developed countries, particulate pollution is a thing of the past."

Max nodded. He put his glass down on a low table and leaned forward. "Yes, the exhaust from your power stations is clean as far as solids go, but it still contains carbon dioxide. That's one of the main greenhouse gases responsible for global warming."

"Man-made global warming is a myth, Dr Hay."

"No, Mr Matternicht, sir, it's not."

"I have a great many scientists working for me, Dr Hay, some with even better credentials than yours. The consensus of these scientists is that human-induced global warming doesn't exist. The climate is in a natural warming trend and the so-called greenhouse gases we produce are having little or no effect."

"If they say that, they're misleading you. They tell you what you want to hear, not what you should hear."

Matternicht regarded Max skeptically. "Why should I believe you and not them?"

"Because in ten years' time it won't matter who you believe--the facts will be obvious to all except the professional ostriches. Then the governments will act--reluctantly I grant, because cheap fuel and electricity have always been election winners--and impose such restrictions on the coal and oil companies that your businesses are materially affected."

"If coal is such a dead-end business, why did you enter it, Dr Hay?"

"The earth's population is increasing and we need all our resources, including coal. We just have to find a way to make it acceptable. If that can be done, then there's no reason you can't go on mining coal to your heart's content."

"And do you think there is a way, Dr Hay, or is this just so much wishful thinking?"

"Oh, there's a way, Mr Matternicht. It's just not very feasible at the moment. That's where the research comes in."

"Enlighten me."

"Certainly, sir. The basic equation we face is coal in, energy and carbon dioxide out. The energy is essential for the economy, but the carbon dioxide is harmful. Unless we want to cut down on the amount of coal burned in our power stations, we must reduce the carbon dioxide released into the atmosphere by other means. We need to capture it and lock it away somewhere where it cannot warm the climate."

"You disappoint me, Dr Hay. I thought perhaps you had some novel approach, but you're just talking about sequestration. We don't have the land to plant the millions of acres of trees needed to absorb all the carbon dioxide waste for even one year."

"I'm not talking about biosequestration, but about geosequestration. The Norwegians have already started on that, pumping carbon dioxide into old oil fields to increase the yield. A side benefit is that the carbon dioxide is sequestered, taken out of the equation. The Sleipner field in the North Sea is successful, but on a tiny scale. If geosequestration is to work it must be multiplied a million-fold. We'd have to find a way to lock millions of tons of gas into geological strata for thousands of years. It's a big task, but not impossible."

Matternicht stared. "Why has nobody else suggested this?"

"The problem is only now becoming apparent," Max said softly.

"Write a report on this, Dr Hay, and I'll read it. Have it on my desk by the end of the week."

Max stifled a laugh. "If you want a document with a bit of meat and not just filled with vague promises, I'll need a bit more time. Three months."

"Three months it is, but Dr Hay, don't waste my time. If you do, you can try your luck with academia again. If not, well, we'll see, but I think you could find yourself heading up a research team. At a substantially increased salary, of course."

Max grinned. He stood and grasped Matternicht's hand, pumping it vigorously. "Thank you, sir. You won't be disappointed, I promise you."

Chapter 2

July 17, 2000

The estate lay in a densely wooded area close to the Danube River in Austria, and the hunting lodge within it was old but secure. On the ground floor, a number of the rooms had had adjoining walls knocked out to form one large conference room now lined in Peruvian walnut and discreetly lit by hidden spotlights. A tall, prematurely balding man stood in the shadows of the conference room and watched as men entered the room and took their places at the long oak table. One or two of the men saw the shadowy figure but did not give him a second glance. Security at James Matternicht's country estate was legendary and none felt at all threatened.

The tall man scanned the faces of the men as they entered and put a name to each, filing away the information in his mind--Per Svenson, Head of Scandinavian Coal; Patrick Boyle, CEO of Appalachian Coal & Power; Thomas Hu, Chairman of Sino-Australasian Coal; and Boris Radinov, CEO of Russian Coal & Power. The four men radiated power and wealth, but the tall man knew that the fifth man, yet to enter the conference room, could buy and sell these men and their companies.

James Matternicht, he thought. *CEO of Northern Coal & Power Corporation--my friend*. He smiled, unseen in the shadows.

The four men took their places at the table and helped themselves to drinks from the array of bottles and flasks in the middle of the long expanse of wood.

The tall man pressed a button in the wall behind him, sending a silent signal to Matternicht that all was in readiness.

A door in the walnut paneling slid open silently and Matternicht entered. He walked to the head of the table and sat down, whereupon the lighting pattern in the room changed. Pools of light now bathed the four coal barons but deep shadow engulfed the head of the table. Matternicht's voice was quiet, almost gentle. He spoke in English, the language of science and commerce, with no more than a trace of his native Austrian.

"Gentlemen, I've brought you here to discuss a matter that concerns us all. Coal is our life-blood and is the foundation of our power and our wealth, yet today we find ourselves being pushed to the edge of ruin. I speak of the environmental movement, the global-warming fanatics and climate change scientists that would halt progress and take us back to the dark ages. This movement is starting to have a profound effect on the governments of the western democracies. I believe this threat is serious enough to warrant a concerted effort to reverse this trend."

There was a protracted silence from the coal barons sitting around the table. At last, one, Boris Radinov, stirred and said quietly, "You are not telling us anything new, Herr Matternicht. There've always been men who seek to destroy what others build up. The environmental movement is nothing in Russia because we understand the economy needs growth, and coal delivers growth."

"Russia is not the world," Matternicht said, "I'm looking beyond the effects on a single country or even a continent. I'm looking at the global situation. Even Russia must listen when the world speaks."

"You could perhaps be right," Per Svenson agreed. "Scandinavian Coal has had few restraints put upon it by successive governments but a court injunction was brought against it recently. Heavy rain washed out a slurry pond, and tailings polluted a river. Apparently, a fish species nobody has heard of was put in danger." He shrugged. "However, this sort of thing hardly warrants your dire warning."

"Same thing happened in Tennessee," Patrick Boyle said. "A bit of dirty water never hurt anyone, but fuckin' commies picketed Appalachian Coal and Power and shut us down for two weeks. No offence, Boris."

Radinov shrugged. "None taken. Russia's moved beyond Communism. We've no such troubles in Russia. The Greens even have a political party, the Kedr, but they're ineffective, and when they get troublesome, they find trouble, nyet?"

"That's not the case in the rest of the world," Matternicht reminded his guests. "The environmental movement is growing stronger and reputable scientists are joining forces with them to limit our profits."

"I think you worry too much," said the only Southern Hemisphere representative, Thomas Hu. "We have more influence than these environmentalists and we can swamp them with drawn-out legal battles if need be. Money talks and politicians listen."

"And when the seas start to rise? When hurricanes intensify and the Gulf Stream shuts off? What then? Do you think our dollars and pounds and euro and roubles will fight for us when governments panic?"

"Unproven. Nobody's been able to show categorically that carbon dioxide causes global warming," Boyle said.

"I merely state realities. Surely, you're aware of what's happening in the world? You all read the newspapers; you know that even if the link is unfounded, governments can lose their nerve, bow to the uneducated voters..."

"I'm as aware of the facts and fallacies as you are, Matternicht," Boyle said. "You're right in one aspect at least. The global-warming lobbyists are a pain in the ass."

"I know you all have your own science advisers and are fully aware of current controversies. Whether you admit it or not, you must be aware of the dangers to us of the global warming movement."

"We know of this in Russia. Our scientists argue all the time. Some point to the arctic sea ice melting, others to a cooling trend. What are we to believe? Is the earth warming or cooling, and does mankind have anything to do with either?" Boris shrugged and smiled. "Does it matter? If it happens, well, we can holiday in Siberia instead of on the Black Sea."

"On the contrary, this is a serious situation and needs to be addressed while we still have time."

Thomas Hu yawned. "Coal's too useful to the world, Matternicht. So what if we contribute to this putative global warming. So do hundreds of other things. I don't have to tell you of oil and automobile emissions, and the burning of the Amazon forests. I say we don't need to worry that our businesses will be curtailed."

"And when the governments shut the coal mines? When they close down our coal-fired power stations as being too polluting? What then? It'll be too late to stop them. That's why we must do it now--prevent it happening."

"They won't do that," Boyle said. "Coal makes too much money for businesses and governments to shut down. Thousands--millions--of jobs depend on coal."

"Remember how much money you spent when the United States Government made you install pollution scrubbers in all your smokestacks? Coal's cheap to mine, but so polluting, especially coal with high sulphur content. Governments could make that happen again--and more."

"That's true," Per Svenson said quietly. "It could happen. We wouldn't be out of business but we'd be hurt badly. We all have too much invested to just let it happen. Can anything be done though? How do we prevent governments from putting so many restrictions on us we must fold?"

Matternicht smiled, though his expression remained unseen in the bright light that surrounded him like a halo. "We beat them to it by putting severe restrictions on ourselves."

"How's that any better?" Radinov asked sourly. "We still take massive losses. I say we take the fight to these environmentalists and stamp out their influence."

"There's a better way, but before I explain I must ask you to sit through a small lecture by my science adviser. I didn't ask you to bring your own advisers, because I wanted to keep this between us for the moment, but I'll send a report back with each of you, so your advisers can vouch for the accuracy of the facts presented." Matternicht held out a hand to indicate the tall man standing in the shadows. "My science adviser, Professor Maxwell Hay. Max, if you'd be so kind..."

The tall man stepped forward into a pool of light beside the table. "Thank you, Herr Matternicht. Gentlemen, I won't take up much of your time. You all have scientists working for you who can tell you all you need to know if you ask the right questions, but I'd like to direct your attention to certain pertinent points.

"First, you all know that certain gases like carbon dioxide, methane, water vapor and ozone absorb thermal energy that would otherwise reflect back into space, and emit some of it back to the earth. This is called the 'greenhouse effect' and was first demonstrated over a hundred years ago..."

"As you say, we know all this, but why is it big news now?" Boyle asked.

"Because for a long time nobody really thought it would make much difference. I mean, industry and log fires can only create so much CO_2 and the atmosphere is huge--really huge. We all thought we could do pretty much as we liked and the earth would cope. Well, no more. Water vapor levels are fairly constant, methane from cow flatulence..."

Boris Radinov snorted. "Perdet," he muttered.

"...and other sources are much the same and the ozone levels are low. What's changed is the amount of CO_2 in the air. Every time we burn something, whether it's a forest in the Amazon Basin, a log on the home fire, the gas when you light up your barbecue, or the coal in one of your power stations, you're adding to the CO_2 burden in the atmosphere. CO_2 levels are measured in parts per million. Before the industrial revolution, when we all started cutting down the forests for fuel and mining coal and oil to drive industry, the CO_2 concentration was around 270 parts per million. Doesn't sound like much, does it? Look around you at this room, look at the high ceilings, the width and the length...alright, and now look at the wooden ruler in front of you. It's 30 centimeters in length--a foot for our American friend--and imagine a cube measuring a ruler length on each side. That cube's filled with carbon dioxide and the rest of the room is made up of nitrogen, oxygen and argon, the other atmospheric gases. That cube represents 270 parts per million in this room.

"But for over a hundred years we've been adding carbon dioxide to the air. Plants take some out during photosynthesis, some is bound up by corals and mollusks, some gets locked up in minerals, but despite all this the level has been rising. This year it stands at around 370 parts per million--add a few cupfuls to your box of CO_2 in front of you. In the next twelve years, we'll add another 30 parts--another cup. Again, it doesn't sound like much, does it? But the effect it has is out of all proportion."

The men in the room sat quietly, frowning slightly, but listening as Max talked about climate change.

"Remember, CO_2 is a greenhouse gas, and greenhouse gases increase the temperature of the earth. Already this is happening, and as the CO_2 level rises, so will the temperature..."

"But we've just had a cold winter," Radinov protested. "In Russia, every winter is cold. Where's this warming you speak of?" He looked round at the other men. "This is why scientists argue about the validity of global warming."

"There'll always be winters, and snowstorms, and ice," Max said with a smile, "But when we talk about global warming, we're talking about the mean temperature of the planet, not the temperature in any one place--and the mean Earth temperature is rising. There's good evidence to suggest that as the CO_2 level continues to rise, the temperature will increase at a faster rate."

"So, we get a bit warmer," Svenson said. "I like being warm. Where's the harm?" He stared at Professor Hay. "I know the arguments, you understand? I want to hear you say it."

"The planet's not a simple thing--it's incredibly complex, and when we start to alter one part, we can only guess at what'll result. Animals and plants are adapted to their habitats, and if it gets hotter, species will vanish. Already scientists think the polar bear is in danger of extinction..."

"Who the hell cares?" Boyle growled.

"Some will care, and environmentalists are becoming increasingly vocal. However, there are other, perhaps more serious, effects of an increasing temperature. The glaciers have been receding for decades and almost every year the polar sea ice is less. The ice is melting, faster than it can grow again the next winter. More ice melting means more fresh water being dumped into the oceans. The sea level rises, swamping low-lying land and altering ocean currents like the Gulf Stream."

"We've all heard about this putative rise in sea levels," Hu said, his precise English distinctive among the other accents. "But it's hardly risen at all, has it? I've heard figures of a centimeter or so. That's hardly catastrophic."

13

"The figure's twenty centimeters--eight inches--in the last century."

"There you go then. What're we worrying about?"

"The official forecast for the next century is something like another fifty centimeters..." Hu opened his mouth again and then shut it. Max continued. "This estimate is likely to be conservative. Sea level rises from melting ice alone could well exceed two meters in the next fifty years, sufficient to inundate low-lying land and cause chaos in major cities around the world. The expansion of deep water as the warmth penetrates is much greater and far less easily reversed. That could cause sea levels to rise by twenty meters."

"Can it even be stopped?" Boyle asked.

"The sea level rise is tied to rising temperatures, and the temperatures to CO_2 increases." Max smiled. "You could try burning less coal."

"Funny man," Radinov growled. "We're all in the coal business. Are you suggesting we all go out of business?"

"Not in the slightest, Mr Radinov. All I am saying is that the root of all the world's environmental problems is carbon dioxide. More of it will kill this planet; less may save it--if the world acts swiftly."

"And us? What's our part in this?" Svenson turned to the shadowy figure at the head of the table. "Why've you brought us all here?"

"You'll see. Pray continue, Max."

Max inclined his head with a smile. "Thank you, Herr Matternicht. Let me speak frankly, gentlemen. For many years, we in the coal sector have made vast profits from this fossil fuel, and we've cared nothing about the enormous amounts of pollution our power stations, and others like them, were belching into the atmosphere. Coal's cheap and present in staggering amounts. We've barely scratched the surface of the earth in our quest for this commodity. We burn it in our power stations to produce the electricity that runs the mills of progress.

"But for every ton of coal burned in our power stations, we add nearly four tons of carbon dioxide to the atmosphere. Last year, in 1999, the world consumed two billion tons of coal--producing eight billion tons of carbon dioxide. This year, I am sure it will be more--and so on. How long can we continue to do this without it having an irreversible effect? More importantly, gentlemen, how long will the governments of the world allow us to continue doing this?"

"They'd better continue," Boyle growled. "I pay the lobbyists in Washington a fortune to keep the wheels turning smoothly."

"Indeed, as do we all," Max said. "And we've a very strong argument on our side - the world needs coal and industry would shut down if coal production ceased. But, here's the thing, if coal is shown to be the villain of climate change, without any redeeming features, governments may introduce policies to phase out coal over a twenty- or thirty-year period."

"They'd never do that," Boyle said uneasily.

"They will. The climate is changing," Max said. "And I don't mean just the weather. The political climate's changing too and, thanks to our environmentalist friends, politicians are becoming aware of the problem. If levels of CO_2, temperature and sea keep rising, the governments will act against those they see as the major polluters--us."

His audience digested this for a few moments.

"They wouldn't dare," Radinov muttered. "We fund them, we bribe them, we make and break governments..."

"They'll dare, if the alternative is worse."

"So what, then?" Boyle asked. "Herr Matternicht, you must have a plan. I cannot believe you brought us all here to tell us our business is finished."

"Indeed, I didn't, and yes, I've a plan. But first, I ask your patience just a little longer. Max?"

"I must ask your patience a moment longer too, Herr Matternicht," Max said. "There's one other thing I haven't mentioned. With all the talk of carbon dioxide, methane, ozone and water vapor, it's easy to overlook other substances being poured into the atmosphere. Nitrogen oxides, fine particulate matter and sulphur dioxide to name a few. We know almost nothing about how these substances affect our climate, whether alone, or in conjunction with other pollutants."

"Then why concern ourselves with them?" Radinov asked.

"Sulphur dioxide cools the climate, apparently. When volcanic eruptions inject sulphur dioxide into the atmosphere, there's a cooling effect."

"Then it's our friend. This sulphur dioxide will prevent global warming and we've nothing to worry about."

"Unfortunately for that scenario, sulphur dioxide's a major pollutant, causing acid rain and smog, and most governments are making strenuous efforts to curb its production. It's entirely possible that the SO_2 in the atmosphere has been masking and slowing the rise in temperature due to CO_2 levels. Now that SO_2 is being removed, we may see the temperatures rise even faster than predicted."

"Seems like you fuckin' scientists don't know everything after all," Boyle rasped. "All we hear are problems, never the solutions."

"Oh, there's a solution." Max fell silent, smiling slightly, and looked at each man in turn.

"Well, what the hell is it?" Boyle asked.

"We must reduce the amount of carbon dioxide in the atmosphere."

"Wonderful," Svenson said. "So, we're to reduce our profits drastically, mining and burning less coal." The Swedish coal baron shook his head. "I think I'll take my chances with politicians and their greed."

"I didn't say anything about reducing output," Max said. "There're two sides to the equation. Reduce the amount you put into the atmosphere, or increase the amount you take out."

"I don't understand," Hu said. "Are you talking about planting more trees?"

"No. If you tried to use trees to soak up excess CO_2, you'd need regional forests planted each year. That's passive sequestration."

"I've heard of that term," Svenson said. "It involves taking carbon dioxide and locking it up so it cannot escape, doesn't it?"

"That's right, but the amounts I'm talking about are far greater than anything you'll find in biological systems. I'm talking about geo-sequestration--storing carbon dioxide in liquid form deep underground."

"Can it be done?" Radinov asked. "Do we have the technology, or is this just some vodka-fueled fantasy?"

"It can be done," Boyle said, nodding. "We've been doing it for years in the oil and gas industry. When you want to get the last oil and gas from an underground deposit, you blow pressurized carbon dioxide into the rocks to flush out the fuel. I presume you're talking about the same thing, Professor?"

"Essentially, yes," Max agreed, "But on a much greater scale."

"Why?" Boyle asked.

"And what's liquid CO_2?" Hu asked. "I thought CO_2 went straight from a gas to a solid--you know, dry ice."

"Indeed it does, Mr Hu, at normal pressures. However, if we subject the gas to sufficient pressure it will liquefy. And to answer your question, Mr Boyle, liquid CO_2 occupies far less space than gaseous CO_2. By pumping it deep underground, you remove it from the biosphere, and if you remove enough of it, CO_2 levels in the atmosphere decrease ... or at least go no higher," he added as an afterthought.

The men sat around the table and considered the scientist's words.

"So, we set up pumps or something to extract CO_2 from the air?" Boyle asked. "It sounds very expensive."

"Not from the atmosphere," Max explained. "That'd be prohibitively expensive. We need to liquefy the CO_2 at a place where the levels are high, like the exhaust from power station furnaces." Max leafed through some papers on the desk in front of him and selected one. "Let's consider an example. A 500-megawatt power station that'll service 300 thousand homes will require a minimum of ten thousand tons of coal per day, more if it's to meet peak demands. This produces about 37 thousand tons of CO_2 every day, or over 13 million tons a year--from one power station servicing one medium-sized city. You see the scale of the problem, gentlemen? Let's say for the moment that we can capture all of the CO_2 produced from this single power station. We then have to find a place to store it. The standard solution is to find a depleted oil or gas field and inject it into the same layers of rock that successfully held the oil or gas. It might work--after all, the rock held the fuel for millions of years. But where're we going to find a sufficient number of suitably sized empty rock strata?

"The Norwegians started playing around with the Sleipner field offshore in 1996, pumping CO_2 into the strata. In the last four years they've stored around two million tons. Not too bad an effort until you compare it to the output from our single power station--fifty million tons in the same time frame. The Germans are looking at injecting CO_2 into an aquifer near Berlin. This project is only in its infancy and won't be operational for at least a couple of years. Other governments are tossing the idea around, but none really seriously."

Boyle grunted. "Sounds pretty damn hopeless to me. Why're you even considering it, Matternicht?"

"Because I believe we can do better. Tell them, Max. It's time to go straight to the heart of the matter."

"As you wish, Herr Matternicht. Gentlemen, the coal companies are being cast as the villains when it comes to pollution and CO_2 levels. We believe it's time to go on the offensive and demonstrate that the governments, that the world, cannot do without us. We have the expertise and the money to solve the carbon capture and storage problem and when we do solve it, no government in the world will be able to curb our businesses. Herr Matternicht proposes that we build a full-scale sequestration plant at a coal-fired power station and demonstrate that we can capture the full carbon output of the station and store it safely."

"When you say we've the money, why do I get worried?" Radinov asked. "What figure are we talking about?"

"A billion dollars to start with, probably more."

"Jesus!" Boyle exclaimed.

Radinov swore, colorfully and unintelligibly, in Russian.

"That's a big chunk of change," Svenson said. "We can't afford that."

Max laughed. "What makes you think you'd have to? The governments will pay, as they always have. Coal-produced electricity's very cheap and no government wants to tell its electorate that they're being noble and taking the more expensive option that will result in higher electricity costs to the public. No, we'll do the sequestration research and make a big song and dance about how responsible we're being, but the governments will fund our research and make us all a handsome profit by paying us to sequester CO_2 instead of releasing it into the atmosphere."

"This'll need careful promotion," Hu said thoughtfully. "We could call the process 'clean coal' or 'green coal' or something."

"Even so," Boyle said, "We still have to come up with the initial money. I'm not sure I can afford that sort of outlay."

"You can't afford not to," Matternicht said quietly. "Anyway, I'll pay half."

"Why would you do that?" Boyle asked suspiciously.

"The vision's mine. I'll determine where the effort is made, and mine will be the name on the letterhead. When the governments of the world clamour to be allowed to fund the project--and they will--half the profits will be mine."

"And you're sure the governments will do this?" Svenson asked. "They will-- how do you say it? Come to the party?"

"Yes, if we do it right.

"And they'll pay?" Hu asked. "How much?"

Matternicht shrugged delicately. "Who can put a figure on it? I am confident we'll all recover our outlay, and much more. Also, what figure would you put on being able to conduct your business without environmental or governmental interference? Gentlemen, we'll no longer be villains, but heroes."

"Where will the first full-scale carbon capture and storage facility be?" Boyle asked. "America would be a good place to start. I can think of suitable sites in Texas, Nevada and Oregon."

"Come to Russia," Radinov insisted. "No bothersome regulations."

"Sweden too," Svenson stated.

"Lots of room in outback Australia," Thomas Hu mused. "Sino-Australasian Coal would be happy to accommodate you."

"I'll examine many sites," Matternicht assured them. "I've places in mind in all your countries, and more besides. We'll do this carefully, gentlemen, and you'll see, within ten years the governments will be in our pockets, within twenty and the world will sing our praises, within thirty and climate change will slow. Then you'll reap your full reward."

Chapter 3

September 7, 2012

September 7 was a cold day but a fine one, and after he had prepared the lodge, Nigel Campion stood outside and filled his lungs with the crisp air, his gaze drinking in the snow-covered slopes of Mount Hood and the contrasting deep green of coniferous forest lower down. The road to the ski lodge had been cleared of snow earlier, a costly exercise to bring the machinery all the way up there but a necessary one for this was an essential meeting. He could hear the growl of powerful cars on the steep gradients that led to the lodge and he moved to the reception area to greet Matternicht's guests.

The cars arrived in a group, their drivers having instructions to do so. The passengers got out and looked at the other people warily. Two of them recognized each other and nodded a perfunctory greeting before being led into the warmth of the lodge. Campion took their coats and ushered them into the main room where refreshments were laid out in preparation.

"Please, gentlemen, help yourselves to anything you desire."

The men took what they desired in the way of food and drink and sat in large over-stuffed armchairs in a semicircle around the fire.

"Why're we here, Campion?" asked a thin, middle-aged man.

"You're here because James Matternicht asked you to be," Campion said pleasantly. "I know you and Andrew know each other, but probably not my other guest, so let me make the introductions. As you all know, I am Nigel Campion,

Aide to James Matternicht. This..." he indicated the thin man, "...is Robert Peale, Assistant to the Vice-President of Oregon Coal and Power. Next to him is Andrew Winton, businessman and Chairman of the Northern Oregon Chamber of Commerce; and Norman Crane of the US Department of Energy. The reason you're here is to put in place the final aspects of the sequestration project."

"It's going ahead then?" Winton asked.

"Most certainly. It was just a matter of putting the last blocks in place. Mr Crane here supplied the last of these a few days ago."

Winton looked at Crane appraisingly. "DOE's decided to come to the party then?"

Crane did not answer immediately, but instead, looked to Campion, an unspoken question in his eyes.

Campion nodded. "You may trust them. They know better than to cross Matternicht."

"The Department of Energy has been examining the proposal in depth for the last three years. We've utilized the United States Geological Survey databases and drawn up a shortlist of sites that we'd be prepared to sanction, provided funding for the capital works involved is in place."

"May we see this shortlist of sites?" Peale asked.

"No," Crane replied. "It's still classified as Confidential."

"However, I can tell you that Rushing River is on the list," Campion said. "Though to be truly accurate, it's the Hood Anticline under Rushing River."

"Will Rushing River be chosen?"

"That isn't up to me," Crane said. "I thought I made that clear, Campion. There's only so much I can do. I got the site shortlisted..."

"And you'll select it in due course," Campion said with a smile. "Your superior, Ernest Withers is retiring at the end of the year..."

"I've heard nothing about this."

"It's not common knowledge, but he'll retire for personal reasons."

"Even so, Richards is a shoe-in for his position. I know for a fact he doesn't favour sequestration."

"Richards won't replace Withers--you will. Withers will strongly recommend you to the new administration."

"If there's a new administration."

"There will be."

Crane stared. "How can you know that, and anyway, why should he? He doesn't like me or support my ideas."

"Shall we just say, he took some persuading, but he'll do it. When you replace him, you'll initiate the final selection process and make sure that Rushing River is given the green light. The GOP, which we confidently expect will be more in favor of projects like this after it wins in November, will create an office of Carbon Capture and Storage. I think you'd be the best man to head this up."

Crane struggled ineffectually to keep his pleasure under control, and Peale scowled at the DOE man's expression. "So Rushing River's chosen. What then?"

"Then we need a dedicated man to fast-forward the construction of the Carbon Capture Plant. I see you as that man, Peale. You'll be CEO of Oregon Power's Sequestration Facility with all that entails. Are you up for it?"

"Damn right."

"And what do you have planned for me?" Winton asked. "Am I, too, to be rewarded with power and position?"

Campion grinned. "You'll have all the support you need, but I believe your coin is literally that. Money will be no problem. In return, I want a concerted campaign in favor of carbon geosequestration."

"You've already had that these past five years."

"I know, and we appreciate your efforts, Andrew, but that support was general. Now we need specific enthusiastic support for the Rushing River site as the proper place for the carbon capture project."

Winton shrugged. "Of course."

"How many papers do you control?"

"Seven. Also, three radio stations, and I have influence on two television stations. Plus, the support of businesses throughout the Northwest."

"Good. I'll make sure Professor Maxwell Hay contacts you after the new President is sworn in next January. Use him; feature him in editorials; get onto talk shows, arrange interviews, opening malls, whatever it takes. I want geosequestration accepted as the next best thing since sliced bread. You'll be the public face of sequestration. Stress the safety of the procedure and how it's going to lead to a cleaner, greener planet--you know the sort of thing."

"Coal and a clean environment don't exactly mix."

"Then change that view. Show people what'll happen if we cut back on coal-- fewer jobs and higher prices. Then hold up sequestration as being the answer. We can burn all the coal we want as long as we soak up all the waste carbon dioxide and store it safely underground. Show them that coal can literally be green."

Winton nodded. "Rushing River will be able to sequester all of its carbon dioxide?" he asked.

Campion looked at Peale. "Why don't you answer that one?"

"Damn near," Peale replied. "It depends which model is accepted, but we could sequester up to ninety percent if we handled up to fifty thousand tons a day. More than that and the percentage falls off, but it'll still be above seventy."

"Good enough, I suppose," Winton said. "And it'll be safe?"

"Absolutely. I've had a scientific team looking at it and the Hood Anticline has an impervious cap. Once the stuff's down there, it's there forever."

"Okay, that's good enough for me. What about you, Crane? Are you going to be able to swing this with the DOE?"

Norman Crane nodded. "In my present position I wouldn't have a hope in hell, but if Campion can deliver as promised and get me in as Administrative Head...well, yes I can do it. After all, geological science backs us up. Or should I say, enough scientists back us up. Sequestration is still a bit of an unknown quantity but if you can deliver a groundswell of public support, Winton, the politicians will listen."

"There'll be plenty of support for you all," Campion assured them. "All you have to do is the part you have been assigned. I've seen the budget on this one, and let me just say that the rewards are substantial. Salaries, share deals and gratuities will be commensurate with your achievements. With approval from the DOE, support from the public sector and press, and the best facilities money can buy...Gentlemen, how can we fail?"

Chapter 4

February 9, 2013

The summons from James Matternicht found Max Hay at dinner with a delightful young lady at the Tantris restaurant on Johann-Fichte-Strasse in Munich. As usual, the food and ambience were superb and the company held promise for the hours ahead. A waiter brought the cell phone to the table and Max heard a laconic message from Matternicht's aide.

"Campion here. He wants you. The usual place."

Max sighed and made his excuses. The young lady pouted, but he found her a taxi and settled up with the restaurant using his Platinum Reserve credit card. Even the high prices for the interrupted meals scarcely scratched the surface of the card's balance.

Matternicht was waiting in his office on the Koniginstrasse overlooking the Englischer Garten. He had the drinks ready--five ounces of warm soymilk for himself and a dry ginger ale for Max.

"Ishkabibble," Matternicht said with a smile, handing him a glass.

"San fairy ann," Max replied. He sipped his soda and sat down in one of the armchairs. "What's so urgent? I was with a rather delectable young lady at the Tantris."

"How the good professor has come up in the world," Matternicht remarked. "Your tastes have become expensive."

"Life is good," Max admitted. "What's so urgent it couldn't wait?"

"I'm afraid Campion was a little enthusiastic. I was surprised you were coming here tonight. Tomorrow would have done. Anyway, seeing as you're here, I'll tell you now. The geosequestration project is officially under way. No more site research needed. Now we just apply ourselves to the task of squirreling away millions of tons of carbon dioxide and watching the money roll in."

"You've decided on a site then. Where?"

Matternicht eased himself into an armchair and regarded his science advisor over the top of his glass. "You tell me. You selected the sites, studied the geomorphology of each and weighed up the pros and cons."

Max settled back in his chair and sipped on his ginger ale while he considered the short list of sites he had submitted five years before, and the repeated updates on them as new data flowed in and governments came and went. "I seem to remember I ranked them as Canada first, then Australia, Oregon, Saudi Arabia and Brazil. Given recent political instabilities, I'd drop the last two so...Bella Lake, Canada."

"Rushing River, Oregon."

"Why?"

"You look surprised, Max. It was third on your list."

"It was third for a very good reason; the capping rock is less than perfect. Why not Bella Lake? The formation is deeper and thus safer."

"And very much more expensive. Max, you have a gift for science but your economic expertise leaves something to be desired. The Canadian option would net us several million dollars less per year."

"Out of billions, Mr Matternicht. The added safety factor is worth that."

"That's debatable. Anyway, the new administration in the United States has made us a very attractive offer, so I have decided to develop the Oregon option. Do you have a problem with that, Max?"

Max shrugged. "I can live with it."

"Good, because you are heading out to Oregon next Tuesday. You'll work with Robert Peale, the new CEO of the as yet unbuilt sequestration installation, to get it up and running."

"That sounds like a long-term project."

"Yes, you'll need to relocate to the West Coast."

Max looked out of the window at the dark vegetation of the Englischer Garten and the lights of the city. He sighed. "I'm a scientist, Mr Matternicht. Wouldn't it be better to send some admin type or engineer?"

"You'll have all the help you need over there, but I want you to oversee the actual sequestration project. Delegate the construction and security aspects. You'll be responsible for ensuring the carbon dioxide is safely stored away underground."

Max frowned. "I can't guarantee that at Rushing River. You've seen my reports on the capping rock."

"Yes, and I've also read the reports by the USGS and DOE. They rate it as safe."

"Safe for oil and gas, yes, but not supercritical carbon dioxide."

"This is not like you, Max, to go looking for trouble. I'm satisfied the capping rock is intact and strong enough. You just make sure the gas can be injected into it quickly and efficiently."

"And if it can't?"

"Then you find a way of doing it. You are my science expert, Max. If you can't do it, no one can. Install whatever safety features you think are necessary, monitor leakages, anything. Just make sure it's up and running by the beginning of 2015. I don't have to remind you that a lot of money depends on this project, and I am prepared to be generous."

Max nodded. "I'll do my best."

"Good man. Now, another soda or do you want to get back to your lady friend?"

"Eh? Oh, I sent her home." Max's mind was already on the Rushing River site in northern Oregon and he saw the layers of rock beneath in his mind's eye. He accepted the fresh glass of ginger ale without comment, his forehead crumpling in thought. *I can do this. It'll be difficult, but I can do it.*

Chapter 5

March 14, 2015

Robert Peale sat in the body of the audience and looked out over the fifty or so people there, clutching his notes. The last five years had seen the culmination of his dreams, with his appointment to the position of CEO of the Oregon Energy's Carbon Sequestration Facility at Rushing River. He felt inordinately pleased with himself, especially now that the geo-sequestration facility was about to go officially online.

From where he sat he could see a young man standing on the stage at the front of the small auditorium, and an older man waiting in the wings. Both looked impatient, and Peale waited for them to call the meeting to order.

"Please be seated," the young man said. Slowly, the noise decreased and people started to look toward the stage. "Gentlemen," he went on, forgetting the presence of half a dozen smartly dressed women in the audience, "Let us begin." He waited a few moments for the last shuffling of feet and creaking of seats to die down.

"This is indeed a red-letter day, a day that will be recognized by all civilized people as the day the United States Government, in conjunction with companies motivated primarily by selflessness and humanitarian concern, took the first real step along the road that will lead to the control of climate change. For years we have listened to the arguments between scientists on both sides of the environmental debate, weighed up the pros and cons of this action and that, and while the world dissolved into acrimony and name calling, we have worked surely and steadily to evolve a response that will solve the world's climate problems.

"I don't have to tell you what this solution is, for you've all been intimately concerned with it these last years. I see before me in the audience, a great body of scientific knowledge, men...and women, with the farsightedness and determination to turn this noble enterprise into actuality. We're represented here today by three of the great estates of modern society--by Government, by Science, and by Commerce. I think we can be forgiven for not inviting the Fourth Estate--the Press..." The young man waited for the ripple of laughter to die down. "The Press has been the reason this debate has dragged on so long, fueling debate for monetary gain. Well, no more. Calmer minds have prevailed and have brought the Great Solution to the brink of fruition.

"I know you're all eager to hear officially that what we've all been working for has come to pass, so I'll yield the podium to the newly appointed Head of the United States Department of Energy's Office of Carbon Capture and Storage. Ladies and Gentlemen, I give you Norman Crane."

Amid enthusiastic applause from the hundred people present, the young man extended a hand to the wings, and then backed away, clapping his hands with gusto. A tall man in an impeccably tailored suit and with a shock of lustrous black hair, strode onto the stage, nodded politely at the officer, and faced the podium.

"Thank you," Crane said quietly. He waited for the applause to die away before continuing. "It was not so many years ago that the heads of governments met to debate climate change and ways to meet the challenge of global warming--and even whether global warming existed. I was there at Kyoto and Copenhagen as an observer; I was a speaker at Sydney, at Rio, at Paris, at Beijing, and at Delhi, and this past year the Department of Energy created the office of Carbon Capture and Storage and committed this great nation to taking a leading role in this fine new technology that promises so much.

"Those of you familiar with the concept will also know that every western nation and a great many of the developing ones has been working to get this technology operating despite seemingly insuperable problems. You will also know that the United States has achieved it first and rightfully takes its place as the leading scientific nation on this planet." He paused, and at once his staff broke into an apparently spontaneous burst of applause, followed an instant later by the other delegates. Crane beamed and raised his hands in a style somewhat reminiscent of President Nixon.

Who the hell does he think he's impressing, Peale thought. Apparently, someone had similar thoughts for a whispered conversation erupted behind him.

"Look at him there," murmured a young man. "He thinks this is another pep rally for the party. There aren't even any TV cameras here to capture his success. If only he knew what a farce this all was."

The young man's companion replied, "Keep it down, Jim. This is not the time."

"Ahh, Kev. Just listen to him. Anyone would think..."

Peale turned his head and looked the younger man up and down. "Anyone would think what?"

Jim raised an eyebrow. "Sorry, bud. Private conversation."

Peale smiled. "Not any longer. I gather you don't think much of our lead speaker."

"Nothing against him as a politician. I just think his science sucks."

"What makes you a science expert?"

"I keep my eyes open. The name's Dr Jim Bellingham." The young man stuck his hand out and after a moment's hesitation Peale grasped it. "I'm with the EIA," Bellingham went on. "I know all about this stuff." He glanced around the room. "Probably more than most people here."

"And with all the arrogance of youth," Peale murmured.

Jim shrugged. "What's your name?"

"Robert Peale. You say you're in the Energy Information Administration? So you must be familiar with this whole concept and our energy strategies. You also know the DOE and USGS have given their full approval. Why do you say Crane's speech is a farce?"

"Well..." Bellingham paused. He glanced across to where Norman Crane was continuing his speech, and shook his head at the outpouring of self-congratulatory phrases. He shook off a warning hand from his friend and leaned closer to Peale. "Well, he talks as if this is all a done deal, as if the science has all been completed, the t's crossed and the i's dotted."

"And it isn't?"

"No way. I'm one of the guys who have to present this technology as if it's as safe as...as crossing the road..." Bellingham grinned. "Tell that to the skunk."

"Skunk? What does that mean?"

"It means that carbon capture and sequestration is about as safe for us humans as crossing a road is for incipient road kill. The skunk thinks the road is flat and easy to walk on, that it's all nice and safe, but when he least expects it...bam! Guts all over the road. It's the same with humans and this CCS technology."

"Jim, that's enough." Kev put his hand on Jim's arm again. "You'll have to excuse Jim's enthusiasm, Mr Peale. He feels passionately about the environment and he gets a bit carried away."

"Bullshit--if you'll pardon my French. They need to be told and..."

28

A man alongside them frowned and raised a finger to his lips. "Please. I'm trying to listen."

Peale grimaced but kept his expression pleasant. "Forgive me, Mr Bellingham, but I fail to see how you fit in here. It seems to me you'd be more at home with the protesters trying to stop all progress than with people committed to saving the planet. That's what we are trying to do with this technology."

"Very commendable intentions, I'm sure, except this CCS is the wrong way to go about it. For Christ's sake! I've gone over the figures, checked the assumptions and done the math. I'm the one who fuckin' supplied the summaries to these bozos and they've completely ignored my recommendations."

"There are a lot of very experienced scientists and administrators in government who..."

"Who don't know their ass from a hole in the ground," Jim snapped.

People looked round with expressions of annoyance and interest. The security guards were looking in their direction and even Jim caught this message. He scowled and leaned back in his chair, crossing his arms. "You'll see," he muttered. "Just don't believe everything you hear today."

Peale nodded pleasantly and turned his attention back to the speaker on stage.

Crane's speech came to a close and the audience rose to its feet in adulation and appreciation. Kev got up, too, and dragged Jim with him, though the young men only offered up a few polite claps before sitting down again. The Head of the Office of Carbon Capture and Storage beamed and waved, soaking up the praise before modestly signaling for silence.

"It is now with great pleasure that I introduce the person who will put all this Government's research and development into action. The United States Department of Energy has named the company that will lead this nation and the world into the challenge of the century, to operate the first full-scale carbon capture and storage facility in the world. I give you the Chief Executive Officer of Oregon Energy's Carbon Sequestration Facility, Robert Peale." Crane gestured toward the audience, and Peale stood up and acknowledged the applause, before making his way down through the delegates.

Peale started with the obligatory round of thanks and praise for every other senior delegate in the room, leading the applause himself as he commended the government heads and administrators for their farsightedness and selfless attitudes that had brought about this great day.

"And so we come to it at last, Saturday March 14, 2015, the day when the decision was made that will launch the first great opportunity mankind have to bring about the saving of our beautiful planet. I'm too young to remember it myself, but I've seen the tapes of that historic day when Neil Armstrong first walked on the moon's surface. He said then that it was a small step for a man but a giant leap for mankind."

Peale smiled deprecatingly. "I do not consider myself in the same league as Armstrong, but I would like to think that this day, too, represented another leap of mankind. Today, a dream becomes a reality. Today, we start to save the world.

"Now, I don't want to run our environmental colleagues down, but planting a few trees, walking to the mall instead of driving, or taking public transport is just a drop in the ocean--the steadily rising ocean..." A ripple of laughter washed over the audience. "...and will never achieve what we need. The requirements of business are too great to just cut back on growth, on jobs, on income. We cannot cut back sufficiently to cure the world. We must protect business, protect jobs, create wealth, but do it in a way that is environmentally sustainable. We have to act, and act decisively if we're to reduce the carbon dioxide content of the atmosphere, if we're to reduce global warming, if we're to prevent the rise of the oceans and ameliorate the impact of technology on our common environment.

"For too long business has been portrayed as the 'bad guy', the villain. Some administrations have even gone so far as to put limits on the companies that produce the wealth of our great nation, seeking to undermine the social structure that has made our country prosperous and powerful. Well, we can thank God that the present administration can see clearly what needs to be done and has moved decisively to implement policies that will be the saving of us all.

"You will all be aware of Oregon Energy and the huge advances it has made in the last twenty years. Once, we were just another energy company committed to the production of plentiful supplies of cheap electricity for the residents and businesses of Oregon. Our coal-fired power stations were even then among the cleanest in the business but as we all became aware of the insidious effects of pollution and carbon dioxide on global warming, we at Oregon Energy initiated research to reduce our emissions still further. Then, in early 2010, using a technology that promised a solution to rising carbon dioxide levels, Oregon Energy opened the new division of Carbon Sequestration, based on CCS technology. This technology, as you all now know, takes the carbon dioxide which is the natural by-product of coal combustion, compresses it enormously, and stores it deep underground where these deposits can remain safe for thousands of years. Carbon dioxide need no longer be added to the atmosphere, there to do its insidious damage, but can be safely stored away, or sequestered. Carbon Sequestration is now part of the largest company in the world designed specifically to capture carbon and sequester it.

"And on this day, ladies and gentlemen, March 14 2015, the Division of Carbon Sequestration has received authorization from the United States

Department of Energy to go into full-scale carbon capture as the flagship company of this great country, and indeed the world."

Peale paused and, a heartbeat later, the delegates responded with a roar of applause that quickly led to a standing ovation. Everyone there knew the decision had been made months in advance, but it was necessary for the play to be acted out, for the announcement to be made publicly. The CEO of Carbon Sequestration stood and smiled at the audience, waiting for the clapping to die away so he could reveal the only aspect of this decision that was not as yet widely known among the delegates.

"As many of you will be aware," Peale went on, "the efficient processing of the enormous quantities of carbon dioxide produced by a coal-fired power station is not an easy task. In fact, it's quite formidable, but we've achieved it. I won't bore you with figures but the constraints put upon us by public safety necessitate the building of the carbon capture facility actually at the power station, and the sequestration site similarly in close proximity. We at Oregon Energy have tested sites near our power stations over the last few years and we, in consultation with the Department of Energy and the United States Geological Survey have determined the safest place for carbon sequestration. This place is the Hood Anticline, a dome of impervious rock lying at a minimum depth of just over one mile..." Peale smiled and nodded at a group of USGS scientists near the front of the room. "...or as my scientific colleagues here like to put it, 1800 meters below the surface. I think that's deep enough to satisfy anyone. By a lucky coincidence, one of Oregon Energy's largest power stations sits atop this geological formation. We have constructed a carbon capture facility alongside it, capable of liquefying 90% of the carbon dioxide produced, and a pumping station that can immediately force this liquefied carbon deep into the earth through specially reinforced boreholes where it is trapped by the impermeable cap of the anticline. This combined production, capture and storage station is the Rushing River facility."

Jim Bellingham leapt to his feet. "A question, Mr Peale. Are you aware that this Hood Anticline, far from being the impervious..."

The delegates turned and stared, the EIA officials groaned, and Peale signaled urgently to the security personnel.

"...cap of rock you portray it to be, is in fact less than secure..."

The security men pushed their way along the row and took hold of Jim. Kev tried to intervene and one of the guards threatened him with a taser. Jim yelled and threw a punch and went down under the weight of two other guards, screaming obscenities.

Five minutes later, after the two young men had been arrested and hauled off in handcuffs, Peale called the meeting to order once more. He could see that several delegates were frowning and possibly even considering the meaning behind the young man's words. Something more had to be said.

"Let us not concern ourselves with these modern-day Luddites. There are always those who long for a simpler life, a life without electricity, running water, medicine, good food and all the amenities that science and technology bring us. A stress-free dream of simpler days perhaps, but it's not real. You cannot turn back time. We shouldn't punish these misguided people, but rather pity them and pray that by example we may show them the error of their ways.

"I don't know what that young man was trying to say, but I sincerely hope that his superiors at the Energy Information Administration will be having words with him. Lest anyone feel the slightest doubt about the Rushing River Facility, let me assure you that the DOE and the USGS has the fullest confidence in both Carbon Sequestration and the chosen site."

Peale felt he had the audience back in control once more but knew that a gesture was needed. "In two days' time, at 9am on Monday March 16, the switch will symbolically be thrown, putting Carbon Sequestration into full production. I invite you all to be on hand to see this and to inspect the site yourself. Let nobody tell you the Rushing River Facility is safe or unsafe--come and see for yourselves. You'll leave knowing the future of carbon sequestration is in safe hands."

Chapter 6

March 16, 2015

T he Oregon Coal and Energy Station at Rushing River threw open its gates at 9 a.m. on the Monday, in readiness for the official throwing of the switch. The main guests at the conference had been in attendance since just after seven, partaking of an impromptu barbecued breakfast before the official business got under way. Robert Peale gave the appearance of a charming relaxed host, though he suspected people could hear him grinding his teeth. Too much rested on this morning for his liking and for the last thirty-six hours he had regretted his invitation for all the delegates to attend the symbolic switching on of the pumping station.

The Public Relations people were much more enthusiastic and Peale suspected they were starting to believe their own hype. They had invited the Press along, as if nothing could go wrong, and even now, Nick Farley, the young PR officer from the conference was extolling the virtues of Carbon Capture and Storage in general, and the Oregon Energy's pumping station in particular. Peale edged closer to listen.

"A marvel of technology," Farley gushed. "Millions have been spent on this one station alone, and billions on overall research into carbon capture and sequestration. All the best materials, installed by the best craftsmen and overseen by dedicated engineers and scientists. The technicians who'll be running the station have received the best training and we can guarantee that when the station is operating, nothing can go wrong. It's totally fail-safe."

"Annaliese Harding, Salem Chronicle," a young brunette reporter said. "Can anything really be completely fail-safe?"

"This station can, Miss...er, Annaliese," Farley said, offering up a winning smile. "You can rest easy at night, knowing we're on the job."

"Are you safe from terrorism?" asked a young man. "Peter Pascoe, Seattle Daily," he added.

"Absolutely. We have one of the finest security firms in the business guarding us."

"What about earthquakes?" Pascoe went on. "Security isn't going to be of much use then, and we get a lot of tremors in the Pacific Northwest."

"Not a problem," Farley said. "As you will already know, I'm sure; the power station itself is built to rigorous standards and the compressing and pumping stations likewise, but with an added safety precaution. The whole facility is built on flexible foundations that are designed to move in the event of an earthquake, allowing horizontal and vertical movements of up to a meter. A system of valves and automatic shutdowns ensures that compressed liquid CO_2 in the borehole cannot escape, even if the pipeline ruptures. I assure you, a facility like this really is fail-safe. Perhaps you'd like to have a look?"

Robert Peale watched as Farley ushered the gaggle of reporters out of the reception building, before joining a group of scientists and administration officials standing in front of a display board.

"Mr Peale," said a smartly dressed grey-haired man as he approached. "When can we expect to get this done? I have to get back to Vancouver."

"I'm sorry, Dr Adams," Peale told the Head of the Geological Survey for the West Coast. "We are waiting for the Head of CCS to arrive."

Adams grimaced and looked at his watch. "Well, I can't stay. Dr Morrison here can stand in for me." He indicated a young man with a mop of unruly hair who was examining the posters on display.

"Eh? Oh, yes, if you like," Morrison said. He waited until his chief had left and then indicated the display. "How accurate is this map?"

Peale glanced at the administrators and scientists standing around wearing expressions of polite interest, then back at Morrison. "What seems to be the problem?"

"No problem, Mr Peale. I was just wondering how accurate the information was on this map."

"Very accurate, I'm told. We've been very careful in everything we do here."

Morrison nodded. "These little green squares are your echo-sounding sites where you probed the integrity of the Hood Anticline?"

Peale had a look at the chart. "Yes, that's correct. As you can see, the coverage is complete."

"That young guy at the conference didn't seem so sure, did he? What was his name--Bellingham? He's with the EIA, isn't he?"

"Not anymore," put in one of the dark-suited administrators. He put out his hand to Peale. "Brad Limstock, Deputy Chairperson of EIA."

"Ah, yes, an unfortunate incident," Peale said. "I'm glad the EIA has cleaned house. Men like that can cause enormous damage with their ill-founded prattle."

"Was it though?" Morrison mused. "You really found the anticline cap was entire? No flaws at all?"

"That's right." Peale turned away from the young geologist, wary of the direction the conversation was going. "I'm sure Norman Crane will be here any moment. Perhaps we could all repair to the control room..."

"You see," Morrison cut in. "I'm certain bore holes were drilled into the Hood Anticline--it's technically a dome, by the way--almost a hundred years ago. Unless those holes were plugged properly, they'd constitute a flaw in the cap rock."

"I can assure you everything was checked."

Morrison nodded and chewed his lower lip thoughtfully. "Who checked it?"

"You did Dr Morrison, or rather the USGS. We have the report on file."

"I don't remember seeing it." Morrison looked at the interested bystanders and smiled. "Look, I'm sure everything is fine. As you say, the USGS passed it. But I was wondering if I could have a word with your own Company geologist."

"Why?"

"Purely for my own interest, Mr Peale." He grinned disarmingly. "I did my doctoral dissertation on salt dome anticlines and I haven't had much chance to work on them since. I'd love to have a chat with your scientists."

Peale grunted. "Hmm, well, that'd be Dr Desmond Twentyman. Just ask at the front desk." He waved a hand toward the foyer and then led the other people away toward the control room.

* * *

Morrison wandered over to the foyer, grabbing a cup of freshly brewed coffee as he passed the refreshment table. There were a few people standing at the front desk and he waited patiently, sipping at his coffee until the man behind the desk turned to him.

"Dr Twentyman please. Mr Peale suggested I talk to him."

The man picked up the telephone and punched in the numbers. "Who shall I say is calling?"

"Dr Matt Morrison, USGS."

The man conveyed this information, listened a moment and replaced the phone in its holder. "He'll be right down, sir."

Morrison nodded his thanks and walked off a few paces to look at a subtle piece of sculpture gracing the center of the foyer. He could not decipher what it was and walked around it carefully, and then stooped to read the small plaque on its base.

"God-awful crap isn't it?" said a voice redolent of Texas.

Morrison turned and grinned at the tall, burly man standing behind him. "It does defy my understanding, I admit. What's it supposed to be?"

"God knows. The plaque reads 'Out of the Cradle', but that doesn't help any." The Texan looked quizzically at the man in front of him. "Dr Morrison, is it? I'm Twentyman. Peale sent you to me?"

"Not so much sent, as suggested I see you. I'm interested in anticlines and I wondered if you could tell me about this one."

"You're from the USGS, Cory tells me." Twentyman nodded toward the man behind the desk. "I'd have thought you'd know all about it already."

"Only the theory. I'd like to see how you've adapted it to the practicalities of carbon storage."

Twentyman hesitated. "Well, I guess it's okay if Peale sent you. What do you want to know?"

"You tested the cap on the anticline. Did you check the old boreholes?"

The Texan looked around the foyer. "We'd better go up to the lab." He led the way up the wide semicircular stairs to the next floor and along a glass and aluminum corridor. He opened the door and ushered Morrison into a large laboratory. The benches were covered in a wide variety of rock and soil samples. Three young men and a woman were peering down microscopes or busying themselves washing samples. In one corner, a technician was grinding down a rock sample and close by, a machine was polishing specimens. "Through here." Twentyman walked into a small office and shut the door behind them. He gestured toward a comfy-looking armchair and sank into another one opposite.

Morrison glanced around the room, noting geological charts on the walls and overburdened bookshelves with their overflow stacked on the floor. He felt a twinge of kinship for a man so obviously in love with geology. "Nice room," he murmured.

"Thanks. What's your interest in the Hood Anticline?"

"I did my PhD on salt dome anticlines and..."

"Where?"

"Berkeley, in '08."

Twentyman nodded. "I thought the name was familiar. I've read your thesis. It's good."

"Thanks...the cap on the Hood Anticline is limestone, isn't it?"

"Yes, recrystallized limestone."

"Recrystallized? I thought the Rushing River bore back in the 1920s only showed softer strata."

"You know your stuff." Twentyman nodded approvingly. "However, as you know, that bore only went to 1800 feet, barely into the cap rock. We've sunk several others which show the cap changes as you go deeper. It becomes harder, more crystalline..."

"More brittle?"

"That too, but that is tough rock down there, overlain by billions of tons of sedimentary deposits."

"How far into the cap did you drill? All the way through?"

"Hell no. That would defeat the purpose. We need undamaged, impervious cap rock. We made damn sure we only went in far enough to check the nature of the rock."

"How far?" Morrison asked. "If you don't mind me asking," he added as the other man frowned.

"About twenty feet. Then we came out and sealed the holes with reinforced concrete, all the way up to the surface, and topped them with a steel cap. Believe me, nothing could get through that."

"Hey, I'm one of the good guys. I believe you. How thick is the limestone cap?"

Twentyman grunted. "Varies. Fifty feet at the north end, down to thirty at the south. We verified this by sonic probes. And before you ask, the sealed boreholes were all in the thicker part. The structural integrity of the cap has not been compromised."

"Could I see this on a map?"

Twentyman crossed to a diagram of the area on one wall. He pointed out the position of the sequestration plant, the limits of the cap rock, and the sites of the exploratory boreholes.

Morrison looked over the sites, nodding pleasantly. "You've taken Draeger measurements to check on CO_2 levels? In case of leakage?"

"Of course, but why are you so het up over it? The stuff's darn near harmless."

"Yeah, well that's good enough for the press, but I wouldn't want to be trapped in a depression with a leak or within a thousand miles if it ever blew out."

Twentyman laughed. "Ain't never going to happen, fellah. This darn stuff's safe as houses. Besides, we take all the necessary precautions and we have a rigorous monitoring program."

"So, you're taking measurements?"

"Sweet Jesus, what've I just been saying?" the Texan exclaimed. "We just started pumping a year ago. There's only about a hundred thousand tons of the stuff down there." He shook his head in exasperation. "But to answer your query again, yes, we've taken measurements."

"May I see the results?"

"Is this an official request? From the USGS?"

"No, Dr Twentyman. At the moment it's just curiosity on my part...but I can make it official if you want."

Twentyman stared at the young man. "You'll have to speak to Dr Roux about that. She did the measurements and wrote the report."

Morrison decided not to suggest that Twentyman, as Head Scientist, must surely have a copy of the report. Instead, he smiled and said, "Where would I find Dr Roux?"

"She's working in the lab." Twentyman opened the connecting door and called out. "Roux, come here a moment."

A tall, slim blonde looked up from her microscope, her initial expression of annoyance giving way to speculative interest as she spied Morrison. She switched the light off in her microscope and walked across the lab.

"Dr Roux, Dr Morrison. He's from the USGS and asking questions about your CO_2 measurements. Reassure him, will you? I have to get downstairs." Twentyman stalked off and Roux turned a look of cool appraisal on Morrison.

"What do you want to know, Dr Morrison?"

"The name's Matt." He reached out and the young woman shook his hand.

"Alright, Matt. What do you want to know? And don't say 'What are you doing tonight?' because I've heard them all."

Matt grinned. "Okay, but do you have a less formal name than Dr Roux?"

"Angelina."

"Nice. You're the one who did the Draeger measurements?"

"You're referring to my measurements of CO_2 levels around the pumping station? If so, then yes. What's your interest?"

Matt grinned again and Angelina looked away and blushed. "I work on anticlines," he explained. "The Survey brought me in to give the Hood Anticline the once over. All just a matter of form, of course. The decision was made long before I got here. But from what Twentyman says, you had something to do with it."

Angelina nodded. "I did, but only in the measuring, not the decision making."

Matt laughed. "I know the feeling. I sometimes think my only contribution to the USGS is to make up numbers at meetings."

"Thirty years ago, I'd have been making the coffee."

"Come now," Matt chided. "Thirty years ago, you wouldn't even have been a twinkle in your father's eye." He was rewarded by another blush. "Can you show me where you tested?"

"What?"

"On a map. Where you did your Draeger testing?"

Angelina said nothing, but led Matt back into Twentyman's office and pointed to the map of the Hood Anticline. "The little red crosses with the numbers are the sites we checked."

"What do the numbers and letters mean...oh, I see, they just identify the site? What were the actual readings?"

"Nothing out of the ordinary." Angelina plucked a slim report out of Twentyman's bookshelf and leafed through to an Appendix Table in the back. "See, six tests at two-monthly intervals for the year following the first injection of liquid CO_2. Forty sites and not a single one above normal."

"These are your measurements?" Matt grinned, and elicited another small blush.

"I took them, yes."

Matt cast his eye across the table. "This one's a bit elevated...and this one."

"Well within error limits. Besides, they're both at site PH3, right next to the injection borehole. I think if you look up the injection dates you'll find those were the actual days when we were pumping."

"Yeah, I can see the difference is small. Were these the last measurements? On November 12 to 17 last year?"

"Last ones to go in the report. I did another set in January and one just last week, but that'll be the last scheduled one."

"And the readings were the same? Nothing out of the ordinary?"

"Yes." Angelina looked at her watch. "I've got work to do, Dr Morrison. If you'll excuse me?"

"Okay," Matt said with a tinge of disappointment. "Can I see you again?"

"If you have some more questions about CO_2."

Matt descended to the foyer and then walked outside to where the Public Relations man was entertaining the journalists. He frowned as he thought back over what he'd heard. *Pretty woman, and I thought I was in there, but then she cooled when I asked if her CO_2 measurements were the same. Why? Did she think I was calling her expertise into question?* He shrugged. His eye caught the presence of a beautiful girl among the reporters and he straightened his shoulders, Dr Angelina Roux fading from his mind.

"So you see," the PR man said. "There really are no safety concerns when it comes to the compression facility and the pumping station."

Matt wandered through the small crowd of journalists to the side of the beautiful young brunette.

"I gather the injection plant is only handling CO_2 produced at this power station," one of the journalists asked. "Are there plans to bring in CO_2 from other stations?"

"Not at the moment," Farley replied. "But it's something we'll consider, as we've a railhead here now to bring coal in. An extension to accommodate liquid CO_2 tankers would be a relatively minor addition."

"Hi," Matt said. "Enjoying the tour?"

Annaliese looked up from the scribbling in her notebook. "Sorry, are you with Oregon Energy?"

"No, I'm one of the visiting scientists. Matt Morrison."

"Annaliese Harding. What exactly do you do, Dr Morrison?"

"Matt, please. I study the geology of the area--the rocks where all this CO_2 is being stored. I was invited along with my USGS bosses to see the official start-up."

"It's all very impressive, isn't it?"

"Sure. All steel and glass and bursting with energy. Let's hope it can be contained."

Annaliese raised an eyebrow. "You think it can't?"

"Well...how much do you know about the process of sequestration?"

"Not much," Annaliese confessed. "I have all the company handouts, but it doesn't mean that much to me. I guess I'll have to get one of the guys at the paper to explain it to me."

"I'd be happy to explain it," Matt said.

Annaliese smiled. "Why would you do that?"

Matt shrugged and matched her smile. "Just naturally helpful, I guess. What about it? I'll buy you lunch."

"I don't think that would be appropriate. We've only just met and...well, you'd already be helping me by explaining all this."

"Okay, you buy me lunch then. Your paper can pay and I'll give you the low-down on sequestration. You'll have an informed source to quote," he added, grinning.

* * *

Dr Angelina Roux watched Matt from a window on the second floor for a few minutes before descending to the foyer and drawing Peale aside.

"That geologist was asking a lot of questions about the Anticline and the carbon dioxide leaks."

"What did you tell him?"

"Don't worry. I know enough not to let anything slip."

Peale nodded and looked across to his guests. "Well, if there's nothing else..."

Angelina smiled and put a slim hand on Peale's arm. "You know, Robert, I could do a lot more if I was Head of Science here."

Peale swallowed. "A lot more?"

"Keeping the scientists off your back, controlling the results of our investigations, and..." She looked into his eyes and slowly licked her lips. "...other things."

"Er, well, yes, that sound's er...great. Perhaps we could er, talk about it."

"Whenever you like, Robert. I'm sure the two of us could arrange something that was good for us both." She turned and walked away slowly, her hips swaying, aware that she had his full attention.

Chapter 7

October 4, 2020

Boris Radinov received the summons at four in the morning, the hour when the body's rhythms run slowest and life is at its lowest ebb. It is the time of day that security agents the world over like to take their victims, and the Russian Federal Security Service (FSB) was no different.

Boris was fast asleep beside his mistress in her Moscow apartment when the door burst off its hinges and armed men cloaked in darkness rushed in, securing the small space in seconds and shaking the sleepers awake.

"On your feet, traitor," the officer in command snapped, holding a gun to Boris' head.

The woman screamed and was dragged naked into the living room where her screams died abruptly. Boris got to his feet, also naked, and sleep befuddled. "What's going on? Do you know who I am, Captain?"

"I know who you are. You're a traitor to Russia and you're summoned before the Minister of Security. Get dressed."

Boris knew better than to argue and hurriedly got dressed. He was marched downstairs and into an unmarked vehicle for the short trip through dark and deserted streets to Lubyanka Square. The FSB building was the same one that the KGB had used in the old Soviet Empire and had lost none of its terrors for those brought against their will to the dingy rooms and concrete corridors beneath it. The security guards bundled Boris into a bare cell and started to leave.

"Wait, Captain, you said I was to be brought before Minister Mendeleev, not locked up."

"You cannot imagine the Minister is up at this hour. Wait here and think about your transgressions, traitor."

"But I've done nothing."

"Then you've nothing to fear." The officer closed the door behind him and the deadbolts clicked into place. A few moments later the single bare bulb in the cell was extinguished and Boris was plunged into a silent stygian darkness.

Time passed. How much time, Boris did not know. He had not been allowed to put on his watch. He tried counting but with nothing except the cold concrete floor to stimulate him, he fell asleep, slept for an indeterminate time and woke to the same all-pervading blackness.

After a while his bladder made its urgent needs known, so he crawled on hands and knees, searching out the confines of his tiny cell. There was no container, so he relieved himself in one corner and crawled as far away from his makeshift latrine as he could before settling down again. Time passed.

Blinding light woke him, and a boot persuaded him to arise and follow his captors into the corridor again. They passed along long echoing concrete passages, where the only illumination came from bare incandescent bulbs, ascended flights of stairs and emerged into wooden-floored corridors. Another floor up and the furnishings became more opulent--carpet covered the floor and potted plants stood at intervals. Pictures of stern-visaged men stared disapprovingly at Boris as he was marched onwards.

They entered a room, where plain wooden chairs lined two walls and a solid oaken door stood at the far end. His guards stamped their feet and returned to guard outside the door, while the Captain accompanied him inside.

"Wait here. Sit and do not move." Boris obeyed.

The Captain walked the length of the room and opened the far door, disappearing inside the room for a short while. The door opened again and the Captain beckoned.

"Come. Minister Mendeleev will see you now."

Boris walked on shaky legs and edged past his captor, blinking at the functional splendor of the room. It was obviously an office--an ordinary office in its contents but anything but ordinary in the quality of its furnishings. The desk was huge and made of polished rosewood, with a high-backed padded swivel chair behind it. The computer was state of the art and even the filing cabinets were of a dark wood, carved, and polished until they shone. The carpet was rich and deep, and the lighting soft and mellow from intricate standard lamps behind the desk that threw their light across the surface of the desk and left pools of shadow in other parts of the room. Only one piece of furniture looked out of place--a simple wooden folding chair facing the desk.

A bearded man in a tailored suit moved out of one of the shadowed pools and pointed at the plain chair. "Sit, Boris Ilyavich Radinov."

"Minister Mendeleev. Thank God. Why have I been brought here like a common criminal?"

The Minister sat in his swivel chair and looked intently at Boris. "I invited you here to discuss a matter of grave import for Russia."

"You couldn't just send for me, Minister? Why did you feel the need to send armed guards to arrest me in the middle of the night and put me in a cell?"

Mendeleev looked past Boris to the officer standing inside the door to the office. "Captain Yakov, did you arrest this man and throw him in a cell?"

"No, Minister. I informed him you wished to speak to him, brought him here at the State's expense and put him in a waiting room as you had not yet arrived."

"There, you see, Boris Ilyavich, it's a misunderstanding, no more. Captain Yakov, bring vodka for my guest."

Yakov exited the room and came back a few minutes later bearing a silver tray on which stood an unmarked bottle and two small glasses. He put them onto the Minister's desk and poured out two shots, handing one to the Minister and the other to Boris. He then saluted and marched across to the door where he saluted again and went out, closing the door behind him.

Mendeleev raised his glass. "Vashe Zdorovie--Your Health."

Boris sniffed the contents of his glass and nodded briefly. "Nu..." he replied, "So..." He tipped his head back and drained the clear liquid, the Minister matching his motion. "Ah, that is good."

Mendeleev poured another round but neither man drank. The Minister folded his arms across his chest and examined Boris in silence for several minutes, while the coal baron did his best to appear unconcerned.

"What is your relationship to James Matternicht, Boris Ilyavich?"

"Matternicht? He's a business associate."

"Tell me more of your business dealings with this man...this foreigner."

"What is there to tell, Minister? He controls a large percentage of the world's coal and he seeks to utilize the coal resources of Russia. I've made business deals with him that have earned Russia valuable foreign exchange."

"And made you many rubles into the bargain."

Boris spread his arms wide. "I'm a businessman, Minister, and for better or worse, we live in a capitalist society. I've made money, but I've also made substantial payments in taxes and contributed to...charities." He forbore to mention that one of the main charities was Minister Mendeleev himself.

"I've never had reason to doubt you, Boris Ilyavich, until now..." the Minister let the sentence hang in the air between them.

"Until now, Minister?" Boris asked nervously.

"Drink up, Tovarishch." Mendeleev waited for Boris to lift his glass and joined him, draining the fiery alcohol. He refilled the glasses.

"What is the nature of your dealings with Matternicht, Boris Ilyavich? It's more than just selling Russia's resources to our enemies, isn't it? There's something else."

"Minister, I do not deal with enemies of Russia."

"Everyone is an enemy of Russia. Even our closest allies would slip the knife between our ribs if we let our guard down for an instant. Boris Ilyavich, your dealings with Matternicht involve more than just coal. Tell me of sequestration."

Boris chewed his lower lip for a few moments. "Sequestration is only a tool whereby we can sell more coal. It's nothing of itself."

"I know what carbon sequestration is, Boris Ilyavich. We're not backward in Russia. What I want to know is why this is so important to you and to Matternicht."

"As I said, Minister, it's only a tool..."

"No!" Mendeleev slapped his hand down on the rosewood desk so hard the vodka glasses shivered. "Don't try to deceive me, Boris Ilyavich, or you'll regret it. We have worse things than the old Soviet gulags for recalcitrants. I know of the argument that if you promise to lock up the carbon dioxide produced by coal-burning power stations, you can increase the amount of coal mined and sold without raising the levels of carbon dioxide in the atmosphere. I know of the billions of rubles and dollars that are to be made, but what I don't see is why every government but one is hanging back on this technology. Why is the United States of America the only one to seriously move forward with carbon geo-sequestration, and why do I hear this damn Matternicht's name associated with this lack of development?"

"Minister, coal is but one source of carbon dioxide. Why do you single out coal? Everyone knows that petroleum used as fuel is far worse. The amount of waste gases that automobiles pour out each year..."

"Petroleum is in decline, as well you know, and coal is fast becoming the main pollutant of our environment. There's coal enough even in Russia alone to supply the whole world for a thousand years. But coal is dirty and either produces fine particulate matter that pollutes everything or, if burned efficiently, produces carbon dioxide gas which leads to global warming. I hear these things, Boris Ilyavich, and I talk to my fellow ministers. I ask them why Russia uses coal instead of researching the use of non-polluting sources of energy like solar and wind and hydroelectric--even nuclear. They say 'Coal is cheap and plentiful'. I ask why we're not researching cleaner fuels. You know what they tell me? They say, 'ask Boris Ilyavich Radinov', so here I am asking him. And I will have an answer."

"Can't you just accept that what I do does not harm Russia?"

"No, I cannot. I want an answer."

Boris sighed and pressed the heels of his hands against his eyes. "You probably already know as much as I, Minister. What do you know of carbon geo-sequestration in other countries?"

"I know that the technology has been around for twenty years or more, but that research in the area is limited. Norway was a leader in the field a dozen years ago with the Sleipner field in the North Sea, and Canada, Germany, Britain, Australia and America had pilot projects under way. But then around 2012, most of the projects were scaled back. Governments concentrated on other methods of carbon capture."

"That is correct, Minister, and even a quick search of the Internet will reveal these projects and a hundred others that died stillborn. Research on sequestering carbon underground in stable strata--geo-sequestration--effectively came to an end, except in America."

"Why?"

"A variety of reasons."

"Such as?"

Boris collected his thoughts. "Norway's Sleipner project was always a pilot program. They operated it for ten years and filled the relatively small space available in the oil field. Since then, they have been evaluating the results and looking at other options."

"And the other countries?"

"Britain's project leaked rather badly, so the emphasis turned to other ways of stabilizing carbon chemically in concrete and as carbonates. Some of those are promising, but only for relatively small amounts--hundreds of tons rather than the hundreds of thousands needed. Italy started well but every time the government changed, there were budget hold-ups or disagreements with the whole concept. Germany did well for a while, but on a very small scale; China...well, China is a bit of a mystery as always, but they suddenly stopped geo-sequestration in 2014 and started planting forests instead, so they must have run into serious problems. Australia had a promising project underway but it leaked badly and the government suspended storage in 2013 until they could overcome the safety problems. Leakage has been the main problem everywhere--Canada, Brazil, France, Romania, India. You must know, Minister, that even solid rock is porous to gases. Everything leaks and a small rate of leakage is acceptable, but time and again, researchers have found that the rate of leakage was unacceptably high. The one project that did not leak was one in Oregon in the United States. They've had no problems, and it's been the one project that has forged ahead."

"What's the reason for their success?"

"Matternicht."

"How?"

"James Matternicht is coal. He controls a good percentage of the world's coal and he has such a huge scale of operations that he can sell coal into the world market at a price with which no other energy source can compete. Perhaps if it was more expensive, less plentiful, governments would look at other power sources, but for any government wanting to keep the populace and big business happy, they must create cheap, clean power. Otherwise, they find themselves voted out of office."

"That's a very cynical attitude, Boris Ilyavich. Not every government is so self-centered."

"Of course not, Minister. Russia is blessed with far-sighted and benevolent leaders...yet coal is still cheap and plentiful...and research on other power sources lag behind."

Minister Mendeleev grunted. "Go on. I'm well aware of how governments act, but I'm curious about any insights you have into the actions of this Matternicht."

"Cheap coal means cheap power, but coal is dirty. Power stations can scrub their effluent to get rid of particulate matter--soot--but carbon dioxide is produced. Every ton of coal produces three and a half tons of carbon dioxide, and carbon dioxide is a greenhouse gas. If coal is to be touted as a cheap energy source, then the CO_2 problem must be answered. Now, as I'm sure you realize, Minister, there are many ways of capturing this carbon."

"Yes, of course. You must not think that because I'm questioning you, I'm ignorant of such matters. I have my own sources for all this information...but, Boris Ilyavich, I want to hear it from your lips."

Boris nodded, sweat beading again on his forehead. He had no doubt the conversation was being recorded. "There have been many methods of capturing carbon put forward, some reasonable, others downright irresponsible. Some scientists say that increasing iron or nitrogen levels in the oceans will foster the growth of algae and mop up excess carbon dioxide. Of course, we tinker with the oceanic ecosystem at our peril. Nobody can forecast the long term effects of algal blooms.

"Soil also is a recognized carbon sink, and farming methods could be changed worldwide to increase CO_2 absorption. Forestry is another method. Plants absorb CO_2, but unfortunately give it off again when they die or are burned for fuel in the third world. Burying carbon in landfills is another option, whether raw vegetation or as biochar--charcoal produced from limited ignition. But we are talking about having to store millions of tons, not just a few thousand truckloads for landfill.

"Then there are chemical methods of sequestration. Metal oxides react with CO_2 to form stable carbonates. This method shows promise, particularly if one was to utilize deep sea basalts, but at the moment, the injection of the necessarily enormous quantities of CO_2 into basalt layers at the bottom of oceans presents enormous difficulties. Land geo-sequestration presents fewer problems."

"Enough," Mendeleev said. "I'm aware of these things. Tell me how Matternicht fits into the picture."

"Most of these methods, except perhaps the basalt injection, require an accompanying reduction of emissions. It's no use hiding away tons if you are producing hundreds of tons at the same time. So Matternicht funds the anti-coal lobby and encourages scientists to explore means of carbon sequestration that require a reduction in coal. Governments can point to this research and say 'We are doing our bit to clean up the world. We are responsible people.' These methods work, but are incredibly expensive, particularly when cheap coal is removed from the equation. So research continues slowly while the governments continue to use cheap coal, proclaiming, 'This is only a stop-gap measure, soon we will solve all our problems.' Meanwhile, Matternicht's money buys the best scientists, the best technology, and they produce the best research on carbon capture and storage. His research team is headed by Professor Maxwell Hay. You've heard of him?" The Minister nodded and Boris continued.

"Matternicht offers to privately fund research on a single geo-sequestration plant and builds that plant at Rushing River in Oregon. The process is secret, and it works. He claims to have solved the leakage problem, reducing it to negligible levels."

"If it works, then why not have many geo-sequestration plants operating?"

"Money, Minister. Money and power. That one station produces billions of dollars in carbon payments from the grateful American government. In the five years it's been operating, over fifty million tons of carbon dioxide has been stored."

"That sounds a lot, but I know it is but a fraction of the carbon dioxide produced from coal worldwide, every year. But your answer proves my point. Surely it would be more profitable to allow sequestration to occur worldwide."

"Only if Matternicht controlled it all. That's why he took advantage of a general failure to develop a safe underground storage method. He funded private research, and made it available to the richest nation--at a price. If anyone else had solved the problem of leakage, then they'd be building sequestration stations, too. It'd be impossible to control who had the technology. Then every nation would be raking in the Pounds, the Euros, the Rupees, Rubles and Dollars, and little of it would stick to Matternicht's hands."

"What is to prevent other nations pursuing geo-sequestration research as well?"

"Nothing, Minister, and some nations still do this, but their steps are hesitant and their will undermined by the difficulties involved and the enormous cost of funding such research." Boris smiled and gestured toward the vodka.

Mendeleev nodded and Boris drained his glass. The Minister refilled it. "Go on."

"Matternicht makes a lot of money and after a while--say in another ten years--when everyone can see how well his process works, he goes public, and every country is invited to join in the noble battle to capture carbon and safely store it underground."

"But how is he better off? In the meantime, a dozen plants would have given him far more money than just one."

"Yes, Minister Mendeleev, but when all countries are invited to join in, the only viable design is that of Rushing River, and that design is his alone. Also, the best of the sites worldwide are those surveyed and claimed by Matternicht's companies. The twenty years the world has lost by turning away from carbon geo-sequestration research can never be made up. Matternicht will control everything."

Mendeleev gestured toward the vodka and Boris gratefully downed his shot. The Minister toyed with his glass, sipping the raw liquid while apparently lost in thought.

"You see now why you're a traitor, Boris Ilyavich? This technology, the kudos for saving the world, and enormous wealth will go to someone else. It belongs to Russia and you, a Russian, have stolen it from our people."

The vodka was starting to have its effect on Boris and he knew he had been backed into an impossible situation. He could argue his innocence but the Minister would not believe him. It seemed all the bribes over the years had come to nothing. All he could do was throw himself on Mendeleev's mercy. No doubt it would cost him a fortune, but that was better than...

"What must I do, Minister Mendeleev?"

"You must make restitution, Boris Ilyavich."

Boris licked his lips. "I'm not as wealthy as people think. The economy..."

"Money will not restore Russia's pride and her pre-eminence in technology. We must become the leader in this carbon geo-sequestration business." Mendeleev smiled mirthlessly. "When Matternicht releases his Rushing River design to a grateful world, the Russian design will prove to be superior. People will come to us, not Matternicht."

"Er, how will our design be superior?"

"You'll make it superior."

"I, Minister? I've no expertise in design. I'm a businessman, a manager, a controller--not an engineer."

"Then you will manage, lead and control, Boris Ilyavich. You'll assemble a team and develop a carbon geo-sequestration plant in Russia that'll be the envy of the world."

"That'll be very costly."

"Luckily, your fortune is very great."

"You expect me to pay for it?" Boris said, aghast.

"Think of it as a sacrifice to prove your loyalty."

Boris knew he was trapped. "Do you have a site in mind, Minister? Or must I find that, too?"

"I've had geologists looking for suitable strata. They've discovered the perfect site."

"May I ask where it is?"

"Outside a village in the Province of Belgorod, about fifty kilometers from the border with Ukraine. A little place called Krasnorovka."

Boris nodded glumly. "I suppose it has to be so far from Moscow?"

"The city of Belgorod is close by, Boris Ilyavich. You'll still be able to find entertainments. Maybe in time you can even move your mistress there. Now, you'll get your affairs in order and move there within the week. Time is of the essence as the Americans have at least a five year start on us. You must catch up and overtake them, which shouldn't be hard to do. We have the best scientists and the best technicians. Drive them hard; I want results." Mendeleev came around the desk and embraced the other man. He poured vodka into the glasses and they raised them in a salute.

"To success."

Chapter 8

April 5, 2028

The advantage of being Matternicht's science advisor was that Max Hay had access to every bit of research carried out under the aegis of the Northern Coal Consortium and its associated companies. No matter where he was in the world, reports were submitted regularly to him from every laboratory and he had a small team of aides who read through the reports and prepared digests for his consumption. This left Max with time to pursue his own scientific interests.

On Wednesdays though, he spent the day at his Santa Monica laboratory on Ocean Avenue, where he perused the digests and chatted with the young scientists who worked there. He was reading a report from Brazil that examined the permeability of metamorphosed and partly-metamorphosed limestone layers when exposed to various gases under high pressure. He frowned and read the passage again before leaning back in his chair to think about what he had just read. After a few minutes, he looked at the article again and noted the author and his address. He picked up the phone and buzzed for the laboratory secretary.

"Kylie, put through a call to an...Eduardo Carvalho..." He spelled the name for her and added the identity of the research establishment in Rio de Janeiro. "That's in Brazil. Ask him if he'll speak to me about his research."

There was a slight hesitation from Kylie. "I think they speak Spanish there, sir."

"Portuguese actually, so ask if he speaks English. They're about four or five hours ahead of us, so you'll have to hurry to catch him in business hours."

It took the secretary about half an hour to locate Dr Carvalho and ascertain that he spoke passable English.

"Dr Hay, what I can do for you?"

"Dr Carvalho. Thank you for making the time to speak to me. I was just reading your paper on the permeability of rock strata..."

"You reading Portuguese, Dr Hay?" The voice sounded surprised.

"No, I'm sorry. I should have said I read a report on your paper. Dr Carvalho, you said that semi-metamorphosed limestone was..."

"Please? That word?"

"Ah, limestone partly altered by heat and pressure."

"Thank you, yes, I understand."

"So, you said that it was generally impermeable to most gases, even under pressure, but not to supercritical gases."

"Yes, that is much what I said."

"The report did not say if you had tested supercritical carbon dioxide."

"No, I did not, testing this one."

"Well, never mind, Dr Carvalho. That was the one I was interested in."

"Ah, sorry I no do this...but you interest in carbon dioxide?"

"Yes."

"I do work since on supercritical carbon dioxide."

"Really? In the laboratory or in the field?"

"In the field. You may know government here consider...how you say? Locking away underground?"

"Geosequestration."

"Yes, that. We have small scale project at Porto Belo, offshore."

"I didn't realize Brazil had a sequestration project."

Carvalho laughed. "We do not. We could not keep the supercritical gas in place. It leaks out very easily."

"Even under metamorphosed limestone?"

"Even then, Dr Hay. Yes."

"How thick was the capping stratum?"

"About five meters."

"And it leaked?"

"Yes. Like a...how you say it? A sieve."

"You're sure? We have a large-scale project here in the States storing supercritical carbon dioxide under limestone and it doesn't leak."

"I am finding that unlikely, Dr Hay. There are no leaks?"

"Only very small ones."

"If you say so."

Max thanked Dr Carvalho for his comments and ended the conversation. When he had hung up he sat and looked out of his office window at Ocean Avenue and the beach beyond, puzzling over what the Brazilian researcher had said.

That can't be right; he must be mistaken or exaggerating. Rushing River has an excellent containment record. Max pulled out the latest figures from the sampling sites above the Hood Anticline and skimmed through the columns of figures. *As I thought, there's nothing here that indicates any sort of problem.* He pulled out the original geomorphology reports and read through them. *That could be it; the limestone is at least twice as thick under Rushing River...still, if Carvalho's right...*

Max came to a decision and put through a call to the Rushing River sequestration facility. He spoke to the CEO of the facility, Robert Peale.

"Robert, how are you?"

"Good, thanks, Dr Hay. I'm sure this isn't a social call so what can I do for you?"

"It's about the carbon dioxide readings from the test sites. The last two sets didn't agree, so I need to check the originals. Could you send them down to me?"

"Did you want the real ones or the ones for public consumption?"

"Actually, both. I need to check on the reduction factors."

"There's nothing wrong is there?" Peale's voice betrayed nervousness. "I mean, we're supposed to reduce the levels for the public reports so people are reassured."

"God, no. Nothing's wrong; it's just that as overall Head of Science I need to see the whole picture. Can you send them down to me by encrypted email?"

The files arrived twenty minutes later and Max opened them using the decryption software. He printed off the pages and started comparing the columns of figures.

My God, this can't be right. The public figures are supposed to be massaged down by a factor of two because the man in the street doesn't understand that twice normal is nothing to be worried about, but some of these public figures are a fifth or...or even a tenth...

There was one site in particular that gave him concern. He referred to his map of the testing sites and found it was in a creek bed on a nearby ranch. *Right above the old Limson shaft.* Max thought about what these readings meant and considered his options.

I could just ignore it and hope it doesn't get worse. Max shook his head. *That would be irresponsible. Something needs to be done, but what? Do I close down the plant? Could I even do that?* There was no real choice when it came right down to it. He picked up his cell phone again and put through a call to James Matternicht.

Chapter 9

February 10, 2030

The Maher family had been planning their vacation for six months. In the first week of February, Randy, a moderately successful used-car salesman of Provo, Utah, was given a promotion and raise. He prided himself on being a family man, and planned on spending the extra income on his wife Karen, his teenage son Cory, and four-year-old Alexa. Randy was also, by his own lights, a fair-minded man, so he allowed his family a say in how they celebrated.

"Disneyland," Alexa cried, clapping her hands and pirouetting in the living room in her pink ballet shoes and tutu. "Mickey Mouse--Pirates of the Caribbean."

Cory grinned. "Seaworld, Virtual World... and we could see a Laker's Game."

"Shopping," declared Karen. "And the homes of movie stars. LA's fine with me."

"Those are all good ideas but I think we should go camping," Randy said. "In August. I have some leave due then. We could go up the Pacific Northwest. I've always wanted to go there."

Alexa objected. "I want to go to Disneyland, Daddy."

Anger flashed in Randy's eyes and Karen pulled Alexa to her. "Camping will be fun, darling. We won't be in tents, will we, dear?" She met Randy's gaze with an unspoken plea.

The muscles in the man's jaw twitched but he deliberately took a calming breath. "We can use cabins," Randy conceded. "It'll still be good. There'll be hiking and cooking over camp fires and..."

"Maybe canoeing, if there's a river," Karen murmured.

Randy glared at his wife for interrupting him. His fists clenched, and the familiar gesture restored his good mood. *I'll be talkin' to you later.* "Horse riding, too. Anyway, that's what we're doing. I know just the place."

"Aw, dad, can't we go to LA? You like basketball and that Virtual World is incred. All the guys at school say so."

Dammit. Has she put them up to this insubordination? "No, son. This family has just decided on a camping trip to Oregon, and you can't go being selfish. Can you?"

Silence fell in the lounge room at the Maher residence, and Randy waited for his son to utter the words that would provoke a beating.

Cory struggled with his disappointment. "No, dad. We'll go camping. It'll be fun."

Karen almost sighed with relief but knew better than to show anything but an impassive demeanor.

Randy grunted, almost disappointed. "Then it's settled. I'll book a cabin tomorrow."

"Where are we going?" Karen asked. "Just so I know what to pack," she added hurriedly.

Randy stared, searching his wife's face for any hint of independent thought. "It's a nice little place called Rushing River, in the Cascades."

Chapter 10

May 20, 2030

S am Jones liked hiking. Every spring, as soon as the snow cleared and the ground firmed enough underfoot, he took his backpack and boots out of his closet and headed for the Oregon wilderness. His job as a stores clerk in a trucking firm in Portland occupied him during the week, when he was at everyone's beck and call, but the weekends were his alone. He drove out into the country in his ancient electric car and for forty-eight hours lost himself in a world where, if he was lucky, the only living things he saw were animals and trees. To his annoyance though, he found himself increasingly out of luck as the years turned. More and more people fled the crowded cities to find solitude in the mountains, gradually turning the lonely trails into highways filled with chattering people and barking dogs. Every year, Sam found himself searching out new trails that had not yet attracted the attention of the masses.

The longer trails were best, like Bull of the Woods Loop or the Three Sisters. After the first few miles Sam could be fairly sure of outdistancing the strollers and finding the relative peace of mountain tracks dotted with other dedicated hikers. In recent years, even these trails were becoming overcrowded. This year, Sam looked for more out of the way places and had discovered almost unused paths in the upper reaches of Rushing River. There was a township nearby and a power station further down the valley, but there were also a lot of woods, rocky ridges, and pasture.

Rushing River was a tributary of the Deschutes River, running in a generally eastward direction from the Cascade Range. Not far upstream from its junction with the Deschutes lay the township of Rushing River and, a mile or so south, lay the only other sign of civilization, the Rushing River Power and Carbon Capture Facility run by Oregon Energy. Fifty miles to the north-northwest, Mount Hood stood guard over the northern borders of the state.

Sam prided himself on his navigation skills, using no more than a rough-drawn map and sign-posted trails, but he carried a 'smart' cell phone which incorporated a GPS in the bottom of his backpack in case of emergencies. He thought this new trail might possibly see him need it, because although the Rushing River 'trail' bordered on farmland and managed forest, the paths were little used and it was always possible to take a wrong turn. Getting lost would not strictly count as an emergency, as he could always just cut across the pastures or follow the creek downstream to the township, but he felt that would be admitting defeat. Better to fix his position and correct his course.

Sam stayed well clear of the power station and skirted the town as he cut south and then west toward the mountains. He marveled that he could be so alone despite the cities of Eugene, Salem and Portland lying only a hundred miles away. The air was fresh, the sun was warm, and he felt at peace with the world as he set off toward the National Forest borders. By mid-morning he lost his happy feeling and knew he had made a mistake. The paths took him away from the forested ridges and into pasture where beef cattle roamed. The only patches of forest he came across were cut-over oak and big leaf maple with a scattering of cedar. None of the trees were large and the undergrowth was thick and apparently filled with poison oak. After discovering the makeup of the understory, Sam rubbed calamine lotion onto his forearm as he walked, and entertained dark thoughts concerning the farmers who had ruined yet another piece of land by indiscriminate logging and clearing.

He stopped a little past midday on the side of a grassy hill and opened a plastic bag that held his lunch--a lettuce and tomato sandwich and an apple. He sat in the long grass with its scattering of early wild flowers and looked down the slope of the land to a silver stream wending its leisurely way through aspens and birch. Just below him, the stream widened out into a broad pond with what looked like a mud and branch dam keeping the water back.

Beavers, he thought. *I wonder if I'll see any*. Conservation efforts had maintained a healthy population of the aquatic rodents in the State, and Sam had come across them before on his hiking expeditions. Their antics amused him, and he hoped he would see them here, too. He was disappointed however, as their arrow wakes did not disturb the breeze-ruffled water.

There was other wildlife present, though, and Sam was glad the cattle herds were grazing elsewhere. Ducks dabbled around the edges of the broad pond and a heron stalked the reed beds searching for frogs. A solitary whitetail buck picked its way slowly from the aspen grove and down to the water's edge. Sam watched, entranced as the animal quivered with suspicion, looking all around for danger, but at last bent to drink.

The sun warmed him and the peaceful scene so relaxed him that Sam lay back in the long grass and closed his eyes. *A short nap and I'll head back. There's nothing of interest out here. Perhaps it's not too late to try Three Sisters.*

He dozed until a gurgling splash awoke him. He stared up at the sky for a minute, trying to decide if he had dreamt the noise, and then sat up. The pond below was calm but had changed drastically. The clear breeze-rippled water was now muddy and roiling and the ducks had disappeared. Then he saw a patch of white in the water near the reed beds and realized that it was the heron, floating unmoving in the water. The ducks, too, had not gone but lay sprawled by the water's edge...*and the deer.*

Sam got to his feet and started down the hill toward the pond. The whitetail buck lay a few feet from the water, head pointing away. *As if it was running...but from what?* He stopped and looked around carefully before continuing. He reached the pond and looked down at a duck, apparently dead, on the grass at his feet. Sam nudged it with his foot, but it did not move. *What killed it? What the hell is going on?* He sat down to think it through.

At once his head swam and he started gasping, a terrible feeling of breathlessness overcoming him. Sam struggled to his feet and walked a few paces, panting as he tried to catch his breath. *What's happening?* He staggered away from the pond toward the stream outlet rather than back up the hill and his breath came a little easier, though he felt very tired and confused. He bent over and at once started gasping again. As he straightened up, he stumbled and fell to the ground, his limbs refusing to cooperate. He tried to get up but only succeeded in rolling on his side. *Oh my God, I'm having a heart attack...* His vision blurred and blacked out.

Chapter 11

August 7, 2030

Annaliese Winton yawned and rubbed her eyes, trying to ease the grittiness that lay behind her eyelids. She fought the desire to just close her eyes and put her head down on folded arms. The screen in front of her beckoned, the cursor blinking incessantly, calling her to finish her article. It did not help that the subject was the latest batch of prosaic recipes from the local Mothers' Institute.

Newspapers had changed in the last fifteen or twenty years. Annaliese remembered that when she had joined the Chronicle back in 2015 they still turned out a print copy every day to match the online version. Today, the paper was completely electronic, being patched together from teams of reporters working in many locations from material that poured in from all over Oregon, the USA and the World. Annaliese's own office was small, half a dozen reporters/columnists, an editor to keep an eye on them all, and a receptionist/manager who screened the calls and emails coming in to the Chronicle, as well as running the office.

Around her in the office, the keyboards clattered and chattered, as seven hands and four minds constructed a portion of the next day's news and comments. Alongside her, Katy grinned as she put together a scathing critique on a play that had opened the previous night. Across the small newsroom, Ben grimly pieced together news of the latest atrocities in a foreign land, and beside him, Tony whistled tunelessly through his teeth as he rhapsodized about the latest vehicle to roll off the production lines of American Daihatsu-Ford. The fourth mind and seventh hand belonged to Foster, a man with strange interests and a unique writing style. He had never learned to type so the forefinger of Foster's right hand pecked rapidly at the keyboard, while the forefinger of his left controlled only the shift key. It looked clumsy and slow, but he turned out good copy in a remarkably short time. At the moment he was working on the astrological forecasts for the paper, for despite the advances of science, or perhaps because of it, their readership still demanded his creative outpourings.

"What sign are you, Annaliese?" Foster called out, his finger still pumping up and down.

"I haven't the faintest idea."

"Of course you do. Everyone knows their sign."

"Pisces then, and don't tell me I'm going to meet a tall dark stranger. I've already had one of those - he was tall and dark and became stranger and stranger - and it didn't work out." Annaliese again felt the tug at her heart when she thought of Peter. It had been five years since he left for good, but she still found herself remembering the early days of her marriage. Since then, she had found the only real antidote to loneliness was a positive attitude. Humor helped, and she often made jokes at her own expense. Life had been a struggle for a while, but her son Adrian had helped--he was the one good thing to have come out of a failed marriage.

"Wouldn't dream of it," Foster replied. "I'll have you know we astrologers don't make generalizations." He grinned. "Our art is an exact science. In fact, you're going to meet a short, tubby, balding man who'll ask you where your copy is. And here he comes."

Annaliese looked up and groaned as she saw the office editor heading in her direction. "Hi, Simon, nearly finished."

"I wanted it twenty minutes ago." He looked over her shoulder at her laptop screen. "There's a split infinitive in line three, a clumsy construction in line seven and your punctuation could use some work. I thought you said you knew how to write."

"You gripe every day, Simon, and you publish my articles every day, too."

"Only because if I didn't, your father-in-law would be on my back."

"That's fewkin' unfair," Ben called out. "She's a damn good reporter and you know it. It's not her fault you only give her crap assignments. She can't help having the Winton name."

"Yeah, yeah, I know," Simon grumbled. "She's good, unlike some here. Now get on with it, we've got a deadline to meet." He stalked away and turned in the doorway. "There's a package for you at the front desk, Annaliese."

"You couldn't have brought it in with you?"

"What am I? Your damn assistant?"

"I don't have one, but if you want the job..." She laughed as the office editor slammed the door behind him.

Annaliese finished her article and emailed it to Simon. She scrolled through the emails on her laptop, hoping that someone had sent something interesting to her, but found nothing she had not already seen. *I suppose it'll have to be the fundraiser at the Elementary School then.* She yawned again and got up to get herself a coffee.

The coffee jug was empty so she changed the filter and added fresh grounds, filling the reservoir and setting it to brew. She waited for it to start, then walked through to the front desk to pick up her package. It was a reinforced mailer, securely taped down. There was no return address on the back. She frowned.

The man behind the desk smiled reassuringly. "It's okay. We put it through the scanner. Looks like it's just a few pages of old-fashioned paper with staples."

"Paper? In this day and age? Why didn't he just email me? How did it arrive? Who brought it?"

"All good questions. A man off the street. That's all I know."

Annaliese poured herself a cup of coffee and took it and the unopened package back to her desk. She sipped and looked at the large slim envelope without making a move to open it. After a few minutes she opened the bottom drawer of her desk and pulled out another envelope, laying it beside the new one on the desk. They were identical, down to her name and address written in felt pen. The only difference was that the first had been opened.

Ben noticed her studious expression and wandered over. "Got something interesting, 'Liese?"

Annaliese shook her head. "I don't know. There's a hell of a lot of technical jargon in it. Scientific terms and things."

"You want me to have a look at it. I've done a bit of science."

"I think I'll have a go at understanding it first. It'll make a change from recipes and fundraisers."

"Yeah, you should have a word with Winton about the crap he shovels into your inbox. You're a better journalist than that."

"Thanks, Ben. Maybe I was once, before I met..."

"No maybe about it. You were good when you were a kid reporter and you're better now. He can't keep blaming you for that retarded son of his. Ask him to give you something you can sink your teeth into. Maybe this thing?" Ben indicated the envelopes.

Annaliese laughed. "Yeah, maybe." She slid the envelopes back into the desk drawer. "Well, I have the exciting world of school fundraising to explore, so if you'll excuse me..."

She had almost forgotten the envelopes by the time she finished work, but as she slipped on her coat, she remembered them and stuck them in her shoulder bag, bending them to fit them in. By the time she reached home, she had entirely forgotten the envelopes and immersed herself happily in her home, preparing dinner for her son Adrian and chatting about school and television.

When they had eaten, Annaliese put the dishes in the washer, poured herself a glass of red wine and adjourned to the living room to watch the news on the large LCD wall screen. Adrian joined her for a while, and when the local news came on, asked her whether any of the stories were hers.

"I write for the Chronicle," she reminded him. "Just an online paper, not TV."

"I know that, Mom. What I meant was, have they picked up any of your stories? You write something brill, they'll be all over you like a rash."

Annaliese laughed. "Language, Adey. But I wish. Have you done your homework?"

"Of course. I did it as soon as I came in." Adrian watched for a few minutes longer and then said. "I think I'll go and play on the computer." He slipped out and left his mother alone.

Annaliese poured herself another glass, reflecting how lucky she was to have produced such a fine son, given the poor quality of his father. That thought led by association to her father-in-law, the Editor-in-Chief of the Salem Chronicle and Chairman of the Chamber of Commerce, State Businessman's Association and a high-flyer in the Republican Party. He had been a senior reporter when she first joined the paper back in '15, and because she tried to emulate him, came to his attention and, after a few months, to the notice of his profligate son Peter. A moment's incautious passion and she found herself carrying the next generation of Winton. She had married Peter, not because she had to, but because she was determined to succeed as a reporter and the Chronicle had seemed the place to do it.

A graphic picture of waves and drowning people washed across her wall screen and she said, "Volume, up three." The sound system obliged and she listened as an environmental group warned that Tuvalu would not be the last Pacific nation to suffer from rising sea levels. Spring tides had submerged sixty percent of the island nation, drowning twenty people and rendering hundreds homeless.

I can't imagine what it must be like to lose one's home through climate change. She watched a little longer but found her mind wandering again. *I need to find something worth writing about.* That had been her problem in 2019, when Adrian was three years old. Her job at the Chronicle, courtesy of Andrew Winton, then Copy Editor, was going nowhere and on the spur of the moment, she had resigned, accepting a job in Portland. Unexpectedly, Peter had supported the move and, for nearly a year, she had imagined he was encouraging her career. Then it emerged that the bright lights and fast women of the city were the real attractions. The marriage limped on another five years before breaking down utterly. When he left, the city apartment had been too much to keep up and she moved back to Salem, her home town. Andrew Winton, now Editor-in-Chief of the Chronicle, had been surprisingly welcoming and had offered her a position as a social reporter. She had accepted, though she knew she was better than that.

I need a story to sink my teeth into. Something that'll show Andrew I'm worth more. Annaliese thought about the tiny scraps of information that had come into her inbox and juggled them mentally, pulling at their boundaries to see if they would expand sufficiently. They all still looked like small stories, even the Councilor sleeping with his secretary. *There's got to be something.* Her gaze fell on the corner of an envelope poking out of her bag and she remembered the package that had arrived that afternoon. She pulled them out and opened the first one, leafing through the half dozen sheets of paper and the brief, unsigned cover letter.

'You know what to do with this,' read the letter. *But that's the trouble, I don't.* The sheets conveyed information, but it was scientific and she really could not make sense of it. Three of the pages consisted of columns of figures in ppm...*whatever that is.* Another talked in terse sentences about cap rock and fractures, anticlines and metamorphosed limestone. The other two had columns of figures, too, but these were dollar amounts and were in the millions...*no, billions.* All names had been carefully removed except for one - Rushing River. She had looked that up online when she first received the package.

Rushing River: township in the Cascades, population 1300 (2025 census). Named for the small river of the same name that bisects the town and is a tributary of the Deschutes River. Income primarily from cattle farming and tourism. Site of the Rushing River Carbon Sequestration Facility, a subsidiary of Oregon Energy and Oregon Coal and Power.

She remembered the Carbon Sequestration Facility--she had been there fifteen years past, on her first reporting assignment when it went online. Annaliese wondered whether the cryptic information she had been sent was anything to do with the facility. *That's silly, it's been fifteen years and there hasn't been a single problem there. And even if there were, why would anyone send me the information? I'm just a social scene reporter in a small city. Something exciting would go to the Washington Post or New York Times.*

Annaliese opened the second envelope, and unfolded the note in it. 'For God's Sake,' it read, 'why haven't you done anything? Every day you delay increases the danger. I'm giving you a last chance to come clean and at least get the credit for it, but I'll go to the Authorities at the end of the month if you don't, and then God help us all.'

She stared at the note as if the intensity of her gaze could wrest information from the page. *He knows me, but what am I supposed to have done wrong that I should confess? Unless...* She put the envelopes side by side and examined the felt tip scrawled address. *They are both addressed the same, to me at the Chronicle...* A frown creased her forehead and she struggled to grasp a thought that flitted past. *A. Winton, not Annaliese Winton. It could as easily be meant for my son Adrian or...or my father-in-law Andrew.*

Annaliese looked at the pages that accompanied the second letter. More columns of figures but these were in tonnages, not the mysterious ppm, and she noticed at once they were steadily increasing--for a while anyway--and then they were small again but with x106 or x109 beside them. Some of the figures had asterisks alongside them, and a note in the margin said, 'First pack, page three.'

I don't have the faintest idea what this is about. Perhaps I should take them to Andrew and see if he can make anything of them. They may have been addressed to him anyway. Then she thought of her bright young son upstairs. He was only fourteen, but his knowledge of science far exceeded hers.

"Adey," she called up the stairs. "Are you busy?"

"Just a moment, Mom." A few moments passed, his bedroom door opened and he peered out. "Sorry, Mom. I had to finish up on 'Blood Planet'. I'm on level five."

"Can you come down and have a look at something, please."

"Sure." Adrian bounded down the stairs three at a time. "What's up?"

"Maybe nothing." Annaliese handed her son the typed paged but kept the notes hidden. "Does any of this make any sense to you?"

Adrian looked at the pages casually, leafing through them quickly, and then turned to the first page again, reading more slowly. "Where did you get them?"

"Someone sent them to me, I guess because I'm a reporter. Do they mean anything?"

"Hard to say. These first few pages are a set of measurements from a number of different places--see, they're sequentially numbered and have dates. There are some from 2014...and 2020...and even some from last year."

"What are they measuring?"

Adrian shrugged. "I don't know, but the figures are in ppm--parts per million."

"That doesn't sound like much," Annaliese said. "Whatever it is, it can't be very important."

"Oh, I don't know." Adrian looked at his mother and grinned. "Cyanide in the air at 300 parts per million will kill you in a few minutes."

"How on earth do you know that?"

"Not on Earth, Mom. On 'Blood Planet', Level Two."

"You're learning all sorts of stuff I don't think a fourteen-year-old should know. What else is in there? It's not all ppm stuff."

Adrian read a bit more. "There's a geology report and what looks like part of a company balance sheet." He whistled. "A very successful company by the look of it--these figures are in billions." He turned to the next set of stapled pages. "Dates again, and another set of figures, measuring something, too, but this lot's huge. We're into the billions again."

"What about the asterisks? Do they make sense?"

"See First Pack, page three," Adrian read from the note in the margin. "First Pack?"

"These pages." Annaliese tapped the parts per million pages.

Adrian grunted, comparing the two sets of figures. "I'm not sure. Can I take them up to my room and study them?"

Annaliese hesitated, and then nodded. "Look after them, though. I'll need them tomorrow morning."

Adrian was already climbing the stairs, his attention fixed on the pages. "Sure, Mom. G'night."

Annaliese watched him until he closed his bedroom door. She felt a surge of pride at her smart son, but also a twinge of worry. She shook her head and went back into the living room, switching off the lights and wall screen by voice commands, and setting the security system. The envelopes still lay on the sofa and she slipped the notes inside them and stuffed them back in her bag. *Perhaps I should show them to Andrew tomorrow--just in case they were really addressed to him. Maybe he can tell me if there's a story here.*

Chapter 12

August 9, 2030

"D id you feel that?"

"Feel what?" The big man stood in the doorway of the kitchen easing off his work boots, toe to heel, first one and then the other. "The only thing I feel is hungry and that bacon sure smells good."

"The earthquake, Marc, what else?" the woman said. "It rattled the crockery and look, the light's still swinging."

Marc looked at the kitchen light on its long cord and yes, it was swinging, but only just. "Are you sure that wasn't me just opening the back door?" The light ceased its tiny motion as he spoke.

"Of course I'm sure. I'm a Pacific Rimmer, aren't I? I know an earthquake when I feel one."

"Easy, Maggie, I believe you. I just didn't feel it out in the yard. It can't have been a big one."

"It was just a cup-rattler, but you know I don't like them."

Marc strode across the kitchen in his stockinged feet and hugged his wife, Margaret. She resisted him for a moment and then smiled, pushed aside her grey hair with the back of one hand and gave him a peck on his unshaved cheek.

"Go get washed up. Breakfast is on the table in ten."

Marc patted his wife on her behind and headed for the bathroom. He emerged ten minutes later, washed and wearing a fresh shirt. He had even passed a razor over the stubble on his face. He sat down at the kitchen table and bent his head in prayer before attacking his bacon, eggs over-easy, and hash browns. As he ate, he eyed the stack of pancakes with anticipation.

Margaret ate less, picking at her toast and eggs, obviously preoccupied. She waited until her husband pushed away his plate and settled back with a contented sigh, coffee cup in hand, before raising the subject again.

"It's not the first one we've had. Remember we had a jolt that woke us up last month."

"You're making too much of it, Maggie. As you said, this is 'quake country.'"

"What if it's one of the volcanoes waking up?"

"That's not very likely."

"It could happen though. Mount St Helens blew fifty years ago, and Mount Hood is nearby, too. What if one of them erupted?"

"We'd still be fine here. Even when St Helens blew her top, we only got a dusting of ash. I was ten then, and my daddy didn't even think it was important enough to let us stay home from school."

Margaret looked doubtful. "If you're sure."

"I am." Marc pushed his chair back, stifled a belch and headed toward the door. "I'll be checking the fences along the creek bed. Should be back early afternoon."

"You want I should fix you a sandwich?"

"After that breakfast?" Marc shook his own grey head and grinned. He hopped over to his wife with one foot half in his boot and kissed her. "If you ever decide to leave me, you'll make one heck of a short-order cook."

Margaret washed the breakfast dishes and set them to dry in the rack. Marc had bought her a new dishwasher not so long ago, but she still liked the feel of warm water and soap, and the good feeling that came from accomplishing something with her hands. She checked her list of chores and started the laundry. While the clothes were swirling, she vacuumed the downstairs, hung the laundry out on the backyard lines--the clothes drier sat unused except on rainy days--and washed the kitchen windows. Around noon, she fixed herself a sandwich and a cup of green tea and carried it upstairs to the spare room, where Marc had his computer.

She switched it on and fed in the password, waiting until the screen settled into its background. "Google," she said clearly, and the voice recognition program immediately opened a window for the search engine. "What now?" she muttered, and then clicked her tongue and said "Clear" when her question appeared on the screen.

"Earthquakes." Thousands of hits appeared and she ran her eye down the list, opening the Wikipedia entry and then the Panpedia one. She closed them as they were too general and thought for a moment. "Earthquakes Oregon Rushing River."

Thousands more hits appeared, including the ones she had read about, and new ones that seemed to have very little to do with the subject. She opened one on Rushing River and found it was related to tremors registered near the Oregon Power and Coal Station the previous year. She closed it with a sigh of exasperation.

"Earthquakes Volcanoes Oregon." The screen flickered and steadied. "Ah, that's more like it," she whispered. Margaret opened entries and read about earthquake swarms and how the movement of magma...magma? "Definition Magma." A new window opened and she read 'Magma is molten rock found beneath the surface of the earth.' She closed the window and returned to her article. Terms bombarded her--tectonic plate motion, faults, basalt, andesite, rhyolite, pyroclastic flows, Juan de Fuca and lateral eruptions--and she had to look up each new word.

She found out that Mount Jefferson and Mount Hood, the two nearest peaks to Rushing River were considered to be dormant volcanoes. Jefferson had erupted a thousand years ago and Hood only two hundred. Mount St Helens, just over the border in Washington State was fully active and had wrought havoc only fifty years before. Earthquake swarms, tiny ones scarcely noticeable without instruments, had occurred back in 1980, and could be indicative of magma rising within the throat of a volcano. Or they could be tremors associated with the Juan de Fuca plate sliding under the North American plate.

Margaret sat back and thought about this, not liking the implications. She ate her sandwich and sipped her cooling tea, looking out the window over rolling fields and forested hills misting into the distance. Mt Hood stood aloof, calm and serene, giving no hint of any disturbance beneath it.

How can I find out whether these earthquakes are normal, or if they are because something is happening? Who'd know?

Margaret turned back to the computer. "Earthquakes Oregon Information Service." Nothing looked useful until she found a reference to the USGS--United States Geological Survey.

"United States Geological Survey" and then she hurriedly added, "Oregon."

"Ah, that's better," she muttered. A major Panpedia article offered a history of the USGS and a breakdown of departments in the State offices in Portland. Margaret scanned the list of departments, not quite knowing what heading to look for, but found entries relating to tectonics and vulcanology. She looked up the terms to make sure of the definitions and then opened them up. From these entries and the links that stemmed from them, she spent nearly an hour rummaging around in the subject.

The subject was much larger than she had imagined. At one point she found herself jumping from one link to another, passing from volcanoes to volcanic rocks to volcanic gases to pyroclastic flows, to gas eruptions and the tragedy at Lake Nyos in the African country of Cameroon. She read about the destruction of Pompeii, Krakatoa (which was West of Java, not East, as the old Maximilian Schell film title claimed), the overwhelming of St Pierre on the Caribbean island of Martinique, the Maori village that disappeared during the Tarawera eruption in New Zealand, and the more recent Mount St Helens catastrophe. The hair prickled on the back of her neck when she found out that Yellowstone National Park was a super volcano that could erupt anytime now. Details multiplied and her head swam with the terms clamoring in her mind.

I'm confused. I don't know whether any of this is relevant. I need to talk to someone. Margaret noticed a contact email address on the USGS site. After a moment's hesitation, she clicked on it and opened an email window.

'Dear Sirs, I am interested in the frequency of earthquakes in the Rushing River region of Oregon. I live near the township and I have noticed two earthquakes recently--one this morning at about 7am, and the other last month (I think around the 20th). Can you please tell me if this is normal for the region, or if I should be taking precautions of some sort? Regards, Margaret Stone, Rushing River Ranch, Rushing River, Oregon.'

She clicked send and then sat and stared at the screen. *They'll never reply, but who else is there?* The corner of a newspaper peeked out from the trash basket near the desk. She pulled it out and leafed through it, a vague idea nagging at her. It was a three-month-old print copy of the Rushing River Gazette, a free monthly online paper filled with the advertising and the inconsequential goings-on of a small community. She had printed out a copy of the paper for the recipes. *But, somewhere...ah, here we go.* She found the recipe for blueberry and maple muffins that included a potentially catastrophic typographical error. Margaret smiled when she read it again and remembered she had written in to the Gazette, who had passed it along to the original writer of the article on the staff of the Salem Chronicle. This woman had actually bothered to write a brief letter of thanks for pointing it out. *What was her name?* She crossed to the filing cabinet and dug into her recipe file. *Annaliese Winton...and her email address.*

Margaret doubted whether a writer of muffin recipes would be interested in earthquake swarms...*but who knows? Maybe someone else at the paper.* She typed up a brief letter along the lines of the one to USGS and sent if off. *It can't hurt.*

She heard the distant growl of her husband's pickup and saw a thin plume of dust in the distance. She switched off the computer, grabbed her cup and plate and hurried to the kitchen to prepare Marc's lunch. She was tidying up when he arrived.

He grinned with delight. "Thanks Maggie," he said, and started into the sandwich. Over coffee and another cup of green tea, they discussed the ranch and its workings. Very soon, the subject of volcanoes and earthquakes slipped from Margaret's mind.

Chapter 13

August 9, 2030

A
nnaliese sat in the waiting room of her father-in-law's office in downtown Salem, the anonymous letters and scientific reports in her purse. She had telephoned for an appointment the previous day and knew that she was lucky to have been admitted so soon--except that the appointment had been at 10 am and it was now nearly noon. The secretary raised her gaze from her computer screen once more and stared at Annaliese until she was forced to look away. The woman then returned to her work with a supercilious smile.

Annaliese cleared her throat. "Er, you did say my appointment was for 10? Perhaps I should reschedule."

"That won't be necessary...Ms Winton. Mr Winton said he is happy to see you today and he asks you to be patient. He will be with you as soon as he can. He is in a very important meeting."

"And you know this...how? You haven't spoken with him for over an hour." The smile again.

Noon came and went and Annaliese picked up another magazine from the coffee table and dropped it back. She opened her bag and took out the papers and re-read them. They would make more sense after Adrian explained what he had found out. She wished she could have talked to him before this meeting, but events had conspired against them. The morning after their talk, she went to his room and found the papers on his desk with a note attached.

'Sorry, Mom, I had to go out early. I'll talk to you about it tonight.'

That night she had been forced to work late when Simon deleted her copy for no good reason and told her to rewrite it. By the time she grabbed a bite to eat and got home she was exhausted. Adrian had seen her state and just said, "Tomorrow. You're going to need a clear head."

Tomorrow was today, but he had said little over breakfast, playing with his cereal and changing the subject when she steered it to the papers.

Perhaps he didn't find out anything. He'll tell me when he's ready. She was determined to see her father-in-law and see if the papers were meant for him, or if he knew anything about their contents.

Annaliese got up to stretch her legs, wandering around the reception area, examining the art prints and photographs of posed businessmen. Andrew Winton was in all of them, standing smiling beside the mayor of Salem, senators and congressmen from Oregon, even a portrait of him shaking hands with the President. *I never knew he walked in such elevated company.* Other photographs were less revealing, and less interesting.

She peered at one where Andrew was smiling, but the other man appeared stern. The name underneath the picture read 'Robert Peale, OC&P' and left her none the wiser. Another showed him with a tall bald man in glasses who stared intently at the camera--Max Hay--*whoever he is.* Annaliese yawned and looked at her watch.

"I think I really should reschedule," she told the secretary.

"No need, Ms Winton. Mr Winton will see you now."

"Now?" Annaliese stood nonplussed for a moment and then grabbed her bag. "Do I...?" She indicated the door to her father-in-law's office.

"Yes, just go in, Ms Winton."

Annaliese took a breath to calm down and opened the door to the office. It was a spacious room with thick carpeting and dark walnut book shelves. A large window showing the city skyline and the distant Cascades threw light over a desk facing the door. Andrew Winton's leonine head was bowed over some documents when she entered, but he glanced up and gestured toward an armchair before bending to his task once more.

"I'll be with you in a moment, Annaliese."

Annaliese took a seat and sat upright, her bag on her knee, waiting for him to finish. At length he did. He put down his pen and leaned back, regarding her coolly.

"Is this about the assignments you are given at the 'Chronicle'? You must realize that I do not concern myself with petty matters like that. I have a lot more to occupy my time than a small newspaper."

Annaliese hesitated, wondering whether she should voice her desires on that point, or stick to her original disclosure. "No...no, that wasn't why I came today."

"Well, spit it out. I haven't got all day." He looked at his watch pointedly.

"I...I was sent a letter...well, two actually...but I don't really know what they're about." Annaliese saw Andrew open his mouth and forged onward. "They're scientific readings of some sort, and a balance sheet. The sender--who is anonymous, by the way--seems to think I should know about the contents as he tells me in a covering note to do something before he does."

"But you don't know what he's talking about?"

"No. That's when I thought of you. The addressee on both envelopes was 'A. Winton' which could be me, or Adrian, or...or even..."

"Or even me. Yes, I get it." Andrew grimaced. "Do you have the letters?"

Annaliese dug into her bag and pulled out both envelopes and held them out.

Andrew looked at her and extended his arm, forcing Annaliese to get up, take several steps forward and place them in his hand. He briefly looked at the address, checked the back of each envelope for a return address and then slipped the contents out onto his desk.

"How did they arrive at the Chronicle?"

"A man brought them in off the street."

"Have you tried to find out anything about him?"

"Nobody can remember anything beyond a vague description. He just put them down on the counter and left."

Andrew grunted and turned his attention to the sheets of paper stapled together, first from one envelope and then the other. "This is all there was? You haven't removed anything?"

"No. Does it mean anything? Was it meant for you?"

Andrew did not answer. He got up and turned toward the window, looking out on the scenery with his hands clasped behind his back. After several minutes he turned back and sat down again. He left the papers on his desk and sat regarding Annaliese over steepled fingers.

"You did the right thing bringing them to me."

"They mean something?"

"Possibly. I'll have to make a few inquiries. However, this is nothing for you to be concerned about."

"I'd like to pursue this, Andr...Mr Winton. There may be a story in it."

A faint smile touched the man's lips. "There may be, but you won't be following it...yet. I want you to leave this in my hands. I've been reviewing your work at the Chronicle, Annaliese, and I think you're ready for a more responsible job. I'd like you to take over the Portland Water Authority scandal from Ben Cummings. He's been treading lightly as there's a possibility the mayor is involved and it's an election year. Well, to hell with the sonofabitch. Dig as deep as you have to and come up with the dirt. I'll publish it." Andrew smiled inwardly at her eagerness. "Are you up for it, Annaliese?"

"Yes, Mr Winton...and, er, thank you."

Andrew's nod was plainly dismissive, so Annaliese arose and moved to the door, where she hesitated and turned back. "About the papers..."

"Forget them, Annaliese. I'll deal with them now."

Chapter 14

August 9, 2030

Matt Morrison sat at his desk in the USGS building in downtown Portland and ignored his computer screen. On it was a half-finished paper on the geological underpinnings of proposed wetlands in the Columbia River estuary, but his heart was not in the subject and he was easily distracted. Matt was a stratigrapher at heart, reveling in the layers of rock beneath them and the way that moving plates buckled and folded them, but he had been seconded a year ago to the Hydrology Division in Portland, rather than the Vulcanology and Seismology offices in Vancouver across the Columbia River in Washington State.

The most recent distraction was an email from a friend in Seattle who was coming down to Portland the following week and hoped to catch up. Matt lost himself in reminiscences of University days and undergraduate escapades. After many minutes he composed a brief reply inviting his friend to stay in his apartment and sent it off.

He stared at the paper for a little while and was moved to insert a comma. A few moments later he deleted the offending punctuation. His work station was in an airy, well-lit, open-plan room with half a dozen other desks, each equipped with a computer and an enthusiastic geologist delving away into the workings of Oregon State. Matt sighed and got up to get himself a cup of peppermint tea. He dunked the bag in hot water, letting the liquid slowly darken to a delicious green, stirred in a heaped teaspoon of raw sugar and carried it back to his desk.

A small window had opened up on his screen telling him an email had arrived, but Matt ignored it, leaning back in his chair and sipping the fragrant tea. *It'll just be Joe accepting my offer.* He opened up the screen with his uncompleted paper and regarded it with distaste. *I really can't be bothered.* He shrugged. *I've got another month--I'll come in and do some on the weekend.*

The email window on the computer blinked again, and Matt moved the cursor and clicked. There was only one new message and the subject line told him it was one forwarded by the Public Relations team. He groaned and looked around the office, calling out to one of his fellow workers.

"Hey, Roz, how would you like a nice interesting email?"

A slim red-head three desks away looked up. "Who's it from?"

"The great unwashed public. It's sure to be interesting."

Roz laughed. "If it's that interesting, why aren't you doing it?"

Matt grimaced and opened the email. It was from a Margaret Stone in somewhere called Rushing River and she was concerned about two small earthquakes...*Two?* "Where the hell does she think she is?" he muttered. "Two a day wouldn't be unusual." As he said it, Matt realized he was being unfair. There were many earthquakes in Oregon, but it had been a while since the last big one, and even a small one could cause jitters. The letter writer went on to name dates--ninth of this month, twentieth of last.

"Hey, Roz," he called out again. "Where's Rushing River?"

"Search me."

Love to. "Mick? Anyone?"

"It's off the Deschutes River, I think."

"Thanks, Kevin. I'll look it up."

Matt did a Google search and came up with the Township of Rushing River on the river of the same name, a tributary of the Deschutes. Another search revealed the location of Margaret Stone's ranch and once he knew its map coordinates, he wandered across to the Earthquake Map on the far wall.

The Earthquake Map was an unofficial piece of whimsy in a time when printed maps were almost nonexistent outside of a museum. Every piece of information imaginable and any photo, map or drawing within the extensive USGS files could be accessed by computer in less time than it took to walk across the office. Matt had introduced the idea, as he was not only the oldest geologist in the office, but also one who remembered working with paper maps in the field. His younger colleagues were utterly reliant on GPS units and the ubiquitous Palm Screens for their information. His idea caught on though and the young graduates thought it a bit of a laugh, but could usually be persuaded to stick a pin in the map for every 'quake that occurred in northern Oregon and southern Washington.

The pins in the map were color-coded by month and seismic intensity, and had the date written on them in tiny letters in another outmoded recording device--ink. Matt cast his gaze rapidly over the sprinklings of pins and after a few minutes found the one from the previous month. He frowned and peered at the pin.

"What the hell is it doing out there, there's no fault line in that region." He looked some more and called out to the room. "Who hasn't entered today's temblors on the map?"

"Sorry, that'd be me," John replied. "Haven't got around to it yet as they're only a bunch of tiddlers. You know, you'd find what you're looking for a lot more quickly if you pulled up the information online."

"I happen to like doing it this way. Where exactly was the one out near Rushing River? I have a member of the public seeking information."

"Okay granddad," John laughed. "Do it the old way. Map reference GC472866, intensity 2.9 at 7.03 am. I'm surprised anyone felt it."

Matt selected a light green pin and carefully inked the date on it before sticking it into the map. It fell very close to another light green one near the Deschutes River on the eastern side of the Cascades. He frowned again and went back to his desk, where he cleared away his other documents and opened up the interactive USGS database. The map coordinates for the most recent 'quake epicenter appeared on a three-dimensional map of the Eastern Cascades and when he clicked on 'Others', a handful of other points flared close by. He rotated the map to show the depth and all but three of the epicenter points receded to the junction with the outer mantle. Two, which he saw by their captions, were the ones reported by the woman from the Rushing River Ranch. "Odd," he muttered. Matt zoomed in on the vertical function and consulted the scale. He whistled softly.

Mick heard him and looked across. "What's up?"

"I've got two surface tremors three weeks apart from the same spot."

"How deep?"

"Fifteen hundred meters, give or take."

"What fault line are they on?"

"That's just it, they're not. Nor is there a dam or a sizeable body of water anywhere close providing lubrication."

Mick got up and wandered across to look at Matt's graphics. "Well, there must be something. Tremors need something to set them off."

"Yeah, but they're tiny, and not causing any damage. I'm inclined to just forget it."

"I thought you said it was a member of the great unwashed who asked. What are you going to tell him?"

"Her."

Mick grinned. "Even better, but you're going to have to tell her something. You remember last month's memo about being nice to taxpayers."

"Yeah, she wanted to know if she should be worried, so I guess I can reassure her at least."

Mick returned to his desk and Matt played around with the graphics a bit more, rotating the image. He knew there were no fault lines in that area, but he could not quite place the finer levels of the subsurface rocks. He minimized the graphics and pulled up the USGS geological maps, zeroing in on the Deschutes region.

"The Hood Anticline? That whole area's stable."

Matt bit his lip and then cut and pasted data from one set of graphics to the other, merging the two sets of data. Presently, the three light green points of the epicenters lay on the curved rock layers of the anticline. He zoomed in again.

"That's ridiculous," he muttered. "That layer's limestone and there are no mapped faults anywhere near. What's going on? Hey, Mick. What do you know about the Hood Anticline?"

"I doubt anything you don't know. Didn't you do your dissertation on it?"

"On anticlines generally, not just the Hood. There's nothing odd about it, is there?"

"Nope. If there was, they wouldn't have used it for that carbon sequestration site. Didn't you tell me once that you were out there when they started up?"

"Yeah, that's right. I'd forgotten. Thanks." Matt sat back and sipped at the rest of his now cold peppermint tea. He thought back fifteen years to the opening ceremony at the sequestration site and smiled. *I seem to remember a sporty girl and a totally wonderful evening. What was her name? Anna something?* Matt tucked his personal memories away and thought about sequestration and the locking away of millions of tons of pressurized liquid carbon dioxide deep underground. *That could be it. All that pressure could have loosened a weakness in the rocks.*

"Mick, can I bug you again?"

"I guess." He walked over and sat on the edge of Matt's desk. "What now?"

Matt showed him the Hood Anticline with the three epicenters marked in its limestone cap rock, told him about the carbon sequestration and the huge pressure of carbon dioxide beneath the cap. "What do you think? Could something be happening to it?"

"Escaping, you mean? I seriously doubt it. There may be millions of tons of pressurized CO_2 down there but there are billions of tons of rock on top of it. Safe as houses, I'd say."

"And the tremors?"

"A bit of rock settling."

"You don't think I should worry?"

"Why? It's not your concern anyway. Put in a memo if you like...but remember Smythe doesn't like to be bothered by crackpot ideas. You need something concrete to back it up with."

"Yeah, you're probably right."

"Damn right I am." Mick looked at his watch. "You want to get some lunch?"

"Give me ten."

Matt regarded the 3-D image of the anticline on his computer, and then extrapolated upward from the epicenters of the tremors, working out what surface feature was right above them. *Not that that's necessarily important. There's still fifteen hundred meters of rock and soil to get through and if* CO_2 *is leaking, it could be well spread out.* He checked a topographical map online and drew a circle about a kilometer across directly above the epicenters. *That's where I start. Rushing River Ranch.*

Chapter 15

August 10, 2030

S aturday was the day when Annaliese caught up with her housework. Although her reporting job did not mean a strict 8 to 5 work regimen, she could generally take the weekends off as her news stories usually required little research that could not easily take place from home. She set the laundry going, programmed the automatic vacuum to cover the first-floor carpets and wood, and tried her hand at fixing a leaking tap in the bathroom. Adrian played his part, too, making sure his room was tidy, emptying the dishwasher and dusting the shelves in the living room.

By mid-morning, all was complete and Annaliese made herself a cup of coffee. She dabbed at the scrape on her knuckles and thought black thoughts about the wrench, but at least could feel a measure of satisfaction at the now silent bathroom tap. Coffee cup in hand, Annaliese went into her study and pulled up the files on the Portland Water Authority scandal. Ben Cummings had been upset at losing the story, but accepted that she had had nothing to do with the change of ownership. She settled down to read, but half an hour later found herself yawning. *Another sordid little tale of corrupt officials and kickbacks. What's worse, nobody's going to care.*

"Mom, you got a minute?" Adrian stood in the doorway of the study.

"Sure, Adey. What's on your mind?"

"Those papers you showed me."

"What papers...oh, yes, I remember. What about them?"

"Did you still want to know what they mean?"

Annaliese hesitated, wondering if Adrian would be upset she'd taken them to his grandfather. "You worked it out?"

"Sure. I had to ask a couple of people--my science teacher and my friend Jace."

"You didn't let on where they came from, did you?'

"Of course not, Mom. I just asked a few leading questions. I didn't even need to show them the figures."

"And you found out what they mean?"

"Sure did."

Annaliese thought her son looked extraordinarily pleased with himself, so she minimized the screen she was working on and gave him her full attention. "Tell me."

"It concerns the Rushing River Carbon Sequestration Facility. It's leaking."

Annaliese cast her mind back several years to when she first knew about such things. She dredged up memories and said, "Everybody said it would leak a bit. No storage system is totally leak-proof. I remember I did a piece on it when it first opened."

"Yes, but this is more than just a bit of gas. It's been leaking slowly for years and if these figures are right, it's getting worse. Some of those readings were a few hundred or so parts per million above normal."

"That sounds bad, but what does it all mean?"

Adrian shrugged. "I don't know enough about the properties of huge amounts of liquid carbon dioxide but CO_2 gas escaped from Lake Nyos in Africa over forty years ago and killed 1700 people."

"That's awful. How much gas escaped from this lake?"

"About a million and a half tons."

"Oh, Adey, you had me going there. A million and a half tons is a colossal amount. Far more than a few hundred parts per million."

"That's a few hundred parts per million of an awfully large amount of air. It adds up, Mom."

"Even so..."

"Did you know that the Rushing River Station has been injecting nearly a million and a half tons of liquid CO_2 into the ground every month on average? And for the last fifteen years. That's one awesome tonnage of liquid gas."

"That was in those papers?"

"Was? You don't have them anymore?"

Annaliese pursed her lips. "I wasn't sure they were addressed to me. I knew you weren't the A. Winton on the envelope, so I..."

"You gave them to gramps?"

"Why not? But it turns out he didn't know much more than I did. He says he'll look into it."

"Yeah, but if he doesn't recognize the significance of them, or doesn't believe it, or...or even doesn't want it known, it could all be covered up."

Annaliese laughed, but with a touch of anxiety. "Cover up? This is your grandfather we're talking about. He and I may have differences, but he's always been your loving gramps."

"What's love got to do with it, Mom? I know he loves me, and I love him, but this could be a big deal. When money's at stake--big money--loyalties change."

"I can't believe I'm hearing this, Adey. Your grandfather is an upright and honest man. Bigoted and a pain in the ass sometimes, I grant, but basically good. He's looked after us since..."

"Since dad walked out on us? Yeah, I know."

"He's not going to do anything dishonest."

"Did you know he's on the board of directors of Oregon Coal and Power?"

"I imagine a lot of top businessmen are..."

"And that Oregon Coal and Power controls Oregon Energy which owns the Rushing River Carbon Sequestration Facility?"

Annaliese slumped back in her chair. "How do you know all this, Adey?"

"Same way anyone knows anything, Mom." Adrian shrugged. "Same way you research your stories, I guess--online. I started with the sequestration facility and followed the links back. Everything you want to know and a whole lot more is out there if you know where to look."

Annaliese shook her head. "I'm sure there's a very good explanation for his business interests, but what do the figures actually show? I can't remember any of the numbers. Can you recall them?"

"I don't have to." Adrian grinned. "First thing I did was scan them into my computer. You want to see them?" He led the way to his room and cleared a spot on the end of his bed for his mother to sit before opening the files.

"My IT teacher recommended a Wolfram search to look for irregularities in the data sets and compare them to anything similar that might be out there already." Adrian waggled one hand back and forth. "Well, maybe, maybe not, but I found this. It's a financial statement released by Oregon Energy two years ago. I'm not sure if it's the Sequestration Plant because the figures don't match the ones in the document you were sent. I suspect those are the real figures, though. If that's the case, then somebody's not being honest."

Annaliese said nothing, but just shook her head helplessly. "How could you possibly know all this? You've never been interested in finance and...and business."

Adrian grinned. "No, but Jace's big brother is doing Business Studies at Washington U. I emailed him and, er, well, hinted I was doing an assignment..."

His mother shook her head. "And I thought I was the investigative reporter in the family. What else?"

"This one is more straightforward. It seems to be the tonnage of liquid CO_2 injected underground. The figures are in millions of tons and absolutely mind-boggling. This last one..." Adrian scrolled through pages of figures, "...is apparently the CO_2 levels in the atmosphere at forty sites, taken every couple of months for the last fifteen years. Most are fairly normal, but a few are higher. I've highlighted those. Now the CO_2 levels are not overly high if you are taking measurements inside a classroom or lecture hall, but a lot higher than you'd expect in the open air. I'd love to know how they were measured."

Annaliese leaned forward and looked at the screen. Most of the CO_2 readings were in the 400 to 450 range, but a few were much higher--635, 654, even one of 1,790. "What's a normal reading?"

"Depends where you are. 500 in the city, 450 in the country."

She tapped the screen over the highest one. "Whereabouts is this supposed leak?"

"Who knows? The sites are marked with a code that seems to include the place...see? S4, and the date--061730--seventeenth of June this year."

"So, we've got nothing? You couldn't make a case that anything bad is happening here. Not with these figures."

"There's always the fraud."

"Supposed fraud. You can't say for definite that this all relates to the sequestration site, can you?"

Adrian scowled. "No, I guess not...but it fits."

"There was nothing else in the document that might identify anything?"

"It did say 'Rushing River' on the tonnage page, but that's not really controversial. The only other thing was this..." Adrian scrolled. "P587/23. I've no idea what it means."

Annaliese stared at the page for a few moments and then shook her head. "Me neither."

"What're you going to do, Mom?"

"I don't know. I don't even know if I should do anything. Your grandfather has the originals; he should be the one to do something."

"And if he's involved?"

"I can't believe he would be."

"I hope not, Mom, but even if he isn't, he may not see the importance of these figures. What if there really is a leak? And what if it gets worse? Somebody could get hurt."

"You think? It's only CO_2 when you come down to it. We breathe it out all the time."

"At these levels, no, it's not dangerous. Normal atmospheric levels in Rushing River are probably around 440, 450, but if the leak gets worse..."

"If there really is a leak."

"Yes, of course, but if there is and it gets worse, then 1,790 parts per million becomes 10,000, then 20,000 or more and that's enough to make a person pass out. If they couldn't get clear, they'd die."

"I suppose I could go and talk to the people at the sequestration site. See if they'll tell me anything."

"Fat chance." Adrian saw his mother's expression. "But hey, you're an investigative reporter. If anyone can dig the truth out of them, you can."

Chapter 16

August 11, 2030

The Maher family arrived in Oregon via Interstate 84, crossing from Idaho at Ontario, Oregon. They continued northwest until they came to the Columbia River and followed the highway westward to The Dalles. Here they turned south along The Dalles-California Highway with the towering bulk of Mount Hood to their right until the Rushing River turnoff. Another ten miles saw them in the township and another two to the campground in the valley.

"Look, Mommy," Alexa cried out. "Horsies."

Cory sniggered. "They've got horns, stupid. They're cows."

"Be nice to your little sister," Karen said. "There are a lot of new..."

"Okay, quiet everyone. I can't hear myself think." Randy halted outside the campground office and went inside, leaving his family in the car. He emerged ten minutes later and, without saying anything, drove the car over the speed bumps and entered the wooded campground. He stopped outside a small cabin near the shower block. "This is it. Everybody out."

"It's quite small," Karen commented. "And so close to the...the amenities." From where they stood they could hear the chatter of people in the showers and toilets flushing.

"It's all we could afford," Randy said shortly. "Are you telling me it's not good enough?"

"Oh, no. It's lovely, really it is. We'll have such fun here." Karen gathered her children to her and hurried inside the cabin, exclaiming loudly at each new wonder of the camping experience. Meanwhile, Randy unloaded the car and brought everything inside. "Bunk beds," Karen enthused. "You can be on top, Cory."

"I wanna be on top," Alexa complained.

"It's too high, darling. We don't want you falling out and hurting yourself."

As soon as Randy had brought the luggage from the car, he left his wife and children to settle in and wandered off to explore the camping ground. He noted the gas-fired barbecue pits scattered through the grounds, the placement of numerous hiking trails and the availability of canoeing and horse-riding. The camp store was a disappointment, for while it stocked a range of food and other groceries at somewhat inflated prices, it did not carry alcohol.

He returned to the cabin and retrieved the car keys. "I'm going in to town. Do you need anything?"

"What do you want for dinner, Randy? Barbecue? You could get some steaks and burger while you're..."

"Get them at the camp store. I'll get a bottle of gas in town." He saw Karen looking at him expectantly but saying nothing. "Jeez, just ask, why don't ya?" He took out his wallet and peeled off a twenty.

Randy picked up a bottle of gas at the general store in Rushing River Township and then visited the liquor store, picking up a case of Coors and a fifth of Bourbon. On an impulse, he added a two-quart bottle of Pepsi for the children and a bottle of cheap red wine for his wife. He paid the clerk and dumped his purchases in the wagon before setting off on foot to see what the town had to offer.

Fifteen minutes later he had written off the place as uninteresting, though a couple of young women in a hairdressing salon looked like they might be up for a bit of fun. Randy was well aware of the interest women had in him--he straightened his back and sucked in his gut at the thought. He eyed his reflection in a store window. *Not bad. You still got it, good buddy*. He thought about coming into town later and finding those young women at the tavern, fantasizing about their reaction to him. *They want it. They all do, no matter what they might say.*

The Information Center was still open, so Randy wandered in. The woman behind the counter was middle-aged and plain by Randy's estimation, but the attraction she obviously felt for him was still there. Sometimes he tired of being every woman's desire.

"What's there to do in this town?" he asked.

"Good evening. My name is Claudia. Welcome to Rushing River. Are you just passing through?"

"I'm up at the campgrounds for a bit. What's there to do up here?"

"Well, that depends on your interests. If you're up at the campground, then you'll be aware of the fine hiking trails. We have some maps here..." She passed over a few sheets of gaily adorned glossy paper, "...that show some of the more popular ones. Or we have these maps on an inexpensive CD that can be used on your Palm Screen. Are you here with your family?"

Randy nodded. "Yeah, brought the wife and kids up to see a bit of wilderness."

"You couldn't have brought them to a better place then. Our hiking trails display a full range from easy one-hour walks to full day hikes for the more adventurous. If you're after something a little less strenuous for younger ones, there are horse trails, canoeing on the river, and a petting zoo. I have here a brochure that shows where each of these activities is held, what times they're open, and costs. It's all on the CD too." The woman passed across a folded paper with a smile. "There are also wonderful opportunities for photography. I do a lot myself and even take a small photography class on Thursdays..."

"Anything else? Any sights, activities for...adults?"

The woman's smile slipped but she quickly regained it. "We're a family-oriented town, but we do have the Rushing River Carbon Sequet...Sequestration Plant." She stumbled over the long word. "Not that the public are allowed in, you understand, but there are some fine views of the buildings from the perimeter fence. Many people are fascinated to see where history is being made, as our own Oregon Power Company does its bit to save the world from global warming."

"That's crap," Randy muttered.

"I beg your pardon?"

"That global warming stuff is a pile of sh...a lie put about by Democrats for political purposes. Thank God we got a tough guy in the White House now. He'll put a stop to all that left-wing plotting. Jeez, you only have to feel the weather to know it ain't true. Wasn't it cold last winter?"

"Well, I'm sure you're entitled to your opinion." The woman erected her smile again. "I have some interesting information on just that subject..."

"Forget it." Randy turned to go, then reached across and scooped up the brochures and maps on the counter. He stuffed them in his pocket and slammed out through the glass doors. *Ignorant bitch, what does she know?*

Randy returned to his wagon and drove around for a while, exploring some of the roads and followed a winding one that led up through thick pine forests before ending in a clearing with a view over town and the whole valley. Randy was not particularly interested in scenery, but even he could appreciate the miles of forest and farmland disappearing into the hazy distance. Sunset was close, and the road dark under the pines, so he turned in the deserted clearing and drove back to the campground. He arrived with the dusk and found his family anxious and hungry by the cabin.

"Have you got everything ready?" were Randy's first words. "Jeez, Karen, get moving will ya." Randy grabbed the gas bottle and a beer from the wagon and headed over to the nearest vacant barbecue pit. Cory hurried after him with a plate of raw meat and a pair of tongs, while Karen disappeared back into the cabin to quickly cut and butter hamburger buns, and prepare a small salad.

They ate inside, rather than contend with the bugs, and that night his only complaint was the lack of onions and fries.

"They'd run out at the camp store, it being Sunday and all," she explained. "Maybe I can go into town tomorrow and stock up."

Randy grunted noncommittally and pointed at the last piece of steak. "Anyone want that?" Without waiting for a response, he took it and demolished it in half a dozen mouthfuls. He leaned back and belched, before opening another beer.

Karen knew her husband's desires and quickly did the dishes and tidied things away. Lacking a 3-D screen in the cabin, she organized the children into a game of cards so that they would not annoy their father. Randy looked on approvingly and continued to drink. At nine o'clock though, he sent the children off to bed.

"We're going to be busy tomorrow. First day of vacation."

The children dutifully said goodnight to their father--Cory with a restrained hug and Alexa boisterously, before disappearing into the bedroom with their mother. She emerged a few minutes later and made herself a cup of tea. Randy refused her offer of a coffee and cracked another beer instead.

"I think I'll turn in," Karen said after finishing her cup. "If that's alright?"

"Sure, go ahead. I'll be in soon." Randy waited until she was just closing the bedroom door behind her. "Karen, honey?"

Karen stopped and looked at her husband cautiously. "Yes, Randy?"

Her husband grinned. "Wear something nice to bed, okay? We'll have some fun to get us in the right frame of mind for our vacation."

Chapter 17

August 15, 2030

Annaliese was tempted to investigate the mystery of the sequestration papers but knew that her job depended on doing the work she was assigned. She researched the Portland Water Authority over the weekend, and on Monday drove into the city and tried to see the relevant players in the story. Mayor Grede refused to talk to her and referred her to his Public Relations officer, who blithely ignored all evidence to the contrary and put the allegations down to political smearing. Annaliese dug a bit deeper and talked to minor characters on the fringes of the scandal, uncovering things previously overlooked. She leaked these other allegations to the Mayor's PR man and was rewarded by a flash of panic crossing the young man's handsome face. She evidently touched a nerve or two, and on Tuesday morning, Andrew Winton telephoned her.

"I had a call from Grede's office," he said without preamble. "He wants me to shut your story down. Claims it's in the national interest."

"I see. What do you want me to do?"

Andrew told her, and despite being limited to an electronic connection with him, Annaliese found herself blushing at his explicit and anatomically impossible instructions. "Seriously though," he added. "Write it as you find it and get it to me by tomorrow at five. I'm going to crucify the bastard." He hung up without waiting for her response.

She worked late that night and started early on Wednesday morning. Draft succeeded draft until by early afternoon she had what she thought might be the final version. *Before Andrew hacks into it, at least.* She minimized the article, meaning to leave it an hour before reading through it once more and sending it. Her email folder contained nothing of great interest except a query from a reader about muffins and earthquakes. She would not have read it then except the reader came from Rushing River and the place had been in her mind recently. *Margaret Stone? I remember her.*

Annaliese reached into her bag and pulled out the sequestration papers. She had had Adrian print off a copy and she now opened it out, trying to decide what, if anything, she should do about it. *Imagine I'm doing a story on it...what do I need to find out? Who do I need to talk to?* She took her Palm Screen and stylus and started making notes.

Find out if the leakage is real.
Talk to Rushing River boss--Who?
Find out the geology of the site.
Talk to...who? USGS?
Finances. Show the financial statement to accountant. Who?
Earthquakes in Rushing River. Related? How?

Shit. This could be a long and complex job. Do I really want to start it? She sighed and saved her notes before putting the Palm Screen back in her bag. "Hey, Ben, you know about scientific stuff. What does sequestration mean to you?"

Ben looked up from his computer. "In what context?"

"Carbon capture and sequestration."

Ben swiveled in his chair and looked across the room at her. "What do they teach youngsters these days?"

Annaliese laughed. "Much the same as you, I suspect. You're only ten years older than me, but I never did science."

"It was cutting edge technology twenty or thirty years ago when the whole greenhouse gas/global warming debate blew up in everyone's faces. Somebody got the bright idea that we could go on burning coal and gas as long as we found a way to hide the carbon dioxide away--or sequester it. Oregon was privileged to host the first really big sequestration attempt, by shoving millions of tons of CO_2 into the rock layers beneath us."

"And it worked?"

"Sure. The Department of Energy did its homework and found the right place to store it--under Rushing River. Now it's fifteen years later and nary a problem.

You should know all this, Annaliese. You were at Rushing River when they turned it on. I even read your piece."

"That thing?" Annaliese gave an embarrassed laugh. "I blush when I think of it. In those days I was a kid reporter impressed by freshly painted concrete and shiny pipes. My piece was no more than window dressing reflecting the company's press release. I've forgotten anything I once knew about it."

"If you say so," Ben said with a smile. "So, what's got you interested now?"

Annaliese shrugged. "Just something I read. Is the place dangerous? I mean, could it blow up?"

"You've been reading too many thriller novels. Nothing much goes on there. They rail in coal, burn it to make electricity, liquefy the waste gas and push it underground. What can go wrong? Carbon dioxide doesn't explode, it's not even flammable. In fact, it'll put fires out--think of fire extinguishers."

"So, what's the worst that could happen? Let your imagination run riot."

"What? A terrorist strike or something? They blow up the plant and we all lose electricity for a few hours until they cut in the other power stations. Don't worry, Annaliese. These things are safe. Not like nuclear power stations, though even they're safe enough."

Annaliese thought for a few minutes. "What if they ruptured the pipe that pumps the CO_2 into the ground? It's under pressure, isn't it?"

Ben nodded. "Yes, you'd get a spray of very cold gas for a few minutes, and it could kill someone unlucky enough to be caught in it, but there are valves in that pipe that prevent backflow. Very little would escape."

"What if gas escaped from underground?"

Ben looked at her quizzically. "You're really getting into this, aren't you? Have you heard something or are you just fishing around for an article?"

"Just something Adrian said."

"Ah." Ben nodded. "A school project. Well, gas will escape from any underground formation, but the DOE estimates about a one percent loss in a thousand years. That's very low. Again, nothing to worry about."

"How would you test to see if CO_2 was escaping?"

"Beats me. I suppose you could do a litmus test or something."

"Litmus?"

"Well, I'm guessing here, but I seem to remember that CO_2 dissolves in water to form a weak acid, and an acid turns blue litmus red...or is it the other way round? Why don't you go out to Rushing River? I'm sure if you tell them it's for your son's school project, they'll give you some information on it."

"I might do that."

That was exactly what Annaliese did. She emailed her article to Andrew without bothering to read it through again, and took the rest of the afternoon off.

Getting to Rushing River was more than an afternoon's jaunt, however, as the place lay on the other side of the Cascades. She would have to drive up to Portland and along the Columbia River Highway to The Dalles before turning south. The Mount Hood route across the Cascades was shorter but would take longer on the winding hill roads.

She drove around on Thursday. After seeing Adrian off to school, she armed herself with recorders and camera, and tucked the print-out of the CO_2 readings into her bag. The trip round to Rushing River took her about four hours, but the scenery was spectacular and she stopped often, just glad to be out of the city. She arrived in the Township around noon and asked directions to the Sequestration Facility at the Information Center.

Tempted though she was to drive straight to the Plant, Annaliese restrained her impulse, telling herself that if all else failed she might be able to generate a human-interest story on the effect of a technical installation on a small community. The woman behind the Information Center counter--Claudia Barrow--was very helpful, and she left armed with brochures and a list of people worth talking to about the Plant.

First things first, she told herself. *See if I can get anything out of the boss at the Sequestration Plant.*

Oregon Coal and Power stood at the end of a railhead about three miles from the township. There was considerable noise from shunting trains and the rattling of great conveyor belts carrying coal to the power station. The sequestration site was on the far side and was clean by comparison, though the pristine concrete walls and gleaming pipes she half-remembered were now tainted by the ubiquitous coal dust. Annaliese approached the guard at the gatehouse and stated her business.

She was met at the main building by a young man. He introduced himself as Timothy Weiss, in Public Relations.

"What can I do for you, Ms Winton?"

Annaliese decided to run with her colleague Ben's mistake. "My son is doing a school project on carbon and the environment and I thought perhaps I could find out a little about carbon sequestration for him."

Timothy nodded. "Wouldn't it have been more useful for him to do this research himself?"

"True, but you know what teenagers are like, they leave it to the last minute and the assignment has to be in tomorrow."

"Well, I can find you some brochures. Was there anything in particular you wanted to know?"

Annaliese laughed lightly. "I'm not sure I know what to ask. Let's see...I understand you take the carbon dioxide given off by the power station and dissolve it in water and pump it underground. Is that right?"

"Close. We don't dissolve it, though. We pressurize it until it becomes a liquid and pump that into rock chambers over a mile underground."

"How much carbon dioxide are we talking about?"

Timothy smiled. "Our power station consumes over ten thousand tons of coal every day, releasing forty thousand tons of carbon dioxide. We pressurize this into something like twenty million liters of liquid CO_2. That's about ten Olympic sized swimming pools full."

"My goodness! And that's in one day?" Annaliese jotted down a few notes on her Palm Screen.

"Yes, every day of the year, vacations included."

"And it's all, well...perfectly safe?'

"Oh, yes, indeed. We've been open for fifteen years now and we've never had an accident."

"That's an extraordinary achievement."

Timothy preened as if it was all his responsibility.

"This must be a very successful business, too," Annaliese went on.

"I'm afraid I cannot comment on that, but we at Oregon Coal and Power, working in conjunction with Oregon Energy, strive to deliver clean electricity to the consumer at the very best price."

"And we appreciate it," Annaliese said with a straight face. "One more question then, and I'll let you go. I read somewhere that carbon dioxide was escaping from the underground storage areas. Can you comment on that?"

Timothy frowned. "I have no knowledge of such a thing happening."

"Could I talk to someone who might know? A scientist perhaps?"

"You'd have to make an appointment."

"Couldn't you ask if someone would see me now? I'm only over here today and I'd hate for my son to put that in his report if it wasn't true."

Timothy hesitated. "I suppose, if you put it like that...wait here. I'll see what I can do." He walked back into the main building and went to the front desk, where he spoke on the phone for a few moments. He waited, and a few minutes later, a woman in a white laboratory coat came down the stairs and walked to meet him. Timothy and the woman walked outside to Annaliese.

"Ms Winton, this is Dr Roux, our chief scientist. She's agreed to meet you and answer your questions."

Dr Roux put out a manicured hand and grasped Annaliese's briefly. "How may I be of service, Ms Winton?"

"It's very good of you to see me. I'll try not to take up too much of your time. I read that carbon dioxide gas was escaping from underground. Is that true?"

Dr Roux glanced at Timothy. "That's true, Ms Winton, but please allow me to put that in perspective. We test atmospheric levels of carbon dioxide regularly at several sites over our storage area. Carbon dioxide levels are measured in parts per million..." She saw Annaliese nod. "Ah, I see you are familiar with this. Well, normal levels are currently about 430 parts per million, but our sites here vary between 420 and 440."

"So you do get higher readings?"

"Yes, but please do not read too much into it. A certain rise and fall is natural and depends on many factors like the time of day, the weather, the season, plant growth at the site..." Dr Roux smiled. "Even if an animal is close by."

"A figure of 1,790 parts per million would be impossible then?"

"In an open-air site? Absolutely. As I said; nothing over 440."

Annaliese nodded and put her Palm Screen away. "Well, thank you very much for putting my mind at rest, Dr Roux. I'll be sure to tell my son not to include that obviously false statement in his school report." She shook hands with Dr Roux and Timothy and backed away a step. "Oh, one other thing..." She watched the scientist's eyes. "Does the term BP4/061730 mean anything to you?"

Dr Roux's eyes narrowed, but she covered it quickly by turning to the young man. "No, it means nothing to me. What about you, Weiss?"

Timothy shook his head. "Sorry, no."

"Never mind. Thank you again for your time." Annaliese turned and walked away, trying not to hurry. *There is something to it. But where do I go from here?*

* * *

Dr Roux and Timothy Weiss watched the woman leave the grounds of the sequestration plant.

"She knows," Dr Roux said quietly. "Who is she really? A reporter? You said she was a mother getting data for her son's school project."

"That's what she told me. You want me to call security?"

"And have them do what? She's leaving the grounds. No, get her license plate number and we'll have her investigated."

Timothy hurried away to the gatehouse and returned a few minutes later with the necessary information. He handed a piece of paper to the scientist and regarded her quizzically. "You said she knows. Knows what? I need to be aware of things if I'm to do my job properly."

"Nothing you need to be concerned about."

"What is this BP4 thing she asked about?"

"Nothing. Forget it." Dr Roux turned and walked back into the building, leaving a puzzled and rather annoyed Public Relations man behind her.

* * *

Annaliese drove away from the Plant triumphant at having discovered something, but annoyed at not knowing precisely what it was she had discovered. The scientist was hiding something, she knew, possibly that CO_2 was escaping, but unless she could find out where the BP4 site was and the CO_2 levels, she had nothing to write about. It was all very frustrating.

The road into town led past the entrance to a cattle ranch--Rushing River Ranch--and Annaliese remembered the email on her computer from Margaret Stone. On an impulse she turned and drove up the long gravel and dirt drive toward the house. *I don't know why...a couple of small earthquakes aren't news.*

The woman of the house came out onto the front veranda as Annaliese parked her car in the shade of a large poplar tree and got out. She introduced herself and the woman at once became effusive, ushering her visitor inside and offering refreshment.

"Have you had lunch?" Margaret asked. "I can fix you a salad if you like. Oh, it's such an honor to have you call. I didn't expect anything at all really, maybe just a brief email, but for you to make such a long trip out to see me...well, that's just wonderful. Will you have coffee? Or perhaps you prefer tea?"

"Er, coffee thanks, with milk and one sugar." Annaliese looked around the living room of the old farmhouse while her hostess busied herself with the coffee pot. "You said you had felt earthquakes recently. Were they bad ones?"

"Oh, no, just crockery rattlers, but the one last month woke us and I think there was one in May also, but I can't remember the date. It was about the time we found that dead hiker."

"Dead hiker? What happened?"

"Nobody knows. We think he passed through on the 20th but my husband found him dead by the Beaver Pond on the 28th. It was rather dreadful; he'd been eaten by coyotes and possibly a bear."

"What was the cause of death?"

"We never heard." Margaret shivered. "Let's talk about something more pleasant. Tell me about your work on the paper. Do you get to meet lots of famous people? And your recipes...which one is your favorite? I try them all, but I let my subscription to the Salem Chronicle lapse, so I have to make do with what's in the Gazette."

Annaliese politely engaged her hostess in conversation, wondering how to turn the subject back to earthquakes and carbon dioxide. She was saved the trouble by the sudden arrival of Margaret's husband. The back door slammed and an angry voice erupted from the kitchen.

"Where the hell is the phone? I need to call the Sheriff. Maggie!"

"Oh, dear, he does sound upset. It's in here, Marc. We have a visitor."

Muffled expletives issued from the kitchen and a moment later a man walked into the room and stared at the two women. Abruptly, the flushed anger in the man's face vanished and he smiled.

"Hello. Who are you?"

Annaliese stood and extended her hand. "Annaliese Winton, Salem Chronicle."

"Marc Stone. Chronicle, eh? You got here damn fast. I've only just found them myself."

"Found what?" Annaliese enquired.

"The dead cattle...you didn't come about them, then?"

"No. I was passing through and thought I'd call in on Margaret. We've never met but she was good enough to help me with a mistake in a recipe a while ago."

Margaret smiled in pleasure. "Oh, I just commented really...what dead cattle are those, Marc? Have there been more?"

Marc nodded. "Another five, up near the Beaver Pond. If you'll excuse me, Ms Winton, I have to get hold of the Sheriff...the vet, too, I suppose." He picked up an old-fashioned cell phone from the sideboard in the living room and left. Annaliese could soon hear him talking in the kitchen.

"There have been cattle deaths here as well as the hiker?" she asked Margaret.

"A couple, but they're not related, I'm sure."

"What was the cause of death?"

"I'm not sure. You'd have to ask Marc."

Marc came back in to the living room. "I've got to go back out to the Pond. I'm meeting the Sheriff and the vet there in half an hour."

"Do you mind if I come with you?" Annaliese asked.

Marc grimaced. "I don't want this splashed all over the front page. I can do without the crazies turning up on our doorstep."

"No article without your permission," Annaliese promised. "I'm just interested."

Marc considered her words and then nodded. "Okay, come along then."

Chapter 18

August 15, 2030

A ndrew Winton had thought long and hard about his response to the leaked documents. He knew some response was necessary, and soon, before his erstwhile friend carried out his threat and notified the authorities.

Why would he do that? Is he so tired of life he'd rather spend the rest of his in jail? And the others? And me? Damned if I'm going to jail.

He examined the documents again, though he knew the contents intimately. Despite viewing them so often, he was shocked afresh when he read the financial statement. *Nobody should know about that. Not even him. If this gets out we're all ruined. The carbon dioxide levels, on the other hand...* Andrew shrugged. *They are nothing to be concerned about. Not really.* He closed the file and swiveled his chair, leaning back in its padded comfort as he looked out over city and forested mountains.

He closed his eyes and gathered his strength and determination, and then he turned and opened the intercom. "I'm not to be disturbed, Janice."

"The Mayor called, Mr Winton. I said you were in a meeting."

"Good. If he calls again, tell him I'll call him at home this evening. Now, open up a line for me."

"Line one, Mr Winton."

The numbers were committed to memory, though he had never had call to use them before. He punched them in and waited while the view screen flickered and displayed a holding pattern. He heard the series of soft clicks that told him the call had gone through and the pattern dissolved into a face.

The man had once been tall and good looking, but age and worry had evidently bowed his frame and robbed him of his hair and skin elasticity.

Winton nodded and waited for the other man to speak.

"You look well, Andrew," said the old man wearily.

"Can't say the same of you. What's this shit you're spreading, Max?"

Max rubbed his chin. "You know very well. It's getting worse, Andrew, and unless we do something..."

"Not on an open line," Andrew warned. "Be fucking careful what you say."

"It's not going to matter soon. But things will go better for us if we try and contain it."

"I'm not going to discuss this here." He thought for a moment. "You know the South Slough Pond in Baskett Slough Wildlife Refuge, west of Salem?"

"No, but I dare say I can find it. Why?"

"Coville Road on the north side of the pond. There's a picnic area there. You can't miss it. Be there at two o'clock on Saturday."

"So soon? You do realize I'm in LA?"

"You are the one that put the time limit on us all by threatening to go public at the end of the month. At least hear me out. Saturday the 17th, 2pm."

Max nodded and reached out to cut the connection. "I'll be there."

Chapter 19

August 15, 2030

Matt Morrison was only a mid-level scientist in the Portland office of the USGS, and while he was allowed considerable autonomy when it came to his everyday work, he could not just get up and follow his interests. First thing on Monday morning, he stopped in to see his supervisor and asked permission to go into the field.

Dr Eugene Gadzicki considered the request and Matt's reasons carefully. He knew Matt was a first-rate researcher on official USGS projects but he was inclined to follow tenuous leads when he got an idea in his head. His first concern was the completion of current projects.

"How are you going with the mapping of the Columbia Point Chemicals leak? I have to have those results by the end of the month."

"You'll have it, boss. I'm just tidying up a few loose ends."

"Has it contaminated the aquifer?"

"Short answer--no. It's been contained. However, I'm taking another set of samples just to be sure."

"You know this carbon dioxide leakage idea is a long shot, don't you?"

Matt shrugged. "It's possible. I'd like to make a quick trip out there, do a few Draeger tests. Something caused those tremors."

"Were you planning on going alone?"

"I thought I might take Mick Cohen with me. A bit of field experience would do him good."

Dr Gadzicki nodded. "Do the aquifer tests first and write up an interim report. When you've done that, you can take two days, no more."

Matt grinned. "Thanks, boss."

He took the aquifer samples that afternoon and put them in the lab refrigerator. Then he pulled together the rough draft of the report and went through it, leaving the conclusions open until he had the results from the latest set of samples. *I'll be surprised if there are any surprises, though.* The next morning he tested the water and soil samples and found that the contaminant levels matched or were lower than previous samples. *As I thought.* Matt sat down at his desk to write the report, which he finished late on Wednesday. He emailed it through to Dr Gadzicki.

"Mick, are you with me tomorrow?"

Mick stretched and yawned. "Doing what?"

"A bit of field work. I'm heading out to Rushing River to check on a few things. How would you like a couple of days away from the office?"

"I suppose you just want me there to carry all your rock samples?"

"Nope, not this time. Just the hand pump and a few packs of Draeger tubes."

"Do we get to camp out in the wilderness?"

"I was thinking of a nice comfortable motel."

"Excellent. A day of tramping about the hills followed by a hot shower and a couple of beers. That's my idea of field work. You have yourself a Sherpa, Matt."

Matt picked Mick up from his apartment in downtown Portland at six the next morning and bought him a cup of pumpkin spice coffee at Starbucks before they set out along the Columbia River Highway. He sipped on his own vanilla and cinnamon coffee and listened to Mick enthuse about a 3D-CD he'd bought the previous week featuring an old-time classic death metal band called the Rancid Stardogs. Matt listened politely but shook his head when Mick asked him if he'd heard the band in question.

"Not my thing," he said. "I'm more into classical and old pop."

Mick laughed. "Yeah, I'd forgotten you were old enough to remember Mozart and the Beatles."

"Have some respect for your elders and betters, please."

"I'll buy you a beer tonight instead."

They reached Rushing River mid-morning and found a motel near the campground. Matt used his USGS card to register while Mick unloaded their luggage. The room itself was dim and paint was peeling in the bathroom, but at least it was clean. They changed into their boots and hiking gear and Matt made sure the equipment was in working order before they set out.

"Where are we going first?"

Matt set up his laptop and pulled up a map of the area. He scrolled through it until he found the Rushing River Township. "This is the Rushing River Ranch, pretty much directly above the tremor epicenters. If there really is a carbon dioxide leakage, I'd expect levels to be higher there."

Mick picked up one of the Draeger tubes. "I thought these were only for testing the CO_2 levels inside buildings and enclosed areas."

"Yeah, that's what they're designed for, but you can still get an idea of levels outside. We're not going to get anything we could testify to in a court of law, but if the levels point to something suspicious, we can do other tests."

"Well, let's saddle up and head on out to the ranch."

"First things first," Matt said. "We need to get some baseline readings first." He took one of the Draeger tubes and clipped it into the hand pump after breaking the ends off the glass tube. He worked the action with one hand while he counted out the number of strokes. "Okay, now we wait sixty seconds...and...we have...a reading of...oh, close to 700 parts per million."

"Is that high? Should we open the doors?"

"That's pretty normal for indoors. Now we can do the same outside." They stepped out into the motel forecourt and repeated the procedure. "There's a bit of a breeze, so the air is mixing well. This should give us a reasonable outdoor baseline." Matt read off the line of blue crystals in the glass tube. "450. That's a trifle high, but that may be because we're in town, or it may be because the scale on these tubes is not terribly accurate."

"If it's not accurate, what's the point?"

"We're not here to scientifically prove or disprove the presence of excess CO_2; just to get an idea of the levels to see whether a more accurate measurement is justified."

"Okay, you're the boss. Lead on."

Matt and Mick walked up to the campground and explained that they wanted to take a few measurements. The campground owner was reluctant, worrying that campers might be upset or scared by officials taking readings with arcane equipment.

"We'll be discreet," Matt reassured him.

They crossed an open area of grass and a few trees, and scrambled down into the boulder strewn riverbed. Then they walked upriver for half a mile or so, past the point where campers were swimming or canoeing. Matt performed the test again, slipping the used glass tube back into his bag when he finished.

"Same again, 450--possibly a little less--and the air is still."

"Why are we measuring it down here instead of on the field above?"

"Come, come, you know the answer to that. You tell me."

Mick thought. "Because of the water?"

Matt grinned. "Think about the properties of CO_2 gas."

"Properties? Oh, you mean its density. The gas is denser than air, so it's going to collect in hollows or riverbeds."

Matt nodded. "There's still going to be a lot of mixing, but this can act as a good basal measurement."

"So where to next? The ranch?"

Matt consulted his map. "I think we should approach from downwind. The prevailing winds this time of year are generally from the north or northwest, so we'll start here and move in toward the ranch proper."

"Shouldn't we get permission to go on the ranch?"

"Yeah, you're probably right. Okay, we'll go up to the ranch house and tell them what they're doing."

They drove to the Rushing River Ranch but found nobody home. Matt even tried the back door but it was locked. They looked around at the neat house, its garden and barn, wondering where everyone was. Mick started calling out, wandering over to the open barn and looking in, while Matt leaned on his car's horn, advertising their presence loudly. Nobody came.

"What now?"

Matt consulted his laptop map again and clicked the mouse. A red circle appeared on the screen. "This is the one-kilometer radius circle I drew that is directly above those three epicenters. Here's the ranch house at the southern perimeter. Take a reading, Mick and let's see what we've got."

Mick took out the pump and opened a Draeger tube, waiting for the blue coloration to appear. "450 again, maybe a bit less."

Matt sucked his forefinger and held it up. "Wind's from the north-northwest, coming straight across the circle. Damn, I was sort of hoping we might find something."

"There's a lot of air to dilute anything. We should find some dips and hollows. Anything on the map?"

"There's this stream that cuts up from Rushing River through the northern part of the circle." Matt peered at the map, angling it to the light. "It says Beaver Pond Creek. That might be worth investigating."

Mick looked at the map over Matt's shoulder. "How are we going to get there? There's no road close by."

"We could cut across the fields."

"What happened to asking the rancher?"

"They could have gone into town or anywhere. I say we make a quick trip cross-country and wrap this whole exercise up."

"Ranchers have guns," Mick said dubiously.

"Don't worry. I'll leave a note on my windscreen and on the house door explaining our actions." Matt scribbled two quick notes, added a USGS card to each, and fixed them in place. "Come on, sooner gone, sooner back."

There was no gate into the fields to the north, so Mick and Matt hopped over the fence, being careful not to put any strain on the wires and being cautious about the barbed wire topper. They set off across lush pasture, concentrating on crossing the open space as quickly as possible. A gate led into the next pasture, and they took care that it closed properly behind them. Half way across, Matt realized they were being followed and turned to confront a small herd of curious cattle.

"Er, Mick, do you know anything about cows?"

"Not much, why? Oh." He saw them and stepped closer to his colleague. "What do we do? Are they going to charge?"

"No idea, but they haven't so far. I think we just back away slowly."

Mick eyed the far fence line and estimated its distance. "I don't like our chances if we have to run for it."

"So we walk slowly." They backed away and for a dozen paces it looked as if they could just walk away. Then the cattle started forward and some of them started a flanking movement. "Shit. Pick up the pace a bit." Matt started to walk faster, but the cattle broke into a run and encircled them, coming to a stop and regarding the two men with large liquid eyes. Matt and Mick stopped.

"Damn, I feel like Custer but I don't see any little horns, only big ones," Mick muttered.

"Funny man. We can't stay here and wait for help, so I think we should continue forward."

"There are some bloody big cows in the way."

Matt pointed. "I don't think they're cows."

"Oh that makes me feel a lot better."

"Come on." Matt started forward and half way to the cattle in front of them, the beasts spooked and stampeded away, before circling back and standing facing them again. "And again." Twice more and the cattle trotted around, away from in front of them and then edged closer as first Mick, and then Matt climbed the fence into an empty field. The men exhaled loudly in relief and looked at the cattle that were now lining the fence.

"We don't have to go back the same way, do we?" Mick asked.

"We'll find another way."

Another half hour brought them to the edge of a shallow valley with a slow stream winding its way down the middle. Mick took another Draeger reading near the water's edge.

"I'd say that's a fraction over 450. What do you think?"

Matt examined the tube carefully. "Perhaps a bit over."

They headed upstream, walking along the meandering rush-lined stream in the summer sun. Birds called, and yellow butterflies flew up from stands of ragweed as they approached.

"Idyllic, isn't it?" Mick said. "Not at all the place I'd expect to find anything wrong."

"Well, we haven't found anything, have we?" Matt prepared another tube and took another reading. "450...or a fraction under."

"Never mind, it's a nice day for a stroll. How much farther do you want to go?"

"The map shows a beaver pond perhaps half a mile upstream--just inside the circle--and some steep-sided gullies a mile beyond that. I'd like to test them. Coincidentally, there's a walking track near there that should circumvent your cows on the way back."

They reached the Beaver Pond with its stand of aspens and birch and continued on past it after taking more Draeger readings. The land grew steeper and the stream leapt and burbled down a rocky course as the valley sides hemmed them in. A faint track led them on until the valley split into three. The stream continued onward but two steep-sided gullies led off on either side. The near-sided one was steeper and less accessible, but Mick clambered into it for about fifty yards before taking a reading.

"Just the same," he called back.

"Okay, we'll try the other gully and then call it a day."

They leapt the narrow stream and trudged into the other gully. The sides were less steep and there were a few stunted trees and shrubs at the entrance. Further in, the ground fell away into a small amphitheater as if the soil had slumped. Grass grew greenly in the depression and Matt clambered down to the bottom and arrived breathing hard.

"Damn, I'm not as fit as I thought I was," he called back up to Mick. "Come on down."

"Why? I'm only going to have to climb back out again. Take a reading and let's head back to the motel for a beer."

Matt nodded and fitted a tube into the hand pump. He stared at the tube and frowned. "This tube must have been cracked or something. It's showing a reading of 900. Bring me down another tube, will you?"

Mick started down the slope and Matt climbed up a few paces to meet him. He took the tube and worked the pump as before. "That's more like it," he said. "The other tube must have been faulty. This one reads high, but not overly so-- only 500."

Mick looked around and then at where his colleague was standing. He handed him another tube. "Try the bottom again."

Matt raised an eyebrow but jumped down to the bottom and redid the test. "Shit--900 again and I know that was an intact tube. Looks like we've got ourselves a CO_2 pool. Question is--did it leak upward from the strata below or spill into here from some other source?"

"We can discuss this once we're out of danger." Mick started back up the slope.

"Relax. 900 parts per million is nowhere near the toxic level. You've experienced higher levels in a lecture theatre. Still, you have to wonder. I guess if animals had been grazing down here, CO_2 could collect. You wouldn't get much mixing of the air. Or micro-organisms could be producing it. We need to do a soil test."

"I didn't bring any baggies with me, did you?"

"No, we'll have to come back."

"Okay, so where's this trail you said we could return on?"

Matt climbed back up to the screen of trees. He pointed up the side of the gully. "Up there."

They climbed to the top of the gully and over a fence and found themselves on a well-used walking trail. The township lay to the south and west so they headed in that direction, wending their way through the edge of a mixed conifer and broadleaf forest. At intervals, they caught glimpses of rolling farmland with scattered herds of cattle. They passed the beaver pond and paralleled the stream beyond the point where they had joined it.

"You see? We're going right past your cows," Matt said with a grin.

"Uh-huh. What're they doing?" Mick pointed.

Below, near the Beaver Pond Stream, two vehicles were drawn up near the bodies of five cattle and a woman and two men were standing or squatting by the beasts.

Matt stared but nothing reasonable came to mind. He acknowledged freely he had a profound ignorance of what occurred on farms. "None of our business."

A little farther on, the trail split in two, one heading up into forest and the other angling down to a gravel road. Matt recognized it as being near to the ranch entrance, so led Mick down to it. Another twenty minutes found them back at their car in the still-deserted yard of the ranch.

"I'll leave the note for the rancher," Matt said. "We could come out and get a soil sample tomorrow."

"You think micro-organisms were responsible?"

"No, I don't--well, not really, but the levels were ambiguous. If there is only a slow leak from the strata it's no big deal anyway. Anything major would have surely shown up by now."

"Is it worth doing the soil test then?"

"Probably not," Matt considered their options and shrugged. "To hell with it. I vote we stay overnight and head home tomorrow."

"Okay, back to the motel then? I noticed a tavern and a couple of fast-food joints in town."

Chapter 20

August 16, 2030

R obert Peale stood as the door to his office opened and Dr Angelina Roux entered. He waved her to an armchair and came round his desk to sit on the edge of it.

"Good morning, Angelina, always a pleasure to talk to you, but...just what is the problem? My secretary said something about a security matter. Surely Major Watkins as Head of Security would be a more appropriate person to see."

"It's not that sort of security, Robert."

"Oh, sounds intriguing."

"A reporter came round yesterday. She talked to Timothy Weiss in PR."

"He's a good man. What's the problem?"

"He called me because she had a question he didn't want to answer. She asked about gas escaping from storage."

"We've never made any secret of the fact that gas will escape. What do we tell people? One percent in a thousand years?"

"Something like that, but that is not what worries me. She knew."

"Knew what?"

"The carbon dioxide readings at our test sites."

Robert looked at his chief scientist, waiting for her to add a rider to her statement, or tell him she was playing some obscure joke. When she said nothing, he laughed nervously.

"That's impossible. It must have been a lucky guess."

Angelina shook her head. "She knew the Beaver Pond Number 4 site was exactly 1,790 parts per million. That's not a lucky guess."

"How could she possibly know that?"

"I would've thought the answer was obvious. We have a mole. Someone is feeding our secrets to the press." Robert eased off the edge of his desk and went back to his chair, sinking into it. "I'd better call Watkins in after all," Angelina went on. "You'll need Security on this."

"No."

"But he'll know how to silence this reporter. I already know who she is. She's Annaliese Winton of the Salem Chronicle. We took her license down and traced it."

"I'm not going to tell Watkins any more than he needs to know."

"If you're sure."

"Annaliese Winton, you said? I wonder if she's any relation to..." Robert frowned and fell silent.

Angelina looked puzzled. "Any relation to whom?"

Robert shook his head. "Never mind, a random thought."

"Alright, but what do we do?"

"I'll attend to it."

"What about me?"

Robert stood, terminating the meeting. "You have a well-appointed laboratory and free rein to conduct any research you want," he reminded the scientist. "I suggest you busy yourself there."

Robert waited until his scientist had left and then told his secretary he was not to be disturbed. He thought about the implications of a reporter investigating the carbon dioxide leaks and what it might mean for the continued existence of the sequestration plant. "Fuck this," he muttered. He punched in numbers on his view phone. "Andrew Winton, please."

The screen flickered and opened to show Winton at his desk. "What do you want, Peale? I'm busy."

"What're you playing at?"

Andrew stared at the image on his view screen. "Would you like to explain what you mean?"

"Who is Annaliese Winton?"

"My daughter-in-law. Why?"

"Did you send her to snoop around Rushing River?"

"Why would I do that?"

"Will you please stop answering my questions with another one? Your daughter-in-law was here yesterday asking questions about carbon dioxide leakage and she seemed to know specifics. Did you send her, and if so, why?"

"What did you tell her?"

"I didn't tell her anything. I didn't see her. A PR man and my chief scientist saw her, but how did she know what questions to ask? Where did she get her information? From you?"

"Not from me."

"Well, what are we going to do about it?" Robert asked. "If she knows that much, she may know more. What if she prints her story? Hell, we could lose billions..."

"This is not a secure line," Andrew pointed out. "There's no need to say anything. I am as aware of the consequences as you."

"Okay, so what do we do?"

"You do nothing. I'll deal with this."

* * *

Andrew broke the connection and opened another one to the Salem Chronicle offices. "Simon, is my daughter-in-law at her desk today?"

"Yes sir," the office editor said. "You want me to put you through?"

"No. Tell her I want to see her at noon."

Andrew got up and poured himself a cup of coffee from the thermos on the sideboard. He stood looking out of his window at the cityscape and sipped at the strong brew while he considered what was to be done. Not for the first time, he wished he did not have a daughter-in-law.

Do I come down hard on her or try to convince her? Hell, I'd get rid of her if it wasn't for Adrian but she's a good mother for all her faults. Why couldn't my fuckwit son stay faithful to her? Then she wouldn't be here in Salem and I'd not have this added problem...

Andrew returned to his desk and got to work on the many other items of business that crossed his desk every day. He got so engrossed in it he was taken by surprise when the intercom buzzed softly and his secretary said, "Ms Winton is here to see you, sir."

Andrew glanced at the wall clock and saw that it was five minutes of twelve. "Send her in."

Apprehension and excitement warred for control of Annaliese's face as she entered the room. She sat where Andrew indicated and said nothing, waiting for him to speak.

"I read your article on the Portland Water Authority," Andrew said. "I made a few editorial changes but it'll go out pretty much as you wrote it."

"Th...thank you."

"That article tells me you have considerable talent for investigative reporting, which makes it strange that you'd so blatantly jeopardize your future."

"What do you mean?"

"I told you to leave the papers to me. You disregarded my...advice, and started poking your nose into the Rushing River Sequestration Facility."

"So, it does have something to do with it. I hit a raw nerve and they're asking you to back off." Annaliese stood up and started walking toward Andrew, her face lit up with excitement. "I knew it. They do have something to hide..."

"Sit down." When Annaliese did not respond, he repeated himself and watched as his daughter-in-law stopped, flustered, and sat again. "That's better. Now, before you go off half-cocked, perhaps I'd better explain something."

Andrew waited until Annaliese was fully attentive before modulating his voice into warm and confidential tones. "The Rushing River Sequestration Facility is of immense importance to Oregon, to the United States and, indeed, to the World. It was the first large-scale sequestration site and has been running trouble-free for the last fifteen years. During this time, it has been closely monitored by the Department of Energy, the United States Geological Survey, Health and Safety, and half a dozen other regulatory bodies. In the last twelve months, the information gained by this Plant has been used to design and start production on fifty similar plants within the continental USA. Those fifty plants will lead to five hundred others and within ten years, over ninety percent of our electricity will be produced by clean coal-burning power stations and well over half the carbon dioxide produced by them will be sequestered. When other nations see our success, they'll copy us. This means that for the first time, mankind will be able to get a grip on climate change and control it."

He regarded Annaliese with what he hoped was a paternal expression. "This is a critical time, Annaliese. If the Senate gets even a hint of trouble, they may just shut the whole thing down. As you know, the Democrats control the Senate and are able to block legislation by filibustering. Now the President can, with difficulty, circumvent the Senate but it would bring far too much attention to bear on the whole thing and slow the process down. Instead of ten years we could be looking at fifteen or twenty...or never. Do you want that, Annaliese? Do you want to jeopardize the best chance we have of controlling climate change?"

"No. No, of course not, but...well, if there really is a leak, don't we have a duty to say something?"

"All facilities leak." Impatience crept into Andrew's voice. "But not all leaks are of equal importance. I've talked to Robert Peale out at Rushing River Sequestration and I can tell you quite categorically that there is nothing to be concerned about. Leakage is well within the acceptable limits set out by DOE."

Annaliese thought for a moment. "If the leaks are acceptable, why did they deny all knowledge of them? Surely it would be better to freely admit them."

"In the early days of sequestration, even a small leak was regarded with some dismay, but as time has gone on, we have come to recognize leaks are commonplace and mean very little. Of course, we monitor them continuously, but more as a means of obtaining data than as a sign of danger. I imagine that the people you spoke to were under orders to be circumspect, rather than secretive."

"You said 'we', Mr Winton. Are you part of this?"

Andrew smiled. "I do have that honor. Twenty years ago, when this site was first mooted, the authorities recognized the need to have men and women in positions of power within the community, so that well-meaning busybodies..." Annaliese blushed, "...would not derail the enterprise before it bore fruit."

"I didn't realize."

"There was no reason why you should."

"And now it's...bearing fruit?"

"Yes. Within six months, the contracts will be signed and the President will announce to the world that climate change is finally under control. You know, Annaliese, when I was a young man I faced the prospect that my children and grandchildren would inherit a world where the struggle to survive would be their daily lot. I thought food and oil shortages, carbon dioxide and sea level rises, pollution and extinctions were a certainty. Then a group of far-sighted men showed me a way out and I grasped it. We are not there yet but we have made the first steps toward a healed planet and a sustainable future. Help me, Annaliese--help us achieve our goal."

"My god, I had no idea. How can I help?"

"By saying nothing. Just for six months. When the President makes his announcement, you can write all the articles you want." Andrew smiled again. "In fact, I can probably help you achieve a real scoop. You could be the first one to publish the inside story."

Annaliese's eyes sparkled. "You'd do that for me?"

"You're family, Annaliese...and a damn good reporter besides. I'm glad you're with us rather than against us. You are with us, aren't you?"

"How could I say no?"

"Good girl. Now, go back to the Chronicle and do your job. I'll make sure you have a heads-up when this is all about to be announced and you can get your scoop ready."

Annaliese stood and, impulsively, embraced her father-in-law. "Thank you, sir...Andrew. I won't let you down."

Andrew sat and stared at the closed door of his office after Annaliese left. He tried to come to a decision on whether he had convinced his daughter-in-law to say nothing. *I hope so, but how much of that hope is because the alternative is more horrifying. Do I want to go there? She's the mother of my only grandchild, after all. What's her life worth?* The Rushing River Project had brought him millions, but if the contracts were signed, billions would flow down to him and a handful of others. *Can I afford a conscience with so much at stake?*

Chapter 21

August 16, 2030

Friday morning was calm and overcast in Rushing River, but despite his family's desire to stay around the campsite, joining in various craft activities on offer, Randy Maher insisted they all go out hiking again.

"We're tired, Randy, and Alexa has the sniffles," Karen ventured. "Why don't we go another time?"

"This'll be our last opportunity," Randy replied, unsmiling. "We have horse riding into the Cascades tomorrow, canoeing on Sunday and we have to leave on Monday. Just when did you imagine this other time would be?"

"But Alexa..."

"Will be fine. She's a big girl and she should do this. You can always carry her."

The disagreement ended the way they always did, with Randy getting his way. He supervised everyone putting on their walking shoes, packing some apples and water, and smearing exposed parts of their bodies with bug repellent.

"Always be prepared. We'll only be on an easy walking trail but we should be ready for any eventuality."

"Which trail are we taking?" Cory asked.

"The one above the beaver pond. Bring your camera; maybe you'll see one."

They set off at an easy pace, matching their speed to that of Alexa toddling along. After a while, Randy grew impatient with the pace and forged ahead a hundred yards or so at a time and waited for his family to catch up. He glared at Alexa and then at his wife. She picked up her small daughter and increased her pace.

The trail led along Rushing River for a mile before a suspension bridge crossed the Beaver Pond Creek. From here, the trail climbed steeply into conifer and broadleaf forest before flattening out and following the contours of the hillside. The light was dim under the canopy, the air humid, and the smells of humus and moss strong. It was quiet too, away from the noise of the river and they could hear only birdsong and the distant hammering of a woodpecker.

"Is that a hairy or a pileated woodpecker?" Cory asked.

Randy stopped dead in the trail and faced his son. "What did you say? Are you trying to make me look bad by using scientific words?"

"I'm sure he didn't mean anything by it," Karen said quickly.

"Can it, Karen," Randy said. "Well, boy, are you being smart with me?"

"N...no, sir. I...I just heard a boy at the camp say they was all pileated woodpeckers hereabouts an'...an' I told him he was talking crap..."

"Watch your language, boy." Randy cuffed the side of his son's head, but lightly. "And you were right, it is crap. That's a...what did you call it? A hairy woodpecker?"

"Yes, sir, that's what I thought. I figured you'd know, sir."

"Damn right."

The trail worked its way to the edge of the forest and soon they could make out farmland in the gaps between the trees. A fence ran along the side of the trail, the hillside dropping away to a small stream that meandered through pasture and scattered shrubs. At one point they saw several cattle lying on the ground and stopped to stare at them. Cory took a few pictures on his digital camera.

"Are they sleeping, Mommy?" Alexa asked.

"Yes, dear, I expect they're tired."

Randy laughed. "They're not sleeping. Look at the damn things. Heads outstretched and tongues lolling out. They're dead."

Cory took a few more pictures. "What killed them, Dad...do you think?"

Randy shrugged. "How the fuck should I know?" Karen winced but said nothing. "Probably disease. These damn ranchers just leave the bodies lying around for anyone to stumble across. I've a good mind to complain when we get back."

They walked on, but the sight of the dead cattle had put Randy in a bad mood. He grumbled and kicked stones off the path, breaking branches off bushes and stripping the leaves from them.

"Bastard ranchers," he muttered. "So fuckin' rich they couldn't care less if they lose cows from disease, when just one of them could feed a family for months."

"Hey, Dad, look. Another body."

The path had angled away from the stream and bordered a steep-sided gully. Directly below was a hollow that looked as if the pasture had just sunk away, subsiding another twenty feet or so, the verdant grass ripping apart to reveal patches of fresh soil. At the bottom of the hollow lay a coyote, on its side, not moving.

"Shit, it's a fuckin' wolf."

"I think it's a coyote, dad," Cory said.

"Watch your fuckin' mouth, boy," Randy muttered.

"I don't like it," Karen said. "There are too many dead things. We should go back."

"That'd make a damn fine trophy pelt." Randy licked his lips. "None of my buddies have a wolf."

"I think you have to have a permit, Dad," Cory said.

"Who the fuck's going to know except my buddies...and they won't say anything if they know what's good for them. Go down and get it, Cory."

"I don't wanna, Dad."

"I don't care what you want. I'm giving you an order, buddy." Randy bunched his fists and glowered at his teenage son.

Cory shot a glance at his mother, but she looked away. He gingerly climbed the fence and swung his leg over, and then stood at the top of the slope.

"Go on."

The boy started down into the gully and half slid down the loose sides until he stood on the gully floor, looking down into the sunken hollow. "How do I get back up again?"

"You walk along the gully a-ways. The sides are lower. Now get on with it."

Cory advanced to the lip of the hollow and lowered himself over the edge. He stopped and looked up at his father, panting. "I don't feel well, Dad."

"Don't be a girl. Just do it."

Cory started down again, but a few feet lower he sat down suddenly and rested his head in his hands. After a minute he collapsed sideways.

"Cory, what the hell are you playing at?" When his son did not reply, Randy swore violently and clambered over the fence. "Don't make me come down there."

Swearing, Randy slid down into the gully and strode across to the hollow. He stared down at his motionless son. "If you're playing tricks, I'll thrash the hide off you, so help me."

Randy jumped down and in a series of leaping steps, reached Cory. He bent over to shake the boy's shoulder and toppled forward with a cry of surprise, somersaulting to the bottom of the depression. He got to his feet and looked around, breathing hard and plucking at the collar of his shirt. "What the fuck..." Abruptly, he fell and writhed around weakly for a few moments. He ended up lying half across the body of the coyote, his face congested and staring.

* * *

Karen leaned over the fence and stared down at her husband and son. "Randy? Cory? What's wrong?" Alexa heard the panic edging her mother's voice and started crying. Karen bounced her daughter in her arms and uttered soothing noises before leaning over the fence again. "Randy. Get up. What's wrong?"

Karen looked around but there was no-one in sight. She thought about running for help but knew that it might take an hour or more to find someone. She came to a decision and lowered her daughter to the ground. The little girl immediately started to wail and held out her arms to be picked up.

"No, Alexa. Stay here, that's a good girl. Mommy will only be a few minutes." She pulled a chocolate bar from her pocket and peeled back the wrapping. The little girl subsided, pushing the bar into her mouth. "Good girl."

Karen climbed over the fence and, having learned from watching the others, slid quickly to the bottom of the gully. She ran to the hollow and looked down. Her son lay only a few paces away and her husband about twenty feet lower. She took a deep breath and stepped down into the depression. Her vision blurred slightly and she felt mildly nauseous. She panted and considered sitting down for a few moments, but the sight of her unconscious son drove her on.

"I'm here, Cory darling. Mommy will take care..." Everything went grey and Karen staggered, going down on one knee before pitching forward to slide head first down the slope. Her foot caught on her son's body and she came to a stop not far above her husband. She got to her feet unsteadily, scared now and panting hard. She climbed the steep slope and got as far as her son before passing out, lying head down beside him.

* * *

Above, on the trail beyond the fence, Alexa finished her chocolate bar and wiped her fingers on her shorts. She looked around for her mommy and uttered an experimental cry. Nobody came running to pick her up, so she started crying in earnest. Half an hour later she lapsed into hiccoughing sobs, her face puffy and running with mucus. She started down the track toward the camp, not because she knew the way, but because it was downhill.

In the gully below, a blowfly tacked to and fro, following the scent of cooling meat. It winged down into the hollow and landed on Cory's leg where it sat and rubbed its legs together. A few moments later it fell over, onto the grass, and buzzed futilely until it fell silent.

Chapter 22

August 17, 2030

Alittle after one pm on Saturday, Andrew Winton climbed into his twenty-year-old but immaculately maintained Mercedes-Benz W212 and eased it out into the traffic flow. The trip out to the South Slough Pond in the Baskett Slough Wildlife Refuge was leisurely. He took Highway 22 west out of Salem toward Willamina. Coville Road came up on the right, but he passed first it, and then a second branch of Coville before continuing along the Highway another three miles to the Cross Creek Golf Course. He pulled over under the shade of some trees and turned the engine off while he waited. It was not yet half-past the hour and Andrew did not believe in being early for any appointment.

He listened to a sound cube of Vivaldi's Four Seasons while he waited, forcing his mind toward calm. Andrew had made no decision yet about the outcome of this meeting, but he knew something would have to be done. Billions of dollars rested on what happened in the next hour. *But I'll be ready for any eventuality. I won't shirk what must be done.*

The alarm on his watch chimed softly. Andrew started up and turned the Mercedes in a smooth sweep across the highway and accelerated back to Coville Road. He turned into the Wildlife Refuge and dropped his speed to twenty as he approached the picnic grounds. Three cars were parked close to the grass, two family vehicles and a rental. He pulled in beside the rental and got out.

A cool breeze from the coast ruffled his hair as he stepped onto the grass and looked around. A man was walking a dog on the far side of the pond and a young couple sat on the grass a hundred yards away with three small children running riot around them. Close to the water's edge was an old wooden bench. A man sat on it, his back to the car park. Ducks squabbled in the shallows as the man flicked pieces of bread into the water. Andrew walked across.

"Hello, Max."

The man on the bench looked up, but did not rise. He was thin and bald with liver spots sprinkled across his pate. Bags hung beneath his eyes and he exuded a miasma of despondency. "Andrew." He indicated a spot beside him on the bench. "Come and feed the ducks."

Andrew sat and accepted a crust of bread. He put it on the bench beside him and looked at the thin man. "What the hell is this game you're playing, Max?"

"No game." Max crumbled some bread and scattered it at the water's edge, the corners of his mouth lifting momentarily as the ducks fought for the crumbs.

"Then why? What do you hope to gain?"

"Peace of mind, maybe." Max pointed at a large mallard that was driving other ducks away, pecking viciously and beating at his rivals with his wings. "He reminds me of you, Andrew. Me, too, when I was younger...and the others."

"Forget the fucking ducks. What are your intentions?"

"I'm tired of the secrecy, Andrew. I think we should go public with what's happening beneath Rushing River--before somebody gets hurt."

"So you just decide, without consulting anyone, to send inflammatory documents to the press."

"Not to the press, Andrew, to you. The information hasn't gone anywhere else...yet."

"Unfortunately, there's another A. Winton at the Chronicle. Your packages were opened by my daughter-in-law."

Max shrugged, his bony shoulders lifting like some terminally ill vulture. "You controlled the situation, though? That's why you're here?"

"Why should you care whether I controlled it? Your stated intention is to release the details at the end of the month. Has that changed?"

Max scattered the rest of his bread. "Are you going to use that crust?" Andrew passed him the stale bread. "I want you to come with me to the State Governor and tell him what's going on. You have influence in Oregon and you could get something done. That's why I sent the information to you."

"Why the hell would I do that?"

Max smiled and broke the bread up into small pieces. The ducks looked expectantly at him and squabbled for position. "Conscience, Andrew. I want a clear conscience and I hope you do, too."

"My conscience is fine. I've done nothing wrong."

"You've made an obscene amount of money."

"As have you and the others, but making money's not a crime."

"It is if you commit fraud."

Andrew frowned. "Fraud?"

"What else would you call it when you promise to sequester millions of tons of carbon deep underground and fail to live up to that promise? We've taken billions of dollars off the government and now we're all set to multiply that a hundred-fold."

"We promised to sequester, and we have. Do you have any idea of how many millions of tons we've pumped underground?"

"Approximately 200 million tons," Max said. He saw the look of surprise on Andrew's face and smiled. "I like to keep up with these things."

"All right, so how can you call it fraud?"

"We said we'd sequester it, and the understanding was it'd be permanently. That's not the case." Max threw a handful of bread into the water and was rewarded by a flurry of feathers and snapping beaks.

"Nothing is permanent."

"Except death. Yes, I know that, Andrew, but the implication was there that this was more than a temporary solution. Instead, the first major attempt to sequester commercially viable amounts of carbon dioxide has failed. The underground storage area is leaking."

"So, it's leaking? So what? The amounts are trifling."

"I sometimes forget your knowledge of science is not great."

"I know enough to get by," Andrew said huffily. "I can afford experts if I need them."

"Yes, but sadly, you don't use them, or listen to them when you do. There are weaknesses in the metamorphosed limestone layers capping the Hood Anticline. I've told you that before. And now those weaknesses are fast becoming failures."

"You exaggerate. The amounts of gas escaping are scarcely noticeable. The carbon dioxide levels rise locally for a few hours until the atmosphere disperses it."

"It'll get worse."

"How much worse?"

Max shrugged again. "Who knows? Nobody has ever been in this situation before. Once the gas, which you recall is under great pressure, finds a channel to the surface, the only thing holding it back is the strength of the overlying rock. The outlet may enlarge slowly or it may rupture suddenly. I can't imagine the outcome if it did either. There's also the possibility of CO_2 reacting with ground water to form carbonic acid. That would dissolve limestone, basalt and the concrete used to plug old drill shafts."

"So, the carbon dioxide returns to the atmosphere."

"I can't imagine the government will be too happy with us. They've paid us billions to lock it up. Don't you think they might want their money back? Or failing that, to lock us up?" Max threw the last of the bread to the ducks and dusted off his hands.

"Shit." Andrew folded his arms and stretched his legs out in front of him. He frowned, searching for a way out of their dilemma. *I should just kill the old fool, but that may not be enough if he's right.* "How long have we got?"

"I don't know. It could take years or it could go tomorrow. That's why I think we should go to the Governor now and get it fixed." Max looked at his businessman friend sympathetically. "I know this is a lot to grasp, Andrew, but it's got to be done. We both do it willingly and maybe salvage something from the mess, or we're forced to it and lose everything."

"Can it be fixed?" *Or should I just cut my losses and run? I've millions salted away off-shore and there would be countries willing to harbor me for a price.*

"I think so. The problem isn't so very different from capping an oil or gas well. We could drill down and flood the leak with concrete. Plug it right up to the surface."

"Sounds expensive."

"It is, but infinitely cheaper than doing nothing."

The man walking his dog came within earshot as his hound chased the ducks flapping into the pond. He apologized and dragged his protesting dog away. Andrew waited until he was well away, grateful for the chance to think.

"You'll wait until the end of month?"

Max looked at his friend with curiosity. "Why wait? Every day we delay could make our task harder."

"I know, but I need to check a few things first. Look, it's the 17th today. Give me to the...the 23rd and then I'll come to the Governor with you. Will you do that, Max? For old time's sake?"

"You're up to something. What can you possibly hope to do in six days?"

Andrew sighed, a touch theatrically. "We could go to jail over this. Let me make some investments that'll take care of my grandson first and settle my affairs. Just that, I promise."

Max nodded. "Very well, but I'll make the appointment with the Governor for the 23rd. If you are not there, I'll see him alone."

"What do the others think about this?" Andrew asked. "Matternicht and Svenson, Boyle, Hu and Peale. Have you consulted them or is this going to surprise them, too?"

"I've talked to Matternicht--the others matter not." Max laughed, but his laughter sounded like a death rattle. "I always thought he had a hell of a name. Anyway, he was appalled I would even consider such a thing, so..." he shrugged, "...this'll all come as a bit of a blow."

Andrew shook his head, a wry smile on his face. "The thought had crossed my mind to just eliminate you."

"Then it's fortunate there are people around. However, it wouldn't make any difference, Andrew. Unless I countermand an instruction to a certain lawyer, the full set of documents will be sent to the Attorney General's office at the end of the month. If I was dead at the hands of my colleagues before then, you could all go to hell."

"Does Matternicht know about these documents? If you're in danger from anyone, it's from him."

"He knows."

"Even so, he might take you out and try to dismiss the documents as the ravings of a senile old fool."

Max smiled. "I intend to be there to demonstrate my sanity and to present additional data."

"He'll kill you anyway, from spite if not in defense of his wealth."

"After the 23rd, it won't matter. I'll be there to back up my assertions with personal testimony." Max rose to his feet and stretched. "I'm glad you'll be by my side, Andrew. Together we can convince them."

Chapter 23

August 17, 2030

D r George Benson, the Medical Examiner for Wasco County, enjoyed his work. His office was above the small morgue in The Dalles, and lying in the refrigerated lockers were three bodies brought in the evening before from Rushing River at the other end of the county. He liked to examine the scene of the crime wherever possible, but he had been attending another incident when the bodies had been found, so had to rely on the man on the spot, the local sheriff, Jack Warner. The sheriff's report was quite comprehensive though, so George felt no qualms about being absent. He scanned the report once more and drained his cup of coffee before walking down to the autopsy room.

Dr Benson's staff members were efficient and had the bodies out on three gurneys, waiting for him. He changed into scrubs and gloved up, while he apologized to his assistant Lou Pudney for dragging him in on a Saturday.

"No sweat, boss. I've got a date, but that's not until tonight. Plenty of time."

"Anyone I know?"

"Nah, met her in Portland last week."

"Okay, you ready?" Benson adjusted his mask and pushed through the swing door into the small autopsy room with Lou a few paces behind. He looked at the three gurneys and shook his head sadly. "I hate family affairs. Right, to business." Benson approached the body of Randy Maher and activated the sound cube recorder.

"Body is that of a white male, age 45, height five foot eleven inches, weight one hundred and eighty-three pounds." Dr Benson bent over the body, examining the outside visually. "The body has already been photographed. There are minor abrasions to the hands, arms and face with a smear of blood near the right nostril." He shone a small penlight up the nostril. "No sign of sustained bleeding, the amount is consistent with a light blow, delivered premortem."

"The body was found at the bottom of a deep depression in farmland," Lou commented. "Perhaps he fell."

"It's possible. There's dirt under the fingernails...I'm taking samples." Benson scraped material from under the nails and put them into a small plastic bag. He sealed it and passed it to his assistant for labelling. "There are a number of small fibers on the body, no doubt consistent with his clothing...I have collected these together for comparison...there are also two dark hairs that appear to be of animal origin..."

"Coyote, Dr Benson. The man was found lying on a dead coyote."

"Really? I didn't see that in the police report.'

"Jack told me when he brought the bodies in."

"Well, that should be in the report. Didn't he think it was important?"

Lou said nothing, deciding not to reveal the sheriff's jovial demeanor as he delivered the bodies.

Benson started palpating the body. "No obvious breaks or bruising, lividity consistent with lying supine...interesting, there is a distinct blueness to the lividity, consistent with asphyxia." He went on to examine the neck region carefully. "No signs of strangulation...the hyoid feels intact. I will examine this when we go in." His thumb raised first one eyelid, then the other. "A few visible petechial hemorrhages in the conjunctiva and inner eyelids...none visible in the mouth. No abrasions around the mouth or nostrils." He opened the mouth as wide as he could and peered into it, moving the tongue aside. "No pharyngeal obstruction." The doctor rubbed his nose with the back of one gloved hand. "In fact, there is no outward sign of death beyond an indication that he may have been asphyxiated, but without manual or mechanical strangulation. Take blood and urine samples, Lou. I want a full toxicology report."

Benson stood aside while his assistant drew blood and inserted a needle to draw urine out of the bladder. He filled several tubes with bodily fluids and labelled them carefully.

"Now we go in." Benson made a Y-shaped incision in the chest, leading from each shoulder and meeting above the sternum before continuing down to the pubic bone, passing to the left of the umbilicus. He took the bone shears and cut through the ribs, folding the body wall back on both sides. "No obvious signs of trauma in the organs in situ, though the liver is enlarged and showing a few necrotic patches." He removed the organs one by one, turning them over in his hands and examining them closely before weighing them and having Lou note down the results.

Benson then dissected out the neck, carefully exposing the hyoid bone and the larynx. "No sign of bruising." The Stryker saw came out and after the scalp had been examined and reflected away from the skull, he made a semi-circular cut through the bone. Tiny fragments of skin, blood and bone flew up, spattering both men in a fine spray. The stink of friction-burnt bone filled the room. He cut through the membranes covering the brain and examined the organ in place before severing the major nerves and lifting it from its bony case. The weight was noted and sections taken for later analysis.

"I don't expect they'll reveal anything," Benson said. "The brain looks much as I'd expect it to look in a man of his age and health. My money's on the tox report showing us the cause of death." He went over the organs again and took samples, saving the stomach contents for analysis, and then packed the organs back in the abdominal cavity before stapling the incision closed.

"Right, let's have a look at his wife." Dr Benson moved over to the next gurney and looked down dispassionately at the naked body of Karen Maher. He ran through a quick physical description before getting into detail. "Extensive bruising to the body and limbs, consistent with blows over an extended period. Some of them are fresh, others older...days...weeks...one on the upper right arm shows what appears to be bruises in the form of fingers and thumb. The spread of these..." He went back to the body of the man and made some measurements. "...is a good match for the husband's hand. My opinion is that we have a case of spousal abuse, regrettably caught too late." Benson sighed and asked Lou to scratch his forehead with the tip of his pencil. "Thanks, Lou. Lividity indicates the woman died in a supine position with her head lower than her feet...and again we have this blueness. Aside from the bruising, and a few petechiae in the eyelids, there are no other outward signs of physical trauma."

The medical examiner spent a long time investigating the airways of the woman, but with the same lack of results. For the record, he voiced his suspicions. "I am of the opinion that both Randolph Maher and Karen Maher died of asphyxiation. This may be due to some asphyxiating agent or simply due to a lack of oxygen. I am searching for some indication that the woman may have been deprived of oxygen manually, either by signs of a hand over her mouth or evidence of a plastic bag taped over her head. I can find neither abrasions nor sticky residue to the skin."

The internal examination of the woman followed much the same procedure as that of her husband, with as few indications of the cause of death. Dr Benson took blood and urine samples and also sections of the major organs for histological analysis. "Not that I think we'll find anything. There's nothing wrong with her."

"Except she's dead."

"Very true, Lou. What would I do without your perspicacious observations?" He smiled to take the sting out of his words. "The bluish tinge to the lividity of both bodies is the only common factor. Asphyxia almost certainly, but no indication as to the asphyxiating agent. I hope toxicology will reveal that. The boy now."

Cory Maher's body was as unforthcoming as those of his parents. Benson took the same set of samples after his thorough examination and closed up the young body. Lou started cleaning up, zipping the bodies back into their bags and wheeling them through into the refrigerated storage area while Benson went over the notes taken during the autopsy. He listened to the sound cube recording and nodded, satisfied that he had covered everything. Lou then packed the samples into three refrigerated containers, sealed and labelled them, before packing them away in a lockable refrigerator.

"I'll give the laboratory a call as soon as I get washed up, Dr Benson."

"Leave it until Monday, Lou. I doubt there's any great hurry."

Benson stripped off his gown and gloves, stuffing the garments into the appropriate bins, and then washed up thoroughly. He took the sound cube and notes back up to his room and sat down at his desk to consider the findings. *Not that there are many*, he thought. *Not yet anyway*. He got up and crossed to his bookcase, running his fingers over the spines of textbooks, bound journals and magazines, before selecting a slim volume entitled simply 'Asphyxiation'. Benson took a plastic-wrapped sandwich from his briefcase and leaned back in his chair, munching slowly through his lunch as he read what he already knew.

Asphyxia came from the Greek term 'absence of pulse' but it generally meant to cover the conditions of anoxia, meaning an absence of oxygen or hypoxia, a low level of oxygen. It could also cover hypercapnia, or an excess of carbon dioxide in the blood, which, as the gas was a product of respiration, could sometimes result when air was repeatedly rebreathed.

Benson ran down the list of categories, quickly ruling out compression of the neck or thorax as a cause of asphyxia. Bradycardia was a possibility, which could result from pressure to the carotid sinus...but in three people at once? The man's face was congested and a touch edemic, as was the woman's, but that could be a result of her head down position. Certainly there was cyanosis present, which would result from a buildup of carbon dioxide in the venous blood but that would again be a natural result if the gas could not be flushed from the system. There had not been many petechial hemorrhages in the eyes or mouth, but that was not nearly as indicative a factor as people made out. You could cause petechiae by any rise in vascular pressure, even by straining on the toilet or by sneezing.

It boils down to a causative agent like nitrogen or helium...or carbon dioxide, I guess. Unless there was a toxic gas...no, I saw no evidence of that. The tox report will show if anything untoward was present. What else? What could I do that I haven't already done?

Dr Benson thought about what awaited him at home. His wife was on the East Coast, visiting her sister and there were no children (infertility) or pets (allergies) to enliven an empty house. *I could do a bit of investigating.* Reaching a decision, Benson drained what was left of a cold cup of coffee on his desk, closed his briefcase and exited his office, and then the building, locking them behind him.

The trip to Rushing River took a little over two hours and he was fortunate to find the sheriff in his office. After an exchange of pleasantries, Benson broached the reason for his visit.

"I'd like to visit the place where the bodies were found."

The sheriff nodded. "Need some extra background before you do the autopsies, Doc?"

"No, I did those this morning."

"And? What was the cause of death?"

Benson hesitated. "I really can't say at the moment, Jack. My medical opinion is asphyxiation, but by what agent, and if there are complicating factors, I can't say until the toxicology report comes back. That's why I thought the site might tell me something."

"I'll run you out there."

Benson fetched his medical bag from his car and joined Jack Warner in his patrol car. The sheriff drove them out to the campground and parked near the river.

"It's a bit of a hike from here, but the paths are good."

As they walked, Benson had Jack fill him in on how the bodies were discovered.

"Some Eagle Scouts found a little girl, a toddler, sleeping beside the path up ahead from here. They took her down to the campground where the owner identified her as Alexa Maher. Somebody said they'd seen the family leave that morning for the Upper Farmland Trail--where we're going. The owner called the police; we responded and organized searchers to cover every trail. We found the bodies around 5 pm yesterday."

"And no obvious sign of how they died?"

"Shit, I thought they'd been shot, being all sprawled down the slope like that. Then I saw there was no blood, no wounds, so we took pictures, collected every fibre and bit of dirt we could think of and hauled the bodies out."

The two men crossed the suspension bridge and climbed the trail at a fast walk into the forest.

"You didn't notice any...well, strange smells or anything?"

"Plenty of smells," Jack laughed. "It's farmland, after all. And there was a dead coyote under the man's head, though to be honest, it hadn't really started to stink."

"Any sign how it had died?"

Jack shook his head. "Not a mark on it, Doc."

"I don't suppose you kept the body."

"Hell, no, but I guess it's still up there. Why? You think it might be important?"

"Possibly. I can't say until I see it."

"If it's dead animals you want, see Marc Stone up at the ranch. He found five of his cattle dead a couple of days ago and not a clue as to what killed them. Our vet, Pat McGugan, hauled one back to his clinic to cut up, but all he found was a whole lot of steaks." Jack guffawed.

"I hope he didn't eat any of them, if he has no idea what killed it."

"Hey, we might live out in the 'sticks', but we ain't no hicks." He pointed ahead. "Nearly there, doc."

The gully, and the depression within it, was surrounded by police tape. Jack and Benson ducked under the tape and squatted at the edge of the hollow, looking down into it.

"What were the weather conditions like yesterday?" Benson asked.

"Calm and sunny for the most part, but by evening a fresh breeze had sprung up. Why?"

"What about when you got here? Did you take any special precautions?"

"Against what? There were three bodies down there...four if you include the coyote. We went straight in to check for signs of life."

"Did you feel okay?" Benson held up a hand. "I know, bear with me here, I'm not really sure what I'm looking for. Did you, or any of your men, feel any ill effects from being down there with the bodies? I suppose I'm thinking of a gas being present."

Jack shook his head. "Parsons--he's a new recruit, he felt queasy and had a headache later, but I put that down to his inexperience. You really think we might have been gassed?"

"It's a possibility, but at the moment I'm fishing for ideas."

"You seen enough, Doc?"

"One more thing." Benson rummaged around in his medical bag and took out a glass tube with a valve tap attached to one end. "A vacuum tube. I need an air sample." He scrambled down to the bottom of the depression and cracked open the valve. Air rushed in with an audible hiss. "There, I'll send that off for analysis and we'll see if there are any traces left."

"Traces of what, Doc? Are we talking cyanide or nerve gas or something?"

"Nothing so exotic. Most asphyxiant gases are lighter than air, but carbon dioxide is heavier. It would collect in hollows like this."

"That's what you get from auto exhausts, isn't it? No, shit, that's monoxide. Where would you get enough dioxide to kill people?"

"Exhaust gases are mostly dioxide, Sheriff, but I have absolutely no idea how you'd get a vehicle out to a remote area like this. I suppose you could bring a tank of it out here, but why on earth would you want to?"

"Could the bodies have been killed elsewhere and brought here? Staged?"

"Unlikely. The lividity suggests they died in exactly the positions they were found in, and the surroundings don't show any signs of disturbance. I think you'd scuff the ground carrying three bodies in and arranging them." Benson took out a large paper bag and opened it. He picked up the dead coyote and placed it in the bag.

"Interesting. There's no obvious insect activity on the body. I think I need to talk to your vet."

Chapter 24

August 18, 2030

Andrew Winton had put through a call to James Matternicht upon his return from the meeting with Max Hay on Saturday. The head of United Coal and Sequestration was unavailable, so Andrew left a brief message and asked that Matternicht call him back at his earliest convenience, stressing the importance of the connection. Nothing happened that day, and Andrew became increasingly worried. He started to entertain serious thoughts about fleeing the country ahead of a Federal investigation, or of hiring an assassin to take out Max Hay before he could ruin everything. He even went so far as to check on which countries did not have extradition treaties with the United States. This filled him with gloom as he envisaged spending the rest of his life in some god-forsaken Third World country. The thought that his wealth might buy him luxury made the prospect a little easier to bear. He made a cautious call to his investment broker, casually inquiring about what investments could be swiftly liquidated.

"I have an opportunity to make a bundle, but I might need funds quickly...ten million? ...Jesus, is that all? ...Well, that might have to do...a week? ...Okay, I'll call you back."

He called Matternicht again on Sunday morning and again left his message. Andrew sat in his library, bourbon in his hand despite the early hour, and waited. The phone rang at noon.

"Mr Winton?" The voice was cultured and very English. "I understand you wish to speak to Mr Matternicht. May I know the subject matter of this intended conversation?"

Andrew hesitated, unsure how much to say to an aide. "It concerns Maxwell Hay."

"Just a moment." The line went dead for nearly a minute, then, "Mr Matternicht will speak with you on voice-line only. Please hold." There was another delay before a whispery voice came over the wireless link.

"What do you want, Winton?"

Andrew winced at the words, partly because of the hostility in them, but also because of the weakness. The last time he had spoken to Matternicht had been a year ago and his voice had been strong and commanding. *Christ, the man's getting old at last. He must be close to ninety by now.*

"I have a matter of grave concern. Are we on a secure line, sir?" Matternicht was the only man in the world Andrew would call 'sir', and it did not bother him in the slightest. Some things just seemed right.

"Of course. I wouldn't be talking to you unless we were."

"I talked with Maxwell Hay on Saturday. He told me that he's about to blow the whistle on us unless we tell the authorities the Rushing River facility is unsafe."

"How did you reply?"

"I stalled for time, sir. I asked him to give me until the 23rd, at which time I would go with him to the Governor of Oregon." The silence from the other end of the connection unnerved Andrew and he hurried on. "I had to tell him something, sir. He sent me papers by courier and they fell into the wrong hands. I managed to salvage the situation but I was afraid that he might send other copies out unless I cooperated with him."

"Whose were these wrong hands?"

"You don't have to worry about that, sir. My daughter-in-law Annaliese thought they were addressed to her and she opened the packets. She could not make sense of them so came to me. I was able to reassure her and convince her to leave everything in my hands."

"You're certain no copies were made? No other eyes saw them?"

Andrew hesitated for only a second. "Absolutely, sir. Besides, the real danger is Max Hay. He says he's placed full documentation in the hands of a lawyer to send to the AG if he doesn't appear before the Governor on the 23rd."

"Is that all?"

"That's not enough? What are we going to do?"

"You're going to do exactly as you always do--nothing. You'll continue to go in to work each day, carry on your social life as if nothing was happening. I need you to appear to be a solid, honest citizen. Can you do that, Winton?"

"Yes, sir, of course." Andrew felt a mixture of chagrin and relief. Relief that he was not expected to do anything dangerous, chagrin at the thought that he was not considered a useful member of the team.

"And, Winton, one other thing...don't even think about liquidating any assets." Matternicht went on to name Andrew's investment broker and the stocks he had asked about on Saturday. "Believe me, Winton; I remember my friends...and my enemies. I don't want you thinking you can evade your responsibilities. Do you understand me?"

There was only one possible answer. "Yes, sir."

* * *

Matternicht broke the connection and leaned back in his chair. The old man's skin was papery, translucent and stretched over prominent bones. His hair was white, and his hands displayed a faint tremor, but the dark eyes beneath bushy eyebrows were alert and predatory, and his mind still operated like a steel trap.

"You heard." Matternicht's words were less a question than a statement, and his aide nodded.

"What do you want me to do, sir?"

"First, you'll find out the present whereabouts of Maxwell Hay. Bring him to me. Second, you'll ascertain which lawyer he entrusted those papers to. Third, you'll send a trusted man to investigate this Annaliese Winton. Have our technicians set up a monitor of her voice and data communications. I need to know if she knows too much about Rushing River. If she has even an inkling of the truth, she must die immediately. Do you understand my wishes, Nigel?" The aide, who had not taken a single note or recorded a single note, knew the utmost value of discretion. Nothing must ever lead back to James Matternicht. "Yes, sir, I do."

Chapter 25

August 19, 2030

Marc Stone had been working on his tractor all morning. He thought the problem was a blocked fuel feed line filter, but even after he had cleaned that out without finding any blockage and reversed flushed it, he still had problems. His wife Margaret had brought him coffee mid-morning and suggested he should call in a mechanic. Marc preferred to use that as a last resort, but by midday he was no nearer finding the fault. He was glad when a car crunched up the gravel driveway and came to a stop outside the barn, giving him an excuse to stop work.

Marc walked out to see who his visitor was, while wiping his oily hands on a cloth. "Pat," he said, as the vet climbed out of his 4WD. "You've got some news for me?"

"Yeah, of a sort. I did the..." Pat McGugan was interrupted by the back door of the farmhouse opening. He turned to see Margaret in the doorway.

"Hello, Pat," she called. "I've just brewed some coffee. Come and have a cup."

Marc nodded his agreement. "I could do with a break myself." The two men went inside and sat down in the kitchen while Margaret poured the coffee. She helped herself to a cup and came and sat with them.

Pat sipped and said, "Good coffee, Margaret. Thank you."

"What have you got to tell us?" Marc asked. "You did the autopsy?"

"Yes, but it wasn't conclusive. I couldn't find any reason for the death beyond saying it was asphyxiation."

"So how the hell does somebody asphyxiate five head of cattle in the open, without restraining them or leaving marks?"

"I'm sorry, I don't know," Pat confessed.

"What exactly do you mean by asphyxiation, Pat?" Margaret asked. "Just so's I know what you're talking about."

"Basically, it just means to deprive them of air, or rather the oxygen in it. You can do this by constricting the windpipe or exposing them to a gas that depletes the oxygen."

"And you found evidence of this when you examined them?"

"No, I didn't. There were no marks on the neck or anything, really, except small blood vessels burst in the corners of the eyes and in the mouth. That can happen in asphyxiation cases."

"So what killed them?"

"He's just said he doesn't know, Maggie," Marc said gently.

"Well, I don't, but there's something else."

They waited for the vet to carry on and when he did not, Margaret prompted him. "What?"

"The Wasco County medical examiner came to see me on Saturday. It seems there were three deaths in Rushing River--tourists--under odd circumstances."

"Why would he come and see you?" Marc asked. "No offence, Pat, but he's a doctor. What could you tell him?"

"None taken, Marc. I couldn't have told him anything about the human deaths but he didn't ask about those. He wanted to know about your cattle. He also had a dead coyote for me to look at."

"How did he know about my cattle? Hell, I don't want everybody knowing my business."

"Sheriff Warner."

"You said he had a dead coyote," Margaret said. "What was that about?"

"He wanted me to examine it to see if I agreed with his diagnosis."

"And?"

"It died of asphyxiation, too. Funny thing is, it had been sitting outside for three days but it wasn't...well, begging your pardon, Margaret...all maggoty and stinking."

"Is that relevant?" Marc asked.

Pat shrugged. "Sorry, I don't know if it's significant but it's odd at this time of year. There was plenty of bacterial decomposition and even dead fleas in its hair, but no live fly or beetle larvae."

"So, you've got no damn idea whether this is going to happen again. Hell, Pat, I can't just go on losing cattle for no good reason. If I don't know why they die, I can't prevent more happening."

Pat said nothing. He finished his coffee and stood up. "I'd best be getting back," he muttered. "Things to do. Sorry I didn't have better news for you."

"Did the medical examiner say what he thought was responsible for the deaths?" Margaret asked. "I presume he saw similarities between the human deaths and the cattle."

"He had no evidence to back it up yet, he's still waiting for test results, but he thought it was carbon dioxide poisoning. Maybe in a few days I'll have something more to tell you." The vet nodded to both Marc and Margaret. "Good coffee, Margaret. Thanks again." He left.

"Well, that's a fat lot of use to us," Marc grumbled. "How can I protect the herd against something like that? If you ask me, he just doesn't know so he's trotting out some lame suggestion to cover his butt. Who the hell heard of carbon dioxide killing cattle?"

"Um, something like that did happen. When I was looking up earthquakes, I came across...oh, what was it? A volcanic eruption in Africa somewhere. A lake, I think...I'll have to look it up again. I can't remember the name."

"Sounds like a waste of time to me, Maggie. This isn't a volcano we're sitting on."

"There are a whole lot of volcanoes in the Cascades."

"Yeah, but we'd have heard if any were erupting." Marc moved to the door. "I'm getting back to that blasted tractor. Call me for lunch, Maggie."

* * *

Margaret washed up the coffee cups and prepared a tuna casserole, putting it into the oven and setting the timer to tell her when it was cooked. She went upstairs to her computer and switched it on, pulling up the Google search engine. "Africa...lake...carbon dioxide."

The Panpedia entry for Lake Nyos headed the page. Margaret opened it and read the article, enlarging the pictures and following the embedded links. "I knew it. It's a volcano starting." She printed off the article for her husband to read and then sat in thought for a while. "Computer, Volcano...birth...gases." She opened a few of the entries but they told her little. Then she came to one on Paricutin, Mexico.

"Oh, my goodness." In 1943, a farmer in Mexico had noticed a plume of smoke issuing from a crack in the ground in one of his fields. Ash followed, and choking gases, and lava, and soon there was a thousand-foot volcano where a farm

134

had once stood. Margaret noticed one other fact that made her shiver. There had been a number of small earthquakes in the weeks preceding the birth of the volcano. She printed out this information, too.

The oven timer rang and Margaret went downstairs to set out and serve lunch. She took the printouts down, too, and laid them beside her husband's plate.

Marc took a mouthful of tuna casserole and complimented his wife on her cooking. "What's this?" he asked, tapping the top sheet.

"I looked up that reference, the one on the African lake. It's true, Marc. We've got a volcano growing on our ranch."

"What are you on about, Maggie? That sounds crazy."

"Read it. The top one's about this volcanic lake in Africa--Lake Nyos. Fifty years ago it belched out carbon dioxide gas and killed hundreds of people and thousands of cattle and goats. Look at the pictures, Marc. Don't they look like our cattle deaths?"

Marc leafed through the few pages of printout and scanned the pictures. "I don't know, Maggie. A dead animal is a dead animal. They look similar, but how else would you expect a dead steer to look? Anyway, there's no volcanic lake around here."

"Not yet, maybe, but look at the other article. It says that Paracutin volcano in Mexico started on a farm. A crack in the ground sent out gases and ash. Maybe the gas was carbon dioxide and maybe the same thing is happening again. There definitely seems to be a connection between volcanoes and carbon dioxide and Pat says it was likely carbon dioxide that killed our steers."

"He said possibly, Maggie. I really think you are making too much of this. The information is interesting, but I don't think it applies to us. The geologists know all about volcanoes and they'd tell us if one was starting."

"Then how is carbon dioxide killing our cattle? Where does it come from?"

"It may not even be carbon dioxide. Pat said we should wait for the results of the medical examiner's tests."

"But it's all adding up..."

"Look, Maggie, it may be as you say, but I really don't have the time to argue right now. I've wasted the morning on that damn tractor and I've work to do. How about we talk this evening, okay?"

When Marc had left the house, Margaret cleared away the dishes and made herself a cup of tea. She took it out on the front porch and sat looking out at rolling paddocks and grazing cattle. In her mind's eye she saw a black volcano rising from the fields and lava obliterating their ranch.

How can I find out the truth of it? Who would know? She remembered the note that had been left on her door a few days back and went inside to find it. It was on her desk, with a faint coffee ring marring its whiteness. Dr M. Morrison...and his phone number. *He's USGS in Portland, surely he'd know.* She called the number on the card and was put through, after a short delay.

"Matt Morrison. How may I help you?" The image on the viewphone showed a man in his thirties wearing a slightly bored expression.

"Hello, Dr Morrison. My name is Margaret Stone. I live out at Rushing River. You left a card saying you were going onto our land..."

"Yes, I remember. I'm sorry I didn't get permission first, but I didn't think you'd mind. We were very careful to close gates and not spook the stock..."

"I'm sure you were, Dr Morrison, but that's not why I'm calling." She hesitated, suddenly aware just how silly she was going to sound. "I...I think a volcano might be starting on our ranch."

"What makes you think that, Mrs Stone?"

"I'm sorry; I shouldn't be wasting your time. I can see by your expression you think I'm mad." Margaret reached out to cut the connection.

"Wait, don't hang up. Mrs Stone, if I appeared disbelieving, I apologize. You startled me, is all. Please tell me why you think this may be happening."

"Well, there have been earthquakes and then I read about Paricutin and how it started just with a crack in the ground and gas..."

"Paracutin? The volcano in Mexico?"

"Yes. Would this gas be carbon dioxide? Do you know? Like Lake Nyos in Africa?"

"It might, but there'd be a lot of other things too if it was volcanic in origin. Ash, sulphur, hydrogen sulphide...is the gas choking or stinking?"

"No...no, I haven't smelled it but...well, it's killed our cattle."

"Really? Have...er, have you notified the authorities?"

"Yes, the local vet and the county medical examiner think it might be carbon dioxide poisoning but where would that come from except a volcano?"

"The medical examiner? What on earth was he doing looking at a dead cow?"

"He didn't look at the dead cattle but he talked to the vet. He was there because of the dead people..."

"People are dead?"

"Yes, three tourists the day after the cattle died. If it really is carbon dioxide poisoning then could it be because a volcano is forming under our ranch? Are we in danger?"

"Mrs Stone, calm yourself, please. I can categorically state that there's no volcano under your ranch. The geology is all wrong."

"But the Cascades are volcanic. I read it on Panpedia."

"Yes, they are, but your ranch is only peripherally on the Columbia River basalts. The rest is sedimentary rock and non-volcanic. Look, what I'd like to do is come out there tomorrow and run a few tests. I'm confident I'll be able to put your mind at rest."

"Would you? I don't want to be a nuisance, but..."

"No nuisance, Mrs Stone. I'm not sure when exactly, but I'll be there sometime tomorrow."

Margaret disconnected the link and sat in thought for a while. The geologist's words had made her feel better but she wondered if she needed some moral support for his visit. He would no doubt overwhelm her with science. Someone who had experience of the ways people used words might be nice to have on her side. She could only think of one person like that.

She opened up her email and sent a quick message to Annaliese Winton at the Salem Chronicle.

'Annaliese, I know what killed the cattle and now three tourists. Can you come and see me? I don't want to talk on the phone. Margaret.'

Chapter 26

August 19, 2030

Annaliese had gone into work as usual on Monday. She had spent the weekend worrying about the papers and what they meant. Adrian's queries had been the hardest to bear, as he was sure his mother was on the brink of some great investigative coup. She refused to lie to him, but also knew she could not tell him the truth. In the end, she said only that his grandfather had asked her not to pursue the story for the time being, as the revelations would harm the United States and that when the time came, she would be part of a much bigger story. Adrian had looked at his mother askance, but said nothing.

The Salem Chronicle was busy, as usual, but Annaliese found it difficult to be enthusiastic about the humdrum stories that landed in her inbox. Her piece on the Portland Water Authority scandal was scheduled for next week's Sunday paper and she received congratulations from some of the staff and grudging praise from others. Even Simon the Copy Editor was deferential toward her, but the good wishes did not buoy her up. She knew the groundwork had already been done before she took over the story. It was not hers. *Rushing River is mine. That's the story I want to do.*

She poured herself a cup of coffee and sat at her desk, reading emails. Nothing attracted her interest so she sighed and dug out the first of the assignment printouts in her in-box--a police report of a gas station hold-up on Grant and Evergreen.

"Why have I got a crime report?" she asked loudly.

"Because I'm working a murder," Ben replied with a grin. "I get to give you the dull stuff."

Annaliese groaned and reached for her coat.

The gas station robbery yielded nothing of great interest. Annaliese interviewed the clerk on duty, managed to view the CCTV footage, and had a quiet word with the detective assigned to the case. She returned to the office and quickly wrote it up as a two-paragraph story and moved on to the next assignment.

By lunchtime, Annaliese had disposed of a minor assault outside a nightclub, the opening of a new supermarket, a road accident involving neither death nor injury, a case of bullying at the local Elementary school, and the release of a new recipe book by a local author. The pile of printouts in her in-box did not appear to be diminishing either. She got up to get another cup of coffee and then took it in to Simon, waiting at the door of his office until he looked up.

"Yes? I'm busy."

"I can see that, Simon. Is there any reason for the pile of junk stories appearing in my in-box?"

"Someone's got to do them." He bent to his work again. As Annaliese turned to go, he added, "I do have a bigger assignment if you want it."

"More interesting?"

Simon shrugged. "Make it interesting. This came down from Mr Winton and he recommended you. An exposé on price-fixing in Salem hardware stores." He held out a file. "Everything you need to get started is in there."

Annaliese took the file reluctantly. "Mr Winton wanted me to do it?"

"That's what he said. Do you want me to tell him you'd rather not?"

"No, don't bother."

"Then do it. I'm busy." Simon returned to his work, ignoring Annaliese.

The file was as uninteresting as it sounded and she could see from her initial perusal that it would be a long and involved investigation. *Guaranteed to keep me busy and not thinking about Rushing River. Damn him, I've already said I wouldn't follow that up so why is he doing this?*

Her email started blinking and she opened it, eager to escape her new assignment. It was from Margaret Stone at Rushing River. *Synchronicity*, she thought.

'Annaliese,' it read, 'I know what killed the cattle and now three tourists. Can you come and see me? I don't want to talk on the phone. Margaret.'

Annaliese's eyes opened wide. She considered the implications of human deaths on the story. *I can't ignore this.* "Has anyone heard anything about the deaths of three tourists in Rushing River?" she asked the newsroom. "Anyone?"

"Check the file," Katy called back. "I think something came in over the weekend."

Annaliese pulled up the office email files and scrolled back through the brief reports that came in from all around the country. Two-thirds of the way down the page she found a reference to three bodies found near a popular hiking trail in Rushing River. The cause of death was not listed, nor any particulars concerning the identity of the bodies. She leaned back in her chair and thought about what she should do. *I said I wouldn't write about it, but I can't just ignore everything. I could find out what's happening, I suppose. I don't have to actually write about it, so I wouldn't be breaking my promise. But what if there really is something...* She typed a quick reply to Margaret and closed down her email.

It was early afternoon and Annaliese knew she could not drive round to Rushing River and back before Adrian got out of school, so her expedition would have to take place on the following day. She sighed and opened up the folder on price-fixing. *I suppose I'd better look as if I'm doing it.*

* * *

Across town, Albert Ruffin sat in a rented apartment. The only furnishings in the apartment were a folding table and chair and a laptop computer. A bucket of fried chicken fragments lay congealing beside the chair and a can of Coke sat on the table within easy reach. The man was surfing, cruising through net porn when the email alarm beeped. He minimized his screen and opened up the message.

"Bingo," Albert muttered. He had visited the offices of the Salem Chronicle over the weekend as part of the cleaning staff and had uploaded a command to Annaliese Winton's computer that automatically duplicated every email message that came to or went from her computer. Albert did not know why this woman was under surveillance, but one of the flagged words had just come up. He took out his cell phone and called a memorized number.

"The flagged words 'Rushing River' have come up," he told the man on the other end of the connection. He read out the whole of Margaret Stone's email and then Annaliese's reply.

The man on the other end talked. Albert listened and nodded, as though the visual function had not been disabled on this phone. "I understand...Limit collateral damage...Yes, I know her car. Yes...tomorrow." The man put his phone away and sipped from the Coke can. *What the fuck has this woman done to get on the wrong side of these jokers?* He belched and dropped the can on the floor. *Ours is not to reason why, ours is but to cause to die.* Albert grinned at his own wit, closed the laptop and exited the apartment with it.

Chapter 27

August 20, 2030

Matt Morrison had checked out one of the USGS vehicles early that morning, deciding that he would visit Margaret Stone at Rushing River Ranch in his official capacity. The woman was obviously concerned about volcanoes for some strange reason and he thought that his denials of volcanic activity would have more weight if backed by the Department's official insignia. There was also the matter of the cattle and now the three tourists dead from what could be carbon dioxide poisoning. If that really was the case it was certainly not because of volcanic gases escaping. He suspected the source of carbon dioxide was altogether more man-made. Proof of his suspicions was another matter.

He had thought about the conundrum all the previous evening and had decided that he needed to talk to the medical examiner to get his take on the deaths. Before he set off that morning, he called the office of The Dalles Medical Examiner and persuaded the county official to meet with him. At nine in the morning, Matt parked his vehicle in the Mid-Columbia Medical Center car park and crossed to the glass doors of the medical examiner's office.

Matt was not sure quite what he expected to find--gloomy halls echoing to the funereal tread of black-suited somber-faced undertakers perhaps, or the stink of death and preservatives like formalin. Instead, he found himself in a brightly lit foyer talking to a cheerful young man in jeans and a tee-shirt.

"I saw you coming, Dr Morrison," said the young man. "I let Dr Benson know. He'll be down to meet you in a few moments."

"How did you know it was me?"

"Well, you phoned ahead to say you were coming and then you pull up in a USGS vehicle."

"Uh, of course."

"You'll be interested in the Rushing River deaths, I suppose?"

"I'm sorry--you are?" Matt let the question hang.

The young man smiled and held out his hand. "Lou Pudney. I'm one of Dr Benson's assistants. I can't tell you anything, of course, it wouldn't be ethical, but... ah, here's Dr Benson now."

A swing door opened and closed with a secure click behind a middle-aged portly man in a fading suit and white laboratory coat. Twinkling eyes with laughter lines in the corners revealed a personality that had not been worn down by the horrors of his job.

"You'd be Dr Morrison from the USGS."

"Yes, Dr Benson." Matt shook hands. "It was good of you to spare the time."

"You do realize there's not much I can tell you before the official report comes out?"

"I understand, but anything you can tell me might help."

Dr Benson thanked Lou for his time and subtly dismissed him, leading Matt through a door into a small break room. They sat down at a Formica-covered table.

"What did you want to know? I cannot volunteer information but if you ask the right questions..."

"The three tourists who died at Rushing River on Saturday--what was the cause of death?"

"I don't know."

Matt frowned. "Really don't know, or not allowed to say?"

Benson smiled. "If I'm not allowed to divulge details I'll say so. I really don't know. I can tell you that the autopsy results were inconclusive and I'm still waiting for the toxicology results."

"What might the toxicology tests show?"

"The presence of alcohol, drugs--legal or illicit--poisons, toxins, asphyxiants, etc."

Matt thought for a moment. *This is like bloody twenty questions.* "Do you, on the basis of your autopsy, expect the toxicology to show the presence of anything?"

Benson smiled again. "If I knew that, I wouldn't need the tests done. No, that's not really accurate; I'd still need to make sure. So, yes, I suspect the blood may show the presence of an asphyxiant."

"What type?"

"That's the problem. If the bodies had been found indoors, or in an enclosed space, I'd say carbon dioxide, though how the levels could rise high enough to be toxic escapes me. But they were found outdoors, which makes me suspect an uncommon toxin."

"Hmm. Where were they found?"

"In a depression in a gully on the Rushing River Ranch."

"No kidding? And you reached it by a gravel path at the top of the gully? The path led down to the campsite?"

"You know the place?"

"I was there last Thursday."

"How extraordinary." Benson regarded the geologist quizzically. "By coincidence, or were you there by design?"

"A bit of both. I was in Rushing River with a colleague doing some Draeger testing..."

"Draeger?"

"For the presence of carbon dioxide. It's usually used indoors but at a pinch it'll give an indication of outside levels."

"And you found something?"

"I found a sunken depression in a gully on the Rushing River Ranch where the carbon dioxide levels were about 900 parts per million."

"That is not a lethal dose," Benson observed.

"Not even close," Matt agreed. "You'd need more than fifty thousand parts per million to do that, and even then you'd have time to move away from the source."

"Unless it quickly rendered them unconscious. Then they would suffocate."

"True. You really think CO_2 did them in?"

"As I said, if this had been indoors, I'd have thought it likely, but how on earth that concentration of gas was present in the open air is beyond me. Remember these days 450ppm is normal, but in woodlands in early summer, we could have 350 - like 50 years ago."

"I understand some animals also died."

"Five head of cattle and a coyote. I cannot swear that they died of the same causes, but the local veterinarian thinks they did."

"He's in Rushing River? What's his name? I might look him up."

"Pat McGugan." Dr Benson stood. "Well, if you have no more questions, Dr Morrison, you will have to excuse me. I have bodies clamoring to be examined."

Matt grimaced. "Sooner you than me." He followed Benson out into the foyer, where they found Lou Pudney arguing with a tall, brunette woman in a smart pantsuit. Matt thought she looked familiar but could not place her.

"What's going on here?" Benson asked.

"I'm sorry, Dr Benson," Lou said. "I was just explaining to Ms Winton here that you were unavailable for comment on..."

"Dr Benson?" the woman interrupted. "I am Annaliese Winton of the Salem Chronicle. Would you care to comment on the cause of death of the three tourists at Rushing River on the weekend?"

"No, I would not," Benson said politely. "I cannot comment on an ongoing investigation."

"Were the deaths suspicious?"

"As I said, Ms Winton, I cannot comment. You will have to wait for the official report. Now I must ask you to leave." Benson turned to Matt and shook his hand. "Good day, Dr Morrison, it was interesting talking to you." He walked across the foyer, tapped in some numbers on the security keypad and pushed through the swing door.

"I must ask you to leave the premises, Ms Winton," Lou said firmly.

"What about him?" Annaliese pointed at Matt.

Matt grinned and raised his arms. "Don't look at me, I'm leaving anyway." Matt held the door open for the woman and followed her outside. He started across the car park toward his vehicle.

"So why were you here?" Annaliese asked.

Matt stopped. "I rather think that's my own business."

"You're USGS," Annaliese said, looking at the logo on the car's door.

"Very observant. Now if you'll excuse me..." He continued toward his car.

Annaliese shrugged and went to her own vehicle, starting it up and throwing it into gear. It lurched forward, stuttered and died, blocking the exit from the car park. She tried to restart but the starter motor refused to do anything but click under the hood.

Matt got out of his car and walked across to the driver's side of the stalled vehicle. "Would you like me to call you a tow-truck?"

Annaliese swore in an unladylike manner. "I can do it myself, thank you."

Matt nodded. "Fine, but could you move your car out of the exit? I need to get out."

"I would, but you might have noticed my car isn't working."

"It'll still roll, won't it? How about I push you into one of the parking spaces?"

Matt pushed and Annaliese steered it into a vacant spot. She got out, locked it, pulled out her vid-phone and called for the tow truck.

"Well, I'd better be getting on," Matt said, looking at his watch.

Annaliese gave him a sour expression. "A gentleman would wait until the truck arrived."

"Good God, we're in the hospital car park. What the hell do you think is likely to happen...?" Matt's voice trailed away. He shrugged and moved to the opposite end of the car, fervently praying the truck would show up soon.

It arrived after about twenty minutes and Annaliese signed the papers and arranged for its delivery to a suitable repair agency. She then called ahead and found out they could have it repaired by five o'clock but no sooner.

"Can you give me a ride to a rental car company?" she asked Matt.

"You'd trust me? I'm no gentleman, remember."

"Yes, Dr Morrison, USGS, I trust you."

"Okay, hop in." Matt went so far as to open the passenger side door for his guest. He drove out of the car park onto East 19th Street and worked his way through the maze of streets to the Mosier-The Dalles Highway.

"Which way? Do you know where there's a rental company?"

Annaliese shook her head. "Go right. I'm heading to Rushing River so I might as well go in that direction."

Matt raised an eyebrow but said nothing. He drove for about ten minutes, passing the Highway 30 and 197 junctions, but without finding a rental company.

"You'd better let me out," Annaliese said. "I'll catch a taxi back into the town and find one."

Matt turned back and then onto Highway 197. "That would be one option. Another would be to let me be the perfect gentleman and drive you to Rushing River."

Annaliese looked at him bleakly. "I'd still have to get back to The Dalles to collect my car."

"I'd be happy to drive you back tonight as well."

"Now I really think you'd better let me out." When Matt did not even slow the vehicle, she opened her purse and added, "I have a can of mace in here."

"It'd be a pity to cause an accident, so let me just say I'm going to Rushing River myself. It's no imposition to take you." Matt fumbled in his pants pocket and took out his wallet. He handed it across. "My Driver's License is in there. As you can see, I'm Dr Matthew Morrison of USGS, Portland. Call the number on the card in there and you can verify my identity."

Annaliese examined the license carefully and handed it back. "Okay, you're who you say you are. I'm Annaliese Winton, reporter for the *Salem Chronicle*."

"Pleased to meet you," Matt said with a grin. "At least, I think I'm meeting you. I have an odd feeling I've seen you before."

"Perhaps you've seen my picture above my by-line."

"I don't think so. I don't read Salem papers as a rule."

"*Portland Star*, then. I've worked for them, too."

Matt shook his head. "It'll come to me. Where in Rushing River is the big story?"

"I'm not sure there is one yet. And if there is, whether I'll be able to write it."

"Sounds intriguing. Anything you can tell me about?"

Annaliese made a non-committal sound. "What do you do at USGS?"

Matt could tell he was being diverted. "USGS Portland is primarily concerned with freshwater sources around north Oregon and south Washington. At the moment I'm on a team investigating the movement of industrial pollutants through the aquifers." He grinned. "Does it sound like anything you might want to write about? I thought not. It's not what I envisaged I'd be doing twenty years out of grad school."

Annaliese recognized a hook when she heard it. "What would you rather be doing?"

"Stratigraphy."

"Okay..."

"Studying rock layers. I did my dissertation on anticlines and..." Matt saw her look of bafflement. "An anticline is a series of layered rocks that bulge upward. They have some economic importance because oil and gas often get trapped in them. There aren't too many decent ones around here because of the volcanic nature of the terrain, but the Hood Anticline beneath Rushing River is a big one, and apparently intact."

"Beneath Rushing River? Is that why you are going there? And what do you mean by intact?"

"I can tell you're a reporter."

"Sorry, but I am interested."

"Okay. Then yes, beneath Rushing River, and yes, you could say I'm going there on related business."

"And intact?"

"Rock is strange stuff. We are used to seeing lumps of it on the surface and think of it as a hard rigid material that shatters if you apply force to it. Underground, though, with the pressure of billions of tons of overlying strata, rock starts to flow and bend. An anticline is a dome made of layers of rock pushed up in the middle under the influence of unimaginable forces. If the pressures aren't too great and if there are no irregularities or flaws in the rock, it stays together and just folds. If there's a flaw though, the rock layers can snap or shear, resulting in a fault line. When that happens, the dome is no longer intact."

"And then it can't hold gas or oil?"

"No, it can still do that. Petrologists, people who look for oil, often investigate faults because pockets of oil can form behind them. No, when I said the Hood anticline was intact, I was thinking of something else entirely."

"And that's why you are going to Rushing River?"

The highway split soon after they left the outskirts of The Dalles, the main branch continuing south to California via Klamath, the lesser road easing westward toward the Cascades and servicing a number of small towns including Rushing River. A few miles along this road, the surface deteriorated and forest started to encroach on the margins. They followed the Deschutes River for a while and then curved away through forest and farm with signs of habitation becoming increasingly sparse.

On one lonely stretch of road, bordering on a wooded creek, the road straightened and halfway along it they spied a car pulled off on the verge. A man in a rumpled suit stood leaning against it, smoking a cigarette. He stood up and turned toward them as they came round the bend, staring intently for a few minutes before lounging back against his vehicle.

"Is he having car trouble or just enjoying the view?" Matt mused.

"Either way, it would be neighborly to stop."

Matt glanced in the rear-vision mirror. "Lonely place," he murmured. Nevertheless, he slowed and indicated he was pulling over.

The man watched them come to a stop and walked over, leather shoes crunching in the gravel. Despite it being a warm day, he held his jacket closed with one hand. His eyes were unreadable behind cheap dark glasses.

Matt wound his window down. "Hello, do you need a hand?"

The man shook his head. "No. I'm waiting for someone." He stooped to peer into the car. "Fuck," he muttered, and let go of his jacket. The fabric swung back to reveal a gun tucked into his trousers. The man grabbed for it.

Matt threw the car into gear and stamped on the accelerator. Gravel showered up as his car fish-tailed wildly before securing a purchase on the hardtop. He felt, rather than heard, a thump as they swung and Matt saw the man sprawled on the ground. "Shit, I hit him," he muttered, but did not stop, and soon they were out of sight of the car and the man.

Annaliese stared at Matt white-faced. "What the hell are you doing? You might have hurt him...or worse. We've got to stop and help him."

"You didn't see it? The gun?"

"What gun?"

"He had a gun in his belt. As soon as he saw you, he went for it." Matt glanced across at the reporter. "Who the hell have you been pissing off?"

Chapter 28

August 20, 2030

Robert Peale was worried and annoyed. For a long time he had fostered the illusion that being CEO of a prestigious establishment like the Rushing River Carbon Sequestration Facility gave him power and influence. It certainly gave him money, and his wealth gave him the trappings of power, but he was finding out that his domain cast a very small shadow in the world at large. That morning, while he was still at home in his robe, drinking coffee and reading the morning papers, he had received a call from Matternicht. Not James Matternicht himself, of course, but from one of his aides speaking with the authority of the great man.

The aide would fly into Rushing River that afternoon by helicopter, and requested that Peale have all the documentation on hand to demonstrate the safety or otherwise of the Plant. A request from Matternicht carried all the force of an order though, and Peale had no illusions as to his fate if he should displease the old man.

Why now? It's been five years since I've heard from him. I thought the old bastard was dead. Peale dressed and drove into work immediately, causing consternation among two shifts as their CEO stalked the corridors with a grim expression on his face.

"Get Dr Roux," he snarled at his secretary, who arrived just after her boss.

"She...she won't be in yet, Mr Peale. It's only eight-twenty."

"Then call her at home and tell her to get her sorry ass in here. And then get me a cup of coffee."

His secretary's mouth thinned to a slash at his words, but she nodded and picked up the phone. Five minutes later, she brought Peale his coffee and set it on his desk.

"Dr Roux is on her way. You also have a meeting with the Rushing River Chamber of Commerce at ten, and..."

"Cancel all my appointments today."

"Yes, Mr Peale."

"A top company official will be arriving by helicopter at one this afternoon. Nigel Campion. Please make sure he's met and escorted to my office."

Peale sipped at his coffee but could not settle. He got up and paced, sat down again, and more than once picked up his phone to ask if Dr Roux had arrived. He managed to control himself, but was in a foul mood by the time the scientist knocked on the door and entered.

"About fucking time. What took you so long?"

Angelina Roux frowned and answered cautiously. "I don't appreciate your rudeness, Mr Peale. I'm not due to start work for another ten minutes. Your secretary indicated there was some urgency. What's happened?"

"James Matternicht happened."

"Who?"

Peale waved a hand dismissively. "You've never met him, almost no one has. To all intents and purposes, he's the owner of this place."

"That's ridiculous. Oregon Energy owns the power station and this plant."

"Yes, and Matternicht owns Oregon Energy."

"It's a public company..."

"With the bulk of its shares controlled by the Northern Coal Consortium--which is in turn controlled by James Matternicht. Now can we stop talking about who he is and concentrate on the matter at hand?"

"How come I've never heard about him?"

"He's a very private person who employs other people to do what he wants. Now pay attention, Angelina. Matternicht is sending one of his hatchet men here today, a Nigel Campion, to find out exactly what's happening in our storage facility. He's heard disturbing rumors."

"Rumors about what?"

"Don't be coy, Angelina. You know exactly about what. He's heard rumors that the Rushing River Carbon Storage Facility is not as secure as we like people to think. Campion will investigate..."

"And do what, exactly?" Roux asked. "Shut us down? That wouldn't be in anyone's best interests."

"I don't know what he'd do, but he expects our cooperation. I want you to go to your office and get hold of every bit of information we have on the history of CO_2 leakage and print it out."

"What? The whole fifteen years' worth? Everything, or only the trouble spots?"

"Everything. You think he's going to believe us if we only show him what we select?"

Roux left to start printing out the data from her personal computer. Peale ordered another cup of coffee from his secretary and tried to lose himself in his work, reading reports and attending to a multitude of minor issues. He had only marginal success as his mind kept returning to the problem of the leaks. At a little after eleven, Dr Roux returned with a thick sheaf of papers.

"That's it," she said, dropping the wad onto Peale's desk.

Peale eyed the printed pages with distaste. "I suppose we'd better go through it before he gets here."

"We could," Roux agreed, "But how much would make any sense to you? You're not a scientist, Peale."

"I'm well aware of that, Angelina, but I should be conversant with the overall results of your monitoring." Peale picked up the first set of stapled pages and started leafing through them. After a few moments, he gave up the pretense of understanding and tossed it back on the pile. "Explain it to me. In detail--as if I was ignorant of the whole business. I dare say Campion will want a full explanation."

Roux smiled contemptuously and sorted through the pile, taking out a summary page. "We've been testing selected sites around the sequestration site for about eighteen years--before we started operations. In the early days we did simple Draeger measurements, but after a few years we switched to the more accurate Wills & Halbert digital readers..."

"Why?"

"They're far more sensitive than the old Draeger testers."

"How do you do the testing?" Peale asked, not looking at her. "Do you just go to the site and take a reading?"

"Hardly. All you'd get would be the generalized atmospheric levels of CO_2. Any gas leaking to the surface would rapidly dissipate into the large volume of air out there..." Roux waved in the general direction of the window. "Any wind blowing--even a gentle breeze--would hasten the mixing. The Draeger testers in particular were designed to measure levels indoors, so we have to recreate those conditions. We carry a small collapsible plastic open-bottomed box of my own creation...I call it the Roux cube. You place the box out in the field and wait for an hour. Then you test the air inside the box. If CO_2 is leaking out of the soil, the level will rise in the box."

"That seems very time-consuming."

"It is, but not as much as you'd think. We carry a dozen boxes and we sample a dozen sites at a time. You set the box up, move onto the next site, and do the same there. When all dozen have been set out you go back to the first and take your reading, and so on."

"Alright, so how many sites do you test?"

"Forty-seven." Roux unfolded a paper map and smoothed it out, weighting the corners with objects from Peale's desk. "I've marked the sites in red. As you can see, there are several around the injection site, the others farther afield, but all within the confines of the Hood Anticline."

"And the reason for that is...?"

Angelina Roux produced a transparent overlay and positioned it over the map. "The central shaded area shows the approximate boundaries of the strata into which the liquid CO_2 is being pumped. The outer area is the area into which leaking gas may escape..."

"I don't see how it can escape there if the storage area is in here." Peale tapped the map. "I'm Campion, remember. Explain it as you would to him."

Roux sighed and took a piece of paper, quickly sketching the salient features which she pointed out as she drew. "Ground surface...underground storage area... Now imagine a leak here...if it didn't rise through rock and soil vertically, it could spread inward thus...or outward like that. This area here is the spread zone. See?"

"Very good. You know, a three-dimensional model of this would look great in the foyer. It's very simple to understand."

"As you can see, most of the sampling sites are in this spread zone or the central area."

"And these ones out here? And here?"

"They cover a few geological anomalies that affect the surface rock layers. It was considered unlikely that any leaking gas would find its way that far, but better to be safe than sorry."

Peale studied the map. "And which are you?"

"I don't understand the question."

"Are you safe or sorry?"

"Damn it Peale. You of all people should know this site is safe. Nothing's going to happen. I'd know about it by now."

"Okay, okay, it's the sort of question Campion might ask. So that covers the placing of the sites and the way you measure the gas content. Now we come to it. What have you found?"

"There's leakage. We've always known there would be--rocks are porous after all--but perhaps we didn't anticipate the scale of the leakage."

"What? I was under the distinct impression everything was under control. Have you been misleading me?"

"No, I haven't. Everything's under control. We've lost, in the last fifteen years, only about two million tons of liquid carbon dioxide."

"Jesus! Two million tons? Are you serious? I had no idea it was so much. I thought it was only one percent or something like that. Why wasn't I told sooner?"

"Relax. You obviously don't understand. Two million tons is less than one per cent of the total pumped underground. That's well within DOE guidelines. The gas is leaking slowly out of thousands of microscopic pores and cracks in the cap rock and seeping up through the overlying strata. This is all perfectly normal and expected."

Peale grunted and examined the map again. "If it's all so normal and expected, why have you become concerned about some of the testing sites? When that reporter came round last week, you were worried enough to come to me. That doesn't sound like a situation under control."

"You and I know it's safe, but all we need is some busybody reporter blowing things out of proportion and we're in trouble. That's why I came to you."

"So, we've never had any serious problems? You'd be prepared to tell Campion that?"

"I would be quite happy to tell him about sites TH2 and 3, and RC2," Roux said carefully. "If you remember, back in the early days we had some anomalous readings from those sites--CO_2 levels up as high as 4000 parts per million, but nothing came of them. They've since died down to normal levels."

"What about site BP4?" Peale tapped the map over the red-marked site. "You had a reading of 9000 there."

"Which I cut by a factor of five in my report. It's high, I grant you, but I've no reason to suppose it's anything more than just a temporary hiccup."

"And if it isn't?"

Dr Roux did not meet Peale's gaze. Instead, she flicked imaginary lint off her jacket. "What's the worst that can happen? The leak gets bigger and we have to cap it."

"Cap it?"

"Same sort of thing the oil and gas people do when they want to seal off a well. They pump tons of mud and concrete down and seal it so there are no leaks."

"And that would work?"

"I imagine so. Nobody's actually tried it but I can't see why not. The principle is the same, after all."

"No danger of...oh, an explosion, say?

Roux uttered a small superior laugh. "You really don't know any science, do you? Carbon dioxide puts out fires. There's no chance of an explosion."

"But it's toxic."

"Only in very high levels--five per cent or higher. Below that, you get breathless and dizzy but you'd have enough time to get clear."

"But it could kill?"

"You're thinking of the tourists on the hiking trail. There's no proof that was carbon dioxide poisoning."

"And the cattle on the Rushing River Ranch. Three dead in May, another five last week."

"Also, not attributable to carbon dioxide."

"Yet. What about when the medical examiner comes out with his report?"

Roux shrugged. "Who's to say where the carbon dioxide came from? CO_2 from our storage strata is exactly the same as any other source of CO_2. You'd have a damn hard job proving it came from us."

"Where else would it come from?"

"Hell, I don't know. Volcanic gases maybe--we're in a volcanic area. That's not the point, Peale. We don't have to prove it didn't come from us--they have to prove it did."

"What about if we have to cap the leaks--say the one at BP4. It's going to look strange if we're denying culpability but going to the enormous expense of capping a leak."

"We'll cross that bridge when we come to it. Marc Stone has never objected to us going onto his land for testing and sampling. I daresay he'll be amenable to letting us on to control a problem without letting the world know about it."

"Maybe not if he's losing cattle because of our leaks."

"So compensate him."

"And admit liability?"

"Hell, Peale, that's your problem. I just deal with the scientific aspects. Work with your PR department, that's what it's there for. Give Stone a good neighbor grant or something, whatever it takes. Just keep them sweet."

Peale started leafing through the pile of papers on his desk. "Is this going to convince Campion?"

"Convince him of what? Why is he coming? If it's because he thinks Rushing River is about to become a liability, this will convince him it's not. The Sequestration Plant and the storage area in the Hood Anticline are as safe as they ever were. Relax, Peale, there's nothing to find. We're okay."

Chapter 29

August 20, 2030

Matt pulled up in front of the Rushing River Sheriff's Office on Main Street. He turned and looked at Annaliese. "We need to do this," he said.

"Alright, if you say so, but I didn't see a gun, only that you knocked him over and drove away."

"And now I'm reporting it. Look, I don't know what's up but that man saw you and went for his gun. I think that's worth telling the cops about."

Annaliese nodded reluctantly and got out of the car, then followed Matt inside the building. He walked up to the counter and asked to speak to the sheriff.

"What's it concerning, sir?" asked the trooper at the counter.

"I'm not sure really," Matt said, "But this man tried to hold us up with a gun."

A few minutes later, Sheriff Jack Warner had Matt and Annaliese inside his office and was taking down a statement.

"...that's it," Matt concluded. "I hit the accelerator and we got out of there."

Sheriff Warner looked at Annaliese. "Did you recognize the man, Ms Winton?"

Annaliese shook her head. "I've never seen him before."

"Would you recognize him if you saw him again?"

"Possibly."

Warner sighed and looked at the notes he had taken. "So, we have a man of average height, hair color possibly brown, eye color unknown, with no obvious distinguishing features except a hand gun in his pants, and a light-colored car of unknown make but possibly Japanese, and unknown registration. You're not giving me much to go on."

Matt shrugged. "I'm sorry; we were a bit busy escaping to take notes. Look, Sheriff, I don't expect you to make an arrest but we thought you should know. It's possible he'll be looking for us when we head back to Portland tonight."

"I'll send a trooper out to take a look, but unless you hurt him when you knocked him over, I doubt he'll find anything. If someone was out to mug you, he'll be long gone."

Matt stood. "Well, thank you for your time, Sheriff."

Warner leaned back in his chair and looked up at Matt. "Of course, if my trooper finds him injured or dead, and no gun, you might find yourself up on charges, Dr Morrison." He looked across to Annaliese. "Please don't leave Rushing River without notifying me."

Annaliese nodded and got up. "We'll do that, Sheriff."

"What's your business in Rushing River? Where are you going to be if I need to get hold of you?"

"Rushing River Ranch," Matt said.

"The Ranch," Annaliese said simultaneously. They looked at each other.

Warner got up and came around the desk. "I know the Stones," he said. "You behave yourselves there, got it?"

Annaliese waited until they were back in the car before asking, "You're going to the Ranch? That's where I'm going."

"No kidding? Why?"

Annaliese considered her answer for a few moments. "I'm a reporter. I'm interested in the deaths over the weekend. Margaret Stone invited me to come and see her. And you?"

"She called the USGS office worried that carbon dioxide gas was erupting on her land. I offered to come and talk it over with her."

"That's quite a coincidence."

"Perhaps," Matt said. He started the car and pulled out, driving through the township and onto the road that led to the ranch. Annaliese called ahead to tell Margaret they were close, and by the time they arrived outside the ranch house, she was on the front porch ready to welcome them.

"I didn't expect to see you arrive together," Margaret said with a smile. "Do you know each other?"

"Her car broke down so I gave her a lift," Matt said.

"And yes, we do know each other," Annaliese added. Matt looked at her strangely.

Margaret ushered them into the living room and bustled into the kitchen to make coffee. Matt asked, "We know each other? Before today?"

Annaliese smiled. "You don't remember."

"I'm sure I've met you, or seen you at least, but I don't recall the name Winton...oh, of course, it's your married name."

Annaliese inclined her head. "Harding. Annaliese Harding...2015...the opening of the Rushing River Sequestration Plant."

"Good God." Matt blushed and grinned uncertainly. "It is you. How the hell are you? Uh...I...meant to call you..."

"Water under the bridge. I could as easily have called you."

"Coffee, black or green tea?" Margaret called out from the kitchen.

"Coffee for me, please," Matt called back.

"And me."

"So...what have you been up to? You're married?"

"Was. It didn't work out but I have a great son. And I'm still a reporter."

"I'm sorry...that's great...I mean..."

Margaret rescued him by coming into the living room with a tray laden with cups of coffee for her visitors, a jug of cream, sugar, a green tea for herself, and a plate of lemon cream cookies. She fussed about for a few minutes, making sure everyone had what they wanted and were seated comfortably.

"Now, what have you got to tell me?"

Annaliese put down her coffee. "I thought you had something to tell me. That's what you said in your email. About the tourists?"

"Oh, yes, of course. Silly me. It's Dr Morrison who has something to tell me, but we'll do your news first, shall we. Now, let's see...oh, yes. Our vet, Pat McGugan, said that our cattle died of asphyxiation, most probably carbon dioxide poisoning... and he thinks the tourists did, too."

"Would he make a statement to that effect, do you think?" Annaliese asked.

"You'd have to ask him but I don't see why not."

"Did the vet examine the bodies of the tourists?" Matt asked. "Otherwise, how can he possibly say it was the same cause?"

"He said he talked to the medical examiner."

"Yes, I talked to him this morning."

"You did? How did you get to talk to him and I couldn't?" Annaliese complained.

"The community of science," Matt said with a grin. "He knew I was after the information for professional reasons, not just to write a story."

"Reporting the news is professional," Annaliese said with a sniff. "Why did you want to know anyway?"

"I'll get to that. Mrs Stone..."

"Margaret."

"...Margaret. So, you've reason to believe carbon dioxide killed some cattle on your property, and also three tourists?"

"Eight head of cattle and four people."

"Four? Who's the other one?"

"A hiker back in May. Actually, I can't be sure how he died as we just found his remains a few weeks later. It was about the time three of our cattle died from unknown causes, so I think they might all be connected."

"Where on the ranch was this?"

"At the beaver pond north of here."

"Damn," Matt said with feeling. "I don't know whether to be pleased I was right or not. That's where we found high levels of carbon dioxide last week when we did that Draeger testing. Strictly, it was a bit farther on up the creek, but carbon dioxide is heavier than air; it would follow the contours of the land as it dissipated."

"Then the Sequestration Plant really is leaking?" Annaliese asked.

"Well, not the Plant so much as the underground storage strata."

"I thought the carbon dioxide came from a volcano," Margaret queried.

"No chance," Matt said.

"Oh."

"I'm sorry to put it so bluntly, Mrs...Margaret. The Cascades might be volcanic in origin but the land under you here isn't. It's made up of Quaternary rocks, layered in the formation known as the Hood Anticline. I can state quite definitely that you have no potential volcano on your property."

"Thank goodness for that. So, there's no possibility of having another Lake Nyos event happen here?"

"What's Lake Nyos?" Annaliese asked.

"It's a lake in Cameroon," Matt said quietly. "A deep crater lake. Carbon dioxide leaked up into it from a magma pocket deep in the earth and dissolved in the bottom layers of water. Then one night in 1986, the water in the lake turned over, suddenly releasing a cloud of CO_2 gas. Because it's heavier than air, the CO_2 travelled as a cloud down the valley for kilometers, snuffing out the lives of hundreds of humans and thousands of livestock."

"Whew. But that can't happen here?" Annaliese asked.

"There's no volcanic lake here."

"There's the beaver pond," Margaret said.

"No good. It's far too shallow and doesn't sit over a magma chamber. Take it from me, a Lake Nyos style eruption couldn't happen here."

Margaret sipped her tea and nibbled on a lemon cream cookie. "So where did the carbon dioxide come from that killed those people?"

"Only one place it can have come from," Matt said.

"The Rushing River Sequestration site," Annaliese finished.

Margaret looked at her two visitors. "What do we do? Report them?"

"We'd have a hard time proving it."

"Surely not?" Annaliese protested. "Where else could it come from?"

"Very true, but we'll still need hard proof, unless we get lucky enough to catch a major emission of gas as it happens...or unlucky enough."

"What do you mean?" Margaret asked.

"If we stood at ground zero, so to speak, when a cloud of CO_2 emerged, we'd have a couple of minutes to get clear--providing we recognized the symptoms. If it was really concentrated, we'd be dead before we knew anything was wrong."

Margaret's cup rattled in her saucer and she hurriedly put them down on the table. "I think I'd rather have an erupting volcano. At least they give you a bit more warning."

"I don't think you need to worry, Margaret," Annaliese said. "I think if you're out in the open, the gas can't collect enough to be dangerous."

Matt said nothing.

"Perhaps we should go to the Plant again and see if they'll stop pumping any more underground."

"I don't think that would help," Matt muttered. Then, "You've been there before?"

Annaliese nodded. "I asked some questions of their PR man and the chief scientist, Angelina Roux. They weren't exactly forthcoming, basically denying everything."

"What day was this?"

"Last Wednesday."

"Before the tourists died...or the cattle. Why were you asking questions then?"

Annaliese hesitated. "I...I'm not sure I should say."

"Protecting your sources, you mean?"

"No, not exactly...well, I don't actually know who my source is." She thought for a few moments and then exhaled her breath in a rush as she made up her mind. "I received two packages by courier that seemed to show that the Rushing River Sequestration site was leaking. Also, that someone had been fiddling the books, though I haven't looked at that aspect yet. I asked questions at the Plant and then I got a summons from my father-in-law, Andrew Winton..."

"He's your father-in-law?" Matt asked.

"Who's Andrew Winton?" Margaret added.

"A big-time entrepreneur in Oregon. He has fingers in a great many pies."

"Including the Salem Chronicle--the paper I work for," Annaliese went on. "Anyway, he summoned me and swore me to secrecy." She flushed. "I guess I've broken that promise."

"How did he know about the leaks?"

"Um...I told him. The packages were addressed to A. Winton, which could have been Andrew, so I told him. I'm sorry; it seemed like a reasonable thing to do at the time. I thought there might've been a good story in it and he's my boss at the paper. He said there was nothing to the documents and told me to keep quiet for six months."

"Shit. Why would he do that? What would he stand to gain? Does he have a stake in sequestration?"

"I think he does. He told me that several big contracts are about to be signed and that any doubt thrown on the safety of Rushing River could jeopardize everything."

"So he took the papers, I suppose."

"Yes, but my son made a copy." Annaliese dug into her purse and pulled out a single sheet of crumpled paper. "The others are at home." She handed it to Matt.

Matt looked it over, scanning the columns of figures. "These are carbon dioxide levels, no doubt about it, at various coded sites. SP, BP, PH, CC, RC...there's a dozen or so letter combinations, and figures. The first figure could be a sub-site, as in TH1, TH2 and so on, but there are six others that mean something...let's see..."

"Adrian said they were dates."

"Could be...month, day, year...last two range between 14 and 30...that would fit. Rushing River came on line in '15. First two numbers...none higher than 12, second two..." Matt looked up and grinned. "Who's Adrian?"

"My fourteen-year-old son."

"Smart kid. Did he say what the front letters meant?"

"No. He thought they were coded for a place."

"Okay, so what does TH stand for? Or SP? Or BP?"

"I suppose they'd be places around Rushing River," Margaret said. "Is there an RR?"

"No, but it's a good idea. Have the Plant scientists ever come onto the ranch to do tests or take samples?"

"Yes, quite regularly. I haven't always seen them but I'd say every couple of months."

"Do you know where they tested?"

"Not exactly. My husband would know, but I think it was mostly out toward Beaver Creek."

"Hmm, there's no BC. Is your husband around? Could we ask him?"

"Sorry, he's out until later today. You could come back."

"We have to get home tonight, but we might need to come out again tomorrow. Would that be alright?"

"Of course."

Matt and Annaliese took their leave of Margaret and drove back into town. They parked by a dingy diner in the main street and ordered soy burgers and salads, eating them in one of the booths overlooking the street. The burgers were barely edible, but the salad vegetables were crisp and tasty. They ate for several minutes before turning to their problems again.

"What do we do now?" Annaliese asked. "Go to the Sequestration site and demand answers?"

"Unfortunately, we're in no position to demand anything. I doubt they'd even let us through the gates. We need some evidence that CO_2 is leaking in dangerous amounts."

"The death of the tourists isn't enough? And the cattle?"

"Until the autopsy report is finalized, CO_2 poisoning is merely supposition," Matt pointed out.

"So, we sit back and do nothing?"

"I didn't say that, but there is probably little we can do today. We need to identify exactly where these sampling sites were and test them ourselves with certified equipment. I can at least get that from USGS. If the levels are higher than they should be, we can make an argument to shut the plant down, even temporarily, while more tests are conducted."

"So, we have to come back tomorrow and see Margaret's husband?"

"Yes. Can you make it?"

"I think so. I'll need to talk to the editor." Annaliese thought for a moment, creating doodles by pushing her finger through a scattering of sugar grains on the Formica surface of the table. "It might be easiest if I take a couple of days off work. I'm owed a bit of leave and that way nobody will ask awkward questions. What about you?"

"Yeah, I can get away. Look, there's damn all else we can do here today, so how about we see the sheriff and head back?"

"I hope the man with the gun isn't waiting for us."

The sheriff shrugged when they told him they were leaving Rushing River. He told them the trooper sent to investigate had found nothing except some scuffed gravel and a few tire treads on the road shoulder.

"Are you going to trace the tire prints?" Annaliese asked.

Sheriff Warner sighed. "I have few enough resources without chasing after wild geese. There are thousands of tires like that out there, and even if we found the right one, what crime has been committed?"

"He had a gun."

"So you say, and he'd no doubt deny it. Leave it, Ms Winton. Nothing's going to come of this."

The drive back to The Dalles was uneventful, though both Matt and Annaliese scrutinized every car they saw by the side of the road. Matt dropped her off at the car repair and offered to stick around for the hour it would take for her car to be fixed. Annaliese refused.

"I'll see you tomorrow, then?" Matt asked.

"Sure."

"You want me to pick you up? We can drive round together."

"Uh, Matt...look, you're a nice guy, but there's no 'together' in this. I'm a reporter and I've got an agenda that's different from yours."

"Okay, no sweat. I didn't mean...I just thought...well, okay, see you tomorrow." Matt turned away, his face burning.

Annaliese grimaced and called out after him. "Meet you at the diner--the greasy spoon--at ten."

Matt turned and grinned, lifting his thumbs in a salute before climbing into his car and driving away.

Chapter 30

August 20, 2030

Nigel Campion had set in motion a variety of enterprises before he climbed aboard the helicopter that would take him to the Rushing River Sequestration Plant. He knew the value of delegation and had built up a cadre of trusted lieutenants over the years, men who answered to him alone, and if anything went wrong, could be relied on to say nothing. In return for this loyalty, they were extremely well-paid and knew that their families would continue to be looked after if they became guests of the State penal system or reluctant visitors to the County Morgue.

One such lieutenant was Pietro Alvani who had the assignment of monitoring a reporter in Salem, called Annaliese Winton. His man on the spot, Albert Ruffin, had already revealed the woman was being indiscreet, so Pietro had given the order to terminate her. He should not have had to give the matter a second thought, but in the afternoon of the next day, the man called again.

"I couldn't complete. She was in company."

"Do it at her home, tonight. Make it look like a burglary gone wrong."

"She lives with her kid."

"You have a problem with that?"

"No."

Pietro Alvani sent a coded email to Campion, telling him the gist of the conversation, and turned his attention to other matters.

Another of Nigel Campion's lieutenants was Sam Liddell, a private detective. To him, he gave the assignment of tracking down Matternicht's scientific adviser, Professor Maxwell Hay. This proved to be a straightforward task as Max Hay had not gone into hiding, apparently being content to just avoid his usual haunts. Sam, accompanied by one of his assistants, caught up with his quarry at a Denny's Restaurant on Burbank Boulevard in Woodland Hills.

* * *

Max looked up with faint alarm as two burly men slid into the booth next to him. His heart beat a little faster when one of the men drew his jacket back to reveal a holstered gun. A glance across at the busy restaurant told him this was unlikely to be a common mugging, so he decided to try and extricate himself.

"You...you're welcome to the booth, gentlemen. I was just about to leave." Max dabbed at his mouth with his napkin before folding it and placing it by his plate. "I can recommend the chicken salad." He started to slide across his seat, but neither man moved to let him out.

"Just stay where you are for the moment, Mr Hay," one of the men said.

"Ah, you know me, so you must come from Matternicht. Well, it'll do you no good. I'm protected."

"I wouldn't know about that, Mr Hay. I just have orders to escort you to Mr Matternicht. It wasn't actually stated, but I'm guessing he wanted you unharmed. However, one way or another, I'll carry out my task."

"Then I've no choice. However, since you don't require my booth for yourselves, I believe I'll finish my lunch. You're welcome to join me." Max lifted his hand and attracted the attention of the waitress. "A slice of your delectable blueberry pie, please, and a latte."

The man who had spoken shrugged and ordered two black coffees. He sat and stared at Max as he slowly worked his way through the pie and drank his coffee. When Max's cup was eventually pushed away, he set his own undrunk coffee to one side and moved out of the booth

"After you, Mr Hay. Please don't try anything funny. I'd hate to see you hurt."

"So, no jokes or comic quips allowed? Where are we going?"

"Out of the door, then left across the car park to a dark blue Lincoln. Then we take a ride. Mr Matternicht wants to see you."

They turned south out of Burbank and ascended the hills along Topanga Canyon Boulevard, the State Forest on their left. A little past the summit, Sam, who was driving, turned left onto an unpaved road leading deeper into the hills. A few hundred yards brought them to a padlocked gate manned by a guard with an automatic rifle. The guard nodded at Sam and unlocked the gate, letting them through. Another twist and a turn of the gravel road revealed a beautifully constructed timber home with a hazy view of the distant Pacific.

Max followed his captors into the house and after a short wait was shown into a small but well-stocked library. Sitting in an over-stuffed leather armchair was James Matternicht.

"Ah, Max," he whispered. "It was good of you to come."

Max gave a wry smile. "How could I refuse?"

"Thank you, Sam. Would you leave us please?"

"Do you think I ought to, Mr Matternicht?" Sam Liddell looked meaningfully at Max.

"I'll be perfectly safe with Max. Whatever else he may do, he won't offer me physical violence. Tell them, Max."

"I won't harm Mr Matternicht."

Sam and his assistant withdrew from the library and shut the door behind them. Matternicht waved his hand feebly toward a drinks cabinet at one end of the room.

"Help yourself to a drink, Max. I'll have my usual."

Max crossed to the mahogany cabinet and folded back the lid. He found the thermostatically controlled flask and poured exactly five fluid ounces of soymilk into a tumbler, poured himself a dry ginger ale and brought the glasses back to his employer. He handed the milk to Matternicht and sat down in an armchair opposite.

"Ishkabibble," Max said, lifting his glass and sipping.

Matternicht smiled and lifted his glass, though he did not drink. "San fairy ann," he replied. He carefully put his glass on a side table. "I was dismayed that you'd turn on me, Max. I thought we were friends."

"Friends," Max mused. "An interesting concept. Certainly we've known each other a long time. We have an employer-employee relationship, I've been at your beck and call for most of my adult life, and we've shared dark secrets, conspired to deceive the world and make you obscenely rich. I wouldn't call what we have friendship."

"I've been generous, haven't I?"

"Certainly. You made sure my loyalty was bought and stayed bought."

"Until now."

"Yes."

"Why now? What has changed?"

"The world has changed. You've changed. I've changed."

"Pah. Life is change. I thought better of you."

"Can't you see that what we're doing is selfish and will ultimately bring ruin on the world?"

"I didn't take you for a liberal, Max." Matternicht lifted his glass from the table and brought it to his lips. When he replaced it, a thin rim of white clung to his upper lip for a few moments until a tongue that looked out of place in such a skeletal face licked it off. "Why should we care about the world? Neither of us has family we care much for."

Max frowned. "You've a daughter and grandsons. Do you care nothing for them? Don't you worry about the world they'll inherit?"

"They're concerned with nothing but material pleasures," Matternicht said contemptuously. "They'll inherit more money than they could ever spend, so why should I spare them a moment's thought? My legacy is greater than family, greater than most nations. I've put together a business empire greater than any that have gone before." He laughed dryly. "Even Wal-Mart and Apple sit in my shade."

"But what's the point of all this? You suck the world dry of its resources but you hoard your gains jealously. What have you ever done for the world?"

"I gave it an abundance of cheap electrical power, millions of jobs, boosted the economies of many nations. How dare you say I've done nothing?"

"But it's all window dressing, Herr Matternicht, you know that. The foundation of your empire is coal, one of the greatest pollutants to mar this planet's beauty. The world took its first faltering steps on the path to clean, renewable energy--solar, wind, hydroelectric, even nuclear--but you cut the economic ground from under them by promoting coal. You promised a way to continue to use coal for another generation by burying the waste products. It could never be more than a short term solution..."

"And one that was embraced wholeheartedly by governments."

"Of course it was. Politicians aren't noted for their farsightedness and clarity of vision. Most can see no farther than the next election, and cheap power was always going to be a vote catcher. Particularly when you promised there would be no damaging waste products."

Matternicht shrugged bony shoulders. "I was right, wasn't I? We've invested fifteen years demonstrating that Carbon Sequestration works, not just in the tiny pilot projects so beloved of administrations around the world, but in a massive injection of liquid carbon dioxide deep underground by a power station that not only supplies power for a million people but removes nearly all of its waste from the environment. I call that a success, and the United States Government calls it a success, too, so who are you to say otherwise? In six months' time--no more-- contracts will be signed that proliferate sequestration stations like the one at Rushing River throughout the States and the rest of the world. Not only will this be immensely profitable for all our investors, but we will, for the first time, push the carbon dioxide levels in the atmosphere back down to manageable levels."

Max sipped at his ginger ale. "You're starting to believe your own press releases," he commented. "Yet you know that underground sequestration is no more than a pipe dream. It's not working and may very well be dangerous."

"Of course it works. Rushing River is sequestering more than fifty thousand tons a day."

"And how much is leaking out? Do you even know?"

"I'm told that the amounts are negligible. Less than one percent in fifteen years."

"Actually, it's closer to two percent a year."

"Even so, the amounts are tiny."

"Two percent means that in fifty years, all the carbon dioxide now down there will have leaked out. We promised to sequester it forever, but in fifty years it'll be as if we did nothing. In the meantime, because of our promise, the world forgot about clean power and put all their eggs in our coal basket. When the CO_2 levels start soaring, it'll be too late. Can you live with that?"

Matternicht laughed and dissolved into a coughing fit. For several minutes he fought for breath, his face red and tears streaming down his cheeks. When he had recovered enough, he wheezed, "I won't have to, and neither will you. Besides, you paint too black a picture. Sequestration technology will improve and all the gas that escapes today will be captured tomorrow. Especially when we have a hundred, a thousand plants capturing carbon dioxide."

"It's dangerous."

"Nonsense."

"Three people...possibly four...have died in Rushing River from carbon dioxide escaping from the storage layers."

"That cannot be proven...and I'd seriously warn you against spreading rumors."

Max smiled. "They won't be rumors when I present the evidence."

Matternicht sipped at his soymilk again and considered the other man. "Why are you doing this?"

"I thought I'd made that clear, Herr Matternicht. I cannot allow this scam, this confidence trick, to continue any longer. If you remember, I first raised my concerns two years ago, but you ignored me..."

"Not ignored, Max. I examined your ideas and dismissed them."

Max shrugged. "It came to the same thing. This time I'll stop you."

"You really think you can?"

"At the moment, Rushing River is the only operational sequestration facility. I'll go to the Governor and present my evidence. At the very least, he'll shut the facility down while checks are made. Those checks will reveal the truth."

"It would be very easy to remove you from the equation, Max."

"So much for friendship. I anticipated that and have deposited a copy of all the evidence needed to shut you down with a lawyer. With or without me, the truth will out."

"Very clever, Max, but lamentably predictable." Matternicht withdrew a slim folder from between his bony shanks and the arm of his chair and held it out. "Do you mean this? Deposited at the Sacramento offices of Morgan, Aarons and Wyzicki?"

Max frowned. He reached out and took the proffered file and opened it, leafing through it rapidly. "How did you get this?" he asked.

Matternicht drained his milk and placed the glass back onto the side table. "Money brings power, Max, and I'm very rich, remember? Lawyers are as greedy as any other sector of society." He licked his lips and watched Max with a predatory eye. "I rather think I have the upper hand now. What's to stop me disposing of you...?" He stopped and stared because Max was now smiling.

"Where's the other copy, Herr Matternicht?"

"Other copy?"

"One copy in an obvious place, one in a hidden place. I should congratulate you on tracking down the obvious copy so swiftly, but...well, it wasn't really too hard to figure out, was it? I play golf with David Aarons after all."

"I think you're bluffing. There is no second copy. I was watching you. I saw your reaction."

Max grinned. "Yes, I might be, but can you take the chance? Shall I tell you what will happen now, Herr Matternicht? You'll get your affairs in order and come with me on the 23rd when I see the Governor of Oregon. Together, we'll ask him to launch an official investigation into Rushing River."

"I can think of no compelling reason to do so," Matternicht rasped. "I'm not going to destroy everything I've worked for."

"Then you'll be seen as culpable instead of public-spirited. Think about it. If you co-operate there's a possibility you may salvage something. Humanity still needs cheap power and they still need a carbon capture system. Put your billions to work and find a lasting solution."

"I may be better off having you removed, Max, and spending a smaller sum blackening your name. I could come out of this looking like a hero. My lawyers could tie up your documents for years and, even if they were released, without you there to defend them, I could make you look like a fool."

Max shrugged and got up, brushing down his trouser legs. "You have until the 23rd, Herr Matternicht. Please do the right thing." He walked to the door and opened it.

Sam Liddell looked in. "Boss?"

"Take Mr Hay back to where you found him, please. I've no further use for him."

Chapter 31

August 20, 2030

nnaliese arrived back in Salem around four and went straight to the Chronicle. She marched through into Simon's office and demanded the next day off. Simon ignored her until he had corrected the page he was working on, then pushed aside his mouse and stared up at her.

"You've got to do some work around here sometime. It's what we pay you for."

"I do work. I emailed a stack of finished articles to you."

"I thought Winton gave you that piece on price fixing. How's that going?"

"It's progressing. So, can I have tomorrow off?"

"Research, I suppose."

Annaliese nodded, telling herself it was true--just not in the way Simon thought.

"Okay, but this article had better be your best."

"Thanks, Simon. It will be."

Annaliese did some shopping on the way home and arrived back at just after six. She let herself in and called out "I'm home," as she lugged the groceries through to the kitchen. Adrian came down from his room and perched on a stool as she pushed her purse to the back of the counter and put the shopping away.

"How was school?"

"Okay...you know."

"No, I don't. That's why I'm asking."

"It was okay, mom. Nothing special. How was your day?"

Annaliese paused, wondering whether she should tell him or not. *He's my son, he deserves the truth.* "I went out to Rushing River. It's true, Adey, just like those papers said. The gas is leaking out and it's killed three people, maybe four."

"Awesome." Adrian saw the expression on his mother's face and hurried to correct himself. "Awesome as in exciting, mom, obviously not a good thing. How did you find out?"

"I went out to the Ranch--remember I told you about Margaret Stone--and she told us about the medical examiner and the vet and what they said."

"Us?"

"Oh...uh, Dr Morrison, a structural geologist from the USGS. He was out there, too, looking for the same thing. We went to the ranch together."

"So, what are you going to do?"

Annaliese blushed. "Nothing, Adey. Just because I know him from years ago doesn't mean we're..." She saw the grin on her son's face and blushed more deeply. "You mean about the gas, don't you?"

"Yes, I did, mom, but if you'd rather talk about Dr Morrison...what's his first name?"

"Matt. And to answer your question, we are going back tomorrow to take some air samples and see if we can't find some evidence of our own."

"Can I come?"

"You've got school."

"Yeah, but hey, I'd be learning investigative journalism and structural geology, so it wouldn't be wasted time."

"Nice try, Adey, but school's more important."

Adrian acquiesced with good grace and set the table while his mother thawed out two steaks, cooked a couple of potatoes in their skins in the microwave, and put together a small salad of lettuce, cherry tomatoes and red onion rings with a drizzle of crushed garlic in olive oil. When it was ready, they split the potatoes and applied the filling of their choice--plain yogurt for Annaliese, butter and horseradish for Adrian.

"Mrs Patel across the street said you had a visitor this afternoon," Adrian said around a mouthful of steak. "It must have been before I got home from school."

"Did he leave a message or anything?"

"Uh-uh. Peered in a window, knocked on the door and left. Mrs Patel was thinking about calling the police but he left. Would he be one of your informants, mom?"

"You've been watching too many holovids. I don't have informants, only pain-in-the-neck editors. Did Mrs Patel say what he looked like?"

"No, just a guy in a suit."

Annaliese laughed. "Not one of my editors then. Ice cream?"

They cleared away the dishes and Annaliese spooned out generous portions of chocolate ice cream, which they carried into the living room and ate in front of the wall screen TV. The news was its usual litany of bad news--murders, robberies, fraud and accidents, and Annaliese found her mind wandering back to something she found altogether more interesting, a certain young--*not so young now*--geologist who had reappeared in her life.

A knock at the door disturbed her reverie and she got up to see who it was. Her hand was on the doorknob when she realized the front porch light was out and the light from the street lamp barely illuminated her front door. She peered through the peephole and saw a shadowed man standing there.

"Who is it?" she called out.

"Delivery, ma'am."

Something in the voice made her uneasy. "Just leave it on the step."

"Gotta sign for it, ma'am."

"Who is it, mom?"

"I don't know," she answered in a hoarse whisper. "He says he has a package. I think it might be the man who came earlier."

"You going to open the door and find out? Maybe you won a million bucks."

"What company are you with?" she asked the unseen man.

"UPS, ma'am."

"Right." Annaliese looked through the peephole again but saw nothing more revealing. *This is stupid.* Her hand went to the doorknob again.

"Hang on, mom," Adrian called out and then a few moments later, "Oh shit, he saw me."

"What?"

"I looked out the living room window and he saw me. That's no UPS delivery man, though."

"He must think us awfully rude..." The front door shook as something slammed into it. Annaliese stared and then another blow sent splinters flying from the door jamb. "Get back," Annaliese screamed. She turned and hustled Adrian ahead of her toward the back of the house. A third blow splintered the door jamb and the door hung lop-sided from its hinges. She heard a muffled oath behind her as she slammed the connecting door behind her, slipping the catch.

"Who is it?" Adrian yelled. "What does he want?"

The connecting door shivered under a heavy blow. Annaliese grabbed hold of her son and backed away, toward the kitchen.

"I think it's the man who tried to stop us today. He had a gun."

"What man? Shit, mom, we have to call the police."

"The phone's back there in the living room."

The connecting door shook and splintered. Annaliese and Adrian ran into the kitchen. Thoughts crowded Annaliese's mind, threatening to overwhelm her decision-making ability. *Should we run outside? Is he alone? Does he really have a gun? Have neighbors already called the police? Maybe he doesn't want to harm us. Should I attempt to reason with him?* A voice cut through into her consciousness.

"Mom! What do we do?"

The connecting door crashed to the floor amid sounds of swearing and breaking glass. A man appeared at the kitchen doorway, red and sweating, his jacket disheveled and pushed back to reveal a holster, and a black snub-nosed gun clutched in his hand.

Annaliese grabbed the dirty dishes from the bench and threw them at the man, who batted them aside, swearing as a fork pricked him in one cheek. He raised the gun but Adrian threw one of the kitchen stools which missed but made the man jump aside. The gun came up again. Annaliese snatched up a heavy skillet and ran forward, swinging it awkwardly.

The gun went off, deafening in the confined space of the kitchen. The skillet rang and slammed back into Annaliese's face, knocking her to the floor. Her head still ringing with the noise, she rolled over onto her back, her vision blurred and unfocused. A foot nudged her and she forced her eyes to focus on the huge barrel of the gun as the man slowly lined up on her head.

There was a chunking sound like a blunt axe biting into wood and the man collapsed on top of her, the gun skittering across the floor and ending up wedged half under the refrigerator. Annaliese pushed the man off with an effort and hauled herself to her knees. She looked at an ashen-faced boy holding a bottle of wine by the neck.

"Is he dead?" Adrian whispered.

Annaliese resisted the urge to say she hoped he was and shook her head, whimpering softly as a wave of pain washed through her.

"Are you sure you didn't hit me with that bottle?" she asked.

"The bullet. It hit the skillet. I thought you were dead."

Annaliese heard the trembling in her son's voice and was on her feet, enfolding him in her arms, soothing him. The bottle fell and, having survived a forceful blow to a man's cranium, shattered on the hardwood floor, splashing their legs with newly-wooded chardonnay.

"We'd better call the police." Annaliese started toward the front of the house, but Adrian held her back.

"What if there are two of them? He could be waiting for us."

"Out the back way then. We can call from a neighbor's house."

Annaliese picked up her purse on the way out of the back door. She almost switched on the outside light but remembered at the last moment to keep the surroundings dark. They walked on the grass, holding hands and keeping to the shadows, as they moved round the side of the house. The muted sounds of the neighborhood were strange in their ears after the events of the last few minutes, and Annaliese found it hard to imagine how the sound of splintering doors, a scream or two and a gunshot could go unremarked. Somewhere behind them a television blared and off to the right a dog barked mindlessly, but apart from those hints, they might have been in a lifeless zone.

"I think we should risk the car," Annaliese whispered. "We need to get right away from here."

"Starting it could bring his buddy running."

"There are no cars on the street, so if there is someone else here he's hidden. We could run into him or be surprised by him just walking to a neighbor's door. I say we get into the car quietly and let the handbrake off. It'll roll back onto the street and I'll start it there. I think it's our best chance, Adey."

"Okay, mom. Whatever you say."

They ran quickly to the car but instead of opening the front doors, they climbed into the back and then over the seats. The dome light thus remained dark. Annaliese let the handbrake off and gravity slowly pulled them down the gentle incline toward the road.

"I don't see anyone," Adrian said. "Go for it, mom."

Annaliese started up, slammed the car into gear and stamped on the accelerator. The vehicle leapt forward with a squeal of tires. She did not slow or turn on the headlights until they were a block away.

"Is anyone following us?"

"There are a couple of cars but they are way back and going slowly...one's turned off. I think we're okay, mom."

"Okay." She drove slowly toward the city center, merging with the evening traffic. "I'm not quite sure what to do, Adey. I thought the police, but now I'm not sure."

"Why not?"

"A man almost waylaid Matt and me on our way round to Rushing River this morning. Matt said he had a gun and he...he looked a bit like that guy back there. If that man back there was the same man...and I think he was, then he's not a simple mugger or thief. He broke in to try and kill me and I have to ask the question 'Why?' I've just written that story on corruption in the Portland Water Authority and maybe I angered somebody." Annaliese shook her head. "But enough to kill? It doesn't seem likely." She pondered the problem. "Or it's something connected with..."

"With what?" Adrian asked after a few moments.

"With the leaks at Rushing River, but it can't be that. Your grandfather's involved but I can't imagine he's angry enough to...to..."

Adrian grinned. "To get somebody to whack you?"

"It's not funny. If you hadn't hit him with that wine bottle..." Her body shook and Adrian scooted across and put his arm around his mother.

"I'm sorry, mom, you're right, it is serious. So, what do we do? If not the police, then what? We can't just go home."

"No. If the man's dead then we have some explaining to do, and if he's not he could be waiting for us."

"You really think he's from the Water Authority?"

"No, but I can't imagine who else might want to hurt me, except perhaps some old ladies from the Baking Guild." Annaliese giggled. "I really ripped into their recipes a few weeks ago."

"Now who's being funny?" Adrian grinned again and lightly punched his mother's arm. "Seriously though, where can we go?"

Annaliese shook her head. "This is all unreal. I can't believe it's happening."

"Mom. Focus. Where can we go?"

"To gramps. I can't think of anyone else."

"Even if he's involved?"

"Who else is there? Besides, we're family, aren't we?"

Andrew Winton lived on the outskirts of Salem, where the land started to rise toward the Cascades. The suburb was select and the houses old, but they reeked of money. Each was set back from the road and screened from one another by remnants of old broadleaf forest, left by the original developers a hundred years before.

Annaliese pulled into the long curving driveway and parked. Lights were on in the downstairs rooms, so she knew Andrew was still awake. They got out and she rang the doorbell.

Andrew answered the door himself. He looked at Annaliese without expression, and then flicked his gaze past her to take in a movement in the night. He saw Adrian and smiled.

"Adrian, my boy. Come in." He stood aside for his daughter-in-law and patted his grandson on the shoulder. "What are you doing out here--and at this time of night?"

"We had a break in, gramps!"

"What? You're alright though? Not injured? Have the police caught him yet?"

"It's a bit more complex," Annaliese said.

Andrew looked hard at her and then at his grandson. He nodded. "Go into the library." He pointed the way. "Patterson!"

A man appeared as if by magic, slight and well-dressed, his manner self-possessed rather than subservient. "You called, sir."

"A pot of coffee to the library. Two cups and...and a Pepsi. Tall glass and a straw."

The man slipped back into the shadows to the rear of the house, and Winton followed his grandson into the library.

"Alright, take a seat and tell me what this is all about. You had a break in, you said?"

"That's right," Adrian said immediately.

Andrew held his hand up. "In a moment Adrian. I want to hear this from your mother. Something doesn't quite smell right."

"You're right, Andrew. A man broke in and tried to kill us, but we killed him instead."

Andrew stared at her. "What did the police say?"

"We didn't call them."

"Why not?"

Annaliese took a deep breath and exhaled raggedly. "Because he broke in to kill me. He battered down the front door and came at us with a gun. It was a mix of blind luck and Adrian's bravery that saved me."

Andrew looked at his grandson with warmth in his eyes. Then his gaze hardened as he looked back at Annaliese. "You should've contacted the police." He got up and left the room, returning after a few minutes. "The police had already been called by neighbors, but they found no one in your house, alive or dead. I know Lieutenant Dodson down at police headquarters. He told me."

"Thank you, Andrew." Annaliese reached out and squeezed her son's hand. "It's a relief to know we didn't kill anyone."

"Why would he be trying to kill you?" Andrew asked.

"I hoped you could tell me."

"Me? How the hell would I know?"

Annaliese just looked at Andrew.

The library door opened and Patterson entered bearing a tray with coffee and a tall glass of Pepsi. He put the tray down and poured coffee, serving Annaliese and Andrew, and then passing the cold tumbler to Adrian.

"Will there be anything else, sir?" When Andrew shook his head, he turned and left, closing the door firmly behind him.

"I repeat, how the hell would I know why someone tried to kill you? Perhaps it was just a guy breaking in who got carried away."

"It couldn't be that, gramps," Adrian put in. "Mom recognized him as the man who tried to attack her this morning in Rushing River."

Andrew turned a stony gaze on his daughter-in-law. "Is this true?"

Annaliese nodded.

"You went round to Rushing River after I specifically asked you not to?"

"Gramps, that's not the point..."

"Be quiet, Adrian. Grown-up talk. Annaliese, did you disobey me?"

"Damn it, Andrew, there's one hell of a lot more to this story than you led me to believe. People are dying..."

"Enough, Annaliese." Andrew turned to Adrian. "Please leave us for a few minutes, Adrian. There are some things I need to discuss with your mother."

"If it's about the leaking gas, I already know."

"You told him?" Andrew's voice dropped several degrees. "What the fuck were you thinking?"

"Please don't use such language..."

"I'll use whatever fucking language I like in my own home. You fool, Annaliese. You just couldn't leave it alone, could you? You've absolutely no idea who you're dealing with. If you've interfered with their schemes, these people won't rest until you're dead. Jesus, Annaliese, it's not just you--you've involved my only grandson and now his life is endangered, too."

"What do you mean? Who are you talking about? Do you know these people?"

Andrew ran his hands through his silvery hair. "Yes, I know them, they're business associates and they're totally committed to their goals. I tried to warn you off in the gentlest way possible, but you had to stick your nose in. Now they want you dead and they'll take Adrian out, too."

Adrian stared at his grandfather, eyes wide. "You're responsible for the killer?"

"No, not me. I wouldn't harm a hair on your head Adrian. Nor on your mother's," he added. "But the people who have invested in Rushing River stand to lose millions--billions even--and they can be quite ruthless."

"But if you know them you can stop them, can't you, gramps?"

"Maybe I can, Adrian, but it'll take time. You need to disappear--you and your mother. Let me think...you need to get out of here tonight, before they can regroup and try again. The West Coast is no good--their power base is here. It'll have to be the East or the Mid-West, depending on the availability of flights."

"I can't just run away," Annaliese protested. "This whole thing is wrong, Andrew, people are dying. We have to expose them."

"I can't do that, Annaliese, and you don't realize the power behind them. They can literally make and break governments. If they find you they'll kill you and hang the consequences."

"So you help us, Andrew. Help us by exposing them to the world. You know these people and you have friends in high places. You even know the Governor. You could do this with us..."

Andrew seemed to deflate as if someone had pushed a pin into him. He rested his head in one hand and looked away. "You don't understand. I'm leaving, too. I'm getting out while I still can. Tomorrow."

"You were leaving and not telling us? Not even saying goodbye to Adey?"

"You're both well provided for. I've opened accounts and put generous amounts in..."

"To hell with the money, Andrew. What sort of example are you setting for your grandson? You make your money and then skip out when things get tough? If you think your colleagues are wrong you should stand up to them."

Andrew shook his head and his eyes glinted with frustration. "You just don't understand. We cannot stand against Matternicht. Not alone; not together."

"That's the man who wants us dead?"

"Yes."

"Then we go to the police with his name, print his name in the paper, get on the Web..."

"Hit the forums, the chats, open a blog, surf the cloud," Adrian put in.

"...do anything we have to..."

"Then you do it, Annaliese. Tomorrow morning, Adrian and I will fly out of here. I can at least ensure his safety."

"I'm staying with mom, gramps."

"Adrian, leave this to the grown-ups."

"I'm not a kid, gramps. I read those papers, I know what's going on in Rushing River and I know that if those leaks aren't sealed, more people will die."

"How the hell can you know that? Don't believe everything your mother says."

"I'm cloud savvy, gramps. I know my way around the virtual world as well as anyone, and I keep my eyes open. This sort of thing has happened before, hasn't it? You knew about it--you and this Matternicht guy--and you're covering up."

"What are you talking about?"

"Krasnorovka in Russia."

Andrew shook his head. "Means nothing to me."

"Three years ago. The Russians had their own carbon sequestration unit, a fraction the size of Rushing River but growing, and then one day it disappeared. The power station shut down, the area was cordoned off, and a news blackout enveloped the whole country. Even satellites could only see unbroken cloud cover. When it cleared--nothing."

"So how do you know?" Annaliese asked.

"Blogs, investigative forums. Once information is posted, it's there forever. You can't keep secrets."

"Rumor and paranoia," Andrew said.

"Maybe, but what if something really did happen? What if there was a large gas leak that wiped out the town of Krasnorovka? The same thing could happen to any of a dozen other prototype carbon sequestration sites around the world-- Britain, Norway, Germany, Italy, India, China, Australia. None of them have been operating long or are nearly as big as Oregon's effort, but hundreds or even thousands of people could die if they leaked. And what if Rushing River experiences a massive leak? What then?"

"Why didn't you tell me this before, Adey?"

"Didn't want to worry you, mom. But, hey, we have to speak out now, don't we?"

"Well, Andrew, what's it going to be?" Annaliese asked. "Are you with us, or do we do this alone?"

Chapter 32

August 21, 2030

Annaliese and Adrian had gone to sleep in the guest bedrooms upstairs, but Andrew Winton sat up in his study, thinking. He had been noncommittal with his daughter-in-law and grandson, avoiding throwing his support behind them in their battle against Matternicht.

They don't know who they're dealing with. Matternicht will never give up. Andrew poured himself another single malt, taking it back to his armchair by the cold hearth. He weighed up his options--*stay and fight an unwinnable fight, or cut my losses and run? I've never gone against him in my life and I've only known half a dozen men who have--and they're dead. But would he let me go? Or would he come after me?* He picked up the vid-phone and tapped in a number.

"Yes?"

"James Matternicht, please."

"Mr Matternicht is not available. I suggest you contact one of his aides during normal business hours."

"Put me onto his aide now."

"I'm sorry, sir; you'll have to call back during normal..."

"Tell him it's Andrew Winton."

There was silence on the line for a moment, then, "Please hold." Minutes passed and the silence at the other end of the connection was so complete,

Andrew started to wonder if he had been cut off. At last a series of clicks and faint scrapes alerted him that his wait was coming to an end.

"Campion here. Why are you calling?"

"Is this line secure?"

"Yes."

"You've taken out a contract on my daughter-in-law and grandson. I want that contract removed."

"Winton, you're being melodramatic. This isn't some Hollywood Mafia movie. I don't take out 'contracts'."

"You deny a man tried to kill them both this evening?"

"How can I deny what I have no knowledge of?"

"Matternicht would not act except through you. The order must have come from you. Admit it."

"Let me pose a hypothetical scenario, Winton. Imagine someone had information that could cost you everything you'd worked for, and was threatening to go public with this information. How would you react?"

"That's not the same..."

"It's exactly the same. Make a choice, Winton. Cut her free or lose everything. And, by the way, I'm aware you're liquidating your assets. Don't think you can flee your responsibilities. We'll find you."

"My grandson..."

"Can be safe. It all depends on you."

"You promise my grandson will be spared?"

"Yes, but not your daughter-in-law, unless you can absolutely guarantee her silence."

"Yes, yes I can."

"If you guarantee her silence and she talks, your grandson won't be protected--neither will you."

"I'll do my best."

"Your best is not good enough."

"Then...then do what you must but...don't traumatize him more than necessary."

"You must separate them."

"I...I'll do it."

"There's one other task we have for you, Winton. You must contact Max Hay again and agree to go to the Governor with him. Say what you must to convince him you've had a change of heart."

"You're kidding. Why would I want to precipitate the thing that would ruin us?"

"You'll have incontrovertible evidence that Max Hay is insane and that the process is safe. I'll get this to you in the next day or so."

"What evidence is this? Why haven't I heard about it before?"

"Need to know, Winton." The amusement in Campion's voice was evident. "Do your job and leave the planning to me." He broke the connection.

Andrew put his head in his hands and thought of his only son Peter--his sole link with the future. He knew Peter was a womanizer and a drunkard and according to his latest information was down in Mexico somewhere, living the high life on his allowance. Andrew had never liked his daughter-in-law Annaliese, and was not completely sure why. Perhaps it was because she showed little interest in the comforts that money could bring, preferring to work to provide for her son. She had raised her son--his grandson--alone, and had done an excellent job. He was all that a man could want, though still lacking the killer instinct that would make him the perfect successor to the Winton Empire. That would come, though. All he needed was the proper training.

Perhaps this is my opportunity to prise him from his mother's apron strings. What will persuade them to separate?

He picked up the phone and called another number. When the connection opened, the screen was dark, shadowy.

"Max? Andrew here."

A bedside light came on, revealing an old, bleary-eyed man in pajamas, sitting up in a rumpled bed. "Jesus, Andrew. Do you know what time it is?" He yawned.

"Yes. I'll come with you on the 23rd."

There was silence for a few moments as Max stared at the tiny image in his phone. "Alright, I didn't see that coming. Why, Andrew? You were none too keen the other day. In fact, I got the impression you were stalling for time."

Andrew shrugged. "Perhaps I was, but I've changed my mind."

"May I ask what changed it?"

"The old man is out of control. He has to be stopped."

"Yes, but he's been that for some time. What changed your mind now?"

Andrew looked away. "He tried to kill my grandson."

"Why on earth would he do that?"

"My daughter-in-law started an investigation of Rushing River, even after I warned her off, so he took a contract out on her. His man nearly killed both of them."

Max shook his head in sympathy. "He won't stop until he gets what he wants--unless we stop him."

"That's what I want."

"Good man. Bring everything you can on the management of Rushing River and the cover-up of the leakages. I've set up the appointment for ten in the morning."

"Why do I need to bring anything?" Andrew asked. "I thought you had it all."

"I do, but it'll be more convincing if it comes from two sources."

"You'd better watch your back, Max. If Matternicht gets to you, that's it. I'm not doing this alone."

"I'll be fine, Andrew. He's already tried and failed."

"I don't believe it. He never fails."

Max laughed. "There's a first time for everything." He became serious again. "Remember, 10 a.m. on the 23rd. Don't be late or you'll be tarred with the same brush as Matternicht." He cut the connection and the screen went dark.

Chapter 33

August 21, 2030

The argument that erupted in the dining room of Andrew Winton's house that morning seemed to thoroughly discomfort Patterson. Used to the calm and ordered service of a predictable man, Andrew's servant was visibly shaken by Annaliese's disrespect. Breakfast had started amicably enough with honey-cured Canadian bacon, free-range eggs and pancakes with genuine New England maple syrup. For several minutes there was little sound except the noises of people enjoying good food. Patterson hovered, coffee-pot in one hand, ready to refill cups, and a jug of freshly squeezed orange juice in the other to top up glasses.

"I made a few phone calls last night," Andrew said. He sopped up a smear of syrup with a piece of pancake and popped it into his mouth. "I think I have your problem solved. We can get you out of sight of this man who's trying to kill you."

"Uh-huh." Annaliese chewed on the last of her bacon. She drained her cup and Patterson darted forward to refill it. "I was doing some thinking, too. I'm going to follow up on this carbon storage story, full steam ahead. Once it's published, there'll be no cause to kill me."

Andrew scowled. "And what about Adrian while you're doing this foolhardy thing?"

"I'm helping mom."

"No, you're not, Adey. It's too dangerous. You're going to stay with Uncle Bill and Aunt Katie over in St Louis."

"No, I'm not, mom."

"I think that's a damn good idea," Andrew said. "As I was saying, I made some phone calls and I can move you up to Portland, Annaliese. You can use an office of mine up there and start some online digging. I'll be able to give you some good leads for your background research. Adrian can go up with you and fly out of Troutdale. A small airport like that won't be watched."

"No way."

Annaliese grimaced at her rebellious son. "And what'll you be doing, Andrew? I take it you've decided to join us?"

Andrew nodded. "It seems like the right thing to do. I'm going to go into my office here in Salem and try and get hold of Matternicht. I hope to be able to prove to him that you're no threat, and to take the contract off."

"You see, mom? There's no good reason for me to run away."

"No, Adrian, your mother's right. You should be out of harm's way until things are settled."

"Well, for once we agree, Andrew, but I think I could do more if I went round to Rushing River again. You know the CEO there, don't you? You could get me in to do some interviews."

"What makes you think I know the CEO at Rushing River? Anyway, that's a damn fool idea. I can't think of anything more likely to attract unwelcome notice."

"Of course you know him." Annaliese frowned. "I've seen a picture of you shaking his hand--in your waiting room. Robert Peale."

"Ah, yes, of course. I just don't think that's a sensible course of action. Stay away from Rushing River, Annaliese; at least until we know what's going on."

"We know what's going on," Annaliese declared. "At least, we've got a pretty good idea. The carbon storage facility at Rushing River is leaking and there's a cover-up. We've just got to figure out why, and who is involved."

"Go mom." Adrian helped himself to another pancake and smothered it in maple syrup. "We know this Metternich person is involved..."

"Matternicht," Andrew murmured.

"Right, Matternicht. He wouldn't be trying to kill you if it wasn't something terribly important to him. Who else have we got? The CEO at the facility? He must be involved. If there's a bad leak he must know."

Annaliese stared at her father-in-law, her coffee cup halfway to her lips. "And you know Robert Peale," she said. "What's your involvement in this? I know you told me that contracts are to be signed soon that will mean a lot for Oregon business, but what do you gain? What're you covering up?"

"Jesus, woman, you'll be accusing me of taking the contract out on you next."

"No, I don't think you'd do that, Andrew. God knows there's no love lost between us, but you'd never risk your grandson finding out."

"Well, thank you for your vote of confidence. May I also point out that if I was so closely involved in a cover-up, I would scarcely be helping you."

"That's true," Annaliese conceded.

"And, what's more, I'll be calling in favors, doing my utmost to plead with the person I think might be behind this, to call off the contract. If I was covering my tracks, I'd just let him go ahead and kill you."

"Gramps..."

"It's alright, Adrian. I'm just trying to make your mother see that I really am on her side...and yours."

Annaliese sipped at her coffee and considered his words. She had to admit they made sense. "Alright, Andrew, you've made your point. I apologize for doubting you."

"Accepted, Annaliese. Now, let's get moving. We have to get you to Portland and Adrian to the airport."

"Hang on; I've a couple more questions. If I'm going to be quietly researching this, I need to be sure of my basics. You've explained to me why doubt cast on the Rushing River facility could jeopardize future contracts, but why is safety being put second to profit?"

"It's not. If there was any actual danger to the public..."

"People have died."

"But the link has not been proven. Look, Annaliese, a scare story at this time could shut down the whole deal, and throw the economy of the US into chaos. If the story is based on insufficient research, that's all it will be--a scare story. And that's not good journalism. Do your research, write your story, but let me edit it before it's published."

"So you can...what? Cover up the truth? Make your pals look good?"

"Damn it, no. Listen to what I'm saying. A scare story will cause panic and shatter confidence in the economy. Write a fair and balanced piece and I'll persuade people to do a full investigation. An official one. That's fair, isn't it?"

"But you must know the truth about the leaks if you're so intimately involved."

Andrew shook his head wearily. "I only know what I've been told--that the leaks are minor. I'm a businessman, not a scientist. If a scientist tells me it's not a problem, I tend to believe him..." Andrew smiled. "...same as he'd be likely to take my advice if I talked to him about stocks and shares." He looked at his watch. "Now, really, you should be making a move."

Annaliese and Adrian washed and tidied themselves before meeting Andrew and Patterson at the front door.

"Patterson will drive you in my car," Andrew said. "He'll drop you off at my Portland office and then take Adrian on to Troutdale airport." He handed each of them a thick envelope. "A bit of cash I had on hand. You can't go back to your house until all this is sorted, so you'll need to buy clothes and things. Don't use your credit card in case there's a watch on it." Adrian immediately opened his envelope and looked inside.

"Thanks, Andrew, but I'm using my car. I need mobility."

"I imagine the killer knows your car. You'd be safer leaving it here."

Annaliese shook her head. "I know, and I appreciate the offer, Andrew, but I'm using my car. I'm not going to let these bastards rule my life."

"Then I'll have Patterson take Adrian to the airport. You can follow him to my office first."

"That's a waste of time and effort. I'll take Adrian myself."

"I can't allow..."

"Don't I get any say in this?" Adrian complained. "Thanks for the big bucks, gramps, but I should be with mom. Besides, I'd rather say goodbye to her than to Patterson...no offense, Patterson."

"None taken, young sir."

"Very well. If you must." Andrew scowled at not getting his way. He took a card out of his wallet and handed it across. "That's the address of my Portland office. It's not well known and is only tenuously connected to me. Use the garage to get your car out of sight. There's a computer terminal there..." He took the card back and jotted down some letters and numbers on the back. "That's the password for the computer, also the garage and security. It's an encrypted line, so you should be untraceable for the next few days. Do your research and email me daily so I know you're okay."

"Thanks, Andrew. I appreciate it." Annaliese gave her father-in-law a quick and rather stiff hug. "Come on, Adey."

"Thanks, gramps."

"Take care, Adrian. Let me know when you get to St Louis."

Annaliese drove out onto the road carefully, after checking for any suspicious looking vehicles. Unfortunately, there were several cars parked near there and she was unfamiliar with the normal pattern of cars, so she could not reach any useful conclusions. She drove away, watching in her rear-view mirror for anyone tailing them. No one was and she relaxed.

They drove north on Highway 5 and Adrian was quiet, staring out of the window at the distant Cascades and the towering bulk of Mt Hood. As they neared Portland, he stirred.

"Mom, I don't want to go to St Louis."

"Oh? What do you want to do?"

"Help you track down the baddies. I could be useful. I'm great with search engines and..."

"Whoa, Adey," Annaliese laughed. "You're not going anywhere. I had to agree with your gramps but there's no way I'm letting you out of my sight. I'll phone the paper and your school this morning and we'll drop out of sight for a few days."

"Awesome!" He looked sideways at his mother. "What about food and stuff?"

"We'll do a bit of shopping this afternoon." Annaliese patted the envelope in her jacket pocket. "Andrew gave us money to be going on with."

Andrew's office was in a select area of Forest Park, in the hills west of Portland. The building itself was small and set back from the road in the midst of manicured lawns and neatly-pruned trees. Mirrored glass reflected back the wooded surroundings and hid the insides. Adrian punched in the password to a keypad and waited until his mother drove into the garage before pressing the close button and ducking under the descending door.

The office was small but luxurious, with a two-bedroom apartment above it. They explored the cupboards and closets and found them well-stocked with cutlery, crockery and linen, but no food beyond instant coffee, tea-bags, creamer and water crackers. Annaliese put the kettle on and chewed on a slightly stale cracker while the water heated.

"I'll get some shopping in," she called out to Adrian, who had gone downstairs to the office. "Anything special you want?"

"Chocolate ice-cream."

"You got it." Annaliese checked her purse for the envelope of money from Andrew. "I shouldn't be long. Don't answer the phone. I'll beep the horn when I get back and you can open the garage door."

"Okay, mom."

In fact, it was close to midday when she returned. Adrian waited for her in the garage and helped her carry her purchases upstairs. As well as a full raft of groceries, she had bought toiletries and a few changes of clothing for both of them. Adrian grabbed a pair of jeans, a tee-shirt and underwear and headed for the shower while Annaliese made them a cheese and tomato omelet for lunch.

"So, what did you do while I was out?" Annaliese asked later, when he'd returned.

Adrian swallowed his mouthful of omelet. "I changed the combination on the entrance locks." He shrugged at his mother's questioning look. "I just feel safer if nobody else knows it. I can always change it back when we leave. Anyway, then I started the online search, looking for Matternicht."

"What did you find?"

"Not much. There's a lot of hearsay and rumor, but nothing concrete. He was born in Austria in 1943 and he either owns or controls a heap of companies, mostly related to coal, oil, and power--or so people say. Nobody really knows much about him, though. That's the problem. He's so secretive it looks like he's managed to scrub his presence from the Internet."

"What about the Rushing River facility?"

"I haven't got there yet. We need to make a list of things to look for. What about this friend of yours from the USGS--Matt? He could probably save us a search for the geology of the area."

"Oh, sh...sugar," Annaliese said, automatically looking at her watch. "I promised to meet him hours ago." She pulled out her cell phone and tapped out his number. It beeped and informed her that the number she was calling was blocked or switched off. "Damn, we were going to meet and investigate the facility. Now he'll be doing that without me."

"You could text him."

Annaliese nodded and sent Matt a quick text apologizing for missing her appointment and asking him to call her or email her when he got the message.

"What now?" Adrian asked.

"We continue with our search. I think we can safely leave matters geological for Matt. He's trained in the subject and anything we learned would probably be fairly basic. We need to concentrate on Matternicht, Rushing River...what else?"

"Oregon Coal & Power? Oregon Energy? They own the facility."

"Good. The CEO out there--Robert Peale."

"Liquified carbon dioxide."

"Good point. Anything else?"

"Krasnorovka."

"What?"

"Krasnorovka. You remember. I told you about that site in Russia that disappeared. It may be related."

"Okay, add it. Also look up carbon capture, carbon sequestration, hell, even coal. We need to get a handle on the scale of this thing."

Adrian jotted down notes on a pad. "What are you going to be doing while I'm hard at work?"

Annaliese gave her son a hug. "I'll do some searching on the phone. I'll call a few people I know and see if there's anything on our break-in and the killer."

Chapter 34

August 21, 2030

Matt arrived at the Rushing River diner promptly at ten, eager to renew his acquaintanceship with Annaliese. He noted her car was not parked outside on the street, so went inside to wait for her. He ordered coffee and a slice of pecan pie, sitting at a window overlooking the street. The minutes dragged out into half an hour, and then an hour without any sign of her.

The waitress came over to refill his cup twice, the second time saying, "Waiting for someone, hon?"

Matt looked up. "Yeah, an out-of-towner. About five-nine, slim build, brunette. I don't suppose she came in earlier?"

"Sorry, hon. You want some more pie?" She looked at the clock. "It's a bit early but I could have the cook fix you a burger if you want."

"Thanks, but just the pie."

When the waitress returned with the pie, Matt noted her name tag. "Have you lived in Rushing River long, Nicole?"

"Most of my life, hon."

"It looks like a nice place. Friendly, and none of the pace of the city."

"It's nice enough. You from Portland, hon?"

"Yes, and it's Matt. Terrible about those dead tourists over the weekend."

Nicole nodded, then looked at him suspiciously. "Are you a reporter?"

189

Matt smiled and shook his head. "No. I'm up here doing some measurements of the gases in the air."

"For the carbon storage plant? I see the guys from there sometimes, with their boxes and tubes, wandering all over the countryside. I always wondered what they were doing."

"Well, the facility stores carbon dioxide underground, so they have to check whether any of it is leaking out. Have you heard any stories of gas leaks?"

"You'll have to excuse me, hon, there's a customer waiting." Nicole sauntered away, pulling her notepad from her apron pocket.

Damn, was I too direct? Matt started eating his second slice of pie, but pushed it away half eaten, and sipped at his coffee. *I can't wait much longer for Annaliese. Pity, I was looking forward to seeing her.* He indulged in a fantasy for a few minutes.

"Sorry, hon, you were saying?" Nicole was back. "Something about gas leaks?"

Matt smiled. "I was just wondering if there'd been any stories about gas escaping from the ground."

"Can't say as how I've heard of any, hon. Is that what killed the tourists?"

"It's possible."

"You don't say. Could this here gas kill animals, too?"

"Certainly. Some cattle died on the ranch, probably from the gas. Have you heard of any other animal deaths?"

"My kitty Pearl died last fall. Not a mark on her. Found her at the bottom of the garden. Sleeping, I thought. Still, she was nearly fifteen."

"Interesting, but as you say, that's a good age for a cat. Whereabouts was this? In the town?"

Nicole gave him a long considering look before nodding. "Take the south road about half a mile. There's a tall oak split by lightning on your right. A little further along and opposite, there's a series of four houses. Mine's the second one."

"Thanks. Do you mind if I go round and take a few air samples from the bottom of your garden?"

"Knock yourself out, hon." Nicole tore off a page of her notebook and slipped it under his pie plate before walking back to the kitchen. It was the bill.

Matt put twelve dollars on the table to cover the pie and coffee and added a generous tip. He smiled and waved at Nicole as he left the diner, but she was busy with another customer and did not respond.

Out on the street, he looked around in case Annaliese had arrived without him seeing, but the only people visible were locals. He drove south, looking for the sky-blasted oak. Nicole's house was neat but unassuming, with the yards of the four houses running together without fences, the boundaries cursorily outlined by shrubs and different patterns of grass mowing.

A woman came out of the last house in the row and stared at Matt as he started toward Nicole's back yard, so he detoured over to her.

"Hi, I'm Dr Morrison," he said. "USGS. I'm here to do some gas measurements."

"She hasn't got gas," the woman said. "None of us do. Only electric."

"Not that type of gas," Matt said. "It's part of an environmental study, looking at possible pollutants in the air."

"Won't find any around here. The air's clean, or haven't you noticed?"

Matt smiled broadly. "I know, it's really lovely round here, but we need to sample clean air, too, so we can see the difference. Nicole at the diner said I could sample in her back yard."

"I suppose that's okay then. You can test my yard, too, if you like."

"Well, thank you, ma'am. That would be very helpful." Matt followed the woman into her back yard and made a big show of unpacking his meter and holding it at various heights, carefully writing down the results in a notebook.

"That's all there is to it?" asked the woman, her tone reflecting disappointment. "Thought there'd be more to this scientific stuff."

"That's because your air is so pure, ma'am. In the city, my measurements would probably set off an alarm."

"That'd be something to see."

"Sure is, ma'am. Well, I dare say Nicole's yard will be the same, but I'd better check it, seeing as I told her I would." He started to walk across the next-door yard, and then turned back. "Ma'am, Nicole said her cat died last year. I don't suppose you know of any other dead animals, do you?"

"Only raccoons and squirrels on the road. Except there was a squirrel dead under that tree..." she pointed, "...about the same time. Figured he fell out of the tree and busted his neck."

"Well, thanks, ma'am. I'd better get on and make these measurements then."

The readings were very similar to those taken in the suspicious woman's yard. Matt had brought a Wills & Halbert electronic digital carbon dioxide measurement meter that showed the CO_2 content of the air in parts per million. The readings were not continuous but a tiny pump sucked air into the meter when he pressed a button. After ten seconds, a figure appeared on the LCD screen. There were three range levels, and so far, the lowest, which measured between zero and one thousand parts per million, had been sufficient. If he wandered into a pool of carbon dioxide, he would need the middle range--between one thousand and ten thousand parts per million. He sincerely hoped he would not walk into a high range pocket as it was possible he would not remain conscious long enough to take the reading.

There was little danger where he was standing though. The back yards sloped down slightly toward the line of shrubs at the edge of the property, and from there fell away more sharply to a fence and pasture beyond, where cattle grazed. The meter gave readings of between 430 and 449...*nowhere near enough to kill a kitty. And nowhere for a heavy gas to collect.*

He packed up and got back into his vehicle, waving to the suspicious woman as he turned and headed into town. The road to the storage facility was just south of the town, and on a whim he turned down it. A mile or so brought him to a locked gate. He sat in the vehicle and looked through at extensive rail yards and a number of freight trains unloading tons of coal into huge hoppers. Moving belts carried the coal in a continuous stream into the power station and huge cooling towers belched white steam into the skies. The carbon capture and storage facility sat alongside, nearest to the locked gate, and looked strangely deserted compared to the hum and bustle of the other parts.

Bloody hell, what a mess. I'd never have guessed all this was here. They've certainly kept it well hidden. I don't remember it was half as big when I was here fifteen years ago.

Matt got out and shouldered his bag. He went to the gatehouse and pushed the buzzer. "Hi," he said to the guard. He identified himself and asked to talk to their scientist.

The guard spoke into the phone and then pointed up the drive toward a glass and steel building. "Head on up there. They're expecting you."

Matt found a tall woman in a spotless lab coat waiting for him at the entrance to the building. He held out his hand and she shook it politely.

"Dr Morrison. I'm Dr Angelina Roux, Head of Science. The guard said USGS. Is this an official visit? We usually get warning."

"No, nothing like that. Is Twentyman still here? I think I spoke to him a few years back."

"Dr Twentyman retired twelve years ago." Dr Roux's eyes narrowed. "I think I remember a Dr Morrison from the opening. You were asking a lot of questions then."

"Still asking," Matt said with a grin. "I have 'satiable curtiosity'." He saw the woman's blank look and explained. "The Elephant's Child...Rudyard Kipling..." No sign of comprehension lit her face and Matt sighed. "Sorry, just my sense of humor."

"So what is it you want, Dr Morrison? I'm very busy."

"I was wondering if I could have a look at your recent readings for carbon dioxide in the atmosphere."

"And why would you want that?"

"Well, just checking. There have been rumors of leaks."

"There are always leaks." Roux said coldly. "They're negligible."

"I certainly hope so, but if I could have a look at your results...?"

"Is this an official USGS request?"

Matt shook his head.

"Then I must refuse. Now, if you'll excuse me..." Roux turned to go.

"One other thing, Dr Roux. Do you mind if I take a few measurements myself? I brought my own Wills & Halbert meter."

"Out of the question."

"Even if it would lay those rumors to rest?"

Dr Roux hesitated, frowning. "What's to stop you claiming they were higher and fuelling the rumors?"

"Come with me. Show me your sites, let me take the readings and you verify the results. If there's nothing to worry about you'll have independent results confirming your position."

"Wait here." Roux turned and entered the building, leaving Matt outside. He sat on the steps and pulled out his meter, taking a recording. It was 449 parts per million. A few minutes later, Roux came back out. She had changed into a jacket and wore boots with her tailored slacks. In one hand she carried a Wills & Halbert meter. "I saw you take a reading. What did you get?"

"449."

Roux pressed the button on her own meter and read off the result. "449. At least your meter is accurate."

Matt smiled. "Okay then, Dr Roux, lead on...or may I call you Angelina?"

"I think we'll keep this professional, Dr Morrison." She led the geologist toward the carbon capture machinery. "This is station CC1."

"CC stands for carbon capture?"

"Yes."

"Ah, I wondered." Matt tried to think of the sites Annaliese had mentioned as having high levels of carbon dioxide, but could not recall them. He took a reading. "460."

"461," Roux confirmed. "You'd expect it to be higher near the source, but it is still well within standard errors."

They moved over to the pump house where the compressed carbon dioxide was liquefied and pumped underground through a massively reinforced bore hole.

"Site PH2. I get 472 parts per million. This is where you'd expect the most leakage to occur and it is minor."

Matt nodded. "469."

The other side of the pump house was site PH1 and the readings were similar. Dr Roux led the way across the grounds, halting every now and then to display a site and take a reading. "Rail yards RY4 and 5. Readings of 452 and 448."

"Confirmed," Matt said.

A dozen sites later, Roux put away her meter and led Matt back to the main gate. "As you can see, there are no high readings. The rumors you heard are just that, malicious gossip. I hope you'll tell people what we just found, Dr Morrison."

"What about sites outside the facility? How often do you check those?"

"Every two months. Results are consistently low."

"So, a reading of 1,790 would be..."

"Fabricated."

"I found a level of 900 last week with a Draeger tube."

"They are notoriously inaccurate outside. They are designed for use within buildings. I'm surprised you even bothered."

"It was near the place where the tourists died," he persisted.

"I can't see how they're related."

"Carbon dioxide poisoning. Just a coincidence?"

"Dr Morrison, I'd be very careful what allegations you make. There's no cause of death recorded for those unfortunate people, and even if there was, there's nothing to tie it to this facility."

Matt remembered one of the codes Annaliese mentioned. "Where would a site referred to as BP4 be?"

"No idea. It's not one of ours. Now, you'll have to excuse me, Dr Morrison. I have work to do." Dr Roux walked away, leaving the guard to escort Matt from the grounds.

Matt sat in his vehicle and pondered his course of action. *There's no apparent leak near the site, but something killed that family and the cattle on the ranch. And I measured high levels there. Time to measure it more accurately, I think.*

He put his car into gear and headed for the Stone's Ranch. Marc was busy somewhere else, but Margaret came out to greet him as he pulled up outside the house. She expressed disappointment that Annaliese had not come with him.

"She was going to, but I guess something must have come up. I was wondering if I could take a few measurements along the creek beds."

"Of course, Matt. If you can wait a few moments, I'll come with you. I could do with a walk."

Several minutes later, Margaret came out dressed for a walk through pastures, in jeans, boots and jacket, with a wide-brimmed hat. She led the way through the gate into the first paddock, laughing at Matt's discomfiture as a herd of steers trotted over to investigate.

"I can see you're a town lad. All you need is a firm hand. They won't stand up to you, you know." She demonstrated, by walking directly at the largest one. It waited until she was a dozen paces away before breaking and plunging away. "They're really quite sweet-natured. I bottle-fed some of these when their mothers died."

They passed through the fields without incident and came out on the slopes above the beaver pond. They stood and looked down at the tranquil scene for a few minutes before walking down to the edge of the pond, a light breeze rippling the nodding grass. Little blue butterflies danced in the grass and a bird called from the stand of aspens on the far side of the pond.

"I was thinking about those codes Annaliese had," Margaret said. "I think BP might stand for Beaver Pond."

"That would fit," Matt agreed. "I was at the facility just now and the scientist there confirmed that the letters stood for places. She denied there was a BP though."

"So you think this is where those high levels were recorded? Around the Beaver Pond?"

"Looks like it." Matt took out his Wills & Halbert meter and took a reading. "Nothing out of the ordinary here at the moment." He showed Margaret the reading of 425 parts per million and explained how the meter worked. "An average figure is around 450, but it could be a bit lower around forest and farmland."

"The hiker was found here, too," Margaret observed. "Just over here, I think." She walked over to a spot near the pond.

Matt squatted and took another reading at the indicated spot, but the carbon dioxide level was the same. They walked around the pond and upstream, Matt leading the way to the gully where the Maher family had died. Police tape still fluttered forlornly from trees and fence, but Matt ducked under and stepped into the sunken depression, taking a reading every few steps.

"Normal. Maybe slightly elevated, but nothing that couldn't be accounted for by bacterial action." He climbed out. "Whatever killed them has dissipated."

"It's a strange looking depression, isn't it?" Margaret said. "I mean, the gully is fairly ordinary but this conical depression looks odd." She looked at Matt. "Or is this geologically common?"

Matt shook his head. "It looks like the ground slumped away. I've seen it in limestone country where groundwater eats away the underlying rock. The ground then collapses and you get a sink hole."

"Is that what happened here?"

"I don't think so. There's limestone, but it's a long way down, and wouldn't cause this. I suppose an underground stream could have this effect, but...well, look, I'm not sure, but..." Matt looked embarrassed. "Sorry, I'm really just thinking aloud. I don't know why this depression formed." He turned and made his way back to the creek that fed the beaver pond.

Margaret pointed at the water as they emerged from the gully at the head of the pond. "Look, it's all muddy and stirred up. It wasn't like that before, was it?

I'd have noticed." She started down toward the water's edge but Matt reached out and stopped her.

"Wait. Let me go first." Matt pulled out his meter again and measured the carbon dioxide content of the air. He frowned. "560. Please, stay here while I check this out. He advanced to the edge of the pond and tested the air again. "Damn, 810."

"What does it mean?" Margaret called out.

"I think some carbon dioxide has leaked out below the pond."

"Is it dangerous?"

"Not at these levels." Matt looked around him, wondering what to do next. He bit his lip and then took a deep breath, squatting by the water's edge and pressed the button on his meter. A squeal from the device almost made him drop it and he stood up hurriedly.

"What is it? What happened?"

"I don't...oh, I think I was using the wrong scale." He switched to the medium range and tried again. The instrument squealed again and he switched to high range, staring at the figure on the LCD screen. "Dear God," he muttered. "13,900." He stood and moved back to where Margaret was waiting. "We need to get back, but we shouldn't go down the valley any farther. Levels are high here-- not dangerous--but there may be pockets down there. It'll be flowing down anyway."

"The town is downstream," Margaret said. "Are they in danger?"

"I don't think so. The gas will have dissipated by the time it gets that far, but I'll phone the sheriff when we get back to my car."

Margaret found a way up the walls of the valley and they cut across elevated pastures, back to the ranch house. Matt immediately called the sheriff and explained the situation, warning him that if anyone felt ill or short of breath, they should seek higher ground. The sheriff did not sound convinced and thanked him curtly before cutting the connection. Matt's next call was to Dr Roux at the Rushing River facility. After a short delay, his call was transferred to her laboratory.

"What do you want, Dr Morrison?"

"Thought you might like to know, there's been a leakage and this time it's no rumor. I was there when it happened and I recorded a value of 13,900 parts per million."

"You're lying...where?"

"The Beaver Pond on the Stones' Ranch. You knew, didn't you? That's the BP site that had the high values."

"I know nothing of the sort, but thank you for calling." Dr Roux rang off.

Matt bid farewell to Margaret, telling her not to worry. "There may be people round to take measurements. Please let them do so. I'll be back tomorrow or the day after. I have to get back to the USGS and talk to some people. We have to figure out what needs to be done."

Chapter 35

August 21, 2030

"Oh, Jesus, no." Peale stared at the report Dr Roux had just put on his desk. It outlined the findings of a quick expedition she and an assistant had made to the Rushing River Ranch that afternoon. "There must be some mistake."

"None at all," Roux said. "I took the measurements myself."

"So these figures..." Peale tapped the sheet of paper, "...are accurate?"

"Yes. The pond was muddy and disturbed; there were dead fish and frogs around the margins and at least one dead water bird."

"What type? A duck?"

"How the hell should I know? I'm not an ornithologist. And what does it matter anyway? Even with a light breeze blowing and getting there an hour or so after the eruption, I still recorded mid-range values in excess of 2000 parts per million. I have no doubt it was much higher earlier."

"So, we really do have a leak?"

"This is more than a leak."

"What do you mean?"

"A leak implies a gradual percolation of gas upward through the overburden, slowly accumulating until dangerous levels are reached. Such a slow seepage would give animals and people time to get away and certainly wouldn't stir up the mud in the pond. That was caused by a bubble of gas escaping."

"I don't see the problem," Peale complained. "Whether it's a slow seepage or a bubble, what harm can it do unless you're unlucky enough to be sitting by the pond? We just put up a fence to keep people away."

"If it was a leak in a pipe or an underground chamber, that might be something we could get away with--for a while at least--but this is something much more serious. Look..." Dr Roux took a pen from her lab coat pocket and started sketching on a piece of paper. "This is a cross-section through the earth...the surface...here's the anticline with millions of tons of compressed carbon dioxide sitting in it. The facility is here, south of centre, and here's Beaver Pond on the northern margin. Now, imagine a very small, almost hairline crack in the capping rock down here...gas escapes, works its way through the earth and out. We're lucky it's not a continuous process--obviously something crumbled or slumped and blocked the crack, otherwise the gas would just continue to pour out. Then the pressure of the gas clears the crack--or a new one forms near this zone of weakness--and another burst of gas escapes. Again, we're lucky; the overburden collapses and blocks the crack. It happens once more...and blocks. How many times can this go on? How many times before the overburden is insufficient to contain what's stored down there?"

Peale looked at the sketch and then at his chief scientist. "Am I supposed to know that?"

"No." Roux shook her head in exasperation. "That's just my point--nobody knows. This slow gas release and block could continue for years or it could just give way suddenly."

"Then what happens?"

"I don't know. Nobody knows. It's never happened."

"Well then, perhaps it never will..."

"Nobody has ever stored anything like this amount of liquid carbon dioxide in rock strata before. It's under extreme pressure and if enough escapes to lighten the overburden..."

"You keep mentioning that. What is overburden?"

"If you don't understand something, ask immediately. Don't pretend you understand if you don't."

"Well, there's no need to be so damn patronizing. Just because I don't have a PhD..."

"Overburden is just the total soil and rock that lies on top of a particular geological feature--in this case the Hood Anticline."

"Thank you."

"As I was saying, if the overburden is lightened enough so it can't keep the pressure on the storage strata, it might...well, it might blow."

"Is this another geological term?"

"No. Imagine a can of soda is the storage strata and the tab is the overburden. Shake up the can and pull the tab. That's what I mean by 'blow'."

"That...sounds bad."

Dr Roux laughed. "Bad might be an understatement. We just don't know what might happen."

"What can we do to prevent it?"

"Nothing."

"I can't believe that. How about we bulldoze tons more soil and rock on top?"

Roux laughed again. "You could add a million tons of soil and that would only be a fraction of what is already on top."

"We could stop pumping."

"It wouldn't help. The problem is what's down there already."

"But we wouldn't be adding to the problem."

"That's true," Roux conceded. "Perhaps I should do some ultrasound scans of the subsurface rocks in the meantime."

"Would that help?"

"It might reassure us that everything's normal. Why don't you at least stop pumping more down while I do that and we consider what to do?"

"I can't make that decision."

"Who can?"

"Matternicht."

"So, call him."

Peale licked his lips and refused to meet Roux's eyes. "You don't just call Matternicht. If he wants to speak to you, he'll call you."

"Then call this Campion who was out here yesterday. Tell him. If he's Matternicht's aide he'll get the message to him."

* * *

Peale delayed making the call to Campion for several hours. He made sure his secretary admitted no one to his office, not even Dr Roux, and he sat in his swivel chair looking out over the grounds of the sequestration facility, a glass of whiskey in his hand. He kept a bottle and a glass in the bottom drawer of his desk for the rare occasions when he needed to make an important decision. He had never before drunk more than two fingers in the glass, but today he had consumed half the bottle. Despite this, the alcohol did not seem to be affecting him.

The five o'clock siren sounded, and through his picture windows, Peale watched the shifts change. His secretary knocked and asked if there was anything he needed. Peale shook his head without turning round.

"Goodnight, Louise. Just transfer the phone connection to my office before you go home."

"Yes, Mr Peale."

Peale put through the call as it got dark outside, deciding he could put it off no longer. "Campion, please," he asked the person who answered. "Tell him it's Robert Peale and it's urgent."

Matternicht's aide was on the line within minutes. "What is it, Peale?"

Peale took a deep breath. "There's been an incident. A bubble of carbon dioxide erupted beneath Beaver Pond on the Stone's Ranch. My scientist, Dr Roux, thinks the leaks may be escalating. I...we...think we should shut down the pumping."

Campion questioned him at length as to exactly what had happened, and the results of Dr Roux's subsequent investigations.

"So, you see, if the crack widens, we could have a much larger escape of gas...or...or even a blowout," Peale said. "We should stop pumping and maybe limit the damage."

"I think that would be precipitate," Campion replied smoothly. "You're not a scientist, and with due respect to Dr Roux, this is outside her experience. Do nothing for the moment. I'll consult our scientific team and talk with Mr Matternicht, and get back to you. Was there anything else?"

"That isn't enough?"

"Goodnight, Peale." Campion broke the connection.

* * *

Andrew Winton received a short email from Annaliese in the evening. It merely said that she was in residence at his office in Portland and that though she had started an Internet search, so far there was nothing to report. Andrew closed his email and immediately made a phone call.

"She continues to dig into the Rushing River scenario."

"I told you what would happen if she continued. Have you managed to separate your grandson from her?"

"Yes, he'll be far away by now."

"Where is she?"

Andrew hesitated, and then made his decision. "At one of my offices in Portland. 1701 Elm Avenue, Forest Park. The doors are coded--531469--Machiavelli's birth date. She drives an old red Kia, License plate 866WCX."

"Describe the place to me, inside and out." Andrew did so, prompted by further questions. "Alright. It'll be carried out."

"H...how?"

"You don't need to know."

"I just meant...she's the mother of my grandson. I don't want him growing up thinking she suffered."

The man on the other end of the line was silent for a space, then, "My operative was somewhat angered by his reception last time. I cannot guarantee his method. Learn to live with it."

* * *

Annaliese was just about to turn in for the night when she checked her email and saw that there was one from Matt.

"Hi, Annaliese, guess you couldn't make it today. A pity, you missed a lot of excitement. See you tomorrow perhaps?"

She thought for a moment and sent a quick reply back. "Hi, Matt, things came up. What happened?" She waited online and was rewarded a few minutes later.

"There was a small eruption of gas. Nobody harmed but it's significant."

"Details, buddy. I'm a reporter, remember."

"LOL. Too much to say in an email late at night. I'm in at the office checking up on a few things...oh damn. My boss has left a voice-mail for me and I just listened as I typed. Wants to see me at 10 tomorrow. Can you wait until day after? 8 am? I want to do more tests and they may take a while. Would appreciate your help."

Annaliese felt a twinge of disappointment but thrust it away. "Okay. I have work to do here. Where do you want to meet? The diner in RR?"

"No. Car park of The Dalles medical examiner. We'll need a 4WD so it'll be easier if you come with me."

"Okay. See you at 8 am on the 23rd."

"Great. 'Night."

"'Night."

Chapter 36

August 22, 2030

Max Hay had booked a flight to Portland for his meeting with the governor on the 23rd, but apart from that, had gone about his usual daily business. He knew that Matternicht might be having him watched, but he did not let it concern him, casually wandering around Woodland Hills and Canoga Park. He stayed in an apartment block in Jordan Avenue most of the time, venturing out only for meals. His sedentary habits made it easy for him to be found when Matternicht ordered Sam to pick Max up and bring him back to the house on Topanga Canyon Boulevard.

"You again," Max said to Sam as he appeared with his men, intercepting him in the car park of a Wal-Mart superstore. "Are you here to kill me this time?"

"No, Mr Matternicht wants to see you."

"Do I have a choice in the matter?"

"No."

Matternicht was in the same room, the same chair as before, and to Max's eyes hardly seemed to have moved. This time, however, another man was present, the great man's personal aide, Nigel Campion.

"Mr Matternicht, Campion." Max nodded an acknowledgement. "Why have I been summoned again? I'm scarcely likely to have changed my mind in two days."

"No, Max, I didn't suppose that to be the case," Matternicht whispered. "However, I have. I'll come with you to the Governor's meeting tomorrow, and together we'll see what can be salvaged."

Max's eyebrows shot up and he whistled softly. "Do you mind if I sit down?" He walked across to an upright chair and pulled it across to where he could face the two men. "That's the last thing I expected from you. Hoped for, yes, but expected? What brought about this change of heart?"

"Tell him Campion."

"Are you sure that's wise, sir? We can still manage this affair."

"Tell him. All of it."

"Yesterday, a bubble of carbon dioxide escaped the Hood Anticline storage strata and made it to the surface. Some wildlife died, but more importantly, it was witnessed by a local woman and a USGS scientist. He notified the Rushing River facility and Dr Roux confirmed his findings with her own investigation."

"So you now accept that the storage strata are leaking?"

"There was never any doubt of that, Professor Hay, only the scale of it and what should be done about it."

"Your position has always been 'minor leaks and do nothing'. Do I take it you're changing to 'quite a bit and go public'?"

"Hardly that, Max," Matternicht rasped. "Nothing would be served by going public, but we can act to limit further leaks."

"I don't see how you can avoid publicity. A local woman and an independent scientist saw the leak."

"The woman will listen to reason and Peter Smythe, the current head of USGS in Portland is a friend of a friend. I think he can be counted on to restrain his youthful colleague."

"It sounds like business as usual, Matternicht, not a change of policy."

"It is business, Max, always business, but this time not quite as usual. Campion, tell Max what else Dr Roux found."

"She carried out an ultrasound survey of the dome..."

"Impossible if she only started yesterday."

"I'm only telling you what she said. Perhaps it was a survey of only part of the dome. May I go on?" Max nodded. "Very well, then. She found that an area of the capping strata--partially metamorphosed limestone, I believe she called it--is more fragmented than the original survey carried out twenty years ago. She describes the rock as being on the edge of failure."

Max put his head in his hands. "If you'd listened to me, we would have picked this up a year ago at least. We have an immense volume of liquefied carbon dioxide under huge pressure, capped by a rock layer that could fail at any time. Do you know what's going to happen next? That gas is going to escape, and all your little leaks over the years are going to look like party balloons deflating. My God!"

"How bad will it be, Max?" Matternicht asked.

"I'm sure all your other tame scientists have already told you."

"They disagree. I would rather hear it from you, Max. I always trusted your opinions."

"Until this one--and look where that's got us."

A smile cracked Matternicht's face, looking as if parchment had ripped. "Despite what others may tell you, Max, I'm only human. Aren't I allowed one mistake?"

"Ah, but what a mistake."

"Come, Professor Hay, you've been asked a question," Campion interposed quietly.

"How bad is this?"

"Remember Radinov's disaster?"

"Krasnorovka? We don't know what happened there."

"Not for sure, but he was trying to emulate Rushing River and he cut corners. Something happened though. Radinov died and whatever the Russians were doing there disappeared."

"And you think the same could happen at Rushing River?"

"I pray it doesn't, but I fear it could."

"What exactly?" Matternicht asked. "You must have some idea."

"You have a huge amount of liquid carbon dioxide under great pressure in the Hood Anticline--two hundred and fifty million tons or more--kept in place by a supposedly impervious cap of rock and 1800 meters of overlying rock and soil. Imagine what would happen if the cap fragmented like Dr Roux says--if the pressure came off, even a little bit. Carbon dioxide expands, perhaps blowing some of the overlying rocks away and the capping pressure drops some more. Two hundred and fifty million tons of liquid carbon dioxide is the equivalent of 100 billion cubic meters of gas. That's 100 cubic kilometers, Matternicht. Have you any conception of that figure? That's five hundred times the volume of ash ejected by Mount St Helens in 1980, five times the size of the Krakatoa eruption of 1883. If those disasters mean nothing to you, think of it in terms of nuclear weapons. The Hiroshima bomb was about 15 kilotons. That's the equivalent of 15,000 tons of TNT. The largest bomb every exploded was 50 megatons, or 50 million tons of TNT. Krakatoa was the equivalent of 200 megatons and Rushing River could be five times larger than that."

Max Hay got to his feet and advanced on Campion. "You asked me. You wanted to know." He trembled and spittle flew from his lips as he rounded on his former employer. "You're a damn fool, Matternicht. You gambled everything and you lost. How many will die for your vanity?"

"You're sure of your figures?" Campion asked. "You're not exaggerating for effect?"

"How can I be sure? Nobody's ever been in this position before. But just looking at the amount of CO_2 down there and the expansion factors, then...yes. I'm sure."

"All of it will go?" Campion persisted. "At once?"

"Again, I don't know. Unless something blocked it...it's a pressure vessel with the valve knocked off...but if the rocks are stronger than we suppose it might hold. Oh, God, I just don't know."

"So we could, even as a worst-case scenario, see only a portion of the gas escaping...like...like steam from a steam kettle?"

Max shrugged and sat down again. He ran his fingers through the thinning hair on the sides of his head. "It's possible, I suppose."

"There we have it then. There's no need to start panicking and assuming there'll be a great disaster. Let's approach this like reasonable men. It won't be the end of the world if some of the gas escapes..."

"It will be for some people. Carbon dioxide doesn't support life. People die when they breathe it. If it escapes in significant amounts..."

"We can evacuate Rushing River--purely as a precaution. Then we cap the storage area, seal it off, and maybe we even come out of this looking good. We'll have actively worked to save lives."

"Having endangered them in the first place."

"The USGS and DOE passed the designs fifteen years ago."

"That just means they share the blame; it doesn't absolve us."

"Do you *want* to take the blame?" Campion demanded. "Is this all some perverted desire on your part to be punished?"

"Enough of this bickering, both of you," Matternicht commanded, his voice hoarse and strained. "I'll go to the Governor tomorrow, with or without you, Max. The Governor has as much to lose as I if Rushing River is shut down. I'm sure we can reach a compromise solution that will reflect our concern for safety rather than any possible flaws in the design."

"Have you given any thought to exactly how you'll ensure people's safety?" Max asked. "The problem doesn't go away if you stop pumping, you know."

"I believe we have the technology already," Matternicht said. "The problem's similar to those already encountered in oil and gas fields. When there's a blow-out or a gas well catches fire, you call in a team that specializes in controlling leaks. I have such teams on my payroll already. I'll call one in and have this field capped and safe within days."

Chapter 37

August 22, 2030

Albert Ruffin was angry and his head ached where he had been hit with the wine bottle. He contained his anger though, because he had learned over the years that anger made you more liable to make mistakes. The prisons were full of people who made mistakes and Albert did not intend to swell their population. Admittedly, he had made a mistake on Tuesday night, but not an irreparable one. He had opted for the fast, furious, terror approach, hoping to stampede the woman and boy into panicked flight. Instead, they fought back and almost killed him.

I won't make that mistake again.

This time the 'hit' would take place in a quiet suburb, in a house set back from the road, and in a place where the victim thought herself secure. It was a pity the boy was not there--Albert would love to have settled that score--but the woman would do. She was a 'looker' and if he could achieve total surprise, he might be able to have some fun before he killed her. Surprise was likely as he had the code for the entrance.

He arrived at Elm Avenue in Forest Park at dawn and drove slowly along the street, taking note of the houses and the cars, getting a general feel for the neighborhood. He passed 1701 Elm, giving it no more than a quick glance down the curved drive before continuing onward. The house itself was invisible from the road and Albert grinned in anticipation.

There was a small park a hundred or so yards from the house, with a section of off-street parking. The park itself boasted only a few benches and a fountain with concrete paths leading away into the trees, but it served as a place for Albert to leave his car without it being too obvious. It was deserted in the early morning hours, so Albert parked, backing into the bay, and took out his work bag. He would have preferred to leave everything in the car and just take the essentials but he did not think any early risers among the good folk of Forest Park would look kindly on a man carrying a sawed-off shotgun and wearing hospital scrubs.

Albert was a man who watched all the crime shows on television, reveling in the forensic pathology reports. He made an effort to be careful in the execution of his crimes, always being aware of the dangers of leaving trace evidence behind. Where he could, he changed out of his clothes into disposable hospital scrubs, wore gloves, overshoes and a shower cap.

Enjoying a morbid sense of humor, he was not above planting a few scraps of evidence that would mislead investigators. On one occasion he had carried the thumb of a homeless man who had subsequently disappeared into the Columbia River. That man's prints had led police on a fruitless search for an impossible perpetrator. Other times, he carried a few cat hairs with him and left them on the body. It all served to muddy the waters.

Albert walked quietly up the concrete drive of 1701 Elm in the first light of day. A walk across the grass would be more enjoyable and direct, but the passage of a person across the early dew could be seen at a glance. He kept to the concrete until almost in sight of the house and then slipped into the shrubbery. The house was concrete and glass, but unfortunately the ground floor was concrete and the upper floor glass, with curtains drawn across. There were two points of access, a double garage door and front door, both with an access keypad.

The sun was rising and Albert decided he would strike early. He unpacked his bag and checked his equipment before stripping naked. The hospital scrubs covered him completely and he added the shower cap, paper overshoes and two sets of latex gloves that extended up over his sleeves. He picked up the shotgun and walked over to the front door.

He tapped in the code--531469--but nothing happened. The little light stayed red. Albert frowned and tried again--nothing. He stared at the touch plate and cursed briefly when he saw the brand name. He went over to the garage door and tried that without result. "Damn it," he muttered, thrusting his anger down.

Back in the cover of the shrubbery, Albert took out a cell phone and called his contact. "The code doesn't work."

"Can you get in without it?"

"Probably, but not without alerting her. This place is built solidly."

"Wait. I'll check the code." The connection died.

Albert sat down to wait. The sun rose higher and the neighborhood slowly came alive. Bird song filled the air and Albert would have enjoyed the cool morning air and the scents of soil and leaves had he not been dressed to kill.

His phone buzzed softly. "Yes?"

"The code is 531469."

"That's what I tried."

"Then she's changed it."

"What do you want me to do?"

"What you're being paid for. Find a way."

Albert cursed and started stripping off. The scrubs and coverings were fine for a break in but if he was going to perform an opportunistic killing, he would need to look as ordinary as possible. Killers, Albert knew, were sometimes striking looking people and drew attention to themselves by their apparel and their behavior. Albert was middle-aged, of medium height, brown hair, brown eyes, of medium complexion and with bland, homely features. People looked at him but rarely saw anything that remained in their memories. His clothes were tidy but ordinary and he varied them to suit his surroundings. This morning, because he was in a decent neighborhood, he wore casual clothes but ones that were obviously well-made. Anyone seeing him would not think twice and invisibility like this was invaluable.

He repacked his bag and settled down to watch the house from the depths of the shrubbery. Sooner or later, the woman would emerge and he could either force his way in or else take her outside. Albert regarded himself as flexible, opportunistic and patient. His patience ran out at noon, when he made another phone call.

"I can't wait here all day."

"Why not? You're being paid."

"I'm paid for results, not sitting around."

"So do something. Can't you bypass the security?"

"If they were external, but these are set into the concrete. I've seen this brand before. They set off an alarm if they're tinkered with."

"Then you'll just have to wait."

Wait he did, though with increasingly bad grace. He had omitted to bring food or drink with him, anticipating a quick result, and he became ill-tempered as the afternoon wore on. Albert recognized the deterioration in his mental state and was dismayed. If he had to act now, he might make mistakes.

I should go and get something to eat, but I won't be able to tell if she's left by the time I get back. He pondered his problem for a few minutes, his stomach growling its protest. *Damn it, I can't risk missing her.*

Albert Ruffin stayed where he was until night fell and the lights inside the house went dark again. He stretched and picked up his bag, walked back to his car and drove off.

Tomorrow, he thought. *And I'll be prepared for anything. I know where she lives and the make and number of her car. I'll get her one way or the other.*

Chapter 38

August 23, 2030

Andrew Winton had spent much of the previous day attending to his financial situation. One of the problems of his involvement with someone like Matternicht was that if the great man foundered, many lesser men would be dragged down by the undertow. He needed to liquidate assets quickly as he was sure his wealth would be frozen by the government while they investigated his involvement. He was not sure exactly how much Nigel Campion knew about his financial affairs and whether he could actually carry out his threats, but he had decided to take no chances. His main shares remained untouched and his chief broker remained unused. Instead, he offloaded small parcels of his stock, and sold off properties at cut-rate prices. The only criterion of sale was that cash must change hands, and immediately. At the prices he offered, he found ready buyers and, by Thursday night, had amassed nearly five million dollars in several accounts unknown to any of his former associates. The properties had been worth five times that but he needed money in hand for his flight into obscurity.

Andrew booked himself on a flight to Los Angeles for eleven the next morning, out of Independence State Airport. He used his real name and determined the last minute he needed to arrive in order to board his flight. Next, he called a friend who worked for a cargo company, and with the aid of a photograph and its negative, persuaded him to allow him on an unscheduled flight out of McNary Field. The flight would leave at eleven also, but its destination was

Missoula, Montana. From there, Andrew planned to hop to Chicago and thence to New York and London before dropping out of sight of Matternicht's cohorts.

On Friday morning, Andrew left his house before dawn, on foot and wearing casual clothes. He carried a single, small suitcase and wore a money belt under his clothes that held the immediate funds he would need to flee the country; coded account numbers and passwords for the money he had transferred the previous day. He walked several miles and then breakfasted at a Denny's restaurant before boarding a bus for McNary Field, where he arrived at ten o'clock.

* * *

Meanwhile, Patterson drove Andrew's Mercedes with the back windows blacked out, slowly and visibly to Independence State Airport. He parked in the short-term parking area and wheeled three large suitcases to the Northern & Canadian desk, where he checked them in and obtained the boarding pass for his employer. Back at the car, he sat in the front seat and listened to the radio as the minutes ticked by to the time of departure. He saw no one watching him, but he knew that he was very likely under observation. Andrew had assured Patterson he was in no danger--that his enemies merely wanted to stop him leaving. That remained to be seen, but Patterson was determined to carry out his assignment. Just before the final boarding call, Patterson climbed into the back of the Mercedes, waited a few minutes, and exited with his coat collars turned up and head down. He hurried into the terminal and attempted to lose himself in the crowds.

* * *

Albert Ruffin was back in Forest Park by five in the morning. He parked in the same place as the previous day and took out his bag from the trunk of his dark green Taurus. This morning, the contents included a small, innocuous looking device made of C4 explosive, a timer and a motion sensor, and magnetic clamps. He had collected the parts of a bomb the previous evening, but had not assembled it as he was undecided where to use it, or indeed whether it would be needed at all. The woman must surely come out today, and he would have to be prepared to rush in and take her in the house, or else follow her and attach the explosives to her vehicle. Albert preferred to kill up close--it was far more fulfilling seeing the terror and knowledge of imminent extinction in his victims' eyes--but he would make the kill one way or another. Business *and* pleasure if possible, but business *before* pleasure if necessary. It was a motto that had stood him in good stead over the years.

212

Albert was fifty yards from the driveway to 1701 Elm when an old red Kia eased out onto the deserted road and turned away from him. He stared, his hand dipping inside his jacket for his pistol, but left it where it was as he realized he could not hope for a certain kill at that ever-increasing range. The thought followed hard on the heels of his realization that she might not be returning. He turned and ran back to his vehicle, throwing his bag onto the back seat and gunning the engine. His car swung onto the avenue, fishtailing as the tires skidded on the road surface. The red Kia was nowhere in sight and Albert accelerated as he headed down the hill toward the city.

At the bottom of the hill, on St Helens Road, he stopped and looked left and right, focusing on every red car, dismissing it and moving on. The Kia was not visible, so Albert made a decision, turning toward the city. There were more places to go in this direction. He drove fast but, mindful of his bag behind him on the back seat, not fast enough to attract the attention of patrol cars. Factories and rail yards occupied the strip of land to his left, the Willamette River beyond, and the hills of Forest Park rising to his right.

"Come on, where are you, bitch?" he muttered, his gaze scanning the road ahead. Twice he saw a red car and closed on it, only to find it was not his intended quarry. Roads opened up on both sides now and Albert knew if he did not find her soon, the task would be hopeless in the maze of streets in downtown Portland. St Helens Road split into two. He wavered and chose Vaughn Street which led toward Highway 405.

Is she going out to Rushing River again? I could just head there. Perhaps I should...405 it is.

He took the on-ramp onto Highway 405 and followed it south and then east to where it merged with Highway 5 on the Marquam Bridge. The traffic was a lot heavier here and his pace was slower. He found and eliminated more red cars, and at last, as he entered the loop that would take him onto the Banfield Expressway, he saw an old red Kia up ahead of him. Moving close enough to make sure it was the right car; he fell back a hundred yards or so and followed at a leisurely pace.

Where the Expressway plunged under 205, it became the Columbia River Highway and Albert smiled and relaxed when the driver of the red Kia confirmed their destination by staying on the Highway. He reached over into the back seat and rummaged in his bag before pulling out a paper bag. The contents had soaked the bottom of the bag and Albert cursed as he juggled the bag and the steering wheel, finally getting the bag open and spread on the seat next to him. Inside was a moist hamburger sandwich, loaded with fried onions and ketchup. He pulled it apart and wolfed it down, licking his fingers when he finished, screwing up the bag and throwing it into the back seat. A little over two hours later, Albert watched as the old red Kia turned off onto the Brewery Overpass Road in The Dalles.

"Where the hell is she going?" Albert muttered to himself. "Has the bitch mistaken the turn to Rushing River?" He followed as the Kia worked its way slowly through the streets to the Hospital grounds and the County Morgue. "What does she want here?"

Albert parked on the road opposite the morgue and watched from his car as Annaliese Winton parked. She got out and leaned against her car, obviously waiting for someone. He considered taking his gun and walking across to waste her or even driving by and popping her, but there were really too many people around. It would do no harm to wait a while; it was only eight o'clock.

* * *

Flight time from Los Angeles in California to Portland, Oregon was a shade over two hours if the conditions were right. If a person was catching a commercial domestic flight, he would have to allow an hour before boarding and another hour upon arrival to clear his bags and catch a cab. However, James Matternicht never used commercial flights. He owned a Learjet 105 that, with a range of nearly four thousand miles, was able to move him around the world in comfort and with ease.

The meeting with the Governor was at ten in the morning, and even with the supersonic jet at his disposal, he was at the Bob Hope Airport in Burbank just after six, with his erstwhile scientific adviser Maxwell Hay, his aide Nigel Campion, two bodyguards who answered to the names of Luther and Maurice, and a pair of secretaries, Rhiannon and Nardee, chosen both for beauty and efficiency. The pilot had already filed his flight plan and together with the rest of his cabin crew, was finishing off his pre-flight checks when the limousines rolled across the tarmac to the waiting jet.

"Good morning, Mr Matternicht, we'll be ready for takeoff in about ten minutes."

"Thank you, Captain," Matternicht replied with a smile. "What's the weather like today?"

"Partly cloudy with a light crosswind. It shouldn't give us any trouble."

"When you're ready, then." Matternicht boarded the jet and made himself comfortable. The bodyguards sat at the rear, out of everybody's way, Campion close to his employer, and Max a few seats down. The two secretaries arranged the files they carried and set up the laptop computers for instant communications.

They took off at 6:20 am and rapidly climbed through the patchy cloud cover to their cruising altitude. Captain Wingate was diligent in his procedures, keeping a close eye on the instruments and making regular radio checks with ground stations as they moved from one air space to another. Nardee served light refreshments as soon as the seat belt light went off, and Rhiannon opened up email communications.

"Contact Ed Dillon at SurgeCon. Find out where he is and his ETA in Portland."

"SurgeCon?" Max queried. "That's the well-capping company?"

"Yes. His main team was in the Philippines. I'm bringing him in."

"I'm surprised he was available. He's in great demand."

"He wouldn't refuse me."

"Mr Matternicht? The SurgeCon team is ready to fly out of Manila this evening, local time," Rhiannon said. "Mr Dillon estimates his arrival at Portland on the 25th. He requests you bring in the necessary supplies--he attaches a list-- and have them ready on site."

"Order them. Priority air freight. I want them here by Monday morning."

"You obviously think Dillon's going to be able to cap the dome, even though there's no defined borehole," Max commented. "Does he know what he's being asked to do?"

"Up to a point. I don't want to reveal everything before he gets here, but we discussed the general features last night. He's cautiously optimistic."

"And if he can't do it, what then? This problem's not going to go away."

"I'm aware of that, Max. We'll do what needs to be done, with whatever tools we can find." Matternicht thought for a moment and then attracted Rhiannon's attention. "Do we have a helicopter on standby in Portland?"

"I don't know, sir. I'll check." The young woman got busy and after a few minutes was able to say, "No, sir, the nearest available one is a Sikorsky 96 in Tacoma, Washington."

Matternicht nodded. "Have it sent down immediately to Hillsboro Airport. Dillon will need it to transport his men out to Rushing River and I'll pay them a visit myself later today. There are personnel who need replacing."

Campion was hunched over his own laptop, keeping his fingers on the pulse of Matternicht's empire. "Winton's done a runner," he said.

"Explain."

"He's not coming to the meeting this morning. Instead, he's on a flight out of Independence at 11. It appears he's been selling assets all yesterday."

"He's a damn fool," Max muttered. "The authorities won't look kindly on his flight."

"I think that's the least of his worries," Matternicht said coolly. "I cannot stand traitors."

"You called me one the other day," Max observed. He glanced out of the small window by his seat. "Am I to make an unscheduled descent into northern California?"

"You still have your uses, Max, but I think Winton has outlived his." Matternicht leaned toward Campion so the secretaries would not hear. "Have him followed. When I'm ready, I'll make an example of him." The old man asked Nardee for a glass of tepid soy milk and sipped at it sparingly for a few minutes. "Max, you made the appointment with Governor Tibbits. What did you tell him? How much does he know of the situation at Rushing River?"

"He knows enough to be concerned. I gave him generalities but not particulars, and advised him to have emergency services people and government geologists on hand."

"And he agreed to see you at such short notice?"

"He's a friend," Max said. "He's a busy man, though, so this'll only be a short meeting unless he decides the situation is critical."

"Let us hope he won't think it so. I've no desire for undue publicity."

"I think it's a little late for that. You know I won't hold back at this meeting, don't you?"

"I know, Max. I wouldn't expect anything less from you."

Campion looked from one man to the other and saw evidence of a long friendship being torn apart. It made him uncomfortable so he sought to distract his companions. "How come we're going to Portland, Professor Hay?" he asked. "Why not Salem?"

"Tibbits is in Portland opening an Electron Microscopy Conference first thing this morning. He's going to stay over to see us rather than return to Salem." Max shrugged. "I encouraged him. We're going to need to work with the USGS scientists, and Peter Smythe of the Portland/Vancouver office can get things done. It made sense."

"Do you really think these geologists and people can do anything?"

"Frankly, no, but we have to try, don't we? We might have put thousands of people in danger. We should at least try and help them."

"You always were too soft, Max," Matternicht said. "That's why you chose science, I think, rather than business."

Max nodded sadly. "Yes, you're right, but I didn't choose a long enough spoon when I sat down to sup with the devil."

The Learjet 105 began its descent to Hillsboro airport. It landed safely at half past eight, and two limousines were waiting to carry them to their meeting with the Oregon Governor, John Tibbits.

Chapter 39

August 23, 2030

Matt Morrison pulled into the parking lot of the County Morgue in The Dalles a little after eight in the morning and saw Annaliese standing by her old red Kia. He touched the horn lightly and slid his 4WD Toyota into the slot next to her.

"Sorry I'm late. Have you been waiting long?"

"About ten minutes. Nice wheels. Yours or the Department's?"

Matt grinned. "You think I could afford this on what they pay me? I've got a bit of equipment with me today and I don't want to have to carry it all over the fields." He looked appraisingly at Annaliese. "Though with a strong woman to act as a pack horse..."

"Dream on, buddy," she laughed. "I'm carrying my own gear." She held up her camera as she slid into the front seat beside him.

Matt drove out of the car park and after a few minutes was on the road south to Rushing River. They chatted about inconsequential things, both flirting and laughing. Matt noticed a Taurus pull out of the hospital car park and start to follow, but it stopped at the town boundary, so he thought no more of it.

Matt and Annaliese arrived at the Stone's Ranch at nine and drove up to the house. Both Marc and Margaret were home and Matt explained what he wanted to do. He took them round to the back of the 4WD and showed them the equipment he'd brought, explaining what each piece was for.

"This is an ultrasound mapper. Basically, it sends pulses of low frequency sound into the earth and picks up the pulses reflected back by the various soil and rock layers. It enables me to get an idea of what is below us."

"That'll go all the way down to this anticline thing?" Marc asked.

"No, I'd need the more powerful one for that. I'd have brought it, but it's being used up in Walla Walla. Maybe next week. Anyway, this little one will look at the surface layers, down a hundred yards or so."

"And these?" Marc pointed at a series of interlocking pipes.

"It's a mini-drill. If I see anything directly below us--say within twenty feet or so--I can drill down by hand and take a sample of the soil. I can test the soil atmosphere and also the acidity of the soil moisture, both of which are measures of the subsurface carbon dioxide levels. I just hope too much hasn't dissipated in the last day or two."

"You may have a fresh lot," Margaret said. "We had another tremor very early this morning, and another larger one not an hour ago."

"So what are these things?"

"Breathing packs," Matt said. He pulled one out and turned it over, showing the dials and tubes that led to a diving mouthpiece. "An update on the old scuba gear but instead of a steel or aluminum tank, this baby is made of Kevlar and resin to hold pressurized air. Lightweight and tough. I wasn't sure how long I might be working in a carbon dioxide pool, so I brought several." He put the pack back and rested his hand on the stack. "Hmm, perhaps too many of them. Never mind, as long as we don't have to carry them. Which brings me to my request, Mr Stone. Can I drive my vehicle across your land?"

"To the Beaver Pond?"

"Yes. I don't mind lugging equipment around but there's rather a lot here."

"As long as you close the gates behind you."

"No problem," Annaliese said. "That's my job."

"I thought I might come with you and do the gates," Margaret said. "I can leave you there and walk back, but I'd like to see if there's more gas at the pond."

Marc laughed. "If there's more, you won't see it. Go on then, I'll be working in the barn again this morning."

The drive to Beaver Creek was only a little over a mile, though they had to go by a more roundabout route than when walking there. Margaret rode up front and hopped out at each gate and let Matt drive through before closing it and climbing into the cab again. The day was calm at ground level though clouds scudded across the summer sky, skimming patches of shadow over the land.

They came through the last fence and turned right along the rim of the creek, heading toward the pond. Matt slowed and then braked, staring down at the creek bed.

"That's odd," he said. "I could've sworn the creek was flowing the other day."

"Well, of course it is," Margaret said, peering past him from the passenger seat. Her mouth fell open. "Wh...where's all the water gone?"

"Do creeks just dry up like that?" Annaliese asked. "I'm not a country girl, myself."

Margaret shook her head. "Not that fast...and not this one. What can have happened?"

Matt switched off the engine and climbed out. He took his Wills & Halbert meter out of the back and started down the slope toward the dry creek bed. Half way down, he hesitated and looked back at the two women, and then continued on. At the bottom of the slope he took a reading, and then carried on, taking more readings every few paces. When he got to the stones and drying mud of the creek, he squatted down and took another reading before returning to the 4WD.

"What did you find?" Annaliese asked.

"Nothing much. I thought this oddity might somehow be related to the carbon dioxide leaking, but the levels are pretty much normal. A little bit elevated, but given that we had a bubble a few days ago, I suppose that's not too surprising."

"Could it have anything to do with the bubble?" Margaret asked.

"It was an actual bubble?" Annaliese asked. "I mean, you actually saw one?"

Matt smiled. "Not in the sense you're thinking of, like a soap bubble. It's what we call a sudden release of a small amount of gas rather than a slow steady leak. It came to the surface in a rush rather than leaking slowly, and disturbed the water in the pond. Speaking of which, let's go and see the pond. I have a pH meter with me to measure the acidity of the water."

"Why might it be acid?"

"Carbon dioxide reacts with water to form carbonic acid. It's a weak acid, but it'll register with a pH meter if it's present."

Matt started up the car again and resumed his slow drive along the creek valley rim. There was no well-defined track, just a slight streak of stunted grass where the earth had been packed solid under intermittent vehicles. He drove slowly, despite the 4WD capability because he was conscious of being on someone else's land and the wife of the owner sitting alongside him. The vehicle lurched and skidded on a sandy spot and Margaret cried out for him to stop.

"Oh, Marc isn't going to be pleased with that," she exclaimed.

"I'm sorry, I couldn't really help..."

"Not that. The fence. Look at it. Who did that to it?"

The fence that ran along the top of the creek rim leaned over at an angle, the divergence from the perpendicular increasing steadily as their gaze ran along its length.

"Cattle?" Annaliese hazarded. "Could they have pushed it over?"

"Not like that, not that much of it. Drive on, Dr Morrison, please. I need to see how bad this is."

Matt did so, but more slowly as the land was no longer level, but dipped down to their left. A hundred yards further on, the fence was down completely, the strands of wire lying shining in the grass.

"I don't understand it," Margaret said. "The posts look as if they've pulled out of the ground."

"Oh shit!" Matt was not looking at the downed fence but farther on, to the place where the creek emerged from Beaver Pond...except that Beaver Pond was no longer there. "Oh shit," he repeated, and pointed.

"Where is it?" Margaret asked, disbelief in her voice.

"Where's what?" Annaliese asked, her head bent over her camera. "What are we looking for?"

"The pond. It's not there."

Where the pond had sat in the summer sunlight two days before was a gaping hole in the landscape. The pastured ground had slumped and pulled apart, grass and trees and rocks and earth tumbling down into a muddy jumble some fifty feet below them. The chaotic depression was nearly a hundred yards across, irregular in shape and contour, and at opposite ends the creek burst over the new lip and cascaded to the bottom where it swirled in a muddy puddle a fraction the size of the original pond.

"That explains what happened to the creek," Matt said.

"But what's happened to the pond?" Annaliese asked. She took the cover off her camera and started taking photographs.

Matt inched closer in the 4WD but stopped well clear of the lip of the depression. "I guess I don't need to sound out the depths now. The bubble burst and the pond collapsed down into it." They all got out and advanced cautiously to the rim, where they stood staring down into the pit, with the water swirling at the bottom. Annaliese walked around the rim several paces and looked back, raising her camera.

"I need you in the frame," she called out. "As a reference scale."

"I don't understand something," Margaret said. "The water's still pouring in, but where's it going? The water level isn't rising."

Matt looked and saw that she was right. "It's still being sucked down. There's still space below. That means this could collapse some more. I think we'd better retreat." He and Margaret stepped back a few feet, but Annaliese shuffled sideways, staring through her viewfinder. "Get back, Annaliese," he called.

"Hang on, another couple, with the car in it, too." Annaliese stepped sideways, right to the edge and the turf tore out under her foot. She fell to her knees and as she did so, the section of rim collapsed, carrying her downward in a slurry of mud and tangled grass. Her scream cut off abruptly and she fell sideways, sprawled awkwardly, unmoving.

"Annaliese!" Margaret yelled, and started forward to help.

"No! Wait!" Matt pulled the old lady back and snatched his Wills & Halbert meter from his pocket. He held it below the crumbling lip of the pit and thumbed the button. It screamed its overload warning and he flipped it to middle range and a moment later to high range. "Eighty thou," he called out. "And that's at the top." He stared down at the figure of Annaliese a dozen feet below him and weighed his chances of getting down there and pulling her back up. *Slim, but I can't leave her.* Matt started taking deep breaths, hyperventilating, in preparation for his dive into the lethal CO_2 pool.

"The breathing packs," Margaret called out.

"Shit, of course." Matt ran back to the vehicle and pulled out two packs, sprinting back to the sink hole. He slung one on his back, fumbling with the straps in his haste.

"Is she still alive?"

"Yes, but she won't be for long at these concentrations. It'll be pure poison down there." He flipped the switch on the pack he wore and slipped the mouthpiece in. With the other pack over one arm, he gave a thumbs up sign to Margaret and eased himself over the edge. The air fed to him through the breathing pack sustained him and he lowered himself into the invisible pool, but he involuntarily inhaled through his nostrils as well and felt his head swimming. Matt pinched his nose with one hand and continued scrambling down.

Annaliese lay on her side facing the slope. She was still breathing, but irregularly, her chest heaving as her unconscious body strove to find oxygen in every empty, asphyxiating breath. Matt bent over her and shoved the mouthpiece of the other breather pack into her mouth and switched it on. At once, her labored breathing eased. Matt fitted the straps of her pack around her, and with head reeling from the effort, hauled her to her feet and up the crumbling slope, one staggering step at a time.

She was conscious by the time Matt hauled her onto the grass at the top of pit. Margaret knelt and supported her as she gulped air, groaning from a headache that was no doubt gripping her temples tightly.

"Thank you," she whispered. "That was horrible. I thought I was drowning."

"You were. Your lungs still pull in air but it was pure carbon dioxide--well, at least 20 or 30 per cent where you were. Enough to knock you out, but not enough to kill you too quickly. You were lucky."

Matt switched on his Wills & Halbert meter and looked at the readout. "Do you feel up to moving, Annaliese? The CO_2 level has risen to two thousand even up here, and I think it's going to get worse very soon. If it does, the vehicle won't start."

Matt and Margaret supported Annaliese and half-carried her back to the 4WD, putting her into the back seat. The engine started, but ran roughly and Matt backed it slowly along the track until it started to run more smoothly. Then he turned it and they drove back, Margaret opening and closing the gates again.

"What's going to happen?" Margaret asked. "How much bigger is it going to get?"

Matt shook his head. "Too many imponderables to even guess. I'd say a bubble of gas formed in the rock and soil between the storage area and the surface and bits have been rising to the surface at intervals--the hiker, your cattle, the tourists. Now the main bubble has burst through and the ground has collapsed into the void. The creek's pouring into the hole and enlarging it, releasing more carbon dioxide. I'm hoping this is just a subsurface bubble and the main storage rocks of the anticline are still intact. If so, then we might have to evacuate the town, but we can contain it."

"And if the rocks aren't intact?" Annaliese asked.

"Then..." Matt glanced at Margaret beside him and ventured a half smile. "Well, no sense in anticipating problems. Let's concentrate on warning the town. You know the area, Margaret. What would be the best way?"

"Sheriff Warner," she said promptly. "I can call him, if you like. Then I suppose I could ring around everyone I know."

"We'll drive into town and see the Sheriff. Maybe I can help coordinate the evacuation efforts. You call around anyone you can on your phone. Tell them that if they feel faint or short of breath to get upstairs or up a slope. Stay away from any low place that might collect carbon dioxide. And get them to pass it on to people they know."

Matt stopped the car outside the house to let Margaret out. She got out and held the door open, looking in at them.

"It's going to be alright, isn't it?" Margaret asked. "This isn't really dangerous, is it?"

"The gas is dangerous, Margaret. Don't treat it lightly. But as long as you stay away from low places where it can collect, you should be safe enough."

The old woman nodded. "Okay."

Matt hesitated. "Look, there's one other possibility. I keep thinking of a bottle of soda when you flip the cap off. It all rushes out. If that happens, it'll come out fast and strong. Don't wait around to see what happens. Get out as quickly as you can."

Matt drove away and Annaliese turned in her seat to look back. "I don't like leaving her. What if this thing does blow out?"

"That's been worrying me. I think it's safe enough if the cap rock is still largely intact. All this gas could just be escaping through a tiny crack. If it was shattered, it'd be another story." Matt turned out of the ranch driveway onto the road into town and accelerated. "Dr Roux out at the storage facility was adamant the cap was intact and I have to believe they wouldn't be so stupid as to cover up that if it wasn't."

"You think the Sheriff will believe us?"

"Why wouldn't he?"

* * *

"You have to admit your story is far-fetched," Sheriff Warner said. "First a man tries to hold you up on your way here the other day, now you say killer gas is leaking out of the ground on the Stone Ranch. Your killer never turned up, maybe the gas won't either."

"Call Margaret Stone. She was there. She saw what happened."

Warner grunted. "Margaret Stone's a nice lady but she's not what I'd call knowledgeable about scientific stuff. She probably only knows what you told her."

"Then go out to the beaver pond. You'll only see a large hole in the ground. Look at the creek that has dried up. But for God's sake be careful, Sheriff. You can't see carbon dioxide or smell it or taste it, but it'll kill you if you stumble into it."

"Well, maybe I will go have a look."

"What are you going to do about the town's people?" Annaliese asked. "We have to broadcast a warning or something."

"I'll do as I see fit, Ms Winton. First, I'll go out to the Stone Ranch and have a word with..."

"But in the meantime..."

"Please don't interrupt me, Ms Winton. I'll deal with this in my own way. Rushing River is my town and my jurisdiction. The townsfolk are people I've known all my life and I'll act in a way that ensures their safety and protection. I don't need big-city folk telling me my duty."

"Perhaps we could help," Matt said. "We could start telling people..."

"No. If you start telling people unsubstantiated rumors about threats to their lives, you'll cause a panic..."

"They're not unsubstantiated. Annaliese here fell in and damn near died. If that CO_2 spills out it'll flow down the river valley right through town. You have to warn people..."

"No. I don't have to do anything. You and Ms Winton here have two options. One of my troopers can take you to a cell until I decide what should be done, or you can leave Rushing River. You have thirty seconds to choose."

"You'll check the pond out though?"

"Twenty-five seconds."

"It's important Sheriff. I'm not just talking for the sake of it. This could be dangerous for everybody."

"Fifteen seconds."

"Damn it, Sheriff."

"Ten seconds."

Matt's shoulders slumped. "We'll leave."

"Good. A trooper will escort you to the town boundary."

"I'm going to contact the USGS. They'll contact the state authorities."

"Fine, you do that. Trooper Erlich, accompany Dr Morrison and Ms Winton to the town boundary, and make sure they keep going."

The trooper drove behind them until they reached the boundary on the main road north and waited until Matt and Annaliese were nearly out of sight before turning back. Matt drove on another mile before pulling over.

"Are we going back?" Annaliese asked. "We can't just leave them all."

"The problem is, if we go back, that damn sheriff will lock us up, and that would serve no purpose."

"Then what? We have a duty to warn people."

"Okay, call Margaret and tell her and her husband to get out of Rushing River. They're too near to the sink hole anyway. I've got a couple of calls I can make, too."

Matt got out of the car and walked a few paces away to make his calls, leaving Annaliese to call Margaret. He called Nicole at the Diner, but she was not on duty. He left a message but had little hope it would be passed on. Then he called Dr Roux at the storage facility.

"I'll look into it," Roux said. "Thanks."

Matt's next call was to his boss at USGS--Peter Smythe. He was passed through several layers before talking to his personal secretary.

"I'm sorry, Dr Morrison, but Dr Smythe is in a meeting."

"There must be some way I can reach him, Katie. It's very important. Could you take a message in to him, perhaps?"

"The meeting isn't here, Dr Morrison, and he really is unreachable, at least for an hour or two." The secretary paused and then said, "He's with the Governor. I tell you this only so you know I can't possibly interrupt his meeting."

"Okay, thanks Katie. You've got my cell number? Please have him call me the moment he's free. It's very important."

Matt's last call was to the State Police. There was a short delay and then a tired voice said, "Oregon State Police. The Dalles station. Sergeant Malone speaking. How may I be of assistance?"

"I want to report a...a gas leak."

"You'll need to contact the Electricity and Gas Company, sir. Is this on a domestic or commercial property?"

"It's on a ranch out in Rushing River."

"At the ranch house?"

"No, in a field. Look, sergeant, it's vital that this is..."

"If it's leaking from a pipe at a distance from a residence, you really will need to speak to the appropriate Gas Company. If you hold, I'll try and find out which company services that area..."

"It's not leaking from a pipe. It's coming out of the ground."

"Probably from a buried pipe, sir. As I said, the Gas Company is the best..."

"It isn't that type of gas, sergeant. It's carbon dioxide."

There was silence for a few moments. "Carbon dioxide? As in fire extinguishers? And soda drinks?"

"Yes, there's a leak from an underground storage area. The Carbon Capture and Storage facility at Rushing River stores it there. You must have heard of it."

"This carbon storage place put the carbon dioxide underground?"

"Yes."

"And now it's leaking out?"

"Yes."

"Then why don't you tell them their gas is leaking...sir?"

"I already have and they're going to look into it, but the stuff is dangerous and we should move people away..."

"Dangerous how? Explosive? Flammable? Caustic? What?"

"It...it asphyxiates, smothers you."

"And it's poisonous in small amounts? What are we looking at, sir, a few ounces will kill people?"

"Only in large amounts, but there are large amounts escaping. It's heavier than air and flows downhill like a liquid. There's a huge pool of it up on the ranch."

"You've notified the local sheriff?"

"Yes, but I don't think he's going to do anything."

"I'm sure he'll do what's needed, sir. Now, if you'll excuse me..."

"Look, my name is Dr Matthew Morrison. I'm a government geologist at USGS--check it out--and I know what I'm talking about. I'd like to come and see you personally, perhaps the officer in charge, too. If I came straight there, I could be there in less than an hour."

"Just a moment please, Dr Morrison." There was a pause of more than a minute. "Dr Morrison? We're short-handed today, sir. Could I ask you to come in at 1 pm? I'll be able to give you my full attention then. In the meantime, I'll call Sheriff Warner in Rushing River and get his thoughts, and I'll also talk to local emergency officials. Do you have any evidence of your story, sir?"

"I have some photos."

"Please bring them. I'll see you this afternoon then."

Matt hung up and joined Annaliese. "Any luck?"

"She won't leave without her husband and he says he's not going to abandon his livestock. He's rounding up cattle now and moving them away from the sink hole. You?"

"Nothing. My boss is in a meeting with the Governor and the State Police are under-staffed. We can go and see them at one o'clock."

"Is that going to be enough?"

"It'll have to be." Matt looked at his watch. "Look, it's five after ten, and we have to get back to The Dalles for one. I suggest we get a bit of early lunch and get our thoughts together for the State Police. I know this great little place across the river in Washington--the Hood Mountain & River View Retreat--great food and a fabulous view. Are you up for it?"

"I guess, if there's nothing more we can do in the meantime." Annaliese shook her head. "Sorry, I'm just a bit worried, but I suppose the State Police will get things done. I'd love to have lunch while we wait. Thank you."

Chapter 40

August 23, 2030

The meeting took place in an upper committee room of the Museum of Science and Technology on SE Water Avenue in Portland. The Governor's aides had requisitioned the room for this unscheduled meeting only two days before. At exactly ten in the morning of August 23, 2030, Governor Tibbits called the meeting to order, and his aide introduced the people sitting around the table.

"Good morning, ladies and gentlemen," the aide said. "You all know Governor Tibbits, but there are two groups here who will each be unknown to the other, so let me introduce each person. My name is Alex Simpson. I am the Governor's aide. Next to me is the Portland Chief of Police, Luen van der Scheff; then the Emergency Services Co-Ordinator, Vereni Lewis. Next to her is our City Communications deputy chairperson, Julie Byrne; City Councilor Samuel Orenson, who is standing in for Mayor Julian; and at the other end of the table, the Head of the United States Geological Survey in Portland, Dr Peter Smythe. On the Governor's right is Robert Peale, CEO of the Rushing River Carbon Sequestration facility. Next to him is Professor Maxwell Hay, chief scientist to the Matternicht Group; Nigel Campion, aide to James Matternicht; and lastly, James Matternicht." Simpson sat down again and started fiddling with the pencil and pad on the table in front of him.

Governor Tibbits cleared his throat. "I want to thank you all for coming at such short notice. I know you have busy schedules..." he inclined his head toward the city officials on his left, "...so I won't spend time in social niceties. A few days ago, Professor Hay asked to speak to me, and as I've made his acquaintance before, I afforded him a few minutes on the telephone. What he had to say shocked me, and I was persuaded to offer him a platform to air his views on a subject which may affect the safety of Oregon. Professor Hay, would you be kind enough to tell these ladies and gentlemen what you told me?"

"Thank you, Governor. As most of you will be aware, some twenty years ago the governments of the world were faced with accelerating climate change partly due to increasing levels of greenhouse gases--mostly carbon dioxide--in the atmosphere. We were faced with the choice of drastically cutting back on carbon emissions which would have put the brakes on economic growth, or of seeking a way to take the carbon out of the atmosphere and lock it away--sequester it--in biological or geological sinks. Taking this option meant that some people made a fortune but the world was given a breathing space in which to look for a long-term solution.

"Mr James Matternicht offered a long-term solution and developed a method of storing liquid carbon dioxide deep underground in geological strata..."

"Sorry to interrupt, Professor," Byrne said. "But did you just say liquid carbon dioxide? I thought carbon dioxide went straight from the gas phase to a solid and vice versa--dry ice, you know."

"Yes, Ms Byrne, that's correct, but only at normal pressures. Subject CO_2 gas to pressures above seventy-three atmospheres and a temperature of thirty-one degrees Celsius and it becomes a supercritical fluid. That's one that will fill any container in the way that a gas does, but has the density of a liquid. This is a very useful property when it comes to storing CO_2 in rock strata.

"Now, as I was saying," Max went on, "The facility at Rushing River developed an apparently safe method for storing large quantities of carbon dioxide. Geological sequestration is nothing new, and many countries have tried it with varying degrees of success, but their ventures have been small or else the strata leaked badly, forcing them to give up. Only Matternicht's venture at Rushing River succeeded--or so we thought.

"Gentlemen, I'm afraid to say the Rushing River facility also leaks and due to the large quantity of carbon dioxide stored underground, we may be facing a crisis of great proportion. Mr Matternicht agreed to come with me today so that we could, together, tell you of this danger and of the way we seek to redress it."

"What do you call 'a large quantity of carbon dioxide', Professor?" Police Chief van der Scheff asked.

"Upwards of two hundred and fifty million tons."

"Jesus."

"Let me get this straight," Deputy Byrne said. "You have two hundred and fifty million tons of pressurized gas buried underground and it's leaking? Is this stuff dangerous? What are we looking at here?"

"It's an asphyxiant," Co-Ordinator Lewis said. "Are these leaks near a center of habitation?"

"The storage strata are under the town of Rushing River and associated farmland," Peale said. "But the leaks seem to be confined to an area of farmland a few miles out of town. There doesn't appear to be any immediate danger to people unless they stray into the area."

"Can it be contained?" Lewis asked. "I need to know if I'm to co-ordinate rescue services."

"If I'm being honest," Max said, "I don't know. We've never faced anything like this before. However, based on what Mr Matternicht says, I'm hopeful."

"Oh? What do you say, Mr Matternicht?" Lewis asked.

"Please, you'll forgive an old man if he just whispers. My strength isn't what it used to be. This problem has cost me many sleepless nights, but I think I know the solution. I have, as you may be aware, diversified interests in the supply of fuel. Coal mainly, but also petroleum and gas. Sometimes, the gas fields are under great pressure and there's a blowout. There are teams that go in and put out the flames, cap the well and seal it permanently. I have such teams on my payroll and one of these--the best of these--is flying in to Portland in two days' time. I've ordered what they'll need and I've no doubt that in a very short time the storage strata will be sealed tight, and utterly safe."

"If this procedure makes it safe, why wasn't it done right from the start? Then we wouldn't be facing this crisis."

"It's also very expensive," Campion put in. "And as the United States Government had agreed to foot the bill for capital works, we strove to keep costs down. Mr Matternicht is flying in this capping and sealing team at his own expense now to save the taxpayers."

"And I'm sure we appreciate that fact," Governor Tibbits said. "I would like to hear from Dr Smythe now. Peter, I thought the USGS had given the green light on the Rushing River storage strata. Why are they leaking now?"

"The USGS and DOE knew of the Hood Anticline as a possible site for carbon sequestration, but it wasn't until around sixteen or seventeen years ago that it was mapped out thoroughly. Up to that point it was a possible; after the survey a probable."

"Who carried out the survey, Dr Smythe? USGS or DOE?"

Smythe shifted in his seat and stared at the table rather than meet the Governor's eyes. "Well, neither really. We had oversight but the work was carried out by the Oregon Coal & Power scientists."

Governor Tibbits looked at Peale. "Your scientists did the work?"

"Under the guidance and oversight of USGS," Peale said hurriedly. "They accepted the findings. The anticline was in excellent condition, unflawed by any faults or fissures, and the capping layer was metamorphosed limestone, thick and impenetrable. It was an ideal site and USGS agreed. So did DOE."

"Based on your findings," Smythe agreed. "You must realize, Governor, that cutbacks had reduced our funding and we outsourced many projects in those years."

"Unfortunately, this one was the most important and, as I've recently come to realize, was also the most flawed," Max said. "Mr Peale, did you know that the capping rock varies in thickness from about thirty feet at the northern end to nearly double that at the southern?"

Peale examined his notes. "Er...yes, we knew that..."

"And that the limestone is only partially metamorphosed? Mostly to the west and south, closest to the basalt intrusions?"

"Yes, but..."

"And that the capping rock at the northern end has one flaw? I'm talking about the Limson shaft."

"That doesn't exist," Peale retorted. "It's an urban legend."

"I would agree with you up to a point, Mr Peale. The legend has it that in 1921, Ebenezer Limson drilled for oil near Rushing River and was only prevented from striking it rich by a lack of funds. He couldn't raise the capital to bring the well in and he died a year later with the well unfinished. Now, the truth of the matter is that there's no oil down there, but more importantly for us, he stopped drilling just after he hit a layer of limestone. About twenty feet in--out of a thickness of thirty feet."

"It doesn't matter," Peale said. "The cap's still intact and there've been no problems...no major problems."

"The Limson well was on the Rushing River Ranch, near a feature referred to as the beaver pond. That's where the leaks are taking place now, isn't it, Mr Peale?"

"Well..."

"What do you think, Dr Smythe?" Max asked. "Would you judge the cap to be intact still?"

"Hard to say. Without doing my own tests, and as nothing much has happened to show otherwise, I'd say it's intact...but possibly weakened."

Max sighed. "That's precisely the point. Something's happened. The cap's leaking."

"Yes, we know that," van der Scheff said impatiently. "That's the whole point of this meeting. Gas is leaking out but Matternicht believes it can be contained. You seem to think so, too, so where's the danger? Seal the damn thing and be done with it."

"I hope it's possible but I fear it's too late. Look, if I may use an analogy. We've all heard the story, apocryphal I'm sure, of the Dutch boy who put his finger in the dyke. You've heard of it? Yes?" There was a series of nods around the table. "So I ask the question, 'Why did he do it?' The hole was only finger-sized. That wouldn't let much water through."

"Well, that's frickin' obvious," Byrne said. "The pressure of the North Sea behind the dyke would have eaten away at the hole and enlarged it. Sooner or later the dyke would collapse and Holland would be flooded."

"Ah, I see," Tibbits said. "You're concerned that though we've only a little leak now, the pressure of stored gas will eventually open up the cap, releasing it all."

"That's it exactly, Governor," Max said. "Thank you."

"So, we've caught it early enough," van der Scheff said. "It can be capped and sealed before it gets worse?"

"I hope so, because the alternative is too frightening to contemplate."

"You alluded to this before," Lewis said, "when you referred to it as a crisis of great proportion. There's a leak, yet the gas is still escaping slowly, and Mr Matternicht has a team flying in to seal the leak. I fail to see where the crisis lies. Are you telling us you cannot put a proverbial finger in the dyke?"

"Of course we can," Matternicht interrupted hoarsely. "Professor Hay is altogether too pessimistic. We can seal the leak."

"Then why was this meeting called?" asked Byrne. "If this is straightforward, then why didn't you just attend to it?"

"Because we've a concern for public safety," Campion said smoothly. "There's a tiny chance--a vanishingly small chance--of more gas escaping as we seal the leak, and if this should happen, we want to make sure the public is protected."

"Very commendable," Tibbits said.

"And totally misleading," Max added. "These leaks have been present for years and for the last year or two they've been getting worse. I alerted Matternicht to the possibility of catastrophic failure six months ago but he did nothing. It wasn't until I threatened to go public and reveal his complicity that he agreed to this meeting. His motive is money, not public spirit."

Matternicht laughed. "Max likes to think he's my conscience, but in reality he's kept silent for many years, content to reap the monetary benefits of his position. Regrettably, he's turned on me and seeks to salve his own guilty conscience by laying the blame at my door. He's been my chief scientific adviser for thirty years or more; surely he'd know of dangers long before anyone else? The truth of it is that he's acting like a spoiled brat, making a big deal out of an insignificant incident."

"An insignificant incident that's killed four people. A hiker in May and a family of tourists last week."

"Is this true?" Tibbits asked.

"Utter nonsense," Campion said quickly. "The remains of a hiker were found, but no cause of death could be ascertained. The family...well, nobody knows what killed them either. It could have been anything."

"A memo landed on my desk this morning," van der Scheff said. "From the Wasco County Medical Examiner. He says the three deaths in Rushing River were from asphyxiation, most likely as a result of carbon dioxide."

"This casts another light on the leaks," Tibbits said. "If people have died as a result of this leak, then we must shut down the facility immediately."

"That's not necessary," Peale protested. "It's safe."

"It's unconscionable," Matternicht added. "There's no proof that the facility is responsible for the deaths. The carbon dioxide could be from some other source--volcanic perhaps."

"Not volcanic," Smythe said, shaking his head. "The area's sedimentary with no underlying magmatic intrusions. That was one of the selling points for the dome in the first place. "

"So, we shut the facility down," Tibbits said. "We throw a cordon around the area, evacuate the residents and send in a team of experts--independent experts--to evaluate the danger." The Governor turned to his officials. "I want you to work together on this and have a working plan on my desk by this afternoon."

"It won't do any good," Max said.

"We have to do something, Professor Hay. People have died. I'm shutting everything down until I'm satisfied the whole thing is safe."

"It won't do any good to shut it down and it'll never be truly safe, no matter what you do. The stuff is already down there. It's like putting a timer on a nuclear weapon, then burying it and hoping if you ignore it, nothing will happen. Shut the facility and add no more CO_2 if you like, but what's already down there could erupt any time--today, next week, next year, in a hundred years. We've very little control over it."

"I don't think we have anything to gain by making hysterical comparisons to nuclear devices," Matternicht said. "Carbon dioxide is not explosive, nor does it support combustion. It's not going to blow up. It's in a stable formation and will remain there. My team will flood the ground with concrete and seal every leak. There's no reason to be concerned."

"Earlier this morning, I told Mr Matternicht what we're looking at in terms of explosive power, but it seems he's forgotten it or chooses to ignore it."

"So tell us, Professor Hay," Tibbits said.

"Hold on." Councilor Orenson spoke for the first time. "I thought carbon dioxide wasn't explosive. Why are you then talking in terms of explosive power?"

"A good point, Mr Orenson. Perhaps I should've said expansive power. Liquid carbon dioxide is only a liquid under pressure. Release that pressure and it immediately expands into a gas, with an expansion ratio of about 3000 per cent. Instantly, not gradually. A liter of liquid becomes 3000 liters of gas..."

"How much is that in gallons?" Byrne asked.

"A gallon becomes 3000 gallons," Max replied, straight faced. "And there's something like 100 trillion liters of liquid CO_2 down there. Take the cap off it and it'll make the Hiroshima explosion look like a party balloon bursting."

"Jesus wept," Lewis exclaimed.

Van der Scheff said something altogether more basic and even Governor Tibbits muttered an expletive under his breath.

"That's...that's impressive, Professor Hay, but you're talking explosions again and carbon dioxide isn't explosive."

"An explosion's caused by a solid or a liquid rapidly expanding to form a gas. If you take 225 grams--about half a pound--of nitroglycerine and detonate it, it'll become gas with a volume of about one hundred and eighty liters. It's that expansion from a small lump of solid into a large volume of gas, instantly, that makes it an explosive, not any ability to combust. The expansion power of liquid carbon dioxide is much greater." Max leaned forward and met the gaze of each of the city officials in turn. "Let me put this in easy-to-understand terms. After three decades of nuclear disarmament, the stockpile of nuclear weapons held by the United States is around two thousand megatons. If you imagine half of those exploding at once, you have some idea of what would happen if the top came off the Hood Anticline. If that happened under Portland, Portland would cease to exist. And there's more."

"More? How can there possibly be more?" Tibbits asked. "We face destruction on this scale and you tell us there's more? What more?"

"Adiabatic cooling."

"What's that?"

"Simply put, if a gas expands suddenly, the temperature drops. If liquid carbon dioxide expands suddenly by the cap being released the expanding gas will cool to about minus seventy-eight degrees Celsius, about minus one hundred and eight Fahrenheit. A blow-out of the Rushing River facility will not only obliterate everything in its path; it'll snap-freeze what's left and poison every living soul for thirty miles around and possibly two hundred miles downwind." Max gave a wry smile. "I won't even touch on the long-term environmental effects."

There was dead silence around the table; discomfiture and anger on the faces of Matternicht, Campion and Peale; stunned disbelief in the expressions of the others.

Tibbits looked at Peter Smythe. "You're the only other scientist here, Dr Smythe. Is what Professor Hay says true?"

"I think he's being a little bit conservative actually. That said, I believe there's some doubt that it'll all blow at once. If there truly has been leakage from the site, why hasn't that leakage led to a catastrophic blow-out already? A quantity of gas escaping through the strata should clear the way for the rest of it. That doesn't seem to have happened."

"I think I know why," Max said. "Say the initial crack is small, like a pinhole size. Gas leaks out and percolates through the overlying rock and soil until it's held up by something impermeable near the surface. Pressure builds there until it blows through as a bubble of gas, and the soil slumps back again blocking further gas until it builds up again. Meanwhile, the pinhole grows and more gas escapes, the surface bubble is larger and more dangerous."

Dr Smythe nodded. "We won't know until we investigate the site but it sounds reasonable."

"But this is all hypothetical," Lewis said. "Your talk is full of 'ifs' and 'maybes'. This has never happened before, so you're guessing."

"Perhaps," Max said.

"There you go again."

"I think it might have happened once before. The Russians started to build a full geosequestration facility at Krasnorovka in about 2022. Then three years ago, something happened. There was heavy cloud cover over the site and when it cleared, satellite imagery showed the facility and two villages had disappeared. There was a total news blackout in Russia--you may remember there were rumors that there'd been a coup. It wasn't that, but they suddenly stopped work on sequestration."

Governor Tibbits shook his head. "I find it hard to believe that something so dangerous and impossible to control was allowed to happen here in Oregon. What I find equally hard to believe is that you, Mr Matternicht, would be so brazen as to ignore the warning signs until now."

Matternicht's hands fluttered as if trying to deflect the Governor's words. "I admit I've been remiss in my actions, but through ignorance of the real situation I assure you. I only wish that Professor Hay had voiced his concerns earlier, so we could have taken corrective action. Well, no matter. As we say, *was passiert ist, ist passiert.*" Aided by Campion, Matternicht rose shakily to his feet. "Gentlemen, ladies...I will leave you now to your deliberations and your decisions about what you must do to satisfy bureaucratic demands. I intend to fly to Rushing River--I have a helicopter standing by at the airport--with my staff to coordinate the shutdown and capping. Come, Peale, Max."

"I won't be joining you, Mr Matternicht," Max said. "I've decided that it does in fact matter. I resign from your organization formally. I'll find my own way from now on."

"As you wish, Max." Matternicht left the committee room with his small entourage and made his way down to the waiting limousines. "The airport," he told the drivers.

Max left the room shortly after, with Dr Smythe. The Governor scarcely noticed their departure as he was deep in conversation with his officials, planning exactly how they would evacuate Rushing River and the surrounding countryside without creating a panic.

"What will you do?" Smythe asked.

"I forgot that I flew up here with Matternicht. I must find my way back down to Los Angeles. A rental car, I think. It'll give me time to consider my future. And you?"

"Well, Tibbits doesn't seem to need my help. I'll go back to work and...hmm, I've just remembered. One of my scientists was looking into Rushing River. I think I might see if he has anything useful to add." He switched on his phone. "Can I interest you in a cup of coffee in the Museum cafeteria before you go?"

"Another time, maybe," Max said. "I've a long way to go."

"Safe journey, Professor Hay."

Chapter 41

August 23, 2030

The Hood Mountain & River View Retreat was a moderate sized structure that was built into the side of a mountain on the Washington State side of the Columbia River. The Dalles Bridge crossed the river just up from the city and a road wound its way up the mountain to the Retreat. At an elevation of two thousand feet, the Retreat commanded spectacular views of the Columbia River Valley, the Deschutes Valley, and the imposing bulk of Mount Hood. The building itself was semi-circular in design with a long thin patio following the curve of the façade and just inside the patio was a dining room that also afforded its diners an uninterrupted view of mountain and valley. Matt asked for a table on the patio and, as the hour was early for luncheon, they were shown to a choice position in the center, where the patio bulged out over the drop to the highway far below.

"It's spectacular," Annaliese said. "I never even knew this place was here." She stared out over the mountainside and into the distance. "Everything looks different when we're above it. What's down there?"

Matt came and stood beside her. His hand swept along the ribbon of water below them. "The great Columbia River, sweeping down to that hazy blob on the horizon which is Portland."

"We can see as far as Portland?"

"No, but you can see its effect on the environment."

"What about Rushing River?"

"About thirty miles in that direction." Matt pointed between the slopes of the mountain and the lowlands of the Deschutes Valley. "That's the Deschutes River, and Rushing River is a tributary. It's tucked up out of sight around the side of Hood."

"A pity, I'd like to see it. What else?"

"Now, as we face Oregon, the Deschutes River joins the Columbia there to our left..." he pointed, "And on the opposite side, but harder to see, is the Hood River with the town of Hood River at the confluence. Dominating everything is Mount Hood, all glorious 11,240 feet of it. It once had glaciers, but the warming climate took care of those."

"It's still beautiful. It's a volcano isn't it?"

"Yup, officially a stratovolcano in the Cascade Volcanic Arc, and though it is classed as dormant, it has been voted the Oregon volcano most likely to erupt."

"You're kidding?"

"Would I kid a reporter? You want a drink?"

They sat down at their table and ordered drinks--an Australian chardonnay for Annaliese and a Coors for Matt. They also put in their orders for the meal--poached quail with a side salad and lamb shanks with thyme. Matt called them sheepshanks, which got a puzzled look from Annaliese and a raised eyebrow from the waiter.

"I used to be an Eagle Scout," Matt explained. "Knots and all that." When Annaliese still looked none the wiser, he added, "A sheepshank's a knot. Just my odd sense of humor."

Annaliese laughed. "My son Adrian would like your jokes. He still watches those antique comedy routines from the Monty Python people."

"I'd like to meet him. He sounds like a great kid."

Annaliese dropped her gaze and blushed slightly. "I thought you'd be a red wine man if you were ordering lamb though."

"Sorry," he said with a grin, "I could never get used to wines. My dad brought me up to drink beer."

"Tell me about your father. What does he do?"

"He's a mining consultant, though he's close to retiring now. He's up in Canada at the moment, advising on iron deposits somewhere, I think."

"Rocks run in your family, then?"

Matt laughed and drank from his bottle of Coors. "Oh yes. My great-grandfather Herbert worked as a roustabout on the Boulder Dam down in Colorado a hundred years ago, and then on the Grand Coulee Dam here on the Columbia River. His son Stephen followed him into the trade but started to study the rocks as well as blast them apart. He studied the physical properties of different types of rock, got his explosives ticket and was in great demand until he got killed in a hang-fire. By then, though, his son Mike, my father, was hooked on the subject and...well," Matt shrugged, "I sort of drifted into geology, too."

"And your mother?"

"An elementary school teacher in Six Rivers in northern California." Matt smiled fondly. "Again, it runs in her family--teachers of one sort or another from way back. Except Uncle Eustace--he was a con-man and died in jail about forty years ago." Matt winked. "The family doesn't talk about him."

"Brothers and sisters?"

"One sister, Lilian. She's married and another teacher. In Fort Worth, Texas. Let's see, I also have no pets--not that I have anything against them, but I'm not home much. I had a cat when I was a kid--an Abyssinian - also a ferret and a hamster. Not all at the same time, though." Matt smiled and gazed into Annaliese's face. "Okay, enough about me. Your turn."

Annaliese blushed again. "Not much to tell, nor very interesting. I'm one of four kids, two brothers and a sister--I'm the second oldest. My dad was in the army, a sergeant, and my mom was a sales assistant when he met her, then a full-time home worker. Let's see...we had dogs...or rather, my brothers did, and we girls shared them. I had a goldfish of my own. Brought up in Seattle, moved down to Salem after I got my journalism diploma from Pacific U. Then I got married, moved to Portland, got divorced and moved back to Salem."

Matt was silent for a few moments. "What happened? Do you mind me asking?"

Annaliese shrugged and looked out over the Columbia River Valley. "I suppose not. Peter was a Grade A dickhead. He was a cheating, no-good scumbag with a gambling problem and I was happy to see the back of him."

"Sorry. I didn't mean to bring up bad memories."

"Every cloud has its silver lining, as the saying goes--and mine's Adrian."

"Your son?"

"Yes. I couldn't ask for a smarter, more handsome, loving son." Annaliese smiled. "I suppose every mother says that of her child, but it's true."

"I can't wait to meet him. How old is he?"

"Fourteen last January." Annaliese looked back at Matt and opened her mouth to say something more but changed her mind. "Ah, here's lunch."

For several minutes, there was little sound from their table except the clatter of cutlery on china, chewing noises and expressions of delight and contentment over the food. Annaliese finished first and watched Matt eat.

"I like a man with healthy appetites," she said softly, sipping her wine.

Matthew almost choked on a bite of lamb, but said nothing, though his thoughts took a whole new turn.

"Another wine?"

"Please."

Matt ordered another chardonnay and a beer for himself, and they sat back as the waiter cleared their plates. They declined the dessert menu, saying they preferred to just enjoy the view for the time being.

A shadow swept over them and they looked up as a bald eagle soared past, angling down toward the river below, its white helmet and leggings gleaming in the sunlight.

"I love those birds," Annaliese said.

"I know a nesting spot on the Deschutes," Matt said. "I'll take you next spring if you like. I go most years and take photos."

"I'd like that." She sat silently for a few moments, then, "Is she...they...going to be alright? Margaret and Marc, I mean. That sinkhole on their ranch is frightening."

Matt sighed and upended his bottle, taking a long pull of the amber fluid. "I don't really know, but I think the sooner the State authorities step in the better. The situation is serious, Annaliese."

"I suppose there's no chance this carbon dioxide is a result of volcanic action?"

Matt shook his head. "Carbon dioxide is churned out by volcanoes, but so are a lot of other gases, notably sulphur compounds. You'd notice them immediately and we haven't detected a trace of those. No, this is all down to the sequestered CO_2."

"Did you test for sulphur gases?"

Matt grinned and tapped his nose. "Used the most sensitive meter I have."

"What's going to happen?"

"Well, if the leak gets no worse, they'll shut down the plant and try and seal the hole with tons of concrete I imagine. If it gets worse, I don't really see what they can do. Either way, I can see the State and maybe National economies taking a battering. Carbon sequestration was supposed to be the light at the end of the climate change tunnel. Now, I don't know what people will do. Even as recently as twenty years ago, the world could have taken another route, but they chose to keep on churning out carbon and working on storing as much of it as they could."

"It wasn't that bad," Annaliese objected. "I remember as a kid my family was right into recycling and reducing our carbon footprint. A lot of people were doing that."

"That's true, but much of it was lip service. We bought more locally grown produce to save on transport carbon, but insisted on travelling far and wide for our vacations. We put up solar panels and eco-toilets but ignored the carbon cost of producing them. Every year there were more people needing housing, food, clothing, and demanding the same luxuries everyone else enjoyed. The world could only play catch-up, never get ahead of the game. Millions of people did a little bit to stop carbon emissions, but the big boys went on doing whatever they wanted. There's a lot of money to be made in power production, coal, oil, transport, and then when the governments offered big bucks for finding ways of carrying on business as usual, up springs the sequestration plant. The one thing I can't understand is why there aren't more of these facilities if they're supposed to be such a good thing."

"Too expensive perhaps."

Matt nodded. "Bloody expensive, I would imagine, but the government subsidizes them. As far as I know, Rushing River is the only major attempt at using land-based rock strata for carbon storage. In the light of what might be happening, perhaps that's just as well."

"You really think something bad's going to happen?"

"You saw the start of it this morning. Exactly how bad it's going to get and how quickly is anybody's guess. If you want my estimate, I'd say 'very bad' and 'very soon'. I just hope the State Police will take our report seriously."

Annaliese stared at Matt and pushed the remains of her wine away. "How bad is very bad?"

"Stay here, I'll be back in a moment." Matt got up and hurried inside, coming back out in a few minutes with an unopened bottle of beer and a bottle opener. "Now, this bottle represents the storage strata underneath Rushing River, and the cap is the capping rock."

"And the opener?"

"The crack in the rocks. Now, let's put some pressure in the strata." He shook the bottle vigorously. "Of course, you know what's going to happen, so this is just a waste of good beer. Still..." Matt whipped the top off and the frothing beer fountained out, cascading over his hand. "Imagine that magnified a billion times." He put the half empty bottle down and wiped his hands on his napkin.

"I find it hard to grasp numbers like a billion," Annaliese said. "I can imagine a great stream of...of gassy water gushing up, but I can't put it into the real world. If it comes out of that pit on the ranch, it won't really affect the ranch house, will it? That'd be too far away--at least a mile."

"It's not frothy water coming out of the ground, Annaliese," Matt said gently. "It's liquid carbon dioxide that's going to flash into a gas as the pressure comes off and the temperature will drop precipitately to minus seventy odd. The gas asphyxiates," he added grimly, "as you nearly found out. It'll be very cold and utterly deadly and the amounts will be so great it'll probably kill everyone for several miles around."

"Dear God. How far? Will...will Adrian be safe in Portland? In Salem? Will we be safe here?"

"I doubt it's going to blow out today. And I really can't guess how large it would be. Carbon dioxide is heavier than air, so it's going to flow down river valleys and cover towns as it goes. The cold would be terrible for a while, but that would pass. I'd say Portland is way too far to be affected except by gas flowing down the Columbia, and I imagine we're too high up here, so stop worrying." Matt glanced at his watch. "I fancy a piece of chocolate cheesecake for dessert, a nice strong cup of coffee, and then we can drive down and see the State Police. You feel like some?"

"I'll pass--just coffee for...what on earth's that?" Annaliese pointed out to the south.

A tall spire of silvery white climbed to the heavens, spearing through the clouds into the high summer sky. There it spread out in all directions, a tall thin-stemmed mushroom with a rapidly growing cap. Veils fell from the cap as if showers of rain marched across the countryside.

"What is it?" Annaliese asked again.

Other diners were now on their feet and staring, talking in low tones as they strove to make sense of the sight. People, staff and guests alike, poured out of the Retreat, congregating on the patio, shouting and gesticulating. Several took pictures on their cell phones. A sound reached them--a rapidly escalating roar.

"It's a bomb," yelled someone. "They've dropped a fucking atomic bomb."

People started screaming and running for their cars. Amidst the confusion, Annaliese started edging away, caught up in the panic, but Matt grabbed her arm and pulled her away from the crush.

He leaned close so she could hear, though neither of them took their eyes off the silvery apparition sparkling in the sunlight. "It's not a bomb," he said, "But it's just as deadly."

"It looks so beautiful--all white and sparkly."

"Dry ice crystals catching the sun. It's spreading fast--faster than I thought. We have to figure out what we're going to do when it gets here."

Annaliese dragged her eyes away from the cloud. "You said it wouldn't get here...or Portland..." She fumbled for her cell phone and punched in the numbers with trembling fingers. "Adrian! Adey it's happened. The whole thing's gone up...you've got to get away...quickly...don't worry about me, I'm a long way...yes, just go...hello...hello. Adey, are you there? Hello..."

Matt was also on the phone--to his boss Peter Smythe. "Dr Smythe, it's Matt...Matt Morrison...yeah, I'm at the Hood Retreat. Boss, it...it's gone up. The whole damn thing has blown...yes, Rushing River. I can see it from here and I'm thirty miles away...no...kiss goodbye to the Deschutes and The Dalles, the cloud is spreading fast...I don't know." He broke off, suddenly fighting for breath. "The cloud's overhead already and it's snowing--dry ice snow. Can you get word to the authorities?" Matt started breathing fast. "Gotta go, boss. Gotta find a safe place..." He hung up and grabbed Annaliese. "We've got to find somewhere to shelter quickly."

The temperature was plummeting as the dry ice storm descended on them. Annaliese was panting and wide-eyed. "Where? The car? We could drive away..." She gestured toward the almost empty car park. "I should try and get to Adrian..."

"Those fools will get halfway down and then their cars will shut down. High CO_2 levels will kill an engine as dead as a person."

"Then where, damn it? What do we do?"

Matt held Annaliese close and watched the dry ice blizzard sweep toward them, feeling the rising carbon dioxide levels start to choke the life out of him. *Will we freeze or suffocate first? What the hell do we do?*

Chapter 42

August 23, 2030

Marc and Margaret had an argument after Matt and Annaliese drove off. Margaret told her husband about the sink hole and the well of carbon dioxide bubbling at the bottom of it. Her description of Annaliese falling unconscious into the hole and being dragged out by Matt wearing a breathing pack was recounted with breathless excitement.

She also said they should leave the ranch for the time being. "We could go to my sister in Virginia City, or if you don't want to go so far, how about a decent hotel in The Dalles? We could treat it as a short vacation. I'm sure we could come back in a few days."

"I'm not being driven off my land by a gas, for God's sake. Besides, there's too much to do to take a vacation. Now, you said yourself the gas collects in hollows, so as long as we keep to high ground we'll be fine."

"We should move the cattle away from there, at least."

Marc grunted. "We could do that, though there aren't any in the creek paddock."

"The fence is down. They could stray in and die like the other ones last week."

The ground shook beneath them briefly and Margaret cried out. "The tremors are getting worse, Marc. We should leave."

"No, but that damn carbon plant is going to be paying me compensation if there are any other losses," Marc said. He shook his head and stared to the north in the direction of the beaver pond. "I suppose I'd better go and have a look."

"If you can wait a bit, I'll come with you. I promised Annaliese and Matt I'd call a few people first and warn them."

"Well, tell them the warning comes from them, not us. I don't want people round here thinking we're nuts." He stomped off into the barn.

Margaret hurried into the house and started calling her friends in and around Rushing River. It was all she could do to fend off normal conversation and keep her words to the matter in hand. Several people wanted to know if she was leaving town and she had to say she was not.

"It can't be that serious then," one friend said.

Annaliese called her between phone calls out, wanting to know if they were leaving, and Margaret had to tell her Marc's reaction to the warning. "Let him get the stock to safety and maybe he'll agree. I'll work on him some more."

By the time Margaret had finished her calls, an hour or more had passed. She went out to find her husband and suggested they go get the cattle moved.

"In a bit." Marc wiped his sweaty forehead with a cloth. "I could do with a drink and a bite to eat first. How about it, Maggie?"

Margaret made them sandwiches, and they ate them in the kitchen with cold root beers. They did not say much, each wrapped in their own thoughts. A little before eleven o'clock, they stacked the dishes and set off for the sink hole on foot. Marc shook his head when Margaret suggested a vehicle.

"It'll be easier to move the stock on foot."

The earth shook again, a long, drawn-out shudder, on their way to the sink hole. They reached the fallen fence adjoining the creek paddock a little after eleven and found a herd of about fifty steers standing staring at what lay beyond. As they drew near, they could hear the rushing, thundering sound of falling water. The cattle drew back as they approached and Marc and Margaret stood on the edge of a broad hole in their land, staring at the sight that confronted them.

The sink hole had widened considerably in the last couple of hours and the bottom was hidden in foam and spray at least two hundred feet below. Even as they watched, sections of the edge gave way and tumbled into the chasm. The dry creek bed that had hung on the lip of the crater two hours before was now a torrent of water cascading into the hole.

"Where's the water coming from?"

Marc stared in amazement. "I'd say the Rushing River itself, but how has the flow reversed itself? Has the land tilted or something?"

Another strong tremor shook the ground and Margaret turned and ran back a few paces. The tremor did not stop, but grew, the vibration becoming sound and the sound building into a deafening roar. Margaret felt her eardrums rupture and screamed in anguish. No longer heard, but felt in every cell of her body, the shaking of the earth grew to a crescendo. Marc fell to his knees and looked on in horror as a great white column of frigid gas and mist and ice blasted out of the pit, hurling earth and rocks high into the air. A tornado of cold carbon dioxide ripped the breath from Marc's lungs and as he fell back, his last sight was of his wife standing a few paces away, covered in a shroud of frost, her eyes shattered from within by ice crystals.

Husband and wife were dead in the instant before a tidal wave of dry ice crystals enveloped them and froze solid the stampeding herd in the field behind them.

* * *

Claudia Barrow worked in the Information Center in Rushing River Township and lived close to the campground. She was an amateur photographer and loved nothing better than to go on long walks, taking pictures of anything that caught her fancy. She had come to her hobby later in life and still remembered the old film photography of her childhood as being expensive and less than satisfactory.

Pictures of people seldom interested her, so she wandered the riverbank or took long hikes into the hills looking for that subtle combination of light and shadow, a leaf back-lit by the dawn sunlight, or water rippling over rocks, that caught her imagination. Animals interested her, too, but not the usual cutesy poses of kittens and squirrels. She saw the beauty in a fallen feather, a hawk harried by a pair of songbirds, and a torn spider web.

Claudia decided on the river that morning, after the first earth tremor rocked her cottage. She set out through the trees at the bottom of the garden, eager to see if the movement of the earth had perhaps shaken some rocks into the river from the high pebbly banks, or brought a tree down with moist earth-covered roots staring starkly at the sky. Instead, she stood and stared at a river that was suddenly shrunken to a trickle.

Rushing River lived up to its name, attracting fishermen and water enthusiasts from all over the State and beyond, but nobody would travel to see these sluggish rills.

"What happened?" she asked herself aloud. "Where did the water go?"

Claudia snapped off a few pictures of turgid pools and stranded fish, before starting along the bank toward the campground. She met other people gawking at the depleted river and stopped for a few minutes to discuss the wonder. Then she carried on, taking pictures as she went, hurrying as she heard the familiar roar of water again. Visions of the Rushing River plunging into a chasm created by the earthquake filled her mind, but the scene that greeted her was stranger.

Where the Beaver Creek met the river, the land seemed to have slumped and slipped and the river poured into the mouth of the creek, rushing along a stony bed that had reversed its inclination. She raised her camera again, angling for shots that would show the incredible change. The roar grew louder, almost unbearable, and she followed the bank of the creek, seeking the source of the sound. A hundred yards further on she stopped, dizzy. She leaned against a young aspen tree, panting.

She shivered in her summer dress as a cold breeze raised goosebumps on her bare arms. Claudia held out her hand to catch a flake and cried out as it burned her palm. The flakes fell faster, carried on a stiff breeze that blew down the creek bed. A deafening roar enveloped her, the trees whipping and swaying as the blast hit them. She felt short of breath and sank to her knees, and after a few moments lay down, struggling to fill her lungs with something her body could use. Snow fell heavily now, freezing snow much colder than normal. Within minutes, the water in the creek froze, damming the valley and pushing the Rushing River back into its former course.

Claudia's body was buried in drifts of carbon dioxide snow.

* * *

Dr Angelina Roux had that happy ability to put concerns and worries to the back of her mind while she got on with her work. She was in the laboratory of the carbon capture facility when the first tremor struck, sending a stack of Petri dishes crashing to the floor. While the technicians cleaned up and checked for further damage, she went to the window and looked out in the direction of the Stone's ranch. Nothing appeared out of the ordinary, but Angelina felt a small frisson of anxiety. *What if...?* she thought, but refused to follow the thread further.

She returned to her work--editing a paper she planned to submit to the Journal of Stratigraphy--but her heart was no longer in it. After a little while, she went into her office and pulled out the file on carbon dioxide levels: not the file she kept for public consumption but the accurate one, the one that showed the unaltered values of every test she had carried out over the past sixteen years. Shorn of doublespeak and the 'buts and maybes' of scientific doubt, it was a frightening document. The millions of tons of liquid carbon dioxide she had helped inject into the rocks far beneath her feet represented a time bomb. It was not a question of if they escaped, but of when they escaped.

It was happening. The leaks had been minor for several years, well within acceptable limits, even unaltered, and she had grown complacent. When the first readings crept into the danger zone, she had massaged them downward, not wanting to admit failure. Later, she could not reveal her dishonesty and accept responsibility, so she kept quiet and downplayed the leaks, assigning them values a fraction of their true scale. She had even come to believe her own lies, and had convinced the CEO, Robert Peale, that revealing the truth would do far more harm than concealing it.

Angelina thought about Robert Peale for a few moments, and even smiled as she remembered. They had had an affair in the early years, brief but tempestuous, and she had ended it rather than let it peter out. It had left Robert wanting more, which was a bonus for her, as he could be easily influenced. His desires were a control device for her, nothing more, and she had no intention of ever renewing their liaison.

The building trembled again, and an alarm went off somewhere. Angelina got up and walked to the window, looking at the now-sleeping compression and injection facility, and the chimneys of the power plant that now belched carbon dioxide as well as water vapor into the atmosphere.

Too late. No purpose is served by closing down the injection facility. The time bomb's ticking and nothing will stop it. She wondered if she should run. *I could just get in my car, send in my resignation and start again somewhere--somewhere safe.* But when the truth came out she would lose everything. *Better to die here...*

The building lurched and she heard breaking glass and shouting. Alarms were going off in the laboratories and the factory, and train klaxons sounded from the freight yards. Across the miles of countryside, of grass and woods, a huge tree grew, a great column of shimmering white, rapidly obscured by sheets of trailing mist as it punched up through the clouds, caught by the wind and mushrooming out as it lost momentum.

Dear God, it's happening.

A shock wave rattled the windows and on its heels came a deafening roar, even across the intervening miles. Angelina turned and ran, obeying instinct rather than the reason that had governed her adult life. She knew she could not outrun it, but she tried anyway--down the stairs, caught up in a crowd of others shouting and running for the doors--out into a car park already dusted with snow and terribly cold. She stumbled over a body lying in the snow and fell to her knees. All of a sudden it was too much effort to get up. She fought for breath but her panic did not last long.

Dr Angelina Roux drifted into unconsciousness and death and within minutes was covered, along with twenty others from the facility, in a deepening shroud of dry ice crystals.

* * *

Albert Ruffin had followed Matt and Annaliese in the USGS 4WD to the border of town but stopped when he saw they were heading for Rushing River. He turned his Taurus and drove slowly back to The Dalles, thinking through the options available to him.

He still wanted to get the boy, but his first duty was to kill his target, the mother. Albert considered laying another ambush, waiting by the side of the road, but the presence of the man had spoiled that one last time and today would be no different as the two of them were together again. Unless he just waited for her to return home, or to the house in Forest Park, his best option was the car park at the County Morgue in The Dalles. A shooting was possible: Albert knew he was eminently forgettable in appearance and unless he drew attention to himself he would likely escape notice, even if bystanders were present.

On the other hand, there was something clean and pure about explosives. He had the makings in his bag and could whip up a decent little bomb in half an hour. Albert pulled into the car park at the Morgue and was fortunate to find a parking spot only four or five slots over from the red Kia.

"First things first," he muttered. Albert locked the bag in the trunk of the Taurus and went looking for something to eat and drink. He considered driving to a restaurant but decided it was not worth losing such a handy park. A short walk brought him to a small mall where he bought a hamburger and a coke. He also bought a paper, not for the news but as a cover should he be disturbed while putting the bomb together.

Back at his car, he took the bag out and got into the front seat, adjusting the central and wing mirrors to give himself maximum coverage of the approaches to his vehicle. Then he opened the bag and took out the explosive, the timer, a 9-volt battery, a wireless relay and magnetic clamps. There were a few different ways he could detonate the explosive, setting it to blow up when the ignition was turned on, or putting a timer on it, or setting relays between the leaves of the car's suspension so it would go off when the car went over a bump. He weighed each option and discarded them all. An ignition trigger pointed immediately to a bomb and Albert knew that the longer you could leave the police guessing, the better. Timers were good, but only if you knew exactly when the target would be using the car; and the suspension could mean an indefinite delay if the target drove carefully. Albert decided on a timed explosion triggered by a wireless signal. He would set the explosives under the driver's seat with a thirty-minute timer, itself triggered by a radio signal which he would only send as she drove the Kia out of the parking lot.

Albert worked quickly, fitting the parts together and binding them with insulating tape. When he was finished, he put the scraps away in his bag and stashed that back in his trunk. He folded the newspaper around the bomb and walked casually over to the red Kia, looking about carefully to make sure nobody was watching him. Satisfied, he slipped between the Kia and the car on the driver's side and knelt. He felt under the car and selected a part of the floor beneath the driver's seat, fixing the bomb carefully in place with the magnets.

He heard a roaring sound but dismissed it at first as being a jet taking off from the Columbia Gorge Regional Airport. The noise went on, increasing in volume, but he could see nothing so he shrugged and went on with his work. As he finished, a shadow fell over him and he looked up to see thin wispy clouds racing over the sky. They were odd enough that he stood and watched them thicken and blot out the light. A wave of frigid air fell upon him and he gasped, suddenly fighting for breath.

"What the fuck?" he muttered, then, "Snow?"

Albert staggered and fell against the old red Kia, the radio sender in his pocket switching on, but he remained unaware of that fact and of the arming light on the bomb switching from red to green as he collapsed unconscious to the ground.

He was dead within minutes.

* * *

A tsunami of frigid carbon dioxide rolled down the Deschutes Valley, with more falling from the skies. Every scrap of moisture in the air froze instantly and precipitated out as a spattering of hail that kicked up little puffs of the carbon dioxide snow. Plants ruptured from the cold as their sap froze, but every animal and human in the path of the wave of toxic gas succumbed in seconds, long before the cold could affect them.

* * *

Adrian Winton said goodbye to his mother and closed the garage door behind her before going into the kitchen and fixing himself a large bowl of muesli with chopped banana. He took it into the living room and slurped and chomped his way through it while he watched early morning television. After a while he got up, left his bowl unwashed in the sink and had a shower, leaving the television on for company. Then he switched on the computer and got busy searching out information on Rushing River and carbon sequestration.

There was a lot of information, and he copied and pasted relevant parts to Word documents and printed them off, arranging them in neat piles for his mother to look at. A couple of hours later he took a break, stretching and pouring himself a Pepsi which he sipped in front of the television. The news programs had finished but after flicking through the channels he found himself some sitcom reruns that amused him.

The phone rang and he picked it up absently, still watching the TV. "Yeah?...What? Slow down, mom...what's gone? Shit!" Adrian did not apologize, nor did his mother ask him to. "Mom...mom...you're breaking up...mom? Hello? Hello?"

He hung up and walked across to the window that faced the mountains, looking southeast. A huge white column rose into the air, its base hidden by the Cascades, but great swathes of mist...*Vapor? Ash?*...drifted down from the pillar. Adrian was reminded of a great pine tree, complete with drooping branches and his mind made the connection with something he had seen that very morning.

"A Plinian eruption," he muttered. This type of volcanic eruption was a very violent one, with ash ascending rapidly before spreading out and falling under its weight to smother the surrounding countryside. It was named after the Roman naturalist Pliny the Elder, who had described the eruption of Vesuvius--and died shortly thereafter from asphyxiation--in 79 C.E. "But this isn't a volcano erupting; it's the carbon dioxide store." Even through the double-glazed windows, he could hear the muted, but growing roar of the eruption.

Despite the distance, movement of the column and descending swathes could plainly be seen, indicating great speed. The column punched up through the scattered clouds, which evaporated instantly as the frigid column hit them. As the ascending maelstrom of dry ice crystals reached the zenith, it started to collapse, and a tidal wave of white snow belched out in every direction, even as the column was renewed from within.

"Holy crap!" Adrian said as he saw the snow drifting over the mountains onto the eastern side. "I've got to get out of here." He started toward the door but then stopped. *Where do I go, and how? I don't have a car.* Instead, he went back to the window and watched the progression of the eruption.

Carbon dioxide is heavier than air, he remembered. *It'll sink, so as long as I remain high up, I should be okay. I'm at about 800 feet here in Forest Park, I think. But the Cascades are higher and it's spilling over them...yes, and they're also a lot closer to the source. That's dry ice at minus a hundred degrees...water pipes will burst, the electricity will go....so; do I run for it or tough it out here? Gramps's house is well built. I have food and the carbon dioxide shouldn't get this far. I should be okay if I stay here...*

Adrian pulled the television across and adjusted an armchair so he could watch the news channel and the developing disaster out of the window at the same time.

I hope mom's okay.

The television broadcast cut abruptly as the power went off, but Adrian continued to watch through the window.

* * *

Mount St Helens is an 8000 foot peak located 90 miles south of Seattle in the State of Washington, about an equal distance from the Pacific coast, and 50 miles northeast of Portland, Oregon. Along with Mount Hood, it is a stratovolcano in the Cascade Volcanic Arc. Mount St Helens is well known for ash eruptions and pyroclastic flows, and famous for a violent eruption that took place in May 1980. Since then, the volcano has been in a state of intermittent eruption and a new cone has formed within the 1980 blast crater.

Keeping an eye on Mount St Helens and its renewed activity is a team of vulcanologists from the United States Geological Survey, based at the Cascades Volcano Observatory in Vancouver, Washington. Some of the checks can be done at a distance, but numerous instruments are set out around the rim of the crater, some actually within the crater itself and others on the mountain slopes. These instruments must be checked regularly, and the data they have collected, downloaded to a computer for later analysis if they have not been broadcasted back automatically. The USGS dispatches two vulcanologists by helicopter every three to four weeks depending on weather conditions.

The weather on August 23, 2030 was fine and clear with maximum visibility. The two geologists on duty that day were Martin Barnett and Frederick Werner. They were both old hands at that particular exercise and both had experience on volcanoes around the world. Vulcanologists are a rare breed; there are hardly any jobs available in the commercial world and most governments only require a few such specialists. It is exciting and often dangerous work, but both men were drawn to it--if they were not employed to study volcanoes, they would climb them for enjoyment.

Martin and Fred loved this particular assignment--a short trip in a helicopter and then hours clambering around the crater rim and deep into the crater itself. Physically, it was demanding work, but both men were fit, despite the fact that Fred, at 55 years old was nearly twice Martin's age.

On this particular day--August 23, 2030--they were dropped off by the USGS helicopter at eight in the morning and would be collected by it an hour before sunset. They worked through the instruments on the lower slopes first, hiking miles along game trails and following colorful plastic tags in the branches of trees. GPS enabled them to pinpoint the exact position, and they checked that the instrument was stable, that the power system was operational and that there had been no disruption in the accumulation of data.

It was a sunny day and Fred and Martin soon worked up a sweat even though the air was cool at that altitude. They had a short break at half past nine, sitting in the sunshine on the bare slopes beneath the crater rim and admiring the view. It would be better from the crater rim, but even there, facing west, they could see the long winding silver ribbon of the Columbia River and, with a bit of imagination, the Pacific Ocean.

Finishing their short break, they picked up their packs and started for the summit, reaching the crater rim an hour later, working their way around, and checking every instrument. By a quarter after eleven they had worked their way round to the southern part of the rim and took another break. It was thirsty work and they guarded their supplies of water for there were no potable sources of water up there. The day was fine, with only a little cloud to the west and east. The view to the south was unobstructed.

On a cloudy day--and there were many--the only thing visible was a wide, rolling plain of clouds spreading in every direction. On such a day, only the high peaks of the Cascades--Adams, Rainier, Jefferson and Hood--floated above the cloud surface, but that day the view to the south was spectacular and even distant Mount Hood stood out sharp and clear.

"What's that?" Martin asked, pointing to the south.

"What?"

"There. Just to the east of Mount Hood."

On the southern horizon, close to the peak of Mount Hood, something white was growing. As they watched, they saw it grow taller than the distant mountain and start to spread out in the upper atmosphere, a tall, thin figure with a wide-brimmed hat.

"If I didn't know better, I'd say it was a nuclear explosion," Fred said.

"What's near Hood? Portland? There's no nuclear reactors there, are there?"

"It's on the wrong side for Portland and anyway, it's white. An atomic blast would be...well, ugly. That thing's beautiful, whatever it is."

Martin rummaged in his pack and pulled out a pair of binoculars. "Brings it a bit closer," he murmured. "It's all white and sparkly. What can it be?"

"Good thought," Fred said. "I've got that mini-theodolite in my pack. It's not really designed for these distances, but it'll give us a bearing and a height at least." He set to with his instrument and presently said, "It's about ten kilometers high and spreading out. By my reckoning, Hood is a hundred kilometers from here and that thing is about ten kilometers further and a little to the east."

"What the hell's there? There're no volcanoes for sure."

"Check the map."

Martin did so and frowned. "It's farmland...nearest town is Rushing River and the nearest mountain is Hood. Are you sure that...that eruption is not from Hood? From a fissure maybe or a new crater. It could even be further away."

Fred stared intently through the binoculars. "That's not ash..." A long low rumble interrupted him and he looked at his watch. "About five minutes since we saw it start to rise...that's 300 seconds. Sound travels at, oh 0.35 kilometers per second so let's say close to 100 kilometers. I'd say that's confirmation. It's Hood or near to it."

"But not ash?"

"Wrong color, consistency. Look." Fred handed the binoculars back. "You remarked on the sparkly bits and how white it is. It's starting to rotate like a cyclonic storm. Come on then, young fellah me lad," Fred grinned. "Why is that relevant?"

Martin shook his head. "The Coriolis force makes cyclones rotate."

"Good man. Volcanic eruptions, too, but the effect is rarely visible as ash is too heavy. Ergo, that rotating cloud is not ash. It's also too white. A violent eruption like that would include massive amounts of rock and cinder but that white sparkly stuff is falling like a snowstorm. That and the location tells me what it is."

Martin stared at the older man. "Go on then, tell me."

"There's a carbon geosequestration plant at Rushing River. It's blown out."

Chapter 43

August 23, 2030

Max Hay hurried out of the Museum and took a taxi to the nearest car hire company. He had no intention of hanging around Portland any longer than he had to, and wanted to get back to his home in Los Angeles. For a few minutes he had considered flying back, but that might bring him into contact with Matternicht again, and he had finally cut himself off from that man. No, the drive down the Pacific Highway would be restful and give him plenty of time to think about what he would do with the rest of his life. He would take Route 5 down through Salem and Eugene as far as Grants Pass before angling across to the coast.

Max hired a large car, one of the last to come out of Detroit before the automobile capital of America succumbed to the wave of cheap economy cars pouring out of Asia. It was a gas guzzler, but today, Max was thinking about comfort rather than carbon emissions. He found the entry ramp to Route 5 and turned south, easing his big car up to the speed limit, settling back into its comfortable leather seats. He turned on the radio, finding a station that played 'oldies' rather than the cacophonous soft porn that passed for modern music. The air conditioner purred softly and he relaxed for the first time in days.

As he crossed the Willamette River at Wilsonville, he thought about the meeting he had just attended and was assailed by feelings of nostalgia for his old life. For more than thirty years--a good portion of his adult life--he had followed

Matternicht blindly for what he could get--scientific honors and great wealth. He had been granted a generous research budget, excellent facilities and staff. All he had to give in return was everything he was. In many ways, Max thought of himself as a modern Dr Faustus, entering into a pact with Mephistopheles, who would grant him every wish in exchange for his soul.

Well, he had revoked the pact with the devil at last, broken free, and Matternicht could flee back to hell without him. Max had seen the look in the old man's eyes at the meeting, but had not recognized it for what it was at the time--defeat--for the first time in Matternicht's long predatory life. Matternicht and his empire might possibly survive the Rushing River debacle, but he had tasted defeat now and that taste would curdle his remaining pleasures. Max felt almost pity for him.

Almost, but not quite. He deserves everything he gets. Max grimaced. *If he does, then so do I. I enabled him. I gave him the means to do this.*

The car shuddered and slipped sideways a fraction. Max looked in the rear vision mirror but the road behind was smooth and unsullied. He had not hit a pothole, nor were there roadwork signs posted.

A truck had clipped a car up ahead and police were just starting to arrive, closing off both lanes and letting traffic through at a crawl on the hard shoulder. Max slowed and came to a stop, drumming his fingers on the steering wheel. He moved forward a few feet and the stopped again. Shouting drew his attention, and he saw people getting out of their cars and pointing off to the left. Max wound the window down and looked out at the northbound lanes, then further at rolling countryside and the rising ramparts of the Cascades. He stared, wondering what he was looking at.

A tall white pillar climbed above the ranges, its top spread out in all directions, and veils of white mist descending from it. Whatever it was, it had its origins on the other side of the Cascades, a little south of the bulk of Mount Hood, close to...

Rushing River. My God, it's happened--and not just a leak, it's a full-blown eruption. That means...that means those veils descending toward me are clouds of frozen carbon dioxide crystals...

Max gunned the motor and twisted the wheel over, clipping the fender of another car and fish-tailing violently as he fought the car back on track, accelerating back toward Portland on the wrong side of the road.

The noise reached him first, a jet engine roar despite the distance and his closed windows. Oncoming cars honked at him and swerved to avoid him as he kept his foot down, building more speed. He came to an underpass and found trucks in both lanes. Swerving to the right, he shattered the guard rail and ploughed onto the median strip, skidding sideways and bursting a tire.

Shakily, he got out of his car and looked to the east. The white veils descended rapidly, a frigid blast preceding them. Other cars had stopped and people were lining the highway, pointing and taking pictures. The first flakes of snow landed, burning his upturned face.

Max got back in his car and turned the engine on. He wasn't going anywhere, he knew, but he also realized he would need heat very soon--and an airtight container. He wound the windows up and turned the air onto recirculate, jacking up the heat. Outside, people were collapsing, clutching at their throats or staggering a few paces before dropping. He felt light-headed himself and recognized the first symptoms of carbon dioxide poisoning. The windows fogged up and he wiped them with one hand, feeling the cold through the glass. Already, the engine of his car was running roughly, deprived of oxygen. The only sound outside now was the muffled roar of the distant blowout, muted by the blizzard that fell around him. The road was littered with bodies, no movement except...

A small red car, almost silent, a late model Chinese electric Mao, buzzed along the northbound lanes, weaving in and out of the stalled traffic. Electricity uses a lot of oxygen when coal is burned to produce it, but the driver of that car might survive long enough to get out of range--if the gas did not get him first.

The engine of Max's car fell silent and at once the cold seeped in. He felt sleepy now, but was panting for breath. *I can suffocate in here or die in the open. At least that way is quicker.* Max thought once more of his wasted life, and then opened the door.

He did not live long enough to get out.

* * *

Andrew Winton was at McNary Field an hour before the flight was due to depart. He found the man who had secured him a seat in the freighter and paid him off. Freight companies, and more importantly, passenger airlines, do not look favorably on people bypassing the system, but they do allow for employees catching flights back to their home base for family reasons. The man at McNary Field had entered Andrew Winton's name in the system as one Greg Oldham, a mechanic from Missoula, Montana and secured for him a seat in the cargo bay of the eleven o'clock Pathfinder 40 twin-jet heading to that city.

The pilot and flight crew nodded to Andrew in a friendly fashion, but refrained from talking; busying themselves with checking the cargo and making sure everything was in readiness for the flight. Andrew strapped himself in, clutching his small suitcase and patting his money belt. He permitted himself a smile as they taxied to the end of the runway, and grinned in triumph as they lifted off.

Twenty-four hours and I'm in London. Then I disappear from Matternicht's radar. He'll never find me and I've enough funds to weather any financial storm.

The course was east-northeast and they climbed rapidly, passing through scattered cloud into bright sunshine. Andrew undid his seatbelt and stood to stretch before walking to one of the tiny windows in the fuselage. He looked out, but had trouble making out anything.

A crewmember came walking down the aisle with a clipboard in his hand. "We're just coming up on the Cascades, pal, but we're well above them, so don't worry. We'll be higher than Hood by the time we pass it."

"Uh, thanks. Everything looks different."

The crewmember nodded. "I'll get you a cup of coffee after I've checked the load. Hang tight, pal." He walked aft to the netted cargo bays.

The clouds parted as the jet passed over the mountain ridges at fifteen thousand feet and climbing. Andrew sat in his seat wishing he'd remembered to bring a book to read, hoping the crewmember would not take long and bring him a cup of coffee.

The intercom system in the plane was live, carrying comments from the pilots and navigator to the two cargo handlers. Mostly, there were weather reports relayed or the co-pilot marking off the increasing altitude. Occasionally, there was a personal comment or a short burst of laughter, and Andrew tuned it out, putting his head back and trying to sleep. He almost missed the first comments from the cabin as they neared the airspace over Rushing River.

"Whoa, what the fuck's that?"

"It looks like a surface explosion...shit, it's rising fast..."

"McNary Field, come in please...we have...Jesus..."

"Turning to course 135...emergency...emergency..."

Andrew was jolted as the plane's right wing dipped sharply in a turn. "What...?" He fell from his seat onto the floor.

Expletives echoed from the crewmembers on their feet and taken surprise by the maneuver. "What the hell's going on, Kev? I damn near..."

A sledgehammer blow hit the left wing of the jet and sheared it off, ripping a gaping hole through the fuselage. Andrew screamed despairingly as he was sucked out into an icy white void.

His last sight as he died high above the Cascades was a glimpse of the jet falling out of the sky.

* * *

August 23 was the worst day of James Matternicht's life. He left the Governor's meeting knowing that his schemes were in ruins. Thirty years before, he had elevated carbon geosequestration as a substantial solution to the problem of global warming, and along the way had been able to extend the profitable mining of fossil fuels by providing a disposal sink for all the waste carbon dioxide. The additional mining had created gigabucks from the national purse through the sham of carbon sequestration and all this had come to an abrupt end. Everything had changed this day--his organization had been challenged and it was certain that the authorities would now be looking closely at his activities. He had seen it coming these last few days and that was ultimately the reason he had agreed to meet the Governor of Oregon--damage control--if he could seal the leak, he could prove his good faith.

If the authorities investigated him, they would find that he knew carbon geosequestration was a scam right from the beginning. A dangerous scam, for how could anyone guarantee a treacherous substance like supercritical liquid carbon dioxide would stay locked up in rock strata when the slightest crack, the smallest earth tremor could threaten to release it.

Governments had supported him at first, eager to find a way out of the corner they had painted themselves into with their uncontrolled burning of fossil fuels. Global warming had fallen upon a blinkered humanity and any way out was viewed as a solution. Wishful thinking by politicians and pundits had stifled opposition; anyone who pointed out the dangers was shouted down or denigrated. Nobody pursued the consequences of a catastrophic blowout, or even questioned the permanence of geosequestration--despite warnings that all the carbon locked away would be back in the environment within a hundred years.

An economy hungry for cheap power and governments eager to provide it showed him the pathway to riches. James Matternicht gave them geosequestration and harvested privilege, wealth and power. It did not matter to him that he had exploited the earth's resources and that he would escape the consequences when the effluence from profligate energy consumption overwhelmed the environment.

His smile of remembrance lasted until his arrival back at the airport. An unpleasant time was looming, and Matternicht knew he would be fighting for survival in the days and weeks ahead. It was essential that this capping procedure work, so he was going out to Rushing River to oversee the operation personally.

At the airport, his limousines drove through to where the Learjet waited and the newly arrived Sikorsky 96 was undergoing its pre-flight checks. He dismissed his secretaries and bodyguards, ordering them back to Los Angeles on the Learjet.

"Peale and Campion will accompany me to Rushing River. Pilot, are you ready?"

"Very nearly, sir. If you'd like to get aboard and strapped in, we can leave in a few minutes." The pilot turned away and continued his unhurried inspection of his helicopter. In ten minutes he was ready, started the engine and went into a whole new series of checks as the engine warmed up. At last, the pilot was ready and got permission from the control tower to take off.

His course was southeast, rising to a thousand feet and following the Mount Hood Highway as it plunged into the barrier of the Cascades. The land rose up under them but the pilot worked off an altimeter that corrected for landforms and maintained a steady altitude.

It was noisy in the cabin of the helicopter, despite baffles and insulation. All three men in the back wore protective helmets with microphone and speaker. At the flip of a switch, any of them could talk to each other or to the pilot, but Matternicht felt disinclined to talk. He was thinking about Max and was filled with feelings of anger, regret and sorrow--anger at his betrayal, regret that his right-hand man was not at his side when he needed him most, and sorrow at losing an old friend.

They started the descent toward Rushing River and the Carbon Capture facility. Campion pointed ahead and slightly to the side, flipping his microphone switch.

"What's that?"

A white plume shot up from the ground, rapidly growing in length and volume and soared past them into the stratosphere. Hard on its heels came the noise, a terrible shrieking roar that blasted through their protective helmets, deafening them. They screamed in agony and Robert Peale slumped back in his seat, blood leaking out from under his helmet.

The pilot reacted by instinct, not knowing what the white column was, but certain it was hazardous. He put the Sikorsky into a sharp turn but it was too late. The engine sputtered and died, starved of oxygen and a bitter cold blasted through the Perspex windows. None of them heard the engine die, but the pilot could read the instruments and fought to restart it. His passengers stared out into the whiteness that surrounded them, feeling the swooping sickness in their stomachs as the helicopter lurched out of control. Then the free-spinning rotors froze solid and there was nothing to hold them up.

The helicopter fell from a thousand feet in seven seconds. To Matternicht it seemed like seven years as time slowed and gelled around him, the bitter cold rasping like razor blades in his throat and lungs, the carbon dioxide flooding his system. The realization that he had caused this to happen hit him hard. His ancient heart pounded in his thin chest and terror gripped him with icy claws.

Please let me die quickly...before...

An instant later the helicopter smashed into the ground and split open. There was no fire despite fuel spilling everywhere--there was no oxygen to support a flame. Robert Peale, the pilot and Nigel Campion died on impact.

James Matternicht survived long enough to scream before the freezing carbon dioxide rushed into his lungs and snuffed the life from him.

Chapter 44

August 23, 2030

"**W**hat do we do, Matt?"

Matt stared at the onrushing blizzard of what he knew was a storm of dry ice crystals, wondering just what was the answer to that question. Already, he could feel the suffocating effects of rising carbon dioxide levels, so perhaps the question was moot. There would not be enough time to do anything. "If we live long enough, we'll be snap-frozen when that blizzard hits us." He had to shout to be heard above the roar of the jet.

"It already feels like a meat locker," Annaliese said, forcing her mind away from thoughts of her son to contemplate her imminent demise.

"Shit. Two things we need--air and warmth...the breather packs. Come on." Matt dragged Annaliese after him as he sprinted for the sole vehicle in the parking lot--his USGS 4WD. He flung open the back and pulled out as many breather packs as he could, tightening the straps of one around himself, and another around Annaliese. They picked up as many others as they could and started back to the Retreat.

"Waay, wha buh cah hea..." Annaliese pulled the mask from her face and tried again. "Wait, Matt, what about the car heater? We could use..."

"No good," he interrupted. "The CO_2 will prevent the engine working. Come on, quickly." The first flakes of burning snow stung their faces and they ran for the restaurant, slamming the doors behind them.

Inside the dining room, Matt took his mask off. "That'll only hold..." He started choking and fumbled his mask back on. Taking several deep breaths, he slipped the mask aside and spoke quickly, breathing out in a steady stream. "We have to go somewhere that will protect..." He took another few breaths from the mask. "...us. You gave me the idea. Look for the meat..." Again, he breathed from the pack. "...meat locker and pray it's a walk-in one."

They walked quickly through the dining room, along a short corridor and up three steps to the kitchen, where they found a large wide white-door refrigerator with dials on the front showing the internal temperature as minus twenty Celsius.

"In here."

"It's a freezer," Annaliese protested. "We'll...freeze."

Matt switched off the power on the wall and the lights above the freezer went out. "It is going to get a lot colder out here very soon. These rooms are well insulated, so with luck, minus twenty is as cold as we'll get. Look around for any towels or coats or anything. We need to bundle up."

Matt found many tea towels and coats left behind by the kitchen staff and waiters, while Annaliese ventured into one of the hotel corridors and found a storeroom with blankets. She gathered up a bundle and hurried back to the kitchen. Matt had opened the freezer door and thrown out a lot of the meat to make room, and then wrestled a small table inside.

"We need to be off the floor...good girl, those blankets are just what we need." He pointed to his other acquisitions. "A couple of flashlights and..." he patted his jacket pocket, "My trusty Wills & Halbert. Now, are you ready? We should get inside before the air fouls up any more or we freeze to death out here."

Matt waited until Annaliese was bundled up in coats and blankets and sitting on the table before closing the door and plunging them into darkness. He turned a flashlight on and played it around the small room.

"Hardly the Ritz, my dear, but it'll do." Matt took his Wills & Halbert meter out and took a reading at chest level, and then another close to the floor. "Still quite breathable as long as we don't lie on the floor. We just have to hope the door seals are airtight." He wrapped himself in the other coats and blankets and joined Annaliese on the table. "In the interests of conserving body heat, we should huddle together."

"I hope not just in the interests of body heat," Annaliese murmured. She shifted toward Matt and leaned against him as he wrapped the last blanket around them both.

"Do you think you can manage without the flashlight? We don't know how long this is going to last and we should conserve the batteries."

She gave him a brave smile and nodded. "Do we have to keep wearing these packs if the air is okay up here? They're quite uncomfortable."

Matt thought for a moment. "Switch it off for now, but keep your mask handy. If you start feeling woozy, use it immediately." He switched the flashlight off and they sat together, huddled in the dark.

"How long are we going to have to be here?"

"I don't know. A few hours probably. There are westerlies forecast for later today, so that should clear the carbon dioxide away from us. We're high up, too. Bad luck for anyone downwind of Rushing River."

"Margaret and Marc are dead, aren't they?"

"Yes."

"And...and the people of Rushing River?"

"Yes."

"What about the people who were here at the Retreat earlier?

"Very likely they are dead, too. I'm sorry, Annaliese, but from the size of the blow-out I'd say that anyone in the Deschutes Valley, and along the Columbia from Umatilla to Portland will be dead or in great danger unless they can evacuate them."

"All those people dead. Who's to blame for all this, Matt, or is it just an Act of God?"

"Nothing divine about this mess, but where do you start when apportioning blame? You could start with the people at the carbon capture facility itself--they seem to have covered up how bad this all was. Then there are the owners of the facility, Oregon Coal & Power and their backers, whoever they are. Go back further--USGS and DOE okayed the initial plans--or further back still to governments that wanted cheap power but didn't want to pay the bill for producing it safely." Matt shrugged, unseen in the darkness but felt by Annaliese. "You could go back further and point to the short-sightedness of governments and companies who locked the world into the downward spiral of burning fossil fuels and reaping carbon emissions as if there was no tomorrow. Well, wake up guys; tomorrow's here. They got us into this mess, but we'll be the ones who foot the bill. Let's just hope the emergency services in Portland and Salem can respond adequately."

"I...I told Adrian to get out of Portland quickly. Do you think he made it?"

"Where was he?"

"In Forest Park. 1701 Elm. At one of my father-in-law's houses."

"That's elevated, Annaliese. He'll be fine if he stays up there. The carbon dioxide should only affect the low-lying riverfront areas--like where I work." Matt grimaced unseen. "I phoned Peter--my boss--just now and he was at work. I hope he can notify the authorities and get to high ground."

"I couldn't live if anything happened to Adey," Annaliese whispered.

Matt heard the terror and anguish in her voice and hugged her close. "He'll be alright, I promise."

They were silent for a long time, sitting together in the dark meat locker. The air slowly grew fouler and they had to resort to breaths from the breather packs more and more often. The air ran low and they shrugged the spent packs off, turning on others.

"What time is it?"

Matt flicked on his flashlight for a moment. "Just after three."

"It's getting worse, isn't it?"

"Not necessarily," Matt said reassuringly. "This is a small room and we generate our own carbon dioxide when we breathe, remember."

"But outside it's all poison now, and frozen?"

"Well...we're probably not too badly off. We had a lot of dry ice dumped on us, but I'd guess by now the main force of the blow-out is over. It'll likely be gushing for days, but I think the blast that carried the snow up here has dropped away. CO_2 is heavier than air and we are on a mountain, so the CO_2 should just slide off into the valley."

"And how cold?"

"Dry ice at normal pressures is at about minus seventy-eight Celsius, but it..."

"What's that in real degrees? I'm not a scientist."

Matt laughed. "Get used to it, Annaliese, it's the future. Fahrenheit is the old way and America's about the only country to use it now. But to answer your question, about minus a hundred and nine."

"Jesus, that's cold."

"Luckily it sublimates--turns into a vapor--very quickly when the temperature rises, but it will be damn cold for a while. We don't have a thermometer in here, but I wouldn't say it's getting colder. This room must be well insulated."

Matt switched on the flashlight again and pulled out his Wills & Halbert. "I think I'd better check the level in here."

"If it's bad news, I don't want to know."

The warning alarm made them both jump, and Matt switched over to the high-range settings. "Actually, that's not bad. When we first came in the level was about 2000 parts per million, a little high for indoors but it was already leaking in from outside. Now it's at 15,400 parts per million. Nothing to worry about. It'll have to get quite a bit higher before it's dangerous." He switched the flashlight off again.

Another long period of time passed in the dark. They finished the second set of breather packs and moved onto the third, the air in the locker getting staler with every breath.

"Are we there yet?"

Matt grinned in the dark and consulted his watch by the noticeably dimmer light of his flashlight. "Five-thirty."

"That late?"

"We'll have to make a move soon," Matt said. "The fourth set is all we have and I figure we still have to get off this mountain."

"Okay."

Matt handed a flashlight to Annaliese, and used the other to guide himself to the door. He pushed the handle down and pushed, but nothing happened.

"The cold must have warped something."

He put his shoulder to the door and pushed hard. It groaned and opened a few inches. Another push and it swung open enough for him to put his head and shoulders through. A gust of cold air entered.

"Damn, it's cold out here." He took a reading on his meter. "The door did keep most of it out; it's a bit over four per cent in the kitchen. Enough to be dangerous if we are in it a long time, but I think we should make a break for it while we still have our breather packs."

"Uh, I gotta pee."

"Use the corner of the locker. I'll stay out here until you finish." Matt heard vague sounds within and hurriedly added. "Annaliese, seriously, before you er...squat; use your breather pack or take a few deep breaths and hold your breath while you go. The CO_2 level will be higher close to the floor."

"Okay."

While she was occupied, Matt found a corner of the kitchen and relieved himself.

"Finished," Annaliese called. "What now?"

Matt helped Annaliese through the half open door and they negotiated their way through the silent corridors and rooms to the dining room and then the patio.

"We're still at nearly four per cent out here. Keep your breather mask on."

Annaliese was not listening; she stared out over a winter landscape through air that had been scrubbed clean of insects, dust and water vapor. As far as the eye could see, the lowlands of the river valleys were covered in a white shroud, the lowering sun tingeing the snow golden and pink. Nothing moved; not a bird, not an insect, except high above in the deepening blue summer sky, a white contrail crawled.

"They're dead," Annaliese whispered. "They're all dead. There's nothing moving down there."

Matt put his arm around her blanket-wrapped body. "It's not all dead." He pointed toward Mount Hood. "See how the upper slopes are green, and some of the Cascades beyond. I'm betting cities like Portland, Salem and Eugene are largely untouched. The carbon dioxide fountain shot high and fell back, sloshing like water over the low country, but it's draining away now. See? The jet out of Rushing River is already smaller, I'm sure. Wind is rushing inward to take the place of that shot high in the air, but the plume itself is drifting eastward away from the major cities. The wind in the upper atmosphere will dilute the carbon dioxide. Give it another day and the worst of the cold will be over, a few more days and the air will be back to normal."

Annaliese shook her head in dismay. "Such a criminal waste of life."

"It was an ill-conceived venture right from the start and I dare say the owners of the Rushing River plant will have a lot to answer for in court." Matt checked the dial on his breather pack. "I'm nearly out of air in this pack and we only have one more. We'd better get moving."

"Where? Down there?"

Matt grinned and turned her around to face the mountain. "Nope, up there."

The road that wound its way up from the Lewis & Clark Highway to the Retreat carried on up the mountain to a spring. The brook that tumbled down the mountainside was frozen, though the spring still leaked a dribble of water. The grass beneath their feet crunched crisply as they left the road and angled up on a walking track to the summit. Annaliese tried to call her son, but the battery in her cell phone was dead.

"We'll use mine from the summit," Matt said. "Better reception anyway."

They finished their third breather packs and shared the single one that was left, taking a few breaths and passing it across, the exertion of their climb driving the pure air quickly from their lungs. They discarded the blankets and then the coats as exercise warmed them and as they passed above the limit of frost-affected vegetation. The slope flattened out and they came to the rounded summit as their last air pack gave out. Matt took out his tester and switched on, smiling as he switched down to the mid-range, and grinning as he used the low-range.

"Down to 760," he said. "Damn near normal." Matt took out his phone and handed it to Annaliese. "Call Adrian."

Annaliese burst into tears when he answered. "Are you alright, Adey? You promise? You...you're still at grandpa's? Did the...the...were you very frightened?"

"I'm fine, mom, really. I sat here looking out the window and watching TV until the power went off. It's back on now, though. It's on all the news. All the regular programs are off and it's just coverage of the disaster. Are you okay? Where are you?"

"I'm safe. I'm on a mountain top with Matt. He saved my life."

"Tell him...tell him thanks and...I want to meet him."

"You will. Adey, I've got to go. Sit tight there until I get back."

"Okay, mom. Love ya."

"Love you, too, Adey."

Annaliese handed the cell phone back to Matt. "How do we get off this mountain?"

Matt called his boss, Peter Smythe, again.

"Hell, Matt, I thought we'd lost you. Where are you?"

"Stuck on the mountain top above the Retreat. We can't go down because of the CO_2."

"We?"

"A good friend of mine. Can you get us off?"

"Yeah, I think so. Stay there and I'll see what I can do. The rescue helicopters are rather busy at the moment."

"We're not going anywhere. How bad is it?"

There was a long pause. "Pretty bad. Your early call probably saved lives, though. I'd just stepped out of a meeting with the Governor and city officials, so it helped having them all in one place. Look, I've got to go, Matt. I'll get someone to pick you up as soon as I can."

* * *

It was close to sunset by the time Peter Smythe called them back. "Sorry, Matt. There's no way I can get a helicopter to you before tomorrow morning. Will you be okay?"

"We'll survive. I'll rescue a few of the blankets we discarded so we should be warm enough, but we're going to get hungry."

"Sorry about that. I'll see you in the morning."

Matt and Annaliese sat in the last rays looking out over a scene of devastation that was starting to emerge from under the sublimating dry ice snow. The evening sun lit the carbon dioxide column over Rushing River, and the plume of crystals billowing out to the south and east under the freshening breeze sparkled in incongruously beautiful shades of pink and gold.

"What'll happen now, Matt?"

"We pick up the pieces and move on. Hopefully, lessons will have been learned and the government won't be quite so quick to..."

"I meant with us."

Matt turned and looked into Annaliese's eyes. "The Chinese believe when you save a person's life, you have a responsibility for that person from then on."

"Is that what you want?"

"Not just responsibility."

Annaliese smiled. "You got it."

They sat for a while longer in silent contemplation of a changed future, both for mankind and for themselves. Then they went back down the mountain to retrieve the blankets and coats they had discarded on their climb to the summit, and arranged themselves in a sheltered hollow out of the cold breeze that now blew across the mountains.

The temperature fell with darkness, but for many minutes the sun, which had dipped below the western horizon, still lit up the towering plume of dry ice. There was no moon that night until just before dawn, but starlight made the snows spreading out from the fountain glimmer with a strange beauty.

They slept for a while, cold and uncomfortable, and woke with the approach of dawn. The muted roar of escaping gas had lessened while they slept and as the light grew in the sky, they saw the fountain was now a quarter of its previous height and shrinking. The landscape had changed overnight. Dry ice snow had spread over hills and valleys, obliterating the Deschutes and Columbia River Valleys and rising halfway up the flank of Mount Hood. The white land merged into the white sky where the plume still spread out.

As the sun's rays touched the plume with daubs of pink, the roar of escaping gas finally faltered, there was a prolonged hiss and a final exhalation before the fountain collapsed. There was silence.

Annaliese turned to Matt with a look of wonderment on her face. "Did you hear it, Matt?" she whispered. "The earth sighed!"

If you enjoyed this author's book, then please place a review up at the site of purchase, and any social media sites you frequent!

You can find ALL our books up on our website at:
https://www.writers-exchange.com

All our Historical Novels:
https://www.writers-exchange.com/category/genres/historical/

All Max's Books:
https://www.writers-exchange.com/max-overton/

About the Author

Max Overton has travelled extensively and lived in many places around the world-- including Malaysia, India, Germany, England, Jamaica, New Zealand, USA and Australia. Trained in the biological sciences in New Zealand and Australia, he has worked within the scientific field for many years, but now concentrates on writing. While predominantly a writer of historical fiction (Scarab: Books 1 - 6 of the Amarnan Kings; the Scythian Trilogy; the Demon Series; Ascension), he also writes in other genres (A Cry of Shadows, the Glass Trilogy, Haunted Trail, Sequestered) and draws on true life (Adventures of a Small Game Hunter in Jamaica, We Came From Königsberg). Max also maintains an interest in butterflies, photography, the paranormal and other aspects of Fortean Studies.

Most of his other published books are available at Writers Exchange E-Publishing, https://www.writers-exchange.com/Max-Overton/ and all his books may be viewed on his website: http://www.maxovertonauthor.com/

Max's book covers are all designed and created by Julie Napier, and other examples of her art and photography may be viewed at www.julienapier.com

Jim Darley was born in East Prussia--before the Russians took that province. He has lived in Australia since 1962, except for a seven-year stint in Canada. His professional life has been at three universities, managing electron microscope facilities. This included extensive use of CO_2 at the critical point. Knowing CO_2's properties well, Jim was incredulous about the claims made for carbon sequestration. He considers the large scale geosequestration of CO_2 as the world's most dangerous experiment. Jim has published the book "Know & Enjoy Tropical Fruit" and wrote the proposal for the Townsville Palmetum in Queensland, Australia.

The Science behind Sequestered

The science behind SEQUESTERED can be examined at www.sequesteredbooks.com

If you want to read more about books by this author, they are listed on the following pages...

A Cry of Shadows
{Paranormal Murder Mystery}

Australian Professor Ian Delaney is single-minded in his determination to prove his theory that one can discover the moment that the life force leaves the body. After succumbing to the temptation to kill a girl under scientifically controlled conditions, he takes an offer of work in St Louis, hoping to leave the undiscovered crime behind him.

In America, Wayne Richardson seeks revenge by killing his ex-girlfriend, believing it will give him the upper hand, a means to seize control following their breakup. Wayne quickly discovers that he enjoys killing and begins to seek out young women who resemble his dead ex-girlfriend.

Ian and Wayne meet and, when Ian recognizes the symptoms of violent delusion, he employs Wayne to help him further his research. Despite the police closing in, the two killers manage to evade identification time and time again as the death toll rises in their wake.

The detective in charge of the case, John Barnes, is frantic, willing to try anything to catch his killer. With time running out, he searches desperately for answers before another body is found...or the culprit slips into the woodwork for good.

Publisher: https://www.writers-exchange.com/a-cry-of-shadows/

Adventures of a Small Game Hunter in Jamaica
{Biography}

An eleven-year-old boy is plucked from boarding school in England and transported to the tropical paradise of Jamaica where he's free to study his one great love--butterflies. He discovers that Jamaica has a wealth of these wonderful insects and sets about making a collection of as many as he can find. Along the way, he has adventures with other creatures, from hummingbirds to vultures, from iguanas to black widow spiders. Through it all runs the promise of the legendary Homerus swallowtail, Jamaica's national butterfly.

Other activities intrude, like school, boxing and swimming lessons, but he manages to inveigle his parents into taking him to strange and sometimes dangerous places, all in the name of butterfly collecting. He meets scientists and Rastafarians, teachers, small boys and the ordinary people living on the tropical isle, and even discovers butterflies that shouldn't exist in Jamaica.

Author Max Overton was that young boy. He counted himself fortunate to have lived in Jamaica in an age very different from the present one. Max still has some of the butterflies he collected half a century or more ago, and each one releases a flood of memories whenever he opens the box and gazes at their tattered and fading wings. These memories have become stories--stories of the Adventures of a Small Game Hunter in Jamaica.

Publisher: https://www.writers-exchange.com/adventures-of-a-small-game-hunter/

Ascension Series, A Novel of Nazi Germany
{Historical: Holocaust}

Before he fully realized the diabolical cruelties of the National Socialist German Worker's Party, Konrad Wengler had committed atrocities against his own people, the Jews, out of fear of both his faith and his heritage. But after he witnesses firsthand the concentration camps, the corruption, the inhuman malevolence of the Nazi war machine and the propaganda aimed at annihilating an entire race, he knows he must find a way to turn the tide and become the savior his people desperately need.

Book 1: Ascension
Being a Jew in Germany can be a dangerous thing...

Fear prompts Konrad Wengler to put his faith aside and try desperately to forget his heritage. After fighting in the Great War, he's wounded and turns instead to law enforcement in his tiny Bavarian hometown. There, he falls under the spell of the fledgling Nazi Party. He joins the Party in patriotic fervour and becomes a Lieutenant of Police and Schutzstaffel (SS).

In the course of his duties as policeman, Konrad offends a powerful Nazi official who starts an SS investigation. War breaks out. When he joins the Police Battalions, he's sent to Poland and witnesses there firsthand the atrocities being committed upon his fellow Jews.

Unknown to Konrad, the SS investigators have discovered his origins and follow him into Poland. Arrested and sent to Mauthausen Concentration Camp, Konrad is forced to face what it means to be a Jew and fight for survival. Will his friends on the outside, his wife and lawyer, be enough to counter the might of the Nazi machine?

Publisher: https://www.writers-exchange.com/ascension/

Book 2: Maelstrom
Never underestimate the enemy...

Konrad Wengler survived his brush with the death camps of Nazi Germany. Now, reinstated as a police officer in his Bavarian hometown despite being a Jew, he throws himself back into his work, seeking to uncover evidence that will remove a corrupt Nazi party official.

The Gestapo have their own agenda and, despite orders from above to eliminate this troublesome Jewish policeman, they hide Konrad in the Totenkopf (Death's Head) Division of the Waffen-SS. In a fight to survive in the snowy wastes of Russia while the tide of war turns against Germany, Konrad experiences tank battles, ghetto clearances, partisans, and death camps (this time as a guard), as well as the fierce battles where his Division is badly outnumbered and on the defence.

Through it all, Konrad strives to live by his conscience and resist taking part in the atrocities happening all around him. He still thinks of himself as a policeman, but his desire to bring the corrupt Nazi official to justice seems far removed from his present reality. If he is to find the necessary evidence against his enemy, he must first *survive...*

Publisher: https://www.writers-exchange.com/maelstrom/

Book 3: Dämmerung

Konrad Wengler is captured and sent from one Soviet prison camp to another. Even hearing the war has come to an end makes no difference until he's arrested as a Nazi Party member. In jail, Konrad refuses to defend himself for things he's guilty and should be punished for. Will his be an eye-for-an-eye life sentence, or leniency in regard of the good he tried to do once he learned the truth?

Publisher: https://www.writers-exchange.com/dammerung/

Fall of the House of Ramesses Series,
A Novel of Ancient Egypt
{Historical: Ancient Egypt}

Egypt was at the height of its powers in the days of Ramesses the Great, a young king who confidently predicted his House would last for a Thousand Years. Sixty years later, he was still on the throne. One by one, his heirs had died and the survivors had become old men. When Ramesses at last died, he left a stagnant kingdom and his throne to an old man--Merenptah. What followed laid the groundwork for a nation ripped apart by civil war.

Book 1: Merenptah

The House of Ramesses is in the hands of an old man. King Merenptah wants to leave the kingdom to his younger son, Seti, but northern tribes in Egypt rebel and join forces with the Sea Peoples, invading from the north. In the south, the king's eldest son Messuwy is angered at being passed over in favour of the younger son...and plots to rid himself of his father and brother.

Publisher: https://www.writers-exchange.com/merenptah/

Book 2: Seti

After only nine years on the throne, Merenptah is dead and his son Seti is king in his place. He rules from the northern city of Men-nefer, while his elder brother Messuwy, convinced the throne is his by right, plots rebellion in the south.

The kingdoms are tipped into bloody civil war, with brother fighting against brother for the throne of a united Egypt. On one side is Messuwy, now crowned as King Amenmesse and his ruthless General Sethi; on the other, young King Seti and his wife Tausret. But other men are weighing up the chances of wresting the throne from both brothers and becoming king in their place. Under the onslaught of conflict, the House of Ramesses begins to crumble...

Publisher: https://www.writers-exchange.com/seti/

Book 3: Tausret

The House of Ramesses falters as Tausret relinquishes the throne upon the death of her husband, King Seti. Amenmesse's young son Siptah will become king until her infant son is old enough to rule. Tausret, as Regent, and the king's uncle, Chancellor Bay, hold tight to the reins of power and vie for complete control of the kingdoms. Assassination changes the balance of power, and, seeing his chance, Chancellor Bay attempts a coup...

Tausret's troubles mount as she also faces a challenge from Setnakhte, an aging son of the Great Ramesses who believes Seti was the last legitimate king. If Setnakhte gets his way, he will destroy the House of Ramesses and set up his own dynasty of kings.

Publisher: https://www.writers-exchange.com/tausret/

Glass Trilogy
{Paranormal Thriller}

Delve deep into the mysteries of Aboriginal mythology, present day UFO activity and pure science that surround the continent of Australia, from its barren deserts to the depths of its rainforest and even deeper into its mysterious mountains. Along the way, love, greed, murder, and mystery abound while the secrets of mankind and the ultimate answer to 'what happens now?' just might be answered.

GLASS HOUSE, Book 1: The mysteries of Australia may just hold the answers mankind has been searching for millennium to find. When Doctor James Hay, a university scientist who studies the paranormal mysteries in Australia, finds an obelisk of carved volcanic rock on sacred Aboriginal land in northern Queensland, he realizes it may hold the answers he's been seeking. A respected elder of the Aboriginal people instructs James to take up the gauntlet and follow his heart. Along with his old friend and award-winning writer Spencer, Samantha Louis, her cameraman, and two of James' Aboriginal students, James embarks on a life-changing quest for the truth.
Publisher: https://www.writers-exchange.com/glass-house/

A GLASS DARKLY, Book 2: A dead volcano called Glass Mountain in Northern California seems harmless...but is it really?

Andromeda Jones, a physicist, knows her missing sister Samantha is somehow tied up with the new job Andromeda herself has been offered to work with a team in constructing Vox Dei, a machine that's been ostensibly built to eliminate wars. But what is its true nature, and who's pulling the strings?

When the experiment spins out of control, dark powers are unleashed and the danger to mankind unfolds relentlessly. Strange, evil shadows are using the Vox Dei and Andromeda's sister Samantha to get through to our world, knowing the time is near when Earth's final destiny will be decided.

Federal forces are aware of something amiss, so, to rescue her sibling, Andromeda agrees to go on a dangerous mission and soon finds herself entangled in a web of professional jealousy, political betrayal, and flat-out greed.
Publisher: https://www.writers-exchange.com/a-glass-darkly/

LOOKING GLASS, Book 3: Samantha and James Hay have been advised that their missing daughter Gaia have been located in ancient Australia. Dr. Xanatuo, an alien scientist who, along with a lost tribe of Neanderthals and other beings working to help mankind, has discovered a way to send them back in time to be reunited with Gaia. Ernie, the old Aboriginal tracker and leader of the Neanderthals, along with friends Ratana and Nathan and characters from the first two books of the trilogy, will accompany them. This team of intrepid adventurers have another mission for the journey, along with aiding the Hayes' quest, which is paramount to changing a terrible wrong which exists in the present time.

Publisher: https://www.writers-exchange.com/looking-glass/

Haunted Trail A Tale of Wickedness & Moral Turpitude

{Western: Paranormal}

Ned Abernathy is a hot-tempered young cowboy in the small town of Hammond's Bluff in 1876. In a drunken argument with his best friend Billy over a girl, he guns him down. Ned flees and wanders the plains, forests and hills of the Dakota Territories, certain that every man's hand is against him.

Horse rustlers, marauding Indians, killers, gold prospectors and French trappers cross his path and lead to complications, as do persistent apparitions of what Ned believes is the ghost of his friend Billy, come to accuse him of murder. He finds love and loses it. Determined not to do the same when he discovers gold in the Black Hills, he ruthlessly defends his newfound wealth against greedy men. In the process, he comes to terms with who he is and what he's done. But there are other ghosts in his past that he needs to confront. Returning to Hammond's Bluff, Ned stumbles into a shocking surprise awaiting him at the end of his haunted trail.

Publisher: https://www.writers-exchange.com/haunted-trail/

Hyksos Series, A Novel of Ancient Egypt

The power of the kings of the Middle Kingdom have been failing for some time, having lost control of the Nile Delta to a series of Canaanite kings who ruled from the northern city of Avaris.

Into this mix came the Kings of Amurri, Lebanon and Syria bent on subduing the whole of Egypt. These kings were known as the Hyksos, and they dealt a devastating blow to the peoples of the Nile Delta and Valley.

Book 1: Avaris

When Arimawat and his son Harrubaal fled from Urubek, the king of Hattush, to the court of the King of Avaris, King Sheshi welcomed the refugees. One of Arimawat's first tasks for King Shesi is to sail south to the Land of Kush and fetch Princess Tati, who will become Sheshi's queen. Arimawat and Harrubaal perform creditably, but their actions have far-reaching consequences.

On the return journey, Harrubaal falls in love with Kemi, the daughter of the Southern Egyptian king. As a reward for Harrubaal's work, Sheshi secures the hand of the princess for the young Canaanite prince. Unfortunately for the peace of the realm, Sheshi lusts after Princess Kemi too, and his actions threaten the stability of his kingdom...

Publisher: https://www.writers-exchange.com/avaris/

Book 2: Conquest

The Hyksos invade the Delta using the new weapons of bronze and chariots, things of which the Egyptians have no knowledge. They rout the Delta forces, and in the south, the unconquered kings ready their armies to defend their lands. Meanwhile in Avaris, Merybaal, the son of Harrubaal and Kemi, strives to defend his family in a city conquered by the Hyksos.

Elements of the Delta army that refuse to surrender continue the fight for their homeland, and new kings proclaim themselves as the inheritors of the failed kings of Avaris. One of these is Amenre, grandson of Merybaal, but he is forced into hiding as the Hyksos sweep all before them, bringing their terror to the kingdom of the Nile valley. Driven south in disarray, the survivors of the Egyptian army seek leaders who can resist the enemy...

Publisher: https://www.writers-exchange.com/conquest/

Book 3: Two Cities

The Hyksos drive south into the Nile Valley, sweeping all resistance aside. Bebi and Sobekhotep, grandsons of Harrubaal, assume command of the loyal Egyptian army and strive to stem the flood of Hyksos conquest. But even the cities of the south are divided against themselves.

Abdju, an old capital city of Egypt reasserts itself, putting forward a line of kings of its own, and soon the city is at war with Waset, the southern capital of the Nile Valley, as the two cities fight for supremacy in the face of the advancing northern enemy. Caught up in the turmoil of warring nations, the ordinary people of Egypt must fight for their own survival as well as that of their kingdom.

Publisher: https://www.writers-exchange.com/two-cities/

Book 4: Possessor of All

The Hyksos, themselves beset by intrigue and division, push down into southern Egypt. The short-lived kingdom of Abdju collapses, leaving Nebiryraw the undisputed king of the south ruling from the city of Waset. An uneasy truce between north and south enables both sides to strengthen their positions.

Khayan seizes power over the Hyksos kingdom and turns his gaze toward Waset, determined to conquer Egypt finally. Meanwhile, the family of King Nebiryraw looks to the future and starts securing their own advantage, weakening the southern kingdom. In the face of renewed tensions, the delicate peace cannot last...

Publisher: https://www.writers-exchange.com/possessor-of-all/

Book 5: War in the South

Intrigue and rebellion rule in Egypt's southern kingdom as the house of King Nebiryraw tears itself apart. King succeeds king, but none of them look capable of defending the south, let alone reclaiming the north. Taking advantage of this, King Khayan of the Hyksos launches his assault on Waset, but rebellions in the north delay his victory.

The fall of Waset brings about a change of leadership. Apophis takes command of the Hyksos forces, and Rahotep brings together a small army to challenge the might of the Hyksos, knowing that the fate of Egypt hangs on the coming battle.

Publisher: https://www.writers-exchange.com/war-in-the-south/

Book 6: Between the Wars

Rahotep leads his Egyptian army to victory, and Apophis withdraws the Hyksos army northward. An uneasy peace settles over the Nile valley. Rebellions in the north keep the Hyksos king from striking back at Rahotep, while internal strife between the Hyksos nobility and generals threatens to rip their empire apart.

War is coming to Egypt once more, and the successors of Rahotep start preparing for it, using the very weapons that the Hyksos introduced--bronze weapons and the war chariot. King Ahmose repudiates the peace treaty, and Apophis of the Hyksos prepares to destroy his enemies at last. Bloody warfare returns to Egypt...

Publisher: https://www.writers-exchange.com/between-the-wars/

Book 7: Sons of Tao

War breaks out between the Hyksos invaders and native Egyptians determined to rid themselves of their presence. King Seqenenre Tao launches an attack on King Apophis but the Hyksos strike back savagely. It is only when his sons Kamose and Ahmose carry the war to the Hyksos that the Egyptians really start to hope they can succeed.

Kamose battles fiercely, but only when his younger brother Ahmose assumes the throne is there real success. Faced with an ignominious defeat, a Hyksos general overthrows Apophis and becomes king, but then he faces a resurgent Egyptian king determined to rid his land of the Hyksos invader...

Publisher: https://www.writers-exchange.com/sons-of-tao/

Kadesh, A Novel of Ancient Egypt

Holding the key to strategic military advantage, Kadesh is a jewel city that distant lands covet. Ramesses II of Egypt and Muwatalli II of Hatti believe they're chosen by the gods to claim ascendancy to Kadesh. When the two meet in the largest chariot battle ever fought, not just the fate of empires will be decided but also the lives of citizens helplessly caught up in the greedy ambition of kings.

Publisher: https://www.writers-exchange.com/kadesh/

Scythian Trilogy
{Historical}

Captured by the warlike, tribal Scythians who bicker amongst themselves and bitterly resent outside interference, a fiercely loyal captain in Alexander the Great's Companion Cavalry Nikometros and his men are to be sacrificed to the Mother Goddess. Lucky chance--and the timely intervention of Tomyra, priestess and daughter of the Massegetae chieftain--allows him to defeat the Champion. With their immediate survival secured, acceptance into the tribe...and escape...is complicated by the captain's growing feelings for Tomyra--death to any who touch her--and the chief's son Areipithes who not only detests Nikometros and wants to have him killed or banished but intends to murder his own father and take over the tribe.

LION OF SCYTHIA, Book 1: Alexander the Great has conquered the Persian Empire and is marching eastward to India. In his wake he leaves small groups of soldiers to govern great tracts of land and diverse peoples. Nikometros is one young cavalry captain left behind in the lands of the fierce, nomadic Scythian horsemen. Captured after an ambush, Nikometros must fight for his life and the lives of his surviving men. Even as he seeks an opportunity to escape, he finds himself bound by a debt of loyalty to the chief...and his own developing love for the young priestess.
Publisher: https://www.writers-exchange.com/lion-of-scythia/

THE GOLDEN KING, Book 2: The chief of the tribe of nomadic Scythian horsemen is dead, killed by his son's treachery. The priestess, lover of the young cavalry officer, Nikometros, is carried off into the mountains. Nikometros and his friends set off in hard pursuit.

Death rides with them. By the time they return, the tribes are at war. Nikometros must choose between attempting to become chief himself or leaving the people he's come to love and respect to return to his duty as an army officer in the Empire of Alexander.

Winner of the 2005 EPIC Ebook Awards.
Publisher: https://www.writers-exchange.com/the-golden-king/

FUNERAL IN BABYLON, Book 3: Alexander the Great has returned from India and set up his court in Babylon. Nikometros and a band of loyal Scythians journey deep into the heart of Persia to join the Royal court. Nikometros finds himself embroiled in the intrigues and wars of kings, generals, and merchant adventurers as he strives to provide a safe haven for his lover and friends. With the fate of an Empire hanging in the balance, Death walks beside Nikometros as events precipitate a Funeral in Babylon...

Winner of the 2006 EPIC Ebook Awards.

Publisher: https://www.writers-exchange.com/funeral-in-babylon/

Sequestered
By Max Overton and Jim Darley
{Action/Thriller}

Storing carbon dioxide underground as a means of removing a greenhouse gas responsible for global warming has made James Matternicht a fabulously wealthy man. For 15 years, the Carbon Capture and Sequestration Facility at Rushing River in Oregon's hinterland has been operating without a problem...or has it?

When mysterious documents arrive on her desk that purport to show the Facility is leaking, reporter Annaliese Winton investigates. Together with a government geologist, Matt Morrison, she uncovers a morass of corruption and deceit that now threatens the safety of her community and the entire northwest coast of America.

Liquid carbon dioxide, stored at the critical point under great pressure, is a tremendously dangerous substance, and millions of tons of it are sequestered in the rock strata below Rushing River. All it would take is a crack in the overlying rock and the whole pressurized mass could erupt with disastrous consequences. And that crack has always existed there...

Recipient of the Life Award (Literature for the Environment): "There are only two kinds of people: conservationists and suicides. To qualify for this Award, your book needs to value the wonderful world of nature, to recognize that we are merely one species out of millions, and that we have a responsibility to cherish and maintain our small planet."
Awarded from http://bobswriting.com/life/

Publisher: https://www.writers-exchange.com/sequestered/

Strong is the Ma'at of Re, A Novel of Ancient Egypt
{Historical: Ancient Egypt}

In Ancient Egypt, C1200 BCE, bitter contention and resentment, secret coups and assassination attempts may decide the fate of those who would become legends...by any means necessary.

Book 1: The King

That *he* is descended from Ramesses the Great fills Ramesses III with obscene pride. Elevated to the throne following a coup led by his father Setnakhte during the troubled days of Queen Tausret, Ramesses III sets about creating an Egypt that reflects the glory days of Ramesses the Great. He takes on his predecessor's throne name, names his sons after the sons of Ramesses and pushes them toward similar duties. Most of all, he thirsts after conquests like those of his hero grandfather.

Ramesses III assumes the throne name of Usermaatre, translated as "Strong is the Ma'at of Re" and endeavours to live up to the sentiment. He fights foreign foes, as had Ramesses the Great; he builds temples throughout the Two Lands, as had Ramesses the Great, and he looks forward to a long, illustrious life on the throne of Egypt, as had Ramesses the Great.

Alas, his reign is not meant to be. Ramesses III faces troubles at home-- troubles that threaten the stability of Egypt and his own throne. The struggles for power between his wives, his sons, and even the priests of Amun, together with a treasury drained of its wealth, all force Ramesses III to question his success as the scion of a legend.

Publisher: https://www.writers-exchange.com/the-king/

Book 2: The Heirs

Tiye, the first wife of Ramesses III, has grown so used to being the mother of the Heir she can no longer bear to see that prized title pass to the son of a rival wife. Her eldest sons have died and the one left wants to step down and devote his life to the priesthood. Then the son of the king's sister/wife, also named Ramesses, will become Crown Prince and all Tiye's ambitions will lie in ruins.

Ramesses III struggles to enrich Egypt by seeking the wealth of the Land of Punt. He dispatches an expedition to the fabled southern land but years pass before the expedition returns. In the meantime, Tiye has a new hope: A last son she dotes on. Plague sweeps through Egypt, killing princes and princesses alike and lessening her options, and now Tiye must undergo the added indignity of having her daughter married off to the hated Crown Prince.

All Tiye's hopes are pinned on this last son of hers, but Ramesses III refuses to consider him as a potential successor, despite the Crown Prince's failing health. Unless Tiye can change the king's mind through charm or coercion, her sons will forever be excluded from the throne of Egypt.

Publisher: https://www.writers-exchange.com/the-heirs/

Book 3: Taweret

The reign of Ramesses III is failing and even the gods seem to be turning their eyes away from Egypt. When the sun hides its face, crops suffer, throwing the country into famine. Tomb workers go on strike. To avert further disaster, Crown Prince Ramesses acts on his father's behalf.

The rivalry between Ramesses III's wives--commoner Tiye and sister/wife Queen Tyti--also comes to a head. Tiye resents not being made queen and can't abide that her sons have been passed over. She plots to put her own spoiled son Pentaweret on the throne.

The eventual strength of the Ma'at of Re hangs in the balance. Will the rule of Egypt be decided by fate, gods...or treason?

Publisher: https://www.writers-exchange.com/the-one-of-taweret/

The Amarnan Kings Series, A Novel of Ancient Egypt
{Historical: Ancient Egypt}

Set in Egypt of the 14th century B.C.E. and piecing together a mosaic of the reigns of the five Amarnan kings, threaded through by the memories of princess Beketaten-Scarab, a tapestry unfolds of the royal figures lost in the mists of antiquity.

SCARAB - AKHENATEN, Book 1: A chance discovery in Syria reveals answers to the mystery of the ancient Egyptian sun-king, the heretic Akhenaten and his beautiful wife Nefertiti. Inscriptions in the tomb of his sister Beketaten, otherwise known as Scarab, tell a story of life and death, intrigue and warfare, in and around the golden court of the kings of the glorious 18th dynasty.

The narrative of a young girl growing up at the centre of momentous events--the abolition of the gods, foreign invasion, and the fall of a once-great family--reveals who Tutankhamen's parents really were, what happened to Nefertiti, and other events lost to history in the great destruction that followed the fall of the Aten heresy.
Publisher: https://www.writers-exchange.com/scarab/

SCARAB- SMENKHKARE, Book 2: King Akhenaten, distraught at the rebellion and exile of his beloved wife Nefertiti, withdraws from public life, content to leave the affairs of Egypt in the hands of his younger half-brother Smenkhkare. When Smenkhkare disappears on a hunting expedition, his sister Beketaten, known as Scarab, is forced to flee for her life.

Finding refuge among her mother's people, the Khabiru, Scarab has resigned herself to a life in exile...until she hears that her brother Smenkhkare is still alive. He is raising an army in Nubia to overthrow Ay and reclaim his throne. Scarab hurries south to join him as he confronts Ay and General Horemheb outside the gates of Thebes.
Publisher: https://www.writers-exchange.com/scarab2/

SCARAB - TUTANKHAMEN, Book 3: Scarab and her brother Smenkhkare are in exile in Nubia but are gathering an army to wrest control of Egypt from the boy king Tutankhamen and his controlling uncle, Ay. Meanwhile, the kingdoms are beset by internal troubles while the Amorites are pressing hard against the northern borders. Generals Horemheb and Paramessu must fight a war on two fronts while deciding where their loyalties lie--with the former king Smenkhkare or with the new young king in Thebes.

Smenkhkare and Scarab march on Thebes with their native army to meet the legions of Tutankhamen on the plains outside the city gates. As two brothers battle for supremacy and the throne of the Two Kingdoms, the fate of Egypt and the 18th dynasty hangs in the balance.

Finalist in 2013's Eppie Awards.

Publisher: https://www.writers-exchange.com/scarab3/

SCARAB - AY, Book 4: Tutankhamen is dead and his grieving widow tries to rule alone, but her grandfather Ay has not destroyed the former kings just so he can be pushed aside. Presenting the Queen and General Horemheb with a fait accompli, the old Vizier assumes the throne of Egypt and rules with a hand of hardened bronze. His adopted son, Nakhtmin, will rule after him and stamp out the last remnants of loyalty to the former kings.

Scarab was sister to three kings and will not give in to the usurper and his son. She battles against Ay and his legions under the command of General Horemheb and aided by desert tribesmen and the gods of Egypt themselves. The final confrontation will come in the rich lands of the Nile delta where the future of Egypt will at last be decided.

Publisher: https://www.writers-exchange.com/scarab4/

SCARAB - HOREMHEB, Book 5: General Horemheb has taken control after the death of Ay and Nakhtmin. Forcing Scarab to marry him, he ascends the throne of Egypt. The Two Kingdoms settle into an uneasy peace as Horemheb proceeds to stamp out all traces of the former kings. He also persecutes the Khabiru tribesmen who were reluctant to help him seize power. Scarab escapes into the desert, where she is content to wait until Egypt needs her.

A holy man emerges from the desert and demands that Horemheb release the Khabiru so they may worship his god. Scarab recognises the holy man and supports him in his efforts to free his people. The gods of Egypt and of the Khabiru are invoked and disaster sweeps down on the Two Kingdoms as the Khabiru flee with Scarab and the holy man. Horemheb and his army pursue them to the shores of the Great Sea, where a natural event...or the very hand of God...alters the course of Egyptian history.

Publisher: https://www.writers-exchange.com/scarab5/

SCARAB - DESCENDANT, Book 6: Three thousand years after the reigns of the Amarnan Kings, the archaeologists who discovered the inscriptions in Syria journey to Egypt to find the tomb of Smenkhkare and his sister Scarab and the fabulous treasure they believe is there. Unscrupulous men and religious fanatics also seek the tomb, either to plunder it or to destroy it. Can the gods of Egypt protect their own, or will the ancients rely on modern day men and women of science?

Publisher: https://www.writers-exchange.com/scarab6/

The Pyramid Builders, A Novel of Ancient Egypt
{Historical: Ancient Egypt}

The third dynasty of the Old Kingdom of Egypt saw an extraordinary development of building techniques, from the simple structures of mud brick at the end of the second dynasty to the towering pyramids of the fourth dynasty. Just how these massive structures were built has long been a matter of conjecture, but history is made up of the lives and actions of individuals; kings and architects, scribes and priests, soldiers and artisans, even common labourers, and so the story of the Pyramid Builders unfolded over the course of more than a century. This is that story...

Book 1: Djoser

King Khasekhemwy has two sons, Djoser and Imhotep, but their destinies are very different. One will become king and the other his architect and the power behind the throne. Together, they plan to build something new, a great tomb that will be the wonder of the world. But not all is peaceful within the kingdoms of Egypt. Djoser's son Sekhemkhet will inherit the throne, but there are others that seek power and set their plans in motion, and they care nothing for the architectural ambitions of their king.

Ordinary men and women inhabit Djoser's Egypt too, living their own lives, dreaming of power or simple happiness, but sometimes these dreams do not harmonise with the plans of kings...

Publisher: https://www.writers-exchange.com/djoser/

Book 2: Sekhemkhet

Sekhemkhet faces the daunting prospect of following on from the glories of his father's achievement. He desires an even bigger pyramid than that of Djoser and orders Imhotep and Den to build it. However, the king finds it easier to build a tomb than to raise heirs to follow him on the throne, and a cousin seeks to take advantage of Sekhemkhet's precarious position and challenge the king.

Not all is well within Den's family. He is married, but love from an unexpected source threatens to destroy the success he has so laboriously built up. Will he sacrifice love for ambition, or can he find a way to have both?

Publisher: https://www.writers-exchange.com/sekhemkhet/

Book 3: Khaba

The throne of Egypt has passed to Khaba, an old man who seeks only to secure his family's position. Construction of a pyramid tomb is a secondary consideration, and the fortunes of those who desire to build them languish as he refuses further innovations. It is left to his grandson and heir, Huni, to dream of greater architectural glories.

Architect Den has achieved love, but at the cost of ambition. He and his burgeoning family struggle to survive, his relatives seeking out love of their own even as they look for opportunities to further their careers. The promise of a return to fulfilment is offered, but will they be able to grasp it?

Publisher: https://www.writers-exchange.com/khaba/

Book 4: Huni

Like a breath of fresh air after a generation of stagnation, Huni becomes king and sets about reorganising Egypt. He divides the land into administrative regions under governors and devises a way to bring the blessings of the gods to all men-- he will build small pyramids up and down the length of the river, reserving a simple tomb for himself.

Even as Den and his sons build for the king, his twin daughters threaten to tear down the king's future. One falls in love with the heir to the throne, while the other seeks the heir's death. Which one succeeds will determine the fortunes of their extended family.

Publisher: https://www.writers-exchange.com/huni/

Book 5: Sneferu

The kings of Egypt are turning from the worship of all gods to raising the sun god Re above them all. Rather than a stepped pyramid for the spirit of the king to ascend to the undying stars, they seek a representation of the beneficent rays of the sun in a smooth-sided pyramid. This brings with it a host of new problems to be overcome by the king's architects. Meanwhile, the king takes several wives and has many sons who vie for power, using murder to achieve their ends.

Den is old and passes the title of architect on to his son Khepankh and grandson Djer, but they make mistakes as they try to learn new techniques of building massive pyramids. Their mistakes threaten to be their undoing, but they find a way to build true and strong, and a new talent arises from a union between Den's family and the heir to the throne.

Publisher: https://www.writers-exchange.com/sneferu/

Book 6: Khufu

Khufu is excited by the pyramids of his father Sneferu and wants to build a great one that will eclipse everything else ever built. The Great Pyramid presents unique challenges that must be overcome if the pyramid is to be built. Architect Hemiunu finds solutions, but even he relies on help from Rait, a woman of great talent. She must battle prejudice even from her own father if she is to achieve ultimate success.

The sons of Khufu vie for power. Their actions will lead to wars between nations, and call into question who has the right to sit on the throne of Egypt. Meanwhile, the family of Den have taken to sailing and trade and find the fabled land of Punt where discoveries will affect the lives of kings yet unborn.

Publisher: https://www.writers-exchange.com/khufu/

Book 7: Djedefre

Djedefre becomes king, with his brother Hordjedef his principal adviser. Breaking with tradition, the king appoints Rait as his architect, gambling that she will be up to the task of building a pyramid. An earthquake damages the Sphinx, and is seen as an omen of the gods' disfavour, but the king makes a decision that might avert disaster, though many view it as added blasphemy. Concerned for the future, those close to the king plot to remove him.

The king's heir is put aside, and a struggle for power breaks out, leading to deadly strife between the brothers Baka and Setka. Death and exile follow, with consequences that threaten Egypt's future.

Publisher: https://www.writers-exchange.com/djedefre/

Book 8: Khafre

Khafre seizes control and takes the throne of his brother, while his nephew Baka flees to Amurru with his uncle Hordjedef. The new king wants a pyramid as big as his father's, appointing a conventional male architect. However, he has cause to regret his decision, bringing back Rait when things go wrong. Others passed over for the position seek to hurt Rait and violate her daughter Neferit.

The head of the Sphinx is rebuilt, with Khafre's features replacing the damaged face of the god Inpu. Hordjedef quarrels with exiled Baka and returns to Egypt, pleading for forgiveness, but as Khafre sickens, Baka seeks revenge. The heir, Menkaure, must battle for the throne of Egypt when his father Khafre dies.

Publisher: https://www.writers-exchange.com/khafre/

Book 9: Menkaure

Menkaure meets Baka in battle and defeats him. Baka returns to Amurru, but Menkaure's reign is beset by troubles at home and abroad. Although Menkaure's pyramid is rising swiftly, the king falls sick with the 'shaking fever', for which there is no cure. Only a medicine brought back from Punt seems to hold out hope, but Shepseskaf assumes the power of regent, ruling in place of his sick father.

An ambitious army officer by the name of Userkaf takes command of the northern army, and he is deeply devoted to the god Re, allying his family with the priests of Iunu. Neferit's daughter Peseshet strives to become a physician in the face of opposition from the medical fraternity.

Book 10: Shepseskaf

Menkaure's health continues to decline and Shepseskaf must now become king. He strives to finish his father's pyramid, but desires something simpler for himself, forsaking the pyramid form. Others desire power in Egypt--the king's sister Khentkaus wants to be king; Userkaf, now a General, dares to think of greater things; and even the priests of Re and Ptah look to increase their status. Shepseskaf's heir dies, and the king must not only rescue his family's future but must fight off Egypt's enemies at home and abroad.

In Amurru, Baka dies, and his son Bauefre desires the throne of Egypt. He leads an army south against Shepseskaf and Userkaf in a final battle.

TULPA
{Paranormal Thriller}

From the rainforests of tropical Australia to the cane fields and communities of the North Queensland coastal strip, a horror is unleashed by those foolishly playing with unknown forces...

A fairy story to amuse small children leads four bored teenagers and a young university student in a North Queensland town to becoming interested in an ancient Tibetan technique for creating a life form. When their seemingly harmless experiment sets free terror and death, the teenagers are soon fighting to contain a menace that reproduces exponentially.

The police are helpless to end the horror. Aided by two old game hunters, a student of the paranormal and a few small children, the teenagers must find a way of destroying what they unintentionally released. But how can they stop beings that can escape into an alternate reality when threatened?

Publisher: https://www.writers-exchange.com/TULPA/

We Came From Konigsberg
{Historical: Holocaust}

Based on a true story gleaned from the memories of family members sixty years after the events, from photographs and documents, and from published works of nonfiction describing the times and events described in the narrative, *We Came From Konigsberg* is set in January 1945.

The Soviet Army is poised for the final push through East Prussia and Poland to Berlin. Elisabet Daeker and her five young sons are in Königsberg, East Prussia and have heard the shocking stories of Russian atrocities. They're desperate to escape to the perceived safety of Germany. To survive, Elisabet faces hardships endured at the hands of Nazi hardliners, of Soviet troops bent on rape, pillage and murder, and of Allied cruelty in the Occupied Zones of post-war Germany.

Winner of the 2014 EPIC Ebook Awards.

Publisher: https://www.writers-exchange.com/we-came-from-konigsberg/

You can find ALL our books on our website at:
https://www.writers-exchange.com

All our Historical Novels:
https://www.writers-exchange.com/category/genres/historical/

All Max's Books:
https://www.writers-exchange.com/max-overton/

www.ingramcontent.com/pod-product-compliance
Lightning Source LLC
Chambersburg PA
CBHW052006020726
47501CB00004B/1025